THE
SHADOW ARTS

A SEQUEL TO MONSTROUS DEVICES

by

Damien Love

ROCK THE BOAT

A Rock the Boat Book

First published in Great Britain, Ireland & Australia by Rock the Boat,
an imprint of Oneworld Publications, 2021

This mass market paperback edition published 2022

Copyright © Damien Love, 2020, 2021

The moral right of Damien Love to be identified as the Author
of this work has been asserted by him in accordance with the
Copyright, Designs and Patents Act 1988

ISBN 978-0-86154-088-4
ISBN 978-1-78607-939-8 (ebook)

Printed and bound in Great Britain by Clays Ltd, Elcograf S.p.A.

Oneworld Publications
10 Bloomsbury Street
London WC1B 3SR
England

Stay up to date with the latest books,
special offers, and exclusive content from
Rock the Boat with our newsletter

Sign up on our website
oneworld-publications.com/rtb

MIX
Paper from
responsible sources
FSC® C018072

"It's taken everything I loved from the first book and **turned it up to eleven**. Clever, funny, exciting, and occasionally downright nasty – terrific stuff!"

Alastair Chisholm, author of *Orion Lost*

"*The Shadow Arts* is **a brilliant sequel**... I love how this series moves so confidently through some truly unsettling places, exploring challenging themes without sacrificing plot or pace. **Zia is delightfully hideous, and any time spent with Alex's Grandfather is a joy** from start to finish. I hope there's more to come."

Jennifer Killick, author of *Crater Lake*

"The breathless action is back...and **fans of the first book will be happy to be pulled along**."

Booklist

"Dark, mysterious, **adrenaline-pumping roller coaster of a story**. You won't be able to stop reading!"

Kieran Larwood, author of The Five Realms

"...chases and wrecks, sudden attacks, desperate battles, and visions... **Breathlessly paced adventure** with truly eerie and icky notes."

Kirkus

"Damien has a fabulous imagination, these books are **truly unique in plot**... **Very happy to recommend both of these books for aged 9 to 109 year olds**."

Independent Book Reviews

"A **superbly assured sequel where detailed settings, a clever plot, and cliffhanging action combine in an unforgettable read**. At 400 pages, it's epic and all-consuming. Car chases, thrilling attacks, desperate escapes, and otherworldly magic will draw you into this roller coaster of a story."

South China Morning Post

"For fans of the first book and **readers who enjoy action mixed in with their supernatural**."

School Library Journal

To Alison

And in memory of Alan

Time and time again, the castle ruin Boll,
also called Neu-Tannegg, was the target of treasure hunters,
who believed immense riches lay buried under the rubble.
But all searching was in vain. . .

Traditional story from the Black Forest

HARD RAIN

RAIN IS FALLING on the Black Forest.

It moves like smoke over the treetops in the last light, beating an endless martial drumroll on branches and leaves, and setting the steep, wooded slopes of the Kandel mountain streaming.

A man runs recklessly down the mountainside in the rain, feet slipping in sucking mud as he stumbles among tree trunks. He gasps for breath, because he is not a young man. Beneath one arm, he clutches a roll of material tightly to his chest. He trips, falls hard, lies without moving. Then:

"Bloody Nora."

Hauling himself up, he blinks back into the darkness, listens, stiffens, then throws himself on down the slope, even more desperately than before.

He comes eventually to a lonely road cut thinly through the woods. A car sits by the track, looking abandoned. Sparing a second to pat the roof, he flings himself inside, then bends to fumble beneath the driver's seat, uncovering a panel in the floor, a shallow compartment. He tosses in his tube of material, flattens the carpet back down.

The engine purrs and he has the car moving fast, steering with one hand, working a phone with the other. He hits SPEAKER, tosses his phone to the dashboard, and grabs the wheel with both hands as the road veers into a ragged bend.

Trees jerk in his headlights. The windshield wipers beat in time with the phone ringing out on the other end. He grits his teeth, glances at his rearview mirror. Finally, the ringing ends, replaced by an ancient tape-recording labouring to life:

"Hello! I'm not here right now. Or if I am, I'm too busy to come to the phone. Mind you, I'm probably out. But you never know. Just in case you're a burglar casing the place: I could be in. You never know!"

The man at the wheel grinds his jaw.

"This is a machine! Can't say I approve, really, but there it is. Comes in handy, I must admit. So. You know what the fellow says: 'At the tone, leave your name and message. I'll get back to you.' So please do. And I will. Unless you're trying to sell me something. In which case, you really should wait until I decide I want to buy something and come to you. Would save us all a lot of time. In any case, leave a message, if you like. Unless you think the machine will steal your soul, like a camer—"

A beep cuts the rambling off. The driver shouts: "It's 'Arry.

2

An' this'd be another good example of one of them times it would be 'andy if you'd agree to carry a bloody phone. I'm still in the forest, but getting out. Uh, road southeast of the Kandel, 'eadin' for—"

Harry Morecambe breaks off. Far back in his mirror, headlights appear, swallowed instantly again by night.

"Gawd. They're comin' after me. Listen: I followed 'em. I saw some of what they're up to. Weird business. For a change. Looks like there are two more paintings still to go. But, 'old on to your 'at: I got one of the others *back*. Pinched it off 'em. I 'ave it with me. Remind me to blow me own trumpet later. Now, I know where the other two are—"

Harry falls silent as he spots some long, low thing behind him, shooting fast along the road on a dim bed of sparks. Then it is gone. He squints ahead. There is nothing but the shuddering patch of ground racing in his headlights.

"Don't like the look of this. Listen. They said something about Shadow Gate. I was 'iding back in the bushes, so I couldn't 'ear clearly, but the girl definitely said it, more than once. Does that mean anything? *Shadow Gate?* And two more things: it's not—"

There is something in the road ahead: a huge, hunched figure, hands held out like buffers.

Harry accelerates. The car hits, and the world pitches and cracks and falls silent and black.

He comes to without knowing how long he has been

unconscious, wrestles open his door, grabs his phone, and stumbles out. The car lies wrecked. One headlight still shines, the beam trembling with rain. Something moves in the darkness beyond, and a figure comes dragging itself into the light. A figure without a head, missing one arm and one leg, a single metal hand clawing the ground. Back along the road, the headlights reappear, coming fast.

Harry runs, plunging into the forest. Soon he is climbing a steep slope. The air quivers and whines and unseen things come flitting through the dark, slashing. He swings his arms wildly, warding them off, but he is hit, falls, crawls on through thorny undergrowth until he can go no further. He lies listening. No sound but rain. The flying things are gone.

Harry stands, bloody, disoriented, staggers on. After a while, he glimpses lights high ahead through the trees. He remembers the phone in his hand, the call still in progress.

"Is this still on? That was close. Car's totalled, but I think I've lost 'em. I'm in the forest, bit lost, but I can see lights, an' I . . . Oh."

He has emerged into a small clearing. The moon breaks the clouds, illuminating the glade like an enchanted stage set. In its ghostly spotlight, the grass shines very green, the dripping tree branches seem very sharp, and a small girl stands smiling very sweetly, her bright moon face framed by long black hair.

"Taah-daaa." She beams, spreading her arms.

High above her, four small tin machines hover on shivering wings, amber eyes shining. As the moonlight disappears, so does her smile. The little robots' eyes flash as they descend, slicing fast with arms like scalpels.

Harry staggers back. A crashing erupts in the trees behind him, and suddenly a tall shadow looms there. Harry turns again. But there is nowhere to turn. He lifts his phone. "Listen! It's not—"

There is a single blunt blow. A crack of bone.

Harry's phone falls to the forest floor and an enormous black boot stamps down on it. This boot has a curious assemblage of straps and springs around the heel. It grinds the phone to pieces, steps away.

Then there is nothing but rain falling on the Black Forest.

Time passes in rain and changing light, until it is pale morning. Another car comes along the lonely road and stops behind the wreck that had been Harry's. A tall figure steps out, elegant in the wilderness. An old man. He wears a long grey coat, a bowler hat, and, oddly, a black mask across his eyes. He carries a cane.

He makes a rapid search of Harry's vehicle before turning away, empty-handed, then snaps his fingers and rushes back to uncover the compartment hidden in the floor. Retrieving the roll of material, he flattens it out over the roof: an oil painting on canvas, depicting a bleak mountain road under a brooding autumn sky. He studies it, then stows it in his coat.

The old man scrutinises the footprints leading into the forest, begins to follow. At the tree line, he stops as his cane touches something in the long grass. A large metal head rolls out. Wires tangle from its neck, dripping brown liquid. The old man kicks it away, then lights a cigarette. He holds his stick ready and walks on, fading among the misty trees.

The rain falls as if it might never stop. Or perhaps, as if it never began. As if it has simply always rained like this, and always will.

I.

THE SOUVENIR

"YOU NEVER HANG out any more, man."

David Anderson cracked his bubblegum in disapproval at Alex as they walked home from school through drizzling British rain. "Come on. Just come over. There's a whole team of us playing online now – it's total slaughter. I need you to get my back."

"I dunno," Alex muttered. "I've got this stuff I have to—"

"What stuff? You don't have any more homework than me. Anyway, it's Saturday tomorrow. You can't work *Saturday*. You're turning into a proper hermit."

"Yeah. I dunno." Alex stole a look behind.

"Just come," David pressed. "It's Mum's gran's birthday, she's like . . . ninety-one or something. Mum's doing her Old Country menu in honour: pumpkin soup, rice and beans, pen patat, the whole Haitian Kitchen Blowout. She's made tons. You'll be doing me a favour. I'll have to eat it for a fortnight. You loved it last time."

"Maybe. Can I text to let you know?"

David popped another disappointed green bubble and shrugged, unconvinced. "Sure."

They walked on, Alex trying to resist the urge to look back again. David turned to him, opened his mouth to speak, then frowned off over his shoulder. "Uh-oh."

Alex spun in alarm and groaned. Far back along the street, Kenzie Mitchell was waving, tripping over his oversized feet in a hurry to catch them.

"Alex!" Kenzie called distantly.

"Guy really seems mighty keen to talk to you these days," David mused. "What's all that about?"

"Don't know." Alex squinted ahead to his bus stop. A bus was approaching through slow traffic. If he sprinted, he might just catch it. "I'm going to try to get this one."

"Just come over, Alex," David called as he set off. "It'll be a laugh."

It felt good to run, and not only to put distance between himself and Kenzie's lumbering figure. But with every step, Alex felt the object in his coat pocket hitting against him, reminding him it was there. As if he could forget. When he jumped onto the half-empty bus and collapsed panting onto the back seat, he pulled it out.

An old toy robot made of tin.

He twisted around to look back. He spotted David, trotting across the road, going to meet his dad. Kenzie alone at the street corner, just standing there, watching Alex's bus roll away. Nothing out of the ordinary. Alex studied the rainy scene a second longer, then turned back to the robot.

He carried it everywhere now. The secret prize he was supposed to have destroyed far away, but which a compulsion he couldn't name had made him keep, sneaking it home like smuggled goods. The scratched little face leered up with its jagged metal grin. Alex stared down into the hollow eyes, closed his own, and concentrated.

The bus vibrated suddenly, violently, rattling his skeleton in his skin. Alex's eyes snapped open. For a second, he sat caught between terror and tingling elation. Then he realised. It had only been a shudder as a wheel hit a pothole. He let the hand holding the toy drop.

In the seat in front, a woman lifted a newspaper, shifting it backward and forward as if trying to focus. Alex read headlines over her shoulder without taking them in: a new discovery about black holes, an old painting stolen from a Cambridge museum, a cat who had become a billionaire and was being sued by its owner. He sighed and gazed out the window.

He wondered what Kenzie wanted. But not enough to stay and find out. In the past, there had been plenty of times he had run from Kenzie to avoid getting a fist in the face. But his former bully left him alone now. In fact, Kenzie had grown oddly quiet in general.

The turning point had come not long after Alex had returned from his trip with his grandfather: the unexpected journey that had become a desperate adventure as he somehow found himself caught in a mad race across Europe, trying to prevent dark forces from resurrecting a medieval monster, a magical creature of clay known as the Golem of Prague. Four months had passed since that demented episode. Four months without a word from the old man who had started it all.

Alex had been dumped back into his humdrum routine so abruptly the normality had hit him like a shock. But a storm of questions had been set raging in him, and his mind was still stuck back in those impossible days, playing it all over. Part vivid dream, part frantic nightmare, it almost felt like it had never happened at all.

Except he still had the robot as proof that it had. His weird souvenir of another, wilder, unseen world. His link back to it. If he could only work out how to make the connection again.

Alex stared at the little toy, picturing the great secret locked within, a hidden cargo he had glimpsed only briefly but which had burned itself onto his mind.

Concealed inside the robot lurked what looked like a lump of dusty old clay. In fact, he sat cradling a powerful fragment of a myth from centuries before. The few who knew the story referred to this ancient clay tablet as the name of God – a mystical artefact imbued with a devastating, unearthly force that had once given the golem life.

Just a crazy old fable. But Alex had seen it all spring to life around him and had encountered people prepared to go to desperate lengths to capture the tablet, wielding uncanny powers of their own.

Memories came crackling, more vivid, more real than the rumbling bus or the homework in his bag. Alex saw himself pursued by shadowy opponents using weird magic to animate a bizarre army of lethal robots, huge tin men, vicious little flying machines. He remembered the moment he had communicated with the golem itself. He could almost – almost – still feel the power locked inside the tablet, the memory of it moving though him, moving at his command. He had stood on the shoulders of an angel and ordered a river to stop running and rise and . . .

And now he couldn't do a thing.

For months now, when he tried to contact the tablet, he felt nothing at all. He turned it over for the umpteenth time, trying to trace what had changed and when.

Only twice since returning from Prague had he felt the power. First, the encounter in the park around Christmas, just after he got home. Kenzie had been getting roughed up by older boys. Alex had stepped in and he . . . he had made it stop. He had sent the boys away.

The second time had involved Kenzie, too. Although a word was never spoken about it, Kenzie had been left badly rattled by witnessing Alex's intervention in the park. When school started again, instead of making his life a misery, like he had for years, Kenzie left Alex alone. But eventually, his little gang began to notice and started goading Kenzie about it.

It came to a head one grey afternoon, when Alex found himself surrounded by an eager circle of boys led by a Kenzie determined to prove a point.

Alex's heart started hammering as they closed in, urging Kenzie on.

"Give him a slap, K."

"Get 'im, Kenz. Slap 'im."

"Little freak," Kenzie said. He swallowed warily, looked around the faces, licked his lips. "Little freak," he repeated, louder, working himself up. He raised his hand. Then he fell to his knees.

Alex stood motionless while the rest glanced uncomprehendingly at one another. Kenzie curled on the ground, helpless. One of the other boys moved uncertainly toward Alex, then grabbed at his own throat, choking. He crumpled, fell, eyes bulging.

Alex stood, feeling far away, feeling the power emanating from him, the old tin toy burning blue-white-gold in his pocket. The circle took a step back. He flicked his mind at them. More boys falling.

"Go away," Alex said.

He stopped it then, felt his mind falling to earth from somewhere else, descending through thick, slow time, and watched them hurry away. All except Kenzie, still moaning on the ground. For some reason the effect was strongest with him. Kenzie hadn't been quite the same since. None of the boys ever mentioned it again. But they left Alex alone.

Until now. Kenzie had been trying to talk to him these past few days, but Alex had worked hard to avoid him. He still felt bad about having used the power on him, even in defence. But ever since that confrontation, Alex hadn't felt a flicker from inside the tin toy, despite long nights of trying.

His stop drew near. Alex stowed the robot away. As he stepped off the bus, he stood gazing back the way he had come. Just weary traffic trickling homeward through lengthening shadows, just his town's familiar streets slanting away in the rain. He searched around, not knowing what he expected to find.

For the past week or so, he had been plagued by a dim feeling of being followed, the faint, nagging sense of eyes on him. He had started to suspect that what he sensed was only his own guilty feelings about having kept the robot when he was supposed to have got rid of it forever.

Beyond the rooftops, a white sun was sinking through smoky blue clouds. Alex shivered, zipped his coat at his throat, and hurried for home. Spring was here, but it felt like winter didn't want to let go.

II.

HOMEWORK

AFTER DINNER, ALEX went to his bedroom, closed the door, then stood considering the overdue homework stacked on his desk. His eyes drifted to the collection of old toy robots on the shelves above, gathered like a bright, waiting little army. Slightly dusty now.

He sat at the desk, and pulled a sheet from the pile.

Quadratic Sequences
1. Determine the nth term of the sequence 3, 8, 15 . . .

He looked at the numbers without seeing them. He heard his mum laughing at something Carl said downstairs. Rain rapped at his window as wind hit the house with sudden violence.

He flipped open his laptop and looked at the real homework that had been consuming his time, private projects of his own. The folder filled with his research on the golem legend was open. He hadn't found anything beyond what he already knew.

Nothing he could understand, anyway. Beside it, in another folder marked SALT, he'd started to compile every strange old superstition he could find about the stuff, folktales about its power to protect and ward against evil. He'd given up. There had been too many.

He keyed in the same news search he checked every night:

Vltava River Prague Bodies

Nothing.

He returned to his maths, then instantly abandoned it. He crossed the room and knelt to reach under his bed, pulling out first the old toy robot, then a piece of plywood that had once been part of a kitchen drawer but now served as a makeshift drawing board. A large sheet of paper taped over it bore sketches for a book cover he was supposed to be designing for art. He removed that, uncovering beneath another project of his own.

At the top of the board, he had pinned a creased photograph of his mother and father, taken years before he was born: a young couple at some dim, happy party, his dad half-turned, blurring into red-black shadows. A vague, tall man, with black hair pushed back from a high forehead. It was the only picture Alex had ever seen of him. He couldn't see him at all.

His father had died months before his birth. That's what he had always been told, anyway. He felt certain his mother believed it. He had believed it like a law of nature himself until recently.

The rest of the board was covered in a mess of smudgy charcoal drawings, dozens, all variations on the same subject: a tall man in a long black coat and black hat. Sketches from memory of the figure who had hunted Alex and his grandfather across Europe with his strange gang and their weird machines, trying to steal back the toy robot and its clay tablet.

The tall man, Alex called him – although he had eventually given him another, secret, name, one he could still barely bring himself to utter. In some of Alex's drawings, the sombre figure was depicted in full, turned away. In others, he loomed in brutal close-up: rough portraits of a head completely swathed in ragged bandages beneath the hat, save for one terrible eye.

This mummified visage was the only way Alex had ever seen him clearly, up close, after the man had used the tablet to summon forces he couldn't control. Alex flinched as he recalled white light falling from the Prague sky, turning poison-black as it struck down. It had burned the man terribly. But it was Alex who had killed him.

His breath caught as he replayed it again, the most intensely vivid memory of all: this tall, wounded figure leaping from a bridge into a raging river, trying to save his daughter, the unsettlingly strange little girl who had jumped first, diving in when she thought Alex had thrown the tablet into the water. The two of them dragged down under the lethal, boiling current.

Their phantom faces were always in his thoughts, the girl's – Zia, the tall man had called her – sharp and clear, the man's always just out of reach. Alex's attempts to capture his likeness, the features beneath the bandages, had become a nightly ritual. But when he closed his eyes and tried to picture the face he had once glimpsed, it receded into the shadows.

Yet Alex felt it was as close as his own skin. Of all the secrets uncovered during his adventure, this was the one that overwhelmed him most. From vague hints dropped in conversations, from his distant impressions of the tall man, from the resemblance he had eventually noticed hidden in his grandfather's face – from clues in his own mirror every morning – he was certain.

The tall man was his father.

That his grandfather had been determined to keep their pursuer's identity hidden from Alex, refusing to answer any questions about who he was, only confirmed it. Just thinking about it set something shivering in Alex's blood.

He studied the photograph of his dad at the party for the millionth time, trying to penetrate the haze. He felt sure he could match this shadowy picture with the tall shadow leaping through his memories. He taped a fresh sheet to the board, fished out his charcoals, and bent to begin another drawing.

He worked for an hour, hunched in concentration, losing himself, until he realised his arms and neck were aching. He stretched and rubbed his eyes, remembering too late his fingers were filthy with charcoal. His eyes stung. Blinking it away, his gaze caught on the robot lying by his side.

He picked it up and stared at it, long and hard. When he closed his eyes, its ghost hung printed in negative behind his eyelids. He concentrated, straining to send his mind out, detect anything reaching back.

Nothing. He shook the robot in frustration. "Where are you?"

Alex set it aside and looked back at his sketch. He had planned to draw the man's face, but it had somehow eluded him again. Instead, this latest picture showed the tall figure leaping away through the air, powered by the curious spring mechanisms he wore around his boot heels. His coat billowed like the cape of some eerie superhero. A silver-handled cane caught the light in one hand. In the other, a blade shone.

Alex sighed and reached for a fresh sheet of paper, then snatched his hand back as the edge sliced into the pad of his thumb. Hissing, he lifted the finger to his mouth, then hesitated, struck by a memory of cutting his finger on the old toy's rough tin in this room once before, his blood leaking inside, a first uncanny sensation creeping over him soon after.

He recalled his grandfather telling him about the other, real robots they had encountered, how the tall man and his followers powered them: . . . *they use* themselves . . . *Pieces of people. . . Bits of their own bodies . . .*

Blood glistened, rich red among the grimy black whorls of his thumbprint. He grabbed the robot before he could change his mind, held one hollow eye beneath his thumb, then squeezed until blood welled up.

There came a knocking at his bedroom door.

"Just a minute!" Alex scrambled to hide the robot and

drawings under the bed. Jumping to the door, he stole a last look around, then pulled it open. Carl stood there, a bundle of fresh laundry under one arm, a mug of tea in each hand. Proffering one, he stopped and laughed.

"Going goth?"

"Huh?"

"Your eyes." Carl gestured at his own with a mug. "You've got, like, panda rings."

"Oh." Alex took the tea, rubbed his eyes with his other wrist. He nodded toward the discarded book cover on the floor. "It's charcoal. Thing I'm doing for art."

"Can I come in a minute?"

Alex sat at his desk while his mum's partner perched on the bed, dumping the laundry beside him.

"So—" Carl stopped, frowning. "Hey, are you bleeding?"

"Oh." Alex sucked at his thumb, wiped it on his jeans. "Paper cut."

"Oooyah. Well, make sure you wash it, get a plaster on. By the way, what happened here?" From the heap of clean clothes, Carl pulled out Alex's black hoodie, then waggled two fingers through a rough little rectangular hole on the back.

"I don't know." Alex frowned. "I've never noticed that."

"A mystery." Carl nodded. "Probably the same thing puts holes in my socks. Gremlins come when they're on the washing line." He smiled at Alex. "So, uh, how you doing?"

Alex sipped tea, nodded, and shrugged. "Yeah, fine." He waited for whatever was coming.

"Getting on okay at school, I mean?"

"Mmm-hm."

"No trouble or anything."

"Nope." Alex shook his head. "Everything's fine."

"Good. Great. It's just, well, your mum. You know: your mum. She worries. She's worried you've been keeping to yourself a bit, and, y'know, we got that letter about you falling behind with homework. . ."

"I've just been a bit tired."

"Ha. Yeah. Tell me about it. God, when I was your age, I was sleeping all the time. Should've heard my dad. But, I mean, Alex, you know, if there ever was anything— I mean . . ."

Alex swigged more tea and sat staring at his bloody thumb while Carl went through all the things he thought might be troubling him. He could just see the old toy robot lying in the shadows under the bed, behind Carl's feet.

". . . remember what it was like," Carl was saying now. "I'm not that old. Alex, what I'm saying is: sometimes there might be things you might not want to talk to your mum about. But I'm here, you know. You can talk to me. About anything. I mean, I know I'm not your dad, but I—"

"That's right."

"What?"

"You're not my dad," Alex muttered, without looking up. As soon as the words were out, he wished he could call them back.

Carl opened his mouth, reconsidered. He smiled, stood, and took Alex's empty mug. At the door, he paused. "I mean it, though, Alex. Any time. Anything." He closed the door softly. Alex sat feeling shabby, listening to footsteps descending stairs, rain at the window.

He looked at the toy lurking beneath his bed. His desk lamp flickered and went out. He pushed absently on the wire at the base, bending it to the angle he knew would work. The lamp glimmered to life. Loose connection. He leaned his head back and sighed, then took out his phone.

"Hey," he said when David answered. "I will come over tomorrow. I mean, if it's still all right."

III.

DON'T LOOK BACK

THE VISIT TO David's was good, until it went bad.

For a few hours, they slumped on beanbags in David's room, carving their way through some paramilitary massacre of a video game, all digital slaughter and laughter over the headsets. After a while, Alex was surprised to realise he had stopped thinking about the robot, the tablet, the tall man, the girl, his grandfather, all of it. For the first time in months, the tension chewing his skull had eased. He concentrated on the game again, before it came back.

Finally, David's dad appeared in the doorway with a regretful grin. "Time to face the sisterhood."

Downstairs, crammed around the kitchen table, sat David's two older sisters, his mother and her two sisters, his grandmother and her sister, and, regally installed at the head of the feast, his great-grandmother.

David had been right: this was her ninety-first birthday.

She sat swaddled in layers of wool bright against papery grey-brown skin, sound asleep amid the chatter of her family and the muted thump from a well-used turntable.

With a few nods and a sternly raised eyebrow at David's elaborately mimed protests, David's mother ordered David and Alex to sit on either side of the dozing old lady. As Alex squeaked his chair into place, she gave one short, snorting snore, causing David to dissolve in giggles, until his mother's eyebrow shut him up.

"Thanks, Mrs Anderson," Alex said, as she handed him a steaming plate.

"It's good to see you, Alex." She shoved his shoulder gently. "You've not been over in too long." She turned to her mother. "Should we wake Granmé to eat?"

"Let her sleep. She's happy. If she wakes, she wakes."

They dug in. Outside, the night was dark and the rain never stopped, but the kitchen was warm and the lights glowed. The windows steamed as the talk, laughter, and music grew louder. The old woman slept, snoring occasionally. David made a face; his sisters smiled. Alex sank into the comfortable atmosphere, soaked it up.

Once, from the corner of his eye, he thought he saw a shadow move at the window. But when he looked around there were only raindrops running on misted glass. Just ordinary life. He'd forgotten how easy it could be. He made a decision: he would put the old robot away for good. When he got home, he

23

would say sorry to Carl and make things up with his mum. Since he'd returned from Prague, he had been increasingly avoiding talking to her, because he simply didn't know what he might be in danger of saying. *Dad. I saw him. Alive.*

He turned his mind from that. So. He would take the old toy away, somewhere remote, bury it deep where no one would ever find it. Just give it all up and forget. Get back to reality. A life that didn't involve his grandfather's world of ancient strangeness and sleeping monsters and salt and sinister machines and secrets and power. His father's world.

It was just as David's dad began serving dessert that Alex became aware of a change in the old woman. She hadn't snored for a while. Looking up, he caught a glint beneath one eyelid. It closed quickly. But she was awake. The eye opened a sliver again. Watching him.

He did his best to ignore it and turned to accept the bowl David's mum was passing. "Thanks, Mrs Anderson."

"Alex. How many times," she said. "It's Laetitia. Here. I made extra sweet potato bread." She slid another slice alongside his ice cream. "I remembered how much you like it."

The stuff was delicious, but Alex barely tasted it. The old woman had both eyes open now, fixing him with an angry stare. No one else seemed to have noticed. He chewed uncomfortably, forced down another mouthful, then almost choked as the old woman slammed both hands hard on the table.

The music bounced happily on as the gathering fell silent. David's great-grandmother was hauling herself to her feet.

"Granmé?" David's mother started out of her chair to help her. Before she could, the old lady straightened, extended one arm, and pointed an accusing finger in Alex's face: *"Bokor!"*

They all looked at each other. A voice from the stereo was singing about a girl in a hat. The old woman drew a shuddering breath, then shouted the word again, still pointing at Alex.

"What?" Alex managed.

"Granmé? Granmé, it's all right. . ." David's mother and grandmother rushed to her side. She struggled to fight them off. Alex stared at the melting ice cream on his plate. He felt conspicuous, under attack. Then, with alarm, he felt something else: the stirring beyond the borders of his mind he had been searching after for weeks.

Something was reaching out from the old toy robot he carried in his pocket. He felt it moving along the edge of his thoughts. He tried to turn away, but it came flooding fast, eerie, then familiar, wonderful. He wanted to surrender to it. He tried not to.

The sounds around him faded, replaced by a hissing on the air. The room was flickering. Things slowed. The glimmering light was vast now, golden white tinged blue, moving through him. Him moving through it. His mind cleared, expanded.

A tiny noise annoyed him from far below. He turned his head and saw himself sitting down there beyond the vibrating light, beside the shouting woman, and began to piece together the command to shut her up. A distant part of his mind was pleading to stop, *not now, not here, not them,* but it was very weak. He looked at the old woman and formed the words.

But there was something else . . . A hand on his arm.

He could stop that, too. He could remember the words that would make them all stop, send them into the corners. But there was still something else. . .

Lost inside his own skull, battered by thoughts from elsewhere, Alex fought to focus on the hand on his arm. He struggled against the tide of light, using the touch on his arm as an anchor, dragging himself toward it. It was David's father. He was saying something. What was he saying? A word. A name . . .

"Alex," David's dad repeated. He made a wincing nod toward the commotion at the head of the table. "You all right? Think maybe we should make ourselves scarce."

The terrible sensation was gone as instantly as slamming a door. Alex felt his mind rushing back into the here and now. It was as if he had been holding his breath under raging water and had forgotten until almost too late, then come bursting up. His legs felt weak as he stood.

Alex, David, and David's dad huddled in the hallway, listening to the impassioned cries from the kitchen. David shuffled his feet, a little embarrassed. He caught Alex's eye and mouthed a slow, silent *Wow*. Alex hoped his own trembling wasn't obvious. The force had ripped through him from nowhere, unbidden. He'd barely managed to control it. A memory of the sensation still fizzed in his limbs.

Gradually, the noises beyond the wall quietened. David's sisters emerged, frowned oddly at Alex, and went upstairs. A minute later, David's mother stepped out, holding a small plastic bag. At her nod, David's dad slipped back into the room behind her, cheerily announcing it was time for rum. She pulled the door closed softly at her back.

"Sorry, Alex." She gave a quick smile.

"What happened to her, Mum?" David said.

"I'm not sure. She's so old. The past and the present can get mixed up for her. When she was a little girl on the island, she heard some weird things. In the town where she grew up, there were all sorts of superstitions way back then. When I was young, she used to tell me some, all these wild bedtime horror stories. Until my mum found out, and put a stop to it. I think maybe she sometimes has, like . . . flashbacks. Y'know?"

"Uh, yeah. Guess. Crazy, though."

"This is not a word we use, David," his mum said.

David shrugged and shot Alex another secret cross-eyed look. Alex just wanted to get away.

"Is she all right, though, Mum?" David's concern was genuine.

"She's fine, she's calm. But maybe it's best if you don't go back in just now."

"No." Alex tried a smile. "I'd better get home, anyway."

At the doorstep, David's mum held the bag out to Alex over David's shoulder.

"Almost forgot. Sweet potato bread. Pretty good toasted."

"Thanks . . . That word she was shouting. Do you know what it means?"

She shook her head quickly. "Just some old rubbish."

"Probably means, like, 'Why's this incredibly ugly guy sitting beside me, get him away.'" David grinned as he closed the door.

Alex hunched into the breeze as he walked, his fingers curling and uncurling around the robot in his pocket. That was it. Tomorrow. He'd get rid of it tomorrow. Take a bus to the end of the line, head up into the hills. Bury it deep.

It was later than he had thought. Spits of rain came dancing through the dark. The street was long and curved out of sight ahead, devoid of life. When he was a few houses away from David's, he heard a rushing, slapping sound racing at him from behind and spun to see a pale shape lurching at his shoulder. Alex ducked away, heart slamming his chest. But after a moment of blind panic he realised he recognised the figure.

"Kenzie?" Breath shuddered out of him in relief.

"Alex," Kenzie puffed. "How you doing?"

"*What?* Where did you come from? What do you want, Kenzie?"

Kenzie fell silent, almost bashful, eyes fixed on his trainers.

"I was just passing," he mumbled. "No, well, all right. I followed you."

"*Followed* me? Wait, was that you I saw looking in David's window?"

"I've been trying to *talk* to you. . ." Kenzie sounded insistent, but his words trailed into silence.

"Kenzie, what do you *want*?"

Kenzie grabbed his arm. Alex recoiled, tried to shake free, but Kenzie's fist tightened. Under the street light, Alex saw he looked exhausted. His eyes were dull, shadowed by dark rings. "Listen, Alex. I keep having these dreams."

"What? Let go, Kenzie."

"*Listen.*" The larger boy gripped tighter, stepped closer. "Just listen, freak, right? I—" He broke off in fright, clamping his free hand over his mouth as though trying to stop the words that had already escaped. "Sorry. Didn't mean that. But listen. I keep having these dreams."

"Kenzie, just let go."

"I can't really remember. Just bits. It's dark. And there's rain, right? It's always raining. But there's fire. Fire above. Like, in the sky. Blue fire. White. There are people in the dark. And people in the fire, or . . . not sure. Things. Behind the fire. And everything's beginning to break. Everything. Above. Below. Alex, everything's breaking." He was speaking faster, growing wild-eyed. "Right? And you're there. But there's something *behind* you, right?"

"Kenzie, let go."

"No, *listen*." Kenzie was almost shouting. "It's every night! I'm trying to tell you there's something behind you, but I can't talk. You don't see it, but it's right behind—"

Alex ripped his arm away.

"Oh." Kenzie fell silent. His frenzy drained away as though a plug had been pulled. He stood blinking like a sleepwalker startled awake. His rheumy eyes settled on Alex again and flashed fright.

"I need to get home," Alex said, massaging his arm where the fingers had dug in. "I think you should, too." He took a few steps, then turned. Kenzie just stood there, looking lost. Alex gestured to him. The older boy responded as if he'd been waiting for instruction. They walked to the corner.

"I'm this way," Alex said, indicating left. "You're down there, yeah?" He pointed in the opposite direction. Kenzie followed the motion and nodded vaguely, as if still not quite certain.

"Kenzie, will you be okay getting home?"

"Yeah." Kenzie shook his head, rubbed at his face, then straightened, composing himself. "Sorry," he said, walking away.

Alex watched him go. After a few steps, Kenzie stopped, just a shadow now.

"In my dream, though." The voice drifted along the street. "There's something behind you."

Alex dug his hands into his pockets, turned away, walked

fast. "Something behind you," he heard himself repeating. Kenzie's sudden appearance and babbling about his dreams reminded Alex forcefully of his own sense of being followed. It was there again now, he realised. He looked back. Only an empty street.

He stalked on toward his bus stop, then decided to keep walking, hoping the cool air might settle his churning mind. A few streets later he regretted not taking the bus. He glanced behind again. The streets were deserted. Something about the rain made the night seem blacker. The silence was sharp, tight. Then he heard it. Footsteps.

He stopped to peer around. Nothing. Street lights made shivering cones of light in the rain. Between them, voids of darkness.

"Kenzie?" His call sounded small and flat against the night, no echo to it. No reply. Another noise now, gone as soon as he heard it. Different. From a different place. Higher? A *click*, maybe. He told himself it was his imagination, and tried to ignore the voice in his head reminding him he had already seen things that he would never have imagined.

Alex walked faster. The footsteps started again. The dark houses seemed to lean back, trying to get clear. The bend of the road was sinister. Pictures crowded his mind, metal men and flying things with slashing wings. He clutched at the old toy robot. Now would be a good time for the feeling, the power. But there was nothing. He ran.

He sprinted along the street and vaulted a gate, tearing through a garden, hurdling the fence into the next. Landing roughly, he looked back. Was that something moving? Or just rain in the air? A narrow path along the side of this house led to another street beyond. He charged across it, on into more dark gardens. Hunkering down beside a hedge, he watched, listened, then, when he was certain there was nothing, moved in a crouch toward the street and squatted by the gatepost.

To his left there was a junction with another, larger road where there was a bus stop. There might be people, anyway. He threw a last look back as he charged for the corner and so didn't see the tall figure until he'd run into him.

Alex struggled as strong hands pinned his arms to his sides.

"Finally," said the voice.

IV.

THE DARK END
OF THE STREET

"LED ME QUITE the merry dance, have to say."

The hands let go as the figure stepped back. Flinching, raising his arm, it took Alex a second to realise he was somehow looking at his grandfather, shadowy under the street lamps.

"Running through people's gardens," the old man muttered, brushing down his long grey coat. Between thumb and forefinger he held up a leafy twig from a hedge that had been caught in his buttonhole. "Not really the done thing, Alex. Still, good to get the old pulse rate up every now and then. A little exercise never hurt anyone. Well, so they insist on telling me, anyway. Can't say I ever fancied it much myself. I mean, the *clothes* they wear."

He shuddered, looked up, and beamed. "So, how are you, young man? Sorry not to have been in touch for a while, but—"

"You," Alex cut him off, panting. His heart pumped out a cocktail of relief and guilt, delight and anger. In the months since Prague he had heard nothing from him beyond a cheque in the post for a new phone, then a hastily signed birthday card with another cheque, and a DVD of an old movie. He had sensed the old man was deliberately avoiding him, much the way Alex had been avoiding speaking to his mum.

"Where have you *been*? You almost gave me a heart attack. Why didn't you get in touch? Wait." Alex frowned. "How long have you been following me?"

"Following you? I've not. I've only just got here. I went to your house, your mother mentioned where you were, so I thought I'd stroll over, see if I couldn't catch you. Need to have a chat, Alex. Rather important. I saw you talking with that boy, and it didn't seem polite to interrupt, but then you started running for some reas—" The old man stopped abruptly and looked off behind Alex.

"Ah, so, why ask? How long have I been following you, I mean."

"Nothing, it's just . . . nothing."

"Alex. It's me you're talking to."

"Just a feeling I've had. Like maybe someone was watching me. I can't really explain it."

The old man's face clouded. He peered more urgently along the street. His eyes narrowed, then widened. Grabbing Alex by the collar, he pulled him roughly into the centre of the road.

"Stand there."

"Wha—"

No reply. The old man was moving in a curious, rapid crouch, circling Alex. As he went, he cast regular looks back.

Alex followed his gaze. Nothing. Although, the darkness seemed particularly dark along there. Puzzling at the scene, he realised what was different. After a certain point, the street lights just seemed to stop. Beyond the last, nothing but black.

The footsteps started again. Louder.

"Those are the footsteps I heard," Alex said.

"I can't hear them, Alex." As the old man completed his circle, Alex saw with alarm he had laid a thin, powdery white line around them. His grandfather straightened, studying his work. "Can you see if I've left any gaps?"

"Salt?" Alex heard his voice rise to a squeak. "Why do we need salt?" Back along the street, the furthest street lamp winked out.

"Not sure." The old man stared grimly into the darkness. "Never hurts to be prepared, though." The footsteps were enormously loud.

"You can't *hear* that?"

Another light snuffed out. The footsteps stopped.

"Behind me, Alex."

Before he could move, the blackness came rushing. It surged at them like a flood wave, a towering, noiseless mass, gobbling up the remaining street lights, blotting out the sky. As it rolled nearer Alex saw it was made of countless small circular particles, about to engulf them. On instinct, he threw himself down. After a few seconds of nothing else, he risked looking up over the crook of his elbow.

They were inside the roiling black cloud. His grandfather

stood over him as the fury fumed around them, pressing close, but somehow not touching them. Alex climbed gingerly to his feet. It was like standing inside a transparent tube on the bed of a seething ocean. None of the raging blackness crossed the salt circle, but it pressed against the invisible boundary as if against glass.

Mesmerised, Alex stepped forward to get a closer look and wished he hadn't. Each of the myriad circular objects that made up the cloud was a tiny, grotesque head, about the size of a small, rotted apple. And each head was the same: wearing a black hat and entirely swathed in dingy bandages, save for one burning, baleful eye.

As Alex stared, the rotten bandages on the things closest loosened, falling away to reveal yawning, oversized mouths, filled with razor teeth. They snapped like flying piranha just beyond his nose. Repulsed yet fascinated, he lifted a finger to the glass, forgetting there was no glass there. Tiny heads massed hungrily around the spot his finger was moving toward, mouths threshing.

"Alex!" His grandfather knocked his hand down. "Not a good idea to break the circle." The gnashing mouths frenzied in frustration, then, in a blink, the swarm was gone. Alex and his grandfather stood in weak rain under quietly buzzing street lights. There was no sign anything had happened at all.

Fresh shock washed over Alex. "What . . . Those *heads*. That *face*."

"How's that?" His grandfather was scanning the road.

"Heads," Alex repeated. "Faces . . . *His* face. M—" He caught himself before he said it aloud. "The tall man."

"Hmm." The old man ground his jaw. "I couldn't really see them, Alex. I saw a lot of murk vibrating, a disturbance. But I'm afraid that was mostly just for you."

"For *me*? What *was* that?"

"Well." The old man was rooting through his coat pockets. He came out with a single, battered little packet of salt, frowned at it, then put it away. "Couple of possible explanations. Actually, I was wanting a word with you about all this kind of thing, old chap. But first." He gave Alex a grave look and rested a hand on his shoulder. "I need to ask you something. And you must promise to tell the truth. Promise?"

Alex nodded. He tried to push fear from his mind and focus. His fingers brushed the tin toy in his pocket. Now the time had come, he was apprehensive about confessing he had kept it.

"Good man." Lowering his voice, Alex's grandfather fixed him with a penetrating stare. "Now: is that a doggie bag?"

"Huh?"

"In your hand." He nodded toward it. "Plastic bag. Had the notion it might have something to eat inside. I'm famished, Alex. Not had any dinner. Been on the road for days."

Alex started to say something, gave up, held out the bundle.

"Good show. Now then, what have we . . ." The old man opened the package eagerly, took a great sniff. His eyes rounded. He grabbed a piece out, popped it in his mouth.

"Good lord. Pen patat. Nirvana. I've not tasted this in years, Alex.

Not since I was in Haiti that time. Let's see, late-fifties it was. Got a little sticky, as I recall. The trip, I mean, not the pudding." He munched on happily, smiling at a memory. "Ha, I remember, Harry, he—"

Alex's grandfather fell suddenly silent. He folded the bag closed and handed it back, picking fussily at crumbs on his coat. "Look at this. I'll be needing a bib soon. Let's get off the street, eh? We need to talk. I seem to remember there's a quite passable café not far from here. Be safer indoors, and I really am hungry, Alex. A body cannot live on pudding alone, exquisite though it may be. Did you get yourself another phone?"

Alex nodded, pulled it out.

"Have their uses, I suppose," the old man muttered. "Well, what say you drop your mother a message, let her know you're with me, and we're off to get ourselves a little late supper."

Alex looked in the direction the nightmarish cloud had vanished, and shivered. Getting inside was an idea he couldn't argue with. They started walking while he texted, turning onto a brighter road.

Neither noticed but, back along the street behind them, a tiny shadow detached itself from a roof and fluttered into the air. It hovered shakily above the chimneys for a moment as if it might fall, then, with a weak whirr, bobbed after them through the rain.

V.

CUSTARD CREAMS

A YELLOW EXPLOSION of yolk dripped to the plate as Alex's grandfather bit into his first roll.

"Marvellous," he mumbled. "Been living on European motorway food recently, Alex. Fine in small doses, but not something to base your life around. There's nowhere like a decent old-fashioned British café. Not that there are many left."

They had passed two coffee shops Alex knew on the way, but his grandfather had dismissed his recommendations, striding on until they reached this greasy hole-in-the-wall, hidden up a small street that Alex had never noticed before.

The man behind the counter thrived in his own steamy microclimate between a chrome-plated coffee machine, a tea-urn the size of a boiler, and a grill on which half a dozen different meals were sizzling. From the empty taxis outside, it seemed most of the customers were cabbies on night shift. Conversations thrummed the air. Alex's grandfather glanced around, then idly stuffed the salt shaker from the table into his coat pocket.

The entire time they had been there, the old man had persisted in burbling about the weather, about an old film, about food, about nothing. Every now and then, though, he fixed Alex with a long, silent, knowing stare. He knew his grandfather was working up to something – but Alex had questions of his own and was determined this was the night he'd finally get some answers. Before they left this place, he would get his grandfather to admit who the tall man really was. He just needed to think how to begin.

"Marvellous," the old man repeated, taking another bite. "You know, last place I tried getting a simple egg sandwich, fellow tried to put an *avocado* on it. I mean, planet's gone mad. Nothing against the avocado, but there's a time and a place. Mind you, Harry said he'd tried something similar and . . ." He fell silent again, considered the roll in his hand, then placed it alongside the other lying untouched on his plate and pushed the plate away. "Ha. Not as hungry as I thought."

Alex wasn't listening. The mention of Harry Morecambe, his grandfather's oldest friend, had called up a memory from the whirl of a few months before.

Alex had been alone with Harry, and had tried to quiz him about the tall man's identity. Finally, reluctantly, Harry had shown him an old photograph from his wallet. Alex had seen it only briefly, yet was certain of what he had seen: his grandfather, supposedly pictured over seventy years earlier, but looking only twenty years younger.

It was an impossible riddle. But Harry had been trying to tell him something that Alex hadn't been able to figure out. He'd become so caught up in his fascination with the tablet that he'd almost forgotten about it. Now it struck him: Harry hadn't shown him the picture as an *answer*. He was trying to tell him the *question*. Harry had shown him the photograph so he would ask his grandfather about it. Harry was giving him the way in.

Alex's grandfather lifted the metal teapot to refill his mug. His face fell. "Empty. Hang on."

The old man crossed to the counter and stood chatting with the man in the steam. Street light made spattered jewels of rain on the black window behind him. Alex's eyes drifted back to the plate on the table, one roll half-eaten, the other untouched. He'd never known his grandfather to leave food unfinished.

He pulled out his phone and tried to remember the word David's great-grandmother had screamed at him, to try a search. Just to take his mind off things. *Bogor* and *Bocker* pulled up nothing that fit. Trying *Bokor*, he froze at the first result:

> *BOKOR*
> *In the Vodou religion, sorcerers who may practise both light and/or dark magic. Their black magic famously includes the making of ouanga (pronounced "wan-gha"),*

voodoo dolls, or talismans, which house spirits. Also, the
creation of animated corpses.

He put the phone away and closed his eyes. When he opened them, a fresh mug of tea had appeared. He watched the old hand stir in four heaped spoonfuls of sugar.

"Get yourself around that. Sugar'll help. Got some biscuits, too." His grandfather put the plate on the table, then surreptitiously splashed something from a hipflask into his own mug and took a swig. "Feeling almost human again," he said. Setting down the mug, he flexed his left hand and massaged it with the right. "Pins and needles." He winced, then switched his gaze to Alex with new intensity. "And so. How about you, young man? How've you been feeling? Aside from tonight's unpleasantness."

"Fine. Just, you know. Getting on with school and stuff."

"Mmm-hm. Anything else been keeping you busy?"

"No, just . . ."

"Hobbies or such?" The old man's eyes never left Alex's. "The old *toy robot* collection, for instance." He started tapping a sharp, relentless rhythm on the table. "How's that these days?" *Tap-tap-tap-tap.* "Anything in particular you might like to tell me about that?" *Tap-tap-tap-tap.*

"Uh . . ."

"Nothing?" *Tap-tap-tap-tap-tap.* "You might like to share?" *Tap-tap-tap-tap-tap.*

"Just . . . Oh." Alex screwed shut his eyes, then surrendered. "Okay, okay. All right."

He took the toy from his pocket and stood it on the table, fighting the urge to snatch it back. The decision to give it up was almost physically painful. But there was also an undeniable sensation of relief.

"Uh-huh," his grandfather muttered. "And there we are."

"Just take it," Alex said. "I don't want it. It's too much. Take it back, throw it in the river. Get rid of it."

"Tell me, Alex." The old man made no move to touch the toy. "What was in the box? That night, on the bridge, I saw you throw it. There was something in there."

"Oh. My phone. My old phone. It was broken, anyway. Just take it."

"Ah, what made you keep it, son?"

"I'm not even sure." Alex tried to be honest. "I just wanted to . . . *know* more. Learn more. I guess part of me thought I could use it to protect myself. I used to get bullied a bit at school. I mean, you remember the guy you saw beating me up."

"Ah . . . vaguely."

"Kenzie. Remember when I was a little kid, when I was really small. The doctors said I wasn't growing properly – you took me and Mum on all those hospital visits for years."

"Of course." His grandfather grew suddenly absorbed in studying the biscuits. "Go on."

"Yeah, well, he started picking on me then, at primary school. Then, dunno. It just became, like, his hobby. I thought, if I had the tablet . . . I just wanted to see what I could do."

He fell silent. This was the first chance he'd had to talk

about the tablet at all, but it occurred to him there was another reason he had kept it, one he couldn't bring himself to say. This old toy and the power it held were his sole connection to the strange other life his father had abandoned everything for. Abandoned him for.

"I wonder if there wasn't something else," the old man mused. "If it was entirely your decision. Maybe the tablet simply didn't want to be destroyed. The power has been woken and doesn't want to go back to sleep and . . ." His grandfather let the thought trail off and sat back, glancing from Alex to the robot. "And so how have you been getting on with it?"

Alex looked up. "Huh? How do you mean?"

"You know *exactly* what I mean, young man. Have you –" the old man leaned forward – "been able to *use* it?"

"Oh. Sort of. A little. At first. If I got in trouble, like a fight. If someone was going to hurt me, I could make them stop. Make them go away. I mean, I wasn't doing anything *bad*." His mouth was dry. He tried more tea. "But I didn't really know what I was doing, how I was doing it. I tried to learn. But then, well. It just went away."

"Went away?" His grandfather was following intently.

"That's the only way I can explain it." Alex shrugged. "When I tried to . . . contact it, I couldn't find it. There was nothing. For weeks now. Months. Well, not until . . ."

"Until?" his grandfather prompted.

"Tonight. At David's." He told his grandfather about it. "The feeling, the power, it just came from *nowhere*. I didn't try to use it, I didn't *want* to use it. It just started, and I almost couldn't stop it. I don't even know what it was going to do. What I was going to do. You really didn't see those heads back there?" Alex blinked around the café. It suddenly felt weird, sitting in a room full of strangers.

His grandfather sat chin in hand, gazing at the toy. "Well. What you just said about not being in control. That's one possible explanation for what happened on the street. That attack. It might not have *been* an attack. Not from outside, I mean. There's a chance you might be doing it to yourself. Playing with things you don't understand, making ripples. Opening doors. You said the heads you saw were all *him*. The, ah, tall man." The old man sighed heavily. "He only had custard creams."

"Huh?" Alex blinked.

"Chap who runs the café." His grandfather nodded to the counter. "Nothing left but custard creams. On the biscuit front. Never was much of a fan of the custard cream, but any port in a storm, eh?" He crunched one and offered the plate. Alex scowled, shook his head, and sat straighter, listening for his chance as his grandfather went on.

"So, yes. It could simply have been a nightmare you conjured up for yourself, Alex, and you gave it the tall man's face because his face has been on your mind. On the *other* hand, if it *was* from outside, it seemed relatively weak, maybe directed at you from afar, or . . ." He broke off, pursuing a thought, then put down his biscuit, only half-eaten. He tapped the robot and smiled sympathetically.

"Really should have chucked it in the river, Alex."

"Yeah. Well, you can do that now. Just take it back over there and get rid of it."

"Hah, yes." His grandfather pulled at an earlobe. "Well, that would be the *long-term* plan, certainly. But, thing is, Alex . . ."

"Everyone thinks it was destroyed, anyway. That night," Alex continued, barely listening. He stared at the toy, weighing the idea of never seeing it again. Not a bad idea at all.

"Mmmm. Well, I had my suspicions. Couldn't put my finger on it, but there was something about you, Alex. Some kind of glow. When you've been around this business long as I have, you develop something of a sixth sense for it. Might have been what David's great-grandmother picked up on tonight. But I felt you'd been through enough without a grilling from me there and then. Alex, I really meant to have this out with you long before now, but my plans got . . . derailed. It was a lot to leave you with. I truly *am* sorry about that, old chap."

"It's okay. I—" Alex couldn't go on. Memories from that night on the bridge in Prague were washing over him again. "After all that," he whispered, "how could you just *leave* me to . . . ? He *jumped*, he . . . I *killed* him. Both of them. Him and the girl. Zia, he called her. Her name was Zia."

"Whoa, wait." The old man grabbed urgently at Alex's arm. "Alex. Listen to me. None of that. It wasn't your fault. My fault, for dragging you into it. You only did what you had to. You *saved me*, son. The girl jumped. He jumped after her. They got themselves in that situation, and they've been in far worse places before. Believe me, they wouldn't have thought twice about—"

"But he was—"

"Alex, listen," his grandfather broke in. "I'm *truly* sorry I've not been in touch. I should have been here to help you. Talk to you. But, well, y'see, things got a little busy. Ever since Prague, Harry and I have been—"

There it was. "Harry," Alex said. "I need to ask you about Harry—"

"Well. That makes two of us. It's Harry I'm here to talk to you about, Alex. Harry's . . . Harry's in a very bad predicament."

"What?"

"Seriously, Alex. Bad trouble. Literally life and death."

The clamour of questions in Alex's head was silenced as thoughts of Harry came slicing through. He had spent only a few intense days with the man, yet he thought of Harry as one of the best friends he'd ever had. Harry had told him they had actually met once years before, at a time Alex couldn't remember, back when he was still that very small and sickly child, the object of curiosity for countless baffled doctors. *Knee-'igh to a baby grass'opper*, Harry had put it.

He thought again of the photograph Harry had shown him: Harry a child himself, maybe six or seven, standing by Alex's grandfather in their vanished black-and-white world. His grandfather wore a military uniform and looked somewhere in his fifties. Harry had been orphaned during the Second World

War, hiding among bombed buildings in London. He'd said Alex's grandfather had taken him under his wing.

It didn't make sense. The old man and Harry looked roughly the same age now. But it suddenly hit Alex: if what Harry said were true, then Harry was more than an old friend to his grandfather. He was practically an adopted son.

"What's wrong? What's happened to Harry?" Alex said.

His grandfather spoke very quietly: "They got him, Alex . . . Your tall man. Zia."

"*What?*"

"They didn't *die* that night. I don't suppose I ever believed for a second they were really gone."

"Alive?"

"Bad as ever," his grandfather went on. "Worse. And they've got *Harry*. We need to get Harry back, Alex. You and I. I need you to *help* me get Harry back. You and that." He pointed at the old toy standing between them on the table. "You've used it before. You can use it again."

Alex tried to answer. But all he could focus on was the robot's reflection in the tarnished metal teapot, the way it stretched and bulged grotesquely, the way it kept grinning out at him from its dim, distorted dimension.

VI.

A GODDESS AMONG
GARAGE CATS

THE NEXT AFTERNOON Alex sat on a train, foggy after a sleepless night. Damp French fields slipped by outside. He could sense other people in the carriage, their comings and goings. None of it seemed real.

He traced his thumb over the toy robot in the pocket of his hoodie, closed his eyes, and tried reaching out to it with his thoughts. He let his body go slack, bobbing to the train's rhythm, but kept his mind alert, tight as a drum skin, poised for the faintest shiver of response. Empty minutes went by, ending in nothing.

Alex abandoned the attempt. He couldn't concentrate. His grandfather's news had sent feelings rippling through him in too many different directions. Excitement, worry, hope, fear. Some emotions he couldn't find labels for.

His mum had been reluctant about letting him skip school to go on a journey so soon after Easter break. But his grandfather had, in his words, "worked the old charm."

"Marvellous luck," the old man had whispered to Alex the previous night, after speaking alone with Alex's mum and Carl in the kitchen. "Your mother has been very worried about you, young man. Shutting yourself away in your room, getting all moody. I told her not to worry: it's just what happens when they become teenagers. But I suggested it might be an idea if you came along with me for a little trip. Get you out of yourself. Told her we were throwing a surprise birthday party for Harry."

Now his grandfather sat spread across the seat opposite, hidden behind a newspaper. Occasionally he would lean forward to cross-reference his reading with a heap of other newspapers and clippings on the table. Sometimes he scribbled in a battered black notebook. Champagne fizzed quietly in a glass near to hand.

Alex could make out some of the scattered headlines, printed in French, German, Italian, one in English:

GERMAN GALLERY PARTIALLY DESTROYED BY MYSTERY THIEVES

BAROQUE MASTERPIECE PAINTING STOLEN IN MUNICH

As his grandfather bent for his drink, he caught Alex's gaze and tapped the newspaper. "Been following this at all? The stolen paintings?"

Alex frowned. He vaguely recalled something in the news.

But that had happened in Britain. Cambridge, maybe. He shook his head.

"Harry and I have spent the past few months chasing this." The old man put down the paper and gestured at the others. "There have been several pieces taken, all across Europe. No one else seems to have spotted any connection. It took me a few weeks to realise: it's *them*, Alex. It's *them* stealing these paintings."

"The tall man?" Alex sat forward. "Are you certain?"

"Without a doubt." His grandfather shrugged. "I just, eh, haven't been able to work out why they're doing it."

"Well – for money?"

"Hmm? Oh, no." The old man shook his head. "He has little need of that. And if he did, he has more subtle ways. That's one of the things that worries me about this, Alex. They're risking drawing attention. And they're getting increasingly reckless. Far as I can tell, eight paintings have been taken since Christmas. They seem in a desperate rush." He stared out over the industrial landscape now flitting by and repeated quietly to himself: *"Desperate."*

After a moment, he started to gather his papers and put them away. "Clearly, it's for some purpose," he continued. "Something on – y'know – *the sinister side*. I have the feeling it's a very bad business indeed." He paused, pursing his lips doubtfully. "Ah, how about *Shadow Gate*, Alex? Ever come across anything about that anywhere?"

"No. What is it?"

"Just an old story I heard one time," his grandfather said. He blinked away his dark look and smiled. "Long time ago. Well, half a story. Not even that much. I've been trying to remember it."

A tinny voice sounded above, welcoming them to Paris.

"Tell you about it when we get to Harry's office." The old man was already standing, pulling on his coat, eager to get moving.

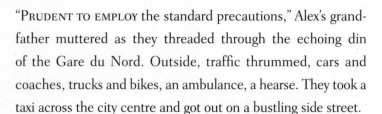

"PRUDENT TO EMPLOY the standard precautions," Alex's grand-father muttered as they threaded through the echoing din of the Gare du Nord. Outside, traffic thrummed, cars and coaches, trucks and bikes, an ambulance, a hearse. They took a taxi across the city centre and got out on a bustling side street.

After a few minutes' walking, the old man hailed another cab for a snaking ride back toward the train station they had just left. He had the driver drop them a few streets beyond, beside a Métro entrance. He paused, scanning the road. Half-hearted rain flitted around them.

"Keep alert," the old man said as he started down the stairs.

It was lunchtime. The underground was busy. Instead of heading for the platforms, his grandfather led him through tunnel-like corridors to another exit and out. After another long, weaving taxi ride, they were standing on a derelict-looking grey street beyond the city outskirts, watching their cab drive away.

"I really don't think anyone's following us," Alex said, scanning the road. Even as he spoke, he realised his own queasy sense of being followed had diminished. In fact, looking around the unfamiliar landscape, he sensed himself coming into focus for the first time in months. Caught in his lonely experiments with the old toy robot, he hadn't realised how much he had wanted to go on another trip with his grandfather. Despite the tumult and danger of their last adventure, and the ominous mood surrounding this new mission, he felt sharper, looser, than he had in a long time. The air seemed sweeter against his skin, an undeniable prickle of excitement.

Shabby walls around eight feet tall ran on either side of the road, shielding the buildings behind. Alex's grandfather stopped at a large, weathered gate. To judge by the flakes of paint clinging to the wood, it had once been green. A smaller door was set into it, beside an unmarked buzzer.

"Top man in Paris," the old man said as he pressed the button. "Harry swears by him. And sometimes at him."

A labourious shuffling of feet on gravel approached from the other side, there was a sound of latches being pulled, and the door opened a crack. A suspicious, bloodshot eye appeared. Beneath it, a hollow cheek sporting grey stubble and a mouth turned down in a sour pout around a half-smoked, currently unlit cigarette. The red eye scowled, scrutinised, then widened.

"Ah!"

The door opened, revealing a skinny man in his seventies, almost drowned by a shapeless blue cardigan and well-worn overalls. A black beret that had known better times sat back on his head. Tucking the cigarette behind his ear, he threw open his arms to embrace Alex's grandfather.

"Albert," Alex's grandfather said, after he had disentangled himself. He indicated Alex. "*Voici mon petit fils*, Alex. Alex, meet Albert, the greatest mechanic left in all France."

Alex held out his hand but was engulfed in a serious bear hug. He staggered as Albert released him and waved them through into a small yard made smaller by teetering mounds of scrap: creeping heaps of tyres, exhausts, engine blocks, and other unidentifiable components in varying degrees of decay.

As they entered, cats scattered in every direction and assumed precarious perches, watching them suspiciously. In one corner, the bright remains of two pinball machines stood lopsided beside the rusted skeletons of two ancient cars propped on bricks, and a low, hulking shape covered by a rain-spattered blue tarpaulin. Along the back wall, garage doors stood pulled back to reveal a large workroom. Albert disappeared inside.

In the middle of the yard, incongruous amid the junk, a long, low car shone blackly, all curves. Alex knew it was old, but it gleamed as though it had just rolled out of a showroom. A Citroën DS, 1961 model. Spoiling the brochure image, a fat, one-eyed white cat lay sprawled on the bonnet, showing off its belly while squinting disdainfully at them. Part of one ear had been bitten away.

"The Goddess," Alex said. "Harry's car." Seeing it without its owner gave him a chill.

"Well, yes and no," his grandfather said. He scratched the cat gently behind its mangled ear. "*Bonjour*, Simone. To be precise, this is Harry's *new* car. Or will be, once we get him back and give it to him. Be a nice surprise for him. Albert here, eh, sourced it for me. He's just been souping it up to Harry's rather particular specifications. Harry's *old* car's over there." He gestured idly with his cane at the shape beneath the tarpaulin. "He crashed it in Germany, when they got him. I had it hauled back. Albert can cannibalise it for spare parts. If there are any useable parts left."

Alex approached the blue shroud and lifted a corner. A scruffy ginger tabby appeared by his side and leapt softly up, curious to see. Alex winced at the smashed remains beneath. He had always been told his father had died in a car accident. Beyond knowing it supposedly happened in Germany – as, it seemed, had Harry's wreck – the details had been left vague. Now he knew why. But looking at the torn and twisted metal still sent something echoing through him.

"Harry was in there? When it happened?"

"Hmmm? Oh. Yes. He was being chased. Then he got stopped. And then they got him."

The cat jumped down and padded away, unimpressed. Alex let the sheet fall back. "Where is he now?"

"Still in Germany. The south." After a moment his grandfather added darkly, "The Black Forest."

Albert reappeared, carrying a half-empty bottle of red wine and two glasses. He gave one glass to the old man, then pulled the cork from the bottle with his teeth and spat it toward a small, oily mound of thick springs on the ground. Splitting the last of the wine between the two glasses, he raised his own in a toasting motion, then stopped, lifting a finger.

"Ah." From his cardigan, he produced a scratched tin and proffered it to Alex, who frowned as he read the greasy label: SINGER SEWING MACHINE OIL.

"Oh," Albert muttered, taking it back. "*Pardon.*" After a moment's more searching, he pulled from another pocket a small bottle of fizzy orange, handing it to Alex with a nod.

"*Bon.*" He raised his glass again. "*Salut.*"

"For friends not here," Alex's grandfather said. Taking a sip, he paused, closed his eyes, then beamed. "Oh, well done, Albert. The '82, is it?"

They began a conversation in French that Alex could not follow, beyond realising from their gestures that the subject swiftly switched from the apparently excellent wine to the car. Albert muttered and gesticulated at the vehicle while the old man squinted and hummed, kicked tyres, and asked the odd question. Finally, Alex's grandfather gestured toward the springs on the ground.

"*Et l'autre?*"

"*C'est chez* Harry," Albert said. The Frenchman produced the oil again, holding it up for inspection, then handed it over, along with a set of car keys, sealing the transaction with a formal crack of bony knuckles.

Alex's grandfather stood regarding the springs on the ground.

With an air of resignation, he nodded and gave Albert a sad smile. Albert laid a consoling hand on his shoulder. The old man pushed the oilcan into his Gladstone, then tossed it inside the car, followed by Alex's rucksack.

"Alex, we're off."

There came another round of hugs, followed by another scattering of cats as Albert hauled the main gate squealing open and Alex's grandfather nosed the car into the street. The engine purred impatiently while he sat for a moment making sure the coast was clear, then they were moving fast.

"Albert's a little on the lugubrious side," the old man said, "but he's done a marvellous job here." The Citroën hummed happily as they swung onto a busy road. Alex's grandfather flexed his fingers around the steering wheel as if loosening a cramp. "Harry'll be over the moon when he sees this car. Although I'm sure he'll find something to complain about."

"Did you say we're going to Harry's office?" Alex said.

"That's right. Need to collect something. I want to check his place over before we head off, anyway. I'm hoping he might have left something useful lying around. Good at keeping notes, is Harry, and he'd made discoveries in recent days." The old man frowned flatly. "Although it might have been better for him if he hadn't."

VII.

DON'T

IT WAS DARK by the time they made it to central Paris and the terrace by the river where Harry kept an office. Street lights flickered on as the old man drove slowly toward the door. He rolled past it without glancing around, pulling in some way down the block.

Alex unclipped his seat belt and reached for the door as the engine cut out. A hand on his arm stopped him.

"Not yet," his grandfather said. He adjusted his rearview mirror and sat back, watching it. "Thought I saw something. Harry's window."

Alex turned in his seat. The elegant street was empty. Fine rain made a champagne fizz around globe lamps. He picked out Harry's doors, set behind a wrought-iron grille, then bent until he could see the third-floor windows above, dark and life-less. Leather squeaked as his grandfather clambered around to join him looking back. They hunched side by side as rain

spattered the rear window. At length, the old man gave a dis-
gruntled sigh.

"I was sure—"

"There." Alex had seen it. A stab of light across Harry's
office ceiling. "Could it *be* Harry?" Alex asked. "Maybe he got
away and made it back!"

"I rather seriously doubt that."

Another thin blade of light flashed. Then gone. The old
man sat tapping his teeth with a thumbnail. He spoke as if
sorting thoughts into order. "Must be them. They got Harry.
They know he was on their trail. They want to find out how
much he knows. Same as we do. So they're searching the place.
We could wait and follow them when they come out. But they
might just destroy anything they find up there on the spot.
Right, well, no two ways about it: I have to go up."

"You can't go in there without knowing what's waiting," Alex
protested, unconsciously speaking in a whisper. He glanced up
to the window, mind racing. "Listen. You know where Harry is,
right? Where they've got him in Germany."

"Well . . . yes."

"Well, if that's the tall man's gang up *there*, or some of them,
that means there are fewer of them guarding Harry, right? So
why don't we try to get *ahead* of them, just go get Harry now?"

"I've no choice." His grandfather shrugged. "If Harry found
out anything about the paintings, I need to see it, Alex. In case
we don't manage to . . . It might not be easy getting Harry back.

Besides, there are other things up there that I need. So. I'll go around the rear alley. There's a drainpipe I can use to get to Harry's back window. I've had to use it before. Bit of luck, they won't see me until I've sized things up. You stay here—"

"I'm not sitting here while you go in alone!"

"Need you to, Alex. Need you to watch the front. If they come out, play it safe, but try to see which way they go. I'll be right behind them, then we can follow. If anyone else arrives and goes *in*, sound a blast on the horn to warn me up there. Got it?"

Alex gave him a grim stare. "Got it. But I don't like it."

"Don't worry." The old man winked, stepped out, hoisted his Gladstone over his shoulder, and headed off, quickly gone from sight as he rounded the street corner.

Sighing, Alex turned to watch Harry's office. Minutes hobbled past. He pulled out his phone. He'd had it switched off, a lesson learned during his last trip to Paris. Two messages were waiting, but he typed a note to his mum first:

> In Paris safe and sound. Helping Grandad get
> stuff ready for Harry's surprise birthday.
> Loads to do! Be in touch soon. Love you. Say
> hi to Carl.

He sent it, scanned the street in both directions for the hundredth time, then checked his messages. Something from David that morning:

```
You OK after the weird biz? Meant to show
you how to do that maths stuff. Do it Monday.
Guess who asked me for your new number? Sort
of had to give him it. Ouch.
```

Then one from Kenzie. Alex frowned. Kenzie used to send him regular greetings along the lines of *you're going to get your face smashed in*, but that had all stopped. He read the message:

```
Don't.
```

Just that. Sent only six minutes ago. Alex stared at the solitary word. Kenzie must have sent it before he'd finished typing. Alex dismissed it, put the phone away, and sat trying to mentally pace out each step of his grandfather's journey. Around the building. Up the wall. Open the window. He must be up there by now.

Alex looked back to Harry's office. Nothing. The dark windows seemed charged with menace. A surge of dread washed over him at the thought of his grandfather up there alone. They already had Harry.

It had been too long. He had to go up. He tried to compose a plan, but his mind felt stuffy and thick. He decided cool air might help and, after checking the street again, stepped out of the car, lifting his face to the rain. A metallic creak chilled his blood.

One of Harry's windows had been pushed completely open.

Alex dropped into a crouch beside the car.

Something was crawling out. *Someone*, in fact, Alex saw, as with stiff, awkward movements, the shadowy shape straightened to stand on the ledge along the building.

A tall man in a long black coat, collar pulled high, black hat tugged low.

Alex stared, frozen, helplessly fascinated. The figure up there seemed taller than he remembered, even larger than the ghost that jumped through his dreams.

Dad.

The word swelled violently in his chest without warning. Conflicting impulses were suddenly pulling him in opposite directions. With a wild lurch of resolve, Alex decided to stand and call out, make his presence known and let whatever would happen just happen.

Then came a noise that killed that notion and rooted him where he knelt. It started low, a bubbling staccato, like treacle coming to the boil, then built to a high, keening howl. The crazed, curdling sound curled horribly around Alex's spine.

The tall man was laughing.

The dark figure lifted his arms triumphantly, coat hanging like wings, as if he were some great black bat-thing perched there. Then, with a joyful shriek and a shuddering creak, he leapt.

Alex flattened against the car as the tall man landed with a mechanical hiss in the road, ten feet away. His boots were huge. The complex spring apparatus around the heels glinted cold. His black coat moved strangely, as though things were seething beneath. Between upturned collar and tugged-down hat, Alex caught a glimpse of dark glasses.

The man raised his right hand and whooped again as he considered what he held there. Something sharp. Sharp and dripping. Dripping something that looked blackish under the street lamps but which Alex feared was really deep red.

Alex tightened his hand around the toy robot in his pocket, tried forcing his mind out to it. Nothing. His grandfather had told him to honk the car's horn if anyone went into the building. What was he supposed to do if anyone came *out*? See which way they went, so they could follow. That was the plan. If only he could persuade his legs to move.

The looming figure abruptly crouched and jumped again, vanishing high into the night. He dropped dimly down some distance away, by the river walkway. Another leap, and he was gone. Alex stood shakily, pulse pounding his temples. How were they supposed to follow that? His eyes went from the black spatter on the ground to the open window above.

Grandad.

He sprinted for Harry's office. He was inside and climbing stairs before he realised neither the security gate nor the doors had been locked. Alex threw himself on up to the third floor.

Harry's door had been recently replaced and still bore only a bare grey undercoat of paint. It stood slightly open. Pale splinters of wood showed where the lock had been ripped out. Trying to quiet his breathing, Alex had a sense of eyes on him and looked up to meet the harsh glare of Marvastro, the fortune-telling automaton still standing guard in his glass cabinet outside Harry's office.

The machine had once promised him power, and power had come. But where had it gone? The penetrating stare gave nothing away. Alex swallowed and crept through the door.

Inside, silence. His eyes adjusted to the meagre light leaking in from outside. The room was large, with a high ceiling. Midway along the right-hand wall, the tall central window hung open. A stir of a breeze touched him.

The last time Alex had seen this sales room it had been wrecked, with Harry's stock of antique toys and mechanical curiosities trashed in a furious fight. A clean-up operation was still underway. Many of the display cases still had shattered fronts and held mangled toys in the process of being sorted. Chairs shrouded in dustsheets huddled against walls like he'd caught them playing ghosts. Boxes, ladders, and paint pots were piled in one far corner. In the other, a door hung ajar, offering a promise of rooms beyond.

Alex weaved warily toward it between display cases. A noise made him flinch. A muffled thud from beyond the door ahead. He stopped, straining to hear. Another, louder thump. A slap. A muted grunt.

Alex dived for cover as the door crashed open and something came flying through. He had a brief impression of a black-clad figure sailing backward and crashing into a set of shelves, tearing them from the wall in a clattering rain.

"Uhhhhhhnnnn."

The voice was female. A flailing arm appeared from the wreckage and the figure hauled herself up: a tall woman, dressed head to toe in black, including a ski mask. The eyes behind the holes blinked dazedly. As she stood shaking her head, there came further crashes from beyond the door, and she was instantly alert. From a long, padded sheath worn strapped across her back, she drew a rapier sword. Thin blade ready, she dropped into a hostile stance and started for the doorway, a prowling, martial shadow.

Halfway there, she stopped, then slowly turned to Alex, where he crouched by a display case. The large eyes narrowed at him. The head cocked to a confused angle. She took a step toward him, then was bowled off her feet as another black-clad figure came tumbling through the door, crashing into her ankles.

As they went down in a heap, Alex's grandfather came hurtling in, holding his cane horizontally between both hands. The second figure, a man, got up, limped painfully backward, then, almost reluctantly, lifted his hands, a knife in each. He dropped into a hobbling, circling motion, feinting one way then the other, before trying a vicious swipe.

Alex's grandfather blocked the blow, knocked the knife-man's hand aside, and drove his stick into his belly. As the figure doubled over, the old man hooked his neck with his cane and dragged him forward, driving his knee into his face. But completing this move, Alex's grandfather stepped blindly on a vintage toy car that had been knocked to the floor. As his foot went skidding away, he fell backward, giving his assailant a chance to make a half-stunned lunge with his blade.

With a reasonably ferocious roar, Alex launched forward, vaulting a cabinet. The black-clad man looked around, confused to find another combatant. In the same instant, Alex's grandfather swung his left leg up in a blunt, arcing swipe that caught the man's head and put him on the floor.

Alex's grandfather got up. The woman launched a kick that sent him sailing back out the door they had all come in through. Pirouetting on the same momentum, she dealt Alex a slap that knocked him just to the edge of unconsciousness. His head hit the floor with a jarring thud. Blackness fell for a second, then, panicking, he jumped to groggily face her, body fizzing with fear, shock, and adrenaline. The faint grey light flickered as his eyes fought for focus. There was a hissing on the air.

The woman was helping her companion up, drawing his arm over her shoulder. Alex searched around in desperation. A broom stood propped against the wall. He grabbed it, then went at them, swinging crazily.

The woman's eyes rounded. She thrust her sword in Alex's general direction but missed by a foot. When he raised the broom again, she swiped madly at the air by his side. He leapt back as she pulled a dagger from a sheath on her leg. She waved it warily as the pair backed out through the door Alex had entered, the man leaning heavily on her and clutching at his thigh. The woman's staring eyes never left the broom Alex held before him.

As soon as they disappeared, Alex made a woozy run through the door after his grandfather, then halted. The space beyond lay in complete darkness. Crouching, he felt cautiously along the floor until he touched a warm hand.

"Grandad?" He explored the arm, a shoulder, a jaw. There was a groan. "They've gone," Alex panted. "Are you all right?"

"I'm okay, Alex. Give us a hand up, though, eh?"

Alex helped him back through into the dim, wavering light of Harry's showroom. The hissing, static sound still popped in his ears.

"They do seem to have it in for Harry's place." Alex's grandfather gestured sadly around. "He's still not had a chance to finish clearing up after—" He broke off, squinted, and stood frowning at something in the gloom beyond Alex's head. "Ah, Alex?"

Alex turned to look. The room was a mess, but he could see nothing out of the ordinary. "What is it?"

His grandfather's eyes widened. He furrowed his brow, stood rubbing his chin, then held out a hand. "Ah. Take my arm again, would you?"

Alex did. "Are you okay?"

"Uh-huh. Now, back this way." They walked through the unlit corridor, into a darkened room beyond. As light flickered on, Alex took in a snug combination of library and office.

Two walls were lined with wooden shelves that would have been filled with books, were it not that most of the books were scattered around the floor, amid a blizzard of papers. The place looked as if a tornado had been trapped there. Behind one exposed section of shelf, a small safe hung open. Inside sat two chunky crystal tumblers and a bottle of amber liquid.

A desk by the open window held a lamp with a green shade, a computer keyboard, and the old man's Gladstone. An expensive-looking computer screen lay on the carpet where it had been knocked over. Automatically, Alex picked it up and set it back on the desk.

"Just keep hold of my arm another second, if you don't mind," Alex's grandfather said, watching him move the screen with great interest. As Alex took his wrist again, his grandfather softly kicked the office door shut. A full-length mirror hung attached to the back.

"Now. See that?" Alex's grandfather lifted the arm Alex held up and down. Alex watched the old man's reflection, the moving arm. There was something wrong about the picture, but he couldn't get hold of it. He stepped closer to the door. It took another second for him to realise he couldn't see himself in the mirror.

The instant the fact registered, he saw himself appear in the glass. The hissing sound was gone. The light grew steady.

"W—" he tried.

"Oh, Harry's single malt," the old man said happily, reaching into the safe. "Twenty-four-year-old. Saves it for special occasions. I think the circumstances qualify." He poured a measure and stood savouring it.

"Wha—" Alex managed. He looked down at himself, then at the pale boy staring dumbly out from the mirror.

His grandfather shrugged. "Golem stuff, Alex. You know. The force you're carrying. According to the legends, the creature had many strange powers. Invisibility, for example. Well, you saw that yourself in Prague. Or, rather, didn't see it, ha."

"What?" Alex would never forget watching the golem fading in and out of sight before his eyes. "But I–I don't know how I did that. I didn't even know I *had* done it."

"No. Gathered that." The old man took another sip and beamed. "Still, it's an encouraging sign, eh?"

Alex had no words. His mind was racing so fast that thoughts were lapping one another, waving as they went past. He suddenly grinned wildly, clicked his fingers, and spun to his grandfather.

"Yeah. *Yeah*. I mean, if I can work out how to—" He paused, skin tingling as the possibilities hit him in a rush. He pictured himself slipping unseen past armies of opponents, creeping undetected into the most guarded strongholds, and he stiffened in alarm as another thought came crashing in. "But what if I *can't* work it out and it happens again? What if I can't . . . get *back*? What if I get stuck being invisible?"

"Alex." The old man tutted. "I don't see the need to dwell on the negative side."

Alex scowled, then turned to check he was still there in

the mirror. He rolled his head on his neck. The woman's slap was still fading on his skin. "She almost knocked me out," he muttered, more to himself, then paused. *Almost knocked me out.* There was something there, a dim idea trying to form.

Once before when the tablet's power had suddenly protected him, Alex recalled, he had been nearly unconscious: dozing almost passed out from exhaustion on a train, when bullies had targeted him. Similarly, when he had finally managed to communicate with the golem itself, he had meditated on the problem so long and hard he finally reached a near-hypnotised point where he had stopped thinking altogether. In fact, the very first time he'd noticed anything strange about the old toy robot at all was when he'd woken in his bedroom to discover homework he'd been struggling with had been finished while he slept.

He turned to tell his grandfather, but stopped. The old man stood with his back to him, pressing his whisky glass against his forehead as if to cool a fever. His shoulders were slumped. Everything about his sagging posture looked achingly weary.

"Are *you* okay?" Alex said.

"Hmm?" His grandfather straightened and looked around, smiling. "Oh, yes. The woman jumped at me as I was coming in the window." He gestured with the glass. "I was out on the ledge, peeking in. She was in here, ransacking Harry's things, then she went running toward the front. Figured I'd take my chance and sneak in, when she came tearing back and caught me. She's an incredible fencer.

"We ended up stuck fighting in the corridor between here and the showroom quite a while. Her companion eventually joined in. Couldn't see who was who, pitch-black. All got rather hectic. But I suspect it was her who got me: got me rather nicely."

He raised his arm to display a bloody slash from knuckles to wrist. With a wince, he splashed whisky over the wound.

"It might not have been her," Alex said with a start. "I saw him."

"Hmm?" The old man began tying a handkerchief around the hand, wriggling his fingers as if to stimulate feeling.

"The tall man. Didn't you see him?"

His grandfather's head snapped up. "You saw *him*? Where?"

"Here. Well, outside. But he came out the front window. Then he . . . jumped away. He had a knife and—"

His grandfather was already gone, dashing toward the main room. Alex found him poised halfway through the open window, one foot on the outside ledge.

"Something's not right," the old man said, leaning into the rain, searching the night. "I haven't actually *seen* him since Prague, Alex. Harry and I, we'd been trying to track them. But I never caught a glimpse of *him*. We saw his machines, tangled with his bald goon and Willy von Sudenfeld – although those two tonight were new. Hard to tell about the chap, what with the mask, but I'm sure I've never encountered the woman before. New recruits, I suppose. He picks disciples up and throws them away. But I haven't laid eyes on *him*, y'see. I had begun to suspect he might still be badly injured after – after what happened in Prague. When he was burned. How was he looking?"

"Just the same. . ." As the memory of the shadowy figure tingled over Alex like static electricity, he shuddered to recall the reckless moment he'd been seized by the mad desire to call out to him. "I hardly saw him, but his face wasn't bandaged any more. Though he seemed stiff when he moved. There was something about the *way* he moved. It was, I dunno. Weird. Weirder than normal. It happened fast, I didn't really take it in. He's even taller than I remembered."

"Coast seems clear for now." Alex's grandfather scanned the road again, then stepped back in. "But there's something. I'm missing something." The old man ran a bloody knuckle over his lips, lost in thought, then absently turned for the light switch on the wall. Nothing happened when he flicked it. Looking up, they saw the bulbs in all the overhead lamps had been smashed.

"Somebody wanted to make sure it was dark," Alex said.

"All the better to hide in," the old man said grimly. "Hide and wait." He clapped his hands. "Still: not as good as turning invisible. Come back through, Alex. We have to get moving, but there are things I need to show you first." He disappeared toward Harry's inner rooms.

Alex reached to close the window, then paused. He thought

he'd heard something. The whoop of a police or ambulance siren sounded from a distance, cutting sharply across the night. Just trouble for someone out there. He locked the window and followed his grandfather, turning away too soon to see a small shadow drop from above and settle weakly on the ledge.

VIII.

NIGHT GALLERY

ALEX FOUND THE old man in Harry's office-library, replacing his bloodied jacket with one from two duplicate suits hanging in a cupboard.

"I always get several made at once," his grandfather said, pulling it on and appraising the cut. "Saves wasting time thinking what to wear." He nodded at Harry's computer. "Reckon you can fire that thing up, Alex? I'm all thumbs with them."

"Uh, think so." Alex hit a key. The sleeping screen lit. He touched the hard drive. Warm. But anyone trying to use it hadn't got far. "It's password protected."

"Ah. Oh, I know: try *The Irons*. Harry always uses that."

Alex tried it a few ways. The third – one word, all lowercase – worked. The desktop was littered with dozens of folders. His grandfather leaned closer.

"There." He jabbed a finger that set the screen trembling. The fingerprint left behind marked a folder labelled ALTE PINAKOTHEK.

"What's that mean?" Alex asked, clicking it open.

"Name of a museum. In Munich. We should go there some time, Alex, highly educational. Now. One of these is a film clip; Harry taped it from the, you know. The websnet. Can you tell which it is?"

Of the five files, only one was a video. Setting it playing revealed a TV news show. A well-groomed man and woman sat talking animatedly in German to a female correspondent on the big screen by their side, reporting from a street somewhere.

"I don't know what they're saying," Alex said.

"Doesn't matter. They don't know what they're talking about. This is from last week. Keep watching, it's coming up."

The reporter stood in drizzling morning rain outside a large, imposing building, its long facade lined with stern rows of tall arched windows. She pointed excitedly to her left. The camera followed the movement until it found an area cordoned by tape, and zoomed in. Between two vans marked POLIZEI, a group of people, some in uniform, stood inspecting the gaping hole where another window should have been. Rubble and glass lay strewn over the ground where the wall had been ripped away.

"Here it comes," Alex's grandfather said.

The picture changed again. This time it was a silent, static, strangely angled black-and-white shot, staring down into a large dim room from a high corner. Huge paintings hung on the walls.

"CCTV," Alex said.

"Inside the gallery. Night before."

The image shook, then settled, as if something had rocked the lens. Stark light fell across the floor. Seconds later, two enormous figures entered, backs to the camera: hulking men in long black coats and black hats. They went straight to the largest painting – Alex estimated it to be around twenty feet in height, maybe fifteen across, but couldn't tell what it depicted in the murky light – grabbed a corner of the frame each, and began to pull it away from the wall.

Another figure came running in, a smaller man, wearing the uniform of a museum guard. He stopped, looked wildly from the pair to some spot out of shot beneath the camera, then started shouting in that direction.

"Someone else there, off-screen," Alex murmured.

"The security guard really shouldn't have tried to stop them." His grandfather sighed. "If anyone breaks in, they're just supposed to wait until police arrive in response to the alarms. Poor chap."

On-screen, the guard sprinted at the figures at the painting. Without turning, one lashed out an arm in a savage blow. Alex felt a sickening twinge of recognition as the gloved fist smashed the man's throat. Lifted off his feet, he landed limp and motionless in the shadows, his head at an odd angle.

The painting was down. Chunks of plaster had been ripped out as they pulled it clear. Each hoisting an end, the thieves began to walk mechanically out of view with their massive prize.

"Do you know how to pause it?" the old man said.

"Uh-huh."

"So . . . now."

Alex froze the scene just as a shaft of light fell across the rear figure. The image was blurred, but he knew what he was looking at. Beneath the hat, an unfinished metal face.

"Life-sizers," he breathed.

"Reporters are talking about *men in plastic masks*," his grandfather said. "The police and newspapers across Europe have tied them to the thefts of two paintings in the past couple of months. But they've missed a trick. As far as Harry and I have been able to work out, they've stolen *eight* paintings now. Most recent was in Britain. Cambridge, just last week."

"I saw something about that." Alex nodded. "From the university, wasn't it?"

"That's right. But, thing is," the old man continued, scratching at an ear, "that's about as much as I can tell you. Clearly, they're stealing these paintings for a reason. But there's just *no* rhyme nor reason to it I can see.

"The pieces they've taken have no connection I can spot. They're all by different artists of different eras, from the fifteenth century to the eighteen hundreds. Different sizes, different subject matter: religious themes, portraits, landscapes. All of wildly different value and renown. I mean, take that." He gestured at the screen. "That's easily the most famous of the lot. Rubens's *Great Last Judgment*. Caused quite the commotion. Hang on."

He glanced around the books on the floor, selected a large

green volume, and riffled the pages. "Here we are," he said, laying it before Alex to display a vibrant reproduction of the enormous painting the robots carried.

> *The Great Last Judgment*
> Peter Paul Rubens, circa 1615
> The dead have risen and assemble awaiting judgment.
> To the left, the blessed ascend heavenward, hoping to
> be saved. To the right, the damned fall helplessly down-
> ward, tormented by demons in the shadows.

"A little garish for my tastes," the old man went on. "Now. That picture has hung in pride of place since the Alte Pina-kothek opened in the 1830s. They actually designed the gallery around it, because it's so big. So you can imagine the fuss. But then, on the other hand, you have something like this . . ."

Turning to his Gladstone, he produced a rolled canvas and spread it out: a hazy oil painting of a lonely mountain pass, desolate beneath a threatening sky.

"See? Utterly different. This one was taken from a private collection in Italy. *On the Way to Béziers*, it's called. From around 1880, painted by an unknown artist."

"Wait," Alex said, struggling to keep track. "That's— You've got one of the *stolen* paintings?"

"Oh, ah . . . Yes. Yes, Harry managed to snatch it back off them and hide it. Just before they got him."

"But shouldn't you give it back? I mean, tell the police . . ." Alex felt the words draining away even as he said them.

"Tell the police?" His grandfather frowned.

"Forget I said anything."

"Tell the police," the old man repeated, tutting. "Honestly, Alex. Whatever's going on here is not something the police would understand. Harry . . . Harry risked everything getting this. No. We have to get Harry back, and we can't waste time trying to explain the situation to people who have no interest in trying to understand it. And we can't just go *giving it back* until we work out why they *wanted* it. With a bit of luck, as long as we have this painting and they don't, they can't . . . Well . . . do whatever it is they're up to.

"I can venture a couple of loose theories. One is that they're after one particular painting and don't yet know which, but they know it's one of the bunch they've been stealing. The other possibility is they need *all* the paintings. The pictures add up to something, or reveal something together. There's some con- nection, some hidden code or . . . I don't know. I mean, look, take me back to all those folders again." The old man squinted at the screen, then: "That one."

Alex opened a folder marked CAMBRIDGE, then a picture labelled SCHALCKEN. Another painting: a young woman, blond and pale, sitting in a dark room, holding out a plate containing what looked surprisingly like a waffle.

"Is that a waffle?" Alex asked.

"Well, quite." His grandfather waved an exasperated hand. "This is the one from Cambridge University. *Lady Holding a Plate* is the title. Sums it up, I suppose. By the Dutch artist Godfried Schalcken. So: you've got your Rubens, a religious scene by a Flemish painter from 1615-ish; an anonymous painting made around 1880; and this, a painting by a Dutch artist in 1680, of a woman holding, as you so rightly say, a waffle. I'm stumped as to what the connection might be. Don't suppose there's anything screaming out at you, is there? I mean, even shapes, colours, anything."

Alex sat chin in hand, looking from one to the other. "How many did you say they'd stolen, eight?"

The old man nodded.

"Does Harry have pictures of them all?"

With his grandfather's guidance, Alex found images of all the stolen paintings: a landscape, a seascape, ruined buildings, figures, faces, the saved and the damned, the sky about to rain, a waffle. Eventually, he had to admit defeat. He turned to his grandfather with a helpless shrug.

"No." The old man sighed. "You know, I even managed to take a quick X-ray of the picture Harry saved. Broke into a dentist's near your mother's the other night. I was convinced there must be some other image or message hidden beneath . . . but nothing I could see. Although, it wasn't the ideal equipment."

As the old man spoke, Alex flicked through the images again, snapping a picture of each on his phone.

"Okay." His grandfather nodded. "Now there's something I want you to listen to." He dug from his bag a small grey box – it took Alex a moment to identify it as an old Dictaphone-style tape recorder. "Harry left two messages on the machine I keep at my place in Paris," the old man said. "He knows I check it. One to tell me he'd got on their trail. Then this. I recorded it over the phone." He clicked PLAY. "Harry's last message."

There was the drone of a car, then Harry's voice, breathless and tense:

"It's 'Arry. An' this'd be another good example of one of them times it would be 'andy if you'd agree to carry a bloody phone. I'm still in the forest, but getting out. Uh, road southeast of the Kandel, 'eadin' for—"

"What does he mean?" Alex asked. "What's the candle?"

"Kan-*del*, with a *K*," his grandfather replied, pausing the tape. "A mountain in Germany. The Black Forest. That's another worrying fact."

"Why?"

"The Black Forest, Alex. Wonderful place. But it's also a place where things have happened." He resumed the tape.

"Gawd. They're comin' after me. Listen: I followed 'em. I saw some of what they're up to. Weird business. For a change. Looks like there are two more paintings still to go. But, 'old on to your 'at: I got one of the others back. Pinched it off 'em. I 'ave it with me. Remind me to blow me own trumpet later. Now, I know where the other two are. . . "

The voice fell silent. Alex opened his mouth to speak when Harry started again, more urgently.

"Don't like the look of this. Listen. They said something about Shadow Gate. I was 'iding back in the bushes, so I couldn't 'ear clearly, but the girl definitely said it, more than once. Does that mean anything? Shadow Gate? *And two more things: it's not—"*

Alex frowned as the voice cut off abruptly. He had an irrational desire to reach into the tape recorder and pull Harry to safety. He strained to hear, but there was nothing except the car, moving faster. His grandfather gently clicked the machine off. The silence felt bleak. Alex exchanged a grim look with the old man.

"Is that all there is?" he asked, as frustrated as he was anxious.

"Ah, yes. That's when they got him."

"What's this Shadow Gate thing?"

"A legend," the old man said, after a moment. He sat forward, hands interlaced, tapping his top lip with his knuckles. "Or a rumour of a legend. Very obscure. I haven't heard that phrase in a long, long time. Even then it was only once or twice. I'd forgotten all about it, dismissed it as a fairy tale. I should know better.

"It was the story of a, well, a medieval sorcerer, Alex. A man who had lived a very long and very wicked life, and whose capacity for evil was matched only by his brilliance as a scholar of his particular dark arts. He had supposedly discovered many strange and terrible secrets, and the story went that he finally found a way to cheat death itself. Eternal life, see? All that nonsense. Supposedly, he conjured up this thing: the Shadow Gate, which would allow him to evade death's grip."

"So . . . what was it?"

The old man shrugged. "Some magical gimcrack. A . . . portal he called into being. An opening. Story went that, when death came for him, the magician opened this gate, then slipped through it and hid. Something like that. It all came at a hideously terrible cost, of course. There's always a price to be paid in these stories, Alex. Always a cost. I've been dredging my memory for more details, but I never heard more than the bare outline, and I've forgotten most of that. I couldn't even tell you where it was supposed to have happened. It's not the kind of history that gets recorded in many books. And most of them were burned long ago."

"Where did you hear about it?"

"Oh, just a story I was told when I was a boy." Alex's grandfather sat staring at the old man staring back from the mirror on the door. "One of the stories."

"Two more things: it's not . . ." Alex repeated Harry's words. "What's not?"

Alex's grandfather shook his head, returning to the present. "Haven't the foggiest. I think he was trying to tell me we'd got something wrong: we thought one thing, but it's . . . not what we thought. Problem *there* is, I hadn't thought much at all. Ha. Well. You know as much as I do now: the tall man is taking these paintings for some reason; it's maybe got something to do with an obscure legend about eternal life; and, eh . . . something isn't something."

He grinned, then darkened. "Shut the computer down, Alex. We need to get moving. We don't have much time left to get Harry back."

Something about the way he said it sent another shiver over Alex. But his grandfather had already gathered up his things and left the room. Alex sent the computer to sleep, then sat for a second gazing around the mess of Harry's ransacked library.

Amid the books and notes scattered under his feet lay a single page from a French newspaper. A red marker had been used to circle a small article. Alex bent to retrieve it, idly curious. The headline read *"Mystérieuse disparition d'un cheminot de l'Eurostar."*

The French he had learned in school wasn't up to the job of translating it all, but from what he could gather the story concerned a railway worker who had mysteriously vanished from the London to Paris train the day before the newspaper was published. One curious element stuck out: the missing man's uniform and equipment had been found discarded on the train, left lying in a heap outside a vandalised toilet.

Alex wasn't sure he was reading it correctly. But it set an alarm bell ringing in his mind that another detail only amplified. The page's December date meant that this disappearance had occurred the same day Alex and his grandfather had arrived in Paris on their last adventure. In fact, Alex was suddenly certain: it had happened on the train they had been on.

He took the page and followed after his grandfather to find him in the display room, poking absently through a tray of smashed old toys on a unit beside the door out.

The old man smiled up. "Almost forgot. Main reason I came." He knelt to the base of the display case and pushed oddly at the wooden skirting. With a rapid clicking, the case swivelled to reveal a safe set into the floor beneath. A numbered keypad lit up as the unit moved aside.

Alex's grandfather keyed in a combination, opened the safe, and pulled out a rough cloth sack weighed down by something heavy inside. "Tools for the job." He waggled his mysterious prize at Alex, stuffed the sack into his Gladstone, then bent to inspect the safe further. Alex leaned over to watch.

"Nothing else." The old man clicked his tongue in disappointment as he stood. "I was hoping Harry might have left some note or clue about what he'd found. I headed for Italy, y'see, to the house where the latest painting was stolen, hoping to find something. Harry stayed here in France, then somehow got on their trail. But he must've left in a rush."

"Is this anything?" Alex brandished the newspaper story. "It was in Harry's library. I mean, it's from earlier, when we came over last time, but—"

The old man glanced over it and hurriedly shook his head. "No," he said firmly. "No, that's nothing." He gently plucked the page from Alex's grip, dropped it into the safe at his feet, then kicked the door shut and pulled the display case back in place. "Let's go."

At the door, the old man paused, considering the broken lock. "Funny," he mused. "I thought they'd come in the same window I did. It was open when I got up there." He frowned, dismissed it. "We'd better get on. Long drive ahead."

As they left the office, Alex touched a hand to the box that held Marvastro. Something his grandfather had told him previously was bothering him, an itch he needed to scratch: *Once you've tried him, he'll always tell you the same thing.*

Obsolete coins still lay in a metal dish attached to the fortune-telling machine. As the old man disappeared down the stairs, Alex quickly fed one into the slot, then watched the imprisoned automaton lurch through its brief, furious imitation of life, a grinding display of rolling eyes and painful-looking breathing.

A small white card finally appeared, sliding out onto a tray as Marvastro fell lifeless. It lay blank side up. Alex felt his skin prickling as he turned it over.

POWER

"Alex!" The old man's impatient voice sailed up from below. Alex stuck the card away in his wallet alongside the identical twin Marvastro had given him before, then hurried down the stairs.

IX.

STOP

"I'VE HAD AN idea," Alex's grandfather said. They were driving through the city, roughly following the bending bank of the Seine. "Just need to make one quick stop."

He turned onto a side street and pulled in.

"Now, I need to nip round the corner. You wait here. By the way, Alex, have you had any luck trying to, ah, connect with the tablet?"

"No." Alex shook his head and looked out the window. The rain had picked up. Blurry people hurried by, heads bowed, umbrellas tilted to the downpour. After his experiences at Harry's office and David's house, his worry over not being able to use the power was now doubled by the fear of it . . . using *him*, without his realising.

His grandfather gave a sympathetic smile, as if reading his thoughts. "Look. You can only give it a go, Alex. Maybe you can do it, maybe not. But I think you can. We know the power is still there for you. That force gave life to the golem, and the golem is a thing that seeks a master for direction – the power *wants* to be used. It wants to be put to work, a . . . *channel*. And, for the moment, you're it, whether you like it or not. Some kind of connection has been made, and you have some aptitude for using it – I saw you that night. On the bridge in Prague. You commanded enormous power, Alex, you *conducted* it. Do it again, and we'll get Harry back easy as pie. It's just a case of, you know, figuring it out."

"Yeah." Alex drew a breath and tried to think about it calmly. His grandfather was right. The power was there. He'd just made himself invisible, after all. That was undeniably pretty cool. All he had to do was work out how he'd done it.

"Easy as pie," Alex repeated. He sat straighter and stole a glance at the old man, still troubled by the sudden look of exhaustion that had come over his grandfather in Harry's office.

The old man was acting as blasé as ever, but Alex knew enough to suspect some of it was just that: an act. His grandfather was worried, and he was really counting on Alex being able to use the power to help him free Harry from whatever prison he was in.

"Okay." Alex nodded. "I'll try. I don't even know what it is you want me to do with it, though."

"Well, I'm not really sure myself. But we can set fire to that bridge when we get to it." The old man opened his door and climbed out, then reached into the back for his Gladstone. He dumped the big bag on the driver's seat and rooted through it, pocketing some implements Alex couldn't identify, before pulling out the cloth sack he'd collected from Harry's office and swinging it over his shoulder. "Back in a jiffy."

Alex watched him disappear around the end of the street, then sighed and pulled out the old toy robot, steeled himself to the task, and concentrated.

He fleetingly recalled the sensation of golem thoughts scratching his mind, the feeling of sending his word out like a living, burning, flying thing. It was like remembering scenes from a film whose title he'd forgotten. He sagged as he remembered more vivid scenes: faces crumbling in fear before him, strangers on a train, bullies in a park. The idea of connecting with that power again suddenly scared him.

The piercing blare of an alarm going off close by pulled him out of his thoughts. Two blue-clad French police ran by, heading in the direction his grandfather had gone. Curious, Alex started to get out, then realised they had parked against a lamp post. He couldn't open the door on his side. With difficulty, he stretched over the bulky Gladstone bag to open the driver's door, then shoved the bag into the street so he could clamber out behind it.

The Gladstone sprang open as it hit the pavement. A large iron crowbar slid out, followed by a hacksaw, an enormous collection of keys strung along a twisted hoop of wire, a half-eaten chocolate bar, and a scratched grappling hook trailing a coil of rope. Cursing quietly, Alex bent to begin packing it away. The alarm kept screaming. He paused, crowbar in hand, looking along the street.

"Hey."

Turning, Alex found a young policeman standing over him, staring at the iron bar he held. A grating voice was issuing urgent reports over the man's radio. One hand was moving toward the holster on his belt.

"Wait, I can explain," Alex said, wondering what he would say next. In response, the policeman opened his mouth, closed his eyes, then sunk to his knees, revealing Alex's grandfather standing close behind wearing a black mask, cane held ready to hit him again. There was no need. The man lay slumped at Alex's feet. The din of the alarm had been joined by sirens, getting closer.

"Oh, that's terrific," Alex said. "That's just great. Let's start assaulting police officers while we're at it. Why not."

"Get in the car, Alex," the old man said. Whipping off his mask, he started scooping up the remaining contents of his bag. "Honestly. Can't leave you on your own for two minutes."

As they sped away, Alex noticed a curious glittering on the old man's coat sleeve. Raindrops caught in the wool, he thought, until he realised it was fragments of broken glass.

"I don't suppose," Alex said, "that you just broke in somewhere for some reason?"

"Bibliothèque de l'Arsenal," his grandfather said, steering fast around a corner. "Big library back there. They don't like to talk about it, but they have a magnificent collection of old magical and occult works. I figured, if there was *anywhere* I might find out more about the Shadow Gate story, it would be in a particular four-hundred-year-old volume I just happen to know is locked in their restricted section. Thing is, you have to apply in advance for access – all sorts of red tape, Alex, forms to fill, and we don't have the time."

Alex closed his eyes and rubbed his forehead. "And?"

"Not much." The old man winced in disappointment. "But there *was* a passing mention of the legend. It supposedly happened around the fifteenth century, at some castle in Germany. Although that hardly narrows it down. Castles galore over there. And, as I said, there's always a price to pay: it seems that when our sorcerer opened this gate, *the sky was torn apart, the earth cracked in protest, a pit opened into the underworld, and the castle fell.* Some rigmarole like that."

"Underworld?" Alex's flesh crept. "What does that mean?"

"Who knows?" His grandfather shrugged. "Doesn't sound too peachy, though. Anyway, this sorcerer had eleven followers. When he opened the gate and the great apocalypse began, they panicked and turned on him. The account is muddy, but the basics seem clear: they sealed the gate, renounced all his works, and changed their ways."

"And you think the tall man wants to open the gate again?"

"Well. Sounds about his style, Alex. Wouldn't you say?"

BEFORE LONG, THEY were out on a motorway heading away from the city, eastward into night and rain. Still busy, the road stretched ahead dotted with moving lights. Every minute or so, the old man scrutinised the traffic behind, tension nibbling the corners of his eyes.

Alex's grandfather pulled out his chocolate bar, bit off a mouthful, and proffered the rest. Alex shook his head.

"Take us most of the night to get where we're going," the old man mumbled. "You could take the opportunity to try the tablet again. Go gentle, but just see if you can, y'know, feel anything?"

"Yeah." Alex turned to his window. "I'll try. I'm just not sure I'll be able—"

"Hang on," the old man said, sounding grim. He switched lanes and accelerated, keeping his foot down almost a minute. Eventually, they moved back into slower traffic. Thirty seconds later, he suddenly repeated the operation, dodging through vehicles at speed.

"Just a test," Alex's grandfather said, after they had settled into a more sedate stream again. "Thought I spotted something. A big car as we were leaving the city. But we're okay." He glanced repeatedly at the rearview. "I think."

Alex sat holding the old toy robot. He tried to push away his anxiety about not being able to do what was needed and turned over his vague theory about some of the times when he *had* experienced the power – moments it had come when he was practically unconscious of it. It was somewhere to start.

"If I could really learn how to control it," Alex began, still thinking aloud, "we could use it to protect us. And then, yeah, if we were *protected* like that, if we could find the tall man we could maybe even talk to him, so—"

"*Talk* to him?" His grandfather shot him an incredulous look.

"Well, yeah. I mean . . ." Alex paused, took a breath, let it go. "You told me the two of you were once friends. You must want that, too. If you could. Don't you?"

"What? Alex, the last thing I want is to ever have to hear his voice again."

"But that night, on the bridge in Prague, he *tried* to talk to me," Alex broke in. "He wanted to talk to me."

"And say nothing worth hearing. Alex, whatever's gotten into you? You sound almost as insane as he is."

"But don't you want to at least try? I mean, he's . . ." Alex's voice dried up. He was suddenly close to saying it, and suddenly close to tears. Finally, here it was, boiling up and out. "He's . . ."

"What, son? What are you trying to say?"

Mouth moving. No words. Alex felt like he was choking. Through his watery eyes, the unknown road outside wavered and winked, lights forming into a shimmering string. His grandfather laid a hand on his shoulder. Alex blinked and caught a momentarily sharp sight of the old man's concerned gaze in the rearview. He swallowed and forced himself on.

"He's . . . my *dad*."

The hand was gone from his shoulder. They swerved sharply

as horns started screaming in an outraged choir. Alex looked up to see a chaos of cars blurring around them while his grandfather cut across traffic in a reckless diagonal, streaking straight for the hard shoulder. He bounced in his seat belt as the old Citroën lurched into a long, skidding stop, tyres squealing in protest. A deep silence settled.

"My dad," Alex eventually whispered again, still amazed he'd said it. "I've known it all along, Grandad. He's *my dad*. That's what you wouldn't tell me. That's *why* you wouldn't tell me."

"Suffering cats." His grandfather slumped over the wheel, burying his face in his forearms. Alex resisted the urge to reach out and touch his shoulder. Now that he'd opened this door, there was no going back. They had to go through this.

"Good old Harry," the old man muttered quietly after a moment. "He said as much. He *told me* you were thinking that. And I told him he was wrong. Rarely wrong, is Harry. I should know that by now."

He sat back and turned to Alex. "But, Alex: really? *That's* what you've been thinking? Now: no. You listen very carefully. That . . . *thing* is not your father. Your father *died*." He broke off and cleared his throat before going on. "Your father died. Thirteen years ago. If anyone knows that, it's me. I was *there*, son. I . . . You know all this. You *know* it—"

"But I *saw* him," Alex broke in, surprised how calm he sounded. He felt sorry for what his grandfather was going through. The old man had carried this secret alone for a long time, shouldering the burden to protect Alex and his mum. Now, even after Alex had told him he knew the truth, his grandfather seemed desperate to keep up the pretence. But Alex was more determined to get it out in the open.

"I saw his *face*," Alex pressed gently. "It's obvious. And the girl. Zia. *Her* face. His daughter . . . my sister. Little sister. Half sister."

"Alex, for the love of— Do you honestly think I would've kept something like that from you? From your mother? Yes, there are things I've not told you, but *this*? Get it through your head: that man is not your father."

"Well, who is he then?" Alex heard his voice explode as patience evaporated. "If he isn't my dad, what's the big deal? Why the big secret? If he isn't my dad, what's it matter? Because he *is*, isn't he?" He folded his arms and stared out at the traffic streaming by.

"Alex. Okay. Listen. He isn't." His grandfather chewed his lip. "Look, I was going to tell you all of this. One day."

Alex refused to look at him.

"Alex. He's not your father – he's . . ." The old man trailed off, looking around as though searching for help, or a way out. Finally, he hung his head, spread his hands in a gesture of defeat, and said something.

One word. It coincided with the angry scream of a horn from a truck rattling past outside. Alex was certain he had misheard.

"What?"

After another heavy pause, his grandfather said it again:

"Mine."

"Mine? What do you mean, *mine*? Your what?"

The old man looked up, smiled sadly.

"He's not your father, Alex. He's mine. He's my father."

X.

FLOWER POWER

THEY HAD BEEN driving again for some time before Alex spoke. He had been thinking carefully about precisely how to frame his next question:

"Whu?"

"Hmm?"

"But." Alex heard his own voice as if from the end of a long tin tunnel. The only word he seemed able to get hold of was *but*. "But. Okay . . . But he looks about forty-something. But you, you must be . . . Right. Grandad: how old are you?"

"Hah. Interesting question. I seem to remember you asked me that once before." Alex's grandfather nodded, then fell silent and became very absorbed in his driving.

Alex felt a scream racing through him. He managed to grab its ankles and drag it back so it came out as a strained whisper:

"So what's the answer?"

"Well, now, you see," the old man said, "this lies in the whole area I've been meaning to talk to you about, Alex. I mean,

Harry, he's been pushing me to fill you in, y'know. *You need to tell the lad, 'e deserves to know* . . . Good old Harry. So, let's see: what age am I. Well, let me think, where are we, this is the end of April now, isn't it? The cruelest month, as they say, so . . ."

He lifted fingers from the steering wheel as though counting. "That makes it, give or take . . . I mean, not precisely *on the button*, but rounding things up . . ."

"*Grandad!*"

"Hundred and ninety. Well, closer to a hundred and ninety-eight. Say two hundred. Far as I know, I was born in 1821."

Another little while passed. Alex had the sensation of his mind folding itself smaller and smaller, packing up to leave. His mouth was open, working slackly, getting ready to speak. He wondered what it was going to say.

"1821."

"That's right. Don't know the exact date. That's why I decided to make January the first my birthday. Keeps things tidy. And it means I can celebrate it the night before, y'know, two birds with one stone. Although, I've been thinking about changing it to summer, to balance the year out. Party-wise."

After another long silence, Alex heard himself saying: "That's impossible." He had probably tried to make it sound decisive, but he was aware that his voice faltered and more painfully aware that, given the amount of impossible things he had experienced, this was hardly an adequate response.

"Impossible, is it?" His grandfather's eyes reflected red lights from the road. "And why is that?"

"Because." Alex gestured at the physical laws of the universe around them, trying to catch the last before they all skipped away. "It's just impossible. A hundred and ninety-eight years old. It's stupid."

"Is that so. Well, tell me this, Alex. Did you know that within a couple of hours' drive from your house, you could put your hands on a living tree that's over four thousand years old?"

"What?" Alex screwed his eyes shut. "No, but—"

"Yes, but. The Llangernyw Yew, in Wales. Magnificent thing. It was already a couple of thousand years old when Caesar invaded—"

"No." Alex cut the old man off before he got started on what sounded like becoming an enthusiastic talk on the natural history of the British Isles. A four-thousand-year-old tree seemed unlikely, but it could wait. He did his best to rally.

"Okay, maybe. Maybe there are trees that are thousands of years old. I don't care. That's trees. That's different from—"

"Well, take the Greenland shark, then."

"The *what*?"

"Greenland shark. *Somniosus microcephalus*. Ugly-looking brute but quite the fellow. It's been estimated the oldest one swimming about today is between three hundred and six hundred years old. Just think: it could've attended the first performances of Shakespeare's plays! Well, if it wasn't a shark. And, you know, there are whales and tortoises around that are easily getting on for two hundred. And, I mean, the Loch Ness Monster, she's at least—"

"No, but . . ."

"But when you consider all that, Alex, is there not just the smallest part of you starts to think, *Well, the* principle *is there*? Life can be sustained in some creatures for several hundred years, so why not in others? Why not in us? Why not longer? That maybe there are things science has yet to learn about ageing? That perhaps it's possible to slow it – maybe stop it?"

His grandfather paused, offering another opening. Alex had nothing except the roaring between his ears.

"Now, the further you go down that line of thought," the old man went on, "the more dangerous it becomes, if you ask me. But, I guarantee you, there are scientists right this moment spending billions trying to crack the code. Just as there have *always* been people trying to unlock the secret, in different ways, for thousands of years. Well, my father is one of them. I told you before: eternal life. It's his obsession. I just *didn't* tell you he'd already gone some way toward achieving it."

The old man fell silent, as though he had explained anything.

Alex sat trying to pull his tattered thoughts together. Rain hit the windscreen in scattered points of light. The wipers ticked back and forth with a steady, comforting *chunk-clunk*, spreading the light out in brief, shining, vanishing arcs.

"You know," his grandfather said happily, "I'd been positively *dreading* telling you about this, Alex. I mean, I would've put it off forever. But now I've actually done it, it's not half as bad as I'd feared. It's a real weight off the shoulders. There's a lesson there: don't keep things bottled up."

Alex barely heard him. He was wondering how much his mind could take before it finally snapped. Maybe it had already happened.

"Right." He grabbed the first question he could, just trying to keep the conversation moving before his thoughts seized up or ran away screaming. "So . . . you're immortal."

"What? Good lord, no. I mean, that's the kind of madness *he* believes in. No, I'm just old, Alex. Just old."

"So, but . . . well, how old is *he*?"

"I can only really guess at that. Always did look young for his age, even before. I've made efforts to find out when he was born, but he's always covered his tracks carefully. I think I can narrow it down to somewhere between 1785 and 1795. Let's say he's about two hundred and thirty. And my sister is around a hundred and eighty-four."

The car shivered as the old man moved out to overtake.

"Sister?" Alex failed to understand. Then he felt his brain buckle and his skin creep as the moon face zoomed in his memory. "The girl. Zia. The little girl. She's your sister."

"Sadly, yes. Ah, are you okay, Alex?" The old man was watching him in the mirror. "I mean, are you okay with *me*, son? I'm still *me*, you know. Still old grandad. Just because I'm maybe a little older than you thought, it doesn't change anything about that."

"No, I'm okay. I think . . ." Alex fell silent, trying to figure out what he thought. It felt like trying to balance at the middle of a seesaw. On one side, the weight of everything he used to think he understood. On the other, his equally heavy certainty that every word the old man had just said was true.

"Right," he said, trying to adjust. Once again, he was struck by how calm he sounded. "But *how*? And I don't understand. You *look* old. I mean, not . . . a hundred and ninety . . . but much older than . . . your father. And Zia, she's just a kid."

"Oh, that's simple enough. I stopped taking the potion when I went away from them. To keep the biological age frozen, you have to keep using it, you see. It's not a one-off thing. You need to top up regularly."

"Potion."

"Brew my father concocted. *Elixir*. You know how he operates. Combination of science and magic and, ah, other learning. He's from the school that doesn't recognise dividing lines between any spheres of knowledge: ancient wisdom or modern developments; science, philosophy, or religion; magic or black magic, or whatever else you might care to call it. What they used to call a magus during the Renaissance, and what we might call a Renaissance man today, ha. Shame he's insane.

"It took him years, but he found his recipe by deciphering various obscure books and manuscripts. He's amassed thousands of rare works, Alex, dating back to medieval times. Some earlier. Strange books. Lots of Latin and runes and astrological symbols. Instructions on communing with angels and demons. Accounts of opening doorways to other places, with handy woodcut illustrations. You get the idea. You've seen some of it yourself. This Shadow Gate business is right up his street.

"That's where I heard that story, of course. My father mentioned it once or twice when I was young: a puzzle he was trying to solve. I've been trying to remember, but I don't think he told me much more. He was already suspicious of me by then – or, rather, he knew I was growing suspicious of him."

"What potion?" Alex prodded, after his grandfather fell into another thoughtful silence. "What's in it?"

"Hmmm? Oh, well, certain elements, gathered at certain times, combined in certain ways, certain words said, certain signs made. Then, y'know: *fire burn and cauldron bubble*. Whiz it all up, leave it to simmer with a sprig of thyme, and Bob's your uncle. And you'll outlive him by several generations. Unless Uncle Bob is taking it, too, of course."

The old man fell silent, apparently studying the road, but Alex saw he was debating how much more to say. He decided staying quiet was his best bet. He tried to remember where he knew *fire burn and cauldron bubble* from. Shakespeare. A play they'd been reading in school. *Macbeth*. Witches casting spells.

"There are several ingredients," his grandfather suddenly continued, straightening his shoulders. "Ah: magnesium, right? Pinch of that. A nip of snake venom. Some others. But those are all trifles, really."

The old man hesitated again, clearly loath to go on. "But the *essential* element is a particular plant. Ah, a flower. It's the centre of it all, Alex. My father keeps it and uses an extract it produces. A ghastly flower. There's only ever been one like it, and getting it was perilous in the extreme. Potentially fatal.

Potentially worse. I was with him the night he went into the forest to take it. The Black Forest, Alex. I've been wary of the region ever since. A horrendous night. 1836, that would have been."

The old man shivered at some phantom and checked his mirrors again.

"I think we should stay off the autoroute. I don't see anyone following but pays to be careful. Be easier to tell out there." He took the next exit off the motorway. They were soon in dark countryside, steering a dim network of smaller roads. Alex's grandfather seemed to know the way instinctively.

"As I said, Harry had been on at me to tell you about all this," the old man resumed. "He was right. You deserve to know, Alex, there are reasons you . . . But I didn't know *how*. And I suppose part of me never wanted to. I just wanted things to be normal between us as long as possible."

Mention of Harry reminded Alex where they were heading, what he had to do. The thought of his grandfather's friend being held in the tall man's clutches somehow seemed even more awful now. But in turn came a memory of the strange photograph Harry had shown him.

"I still don't understand, though. About your age, and—"

"Ah, if you wouldn't mind, Alex," his grandfather said, rubbing one wrist wearily across his forehead, "I need to concentrate on driving. We can talk more, I promise. But I'm a little tired now, and these small roads can be difficult in the dark.

We've probably had enough to chew on for the moment, anyway. Is that okay, son?"

"Okay." Alex nodded. He felt exhausted himself.

"Good man. Maybe you could try more with the tablet? I'll let you know if you, y'know. Disappear. Ha." The old man flexed his left hand repeatedly on the wheel, as if trying to ease a cramp. He sounded his cheerful self, but Alex caught the uneasy undertone.

"I'll try."

The toy robot on his lap grinned through the gloom. Alex took a breath, tried to put everything else aside, and forced himself to consider the problem calmly. He had done it before, as the old man had said. He could do it again. He focused on the empty eyes.

He gave up after a minute. His simmering brain felt close to boiling over. The madness of his grandfather's conversation was one thing. But there was something else. For months, Alex had lived with the belief that the tall man was his father. It had been practically the only thing he had thought about. There had been fear, confusion, and guilt in it, but also one sharp, solid truth: that, just for a moment, they had spoken.

Now, if he were to believe his grandfather's story, he would have to go back to thinking about his dad the way he used to. But when he tried to remember quite how that had been, he realised all he could find there now was an empty space. The distant figure had been pushed further away. Meanwhile, the tall man loomed larger, even more hideously strange.

The engine hummed as they crested a rise. Everything felt eerie. Shadowy trees brooded along the roadside, framing enormous flat fields, vague vineyards. Ghost clouds hung frozen in the towering black sky. No stars. It seemed they were the only vehicle on these roads.

Alex rested his head against the window, hoping the coolness might calm the buzz of his thoughts. As he looked down at the old robot again, something else his grandfather once said drifted across his memory. The best advice the old man had ever given him.

Sometimes you just have to accept what's happening and get on and deal with it.

Deal with it. He rubbed his fingers over the tin toy and yawned, barely aware he was doing it. He let his eyelids close. He just had to find a way to focus his thoughts.

Gradually, he assembled a plan to help himself: he would build a careful, detailed mental picture of each element in the process of contacting the power, a kind of map of the path his mind had to follow: first came the shell of the old tin toy; next, the ancient clay tablet inside, bearing its strange words written in illegible scratches; then, finally, the roaring white light tinged blue and gold.

He would line each image up, one after the other, like a series of doors. Then he would carefully attempt to approach, feel, and pass through each door in turn. Just a series of doors. He set his mind walking slowly toward them.

First the toy robot.

Then the tablet.

Then the light.

Nodding over the toy, trying to move his mind, he lost all track of time. Somewhere along the border of sleep, something flickered, a sudden sense of the tablet's presence, a feeling that what he was looking for was glimmering ahead.

With the distant feeling of trying not to wake himself, he just let it be there for a while. Then, softly, he pushed after it, pushed deeper, slipping through one door, then the next, like a thief tiptoeing through a house.

As he approached the final door that would reveal the light, he saw a vague, unexpected figure, standing between him and the door, back to him. As the figure turned, he saw a face he recognised. The mouth was moving:

"Alex? Wake up, son."

XI.

SPRING MORNING

ALEX'S GRANDFATHER STOOD outside, leaning through the car's open door. They were parked off the road on the edge of a thick forest. It was early morning, still dim. Spotty rain fell.

"Uh . . . where are we?" Alex blinked and stretched. Aside from fields and trees, the landscape was empty. He could feel a dream draining away and tried to remember what it had been. The sleep had been deep.

"We've crossed into Germany," the old man said. "Close to where Harry is. There's a hotel I know not far from here. But there's something I need to do first, and it needs a little privacy. Come on."

He led Alex into the woods. The first unseen birds were already chipping away at the big silence. Tall trees arched together to form a vaulted ceiling above, the light shaded grey green as it came filtering through.

"Any luck?" his grandfather asked as they walked. "With the tablet?"

"Not sure." Alex frowned, beginning to remember. "I thought there was something. Maybe. I was getting closer. But I couldn't get to it."

"You'll do it."

"I've been thinking about it," Alex said. As best he could, he shared his half-formed idea, about moments when he had accessed the power without being aware he was doing it. "Almost like a . . . an unconscious reflex," he concluded. "Or subconscious. But it's like, when I *try* to do it, I can't."

"Mmm. Might make sense," his grandfather mused. "Deeper spots in the mind. You're trying too hard but don't really know *what* you're trying, so you wind up getting in your own way. You have to relax, think less."

"Yeah. I've got a . . . technique I'm trying to work out. To lead me through, and kind of tune out. I'm still trying to figure it out. I don't know if it makes sense."

"Can but try, Alex," his grandfather said. "But, then, there *have* been times when you've used it consciously, no?"

"Yeah," Alex said. "In Prague, on the bridge."

The old man chewed his lip, thinking. "There's a chance Prague might have helped you there. There are places on Earth where, ah, things can get thin, Alex. Between the world we know and – you know. Whatever else. The unknown. Some maintain Prague is one. The bridge we were on, the Charles Bridge, there are strange stories about how it was built. Theories that the whole area was all designed as a kind of alchemical equation: that the very layout of the Old Town is a magical code. A powerful place.

And the presence of the golem itself, of course, seeking a master . . . All that might have helped amplify things, helped you make the connection. The distance you had to travel wasn't so far. It met you halfway."

"Okay, I get it. Sort of." Alex nodded. "But there were other times, back home, when I could use the power when I wanted it, *how* I wanted it. I was conscious, awake, and there was nothing amplifying it there, was there? Like, there was a boy getting beaten up, and I helped him. And then someone was going to beat me up, and I made him stop. Actually –" Alex frowned – "it was the same boy."

"Go on," his grandfather urged.

"But then, the other night, at David's," Alex continued, tripping up over a new thought. "The old woman was shouting at me, and, yeah, I wanted her to stop. But I didn't, y'know – *command* it. It just came out of nowhere and kept getting stronger. I mean, I was wide-awake, and . . ."

"Yes?"

"I dunno." Alex shrugged, bothered by a feeling of having mislaid something important. He nodded determinedly. "I'll keep thinking. I'll keep trying."

They came to a bare place encircled by trees. His grandfather stopped by a large mossy rock and dropped his Gladstone. "This'll do."

He knelt to the bag and pulled out the sack he'd collected from Harry's, upending its contents onto the ground. Two objects fell out: complex, heavy-looking mechanical assemblages of iron and brass, thick springs, cogs and coils held together by metal links and leather straps with buckles. Grunting, he began fixing one over his boot, covering the heel.

With a start, Alex realised where he had seen them before.

"Those are . . . Wait, are those *his*?"

"Hmmm?" His grandfather was working his other foot into the second device. "No. Well: yes. He built them – but I stole them, long time ago. Not used them in a while, though. Let's see, good lord, must be sixty years. Last time was . . . down around Cannes. Ha." He smiled distantly. "There was a masked ball, movie stars in town, a lot of jewellery, and . . . Well, it was a long time ago. Swore off them after that. But needs must when the devil drives."

The old man stopped fussing with the apparatus and smiled up. "Thing is, Alex, I've been feeling a little . . . tired lately. Too much running around, I suppose. So I thought I might use these for a little help, if my energy gets low. Put a spring in my step, as it were. Ha. I had Albert tuning them up for me. Harry collected them while I was away."

He stood, took a tentative step, frowned at the squeal it produced. He turned back to his Gladstone, found the oilcan Albert had given him, applied a few drops and pumped his foot until it was silent.

"Thought it best to get a little practice in. When I broke into the library back there, I overshot, wound up at a window a floor above. But I remember the real trick was *walking* in them. The jumping stuff's quite easy, once you get the hang of it.

The spring-heels multiply the force of your leap, basically. Although it gets a little exponential after a certain point." He stood flexing his knees, looking upward and ahead. "Okay. Right."

He crouched and swivelled his feet quickly toward each other, almost as if he were clicking his heels. Then he was gone.

Alex gawped at the spot where his grandfather had been. He spun, looked around, looked up, hunting the canopy overhead. He finally located him balanced on a branch about thirty-five feet up a tree around thirty feet away.

"That's amazing," Alex breathed. "That was amazing!" he shouted now, running to stand beneath the tree.

"I was actually aiming for the next one down," his grandfather called, gesturing to a branch some ten feet below. "But, no, not bad after six decades. Getting down's the real test. Stand back, please."

Alex retreated, then caught his breath as the old man stepped casually from the branch. He fell tombstoning down, yet landed as though bouncing lightly on a mattress. The springs at his heels gave out a hissing sigh.

"Let's see." He crouched, creaked, and vanished once more in a grey upward blur, to land on the lower branch he had previously indicated.

"Like riding a bike." The old man beamed as he touched down following his fourth test leap. He nodded, satisfied, then knelt to unstrap the contraptions. As he bent to stow them back in his Gladstone, he hesitated, set them aside on the ground, and pulled out the painting Harry had salvaged. The old man unrolled it and moved into better light to stand scrutinising it.

"Can you show me those pictures you took of the others, Alex?"

While Alex found the images on his phone, his grandfather spread the canvas on the grass. Alex showed him yet again how to flip from one picture to another. After some grumbling, the old man got it, then crouched over the painting, stabbing at the screen.

"What am I missing?"

"Well, we don't know if it's all of them, do we?" Alex asked. "Like you said: we don't know if they need all the paintings or just one, or what. Maybe there's a connection between just *some* of them. So, like, uh: some have got people, and some don't. Some have got trees, and some don't." Alex looked at the trees around them, thinking hard. "Maybe it's to do with the different types of trees? You can make a recipe using leaves or . . . bark or something. Like with that flower you mentioned. The potion."

"Hmm." His grandfather sounded unconvinced. He pushed back his hat as he swiped rapidly at the phone, muttering.

Alex stood looking on over the old man's shoulder. "Maybe it's not . . . the *pictures*," he said.

"Eh? How do you mean."

"I mean, not the . . . images. Like, if it was some coded message in the images – to do with the trees, or whatever – they wouldn't need to physically take the *paintings*, would they?

They could just, y'know –" he gestured at the phone's display – "look at copies."

"That's a point," the old man said. "But then, there are minute details in the originals that might not be apparent in reproductions. And also, unless you were very careful and did them yourself, copies wouldn't all be at the right scale to each other. These pictures on your phone certainly aren't. What I'm saying is, you might need to arrange the originals together in a certain *way*, so that things line up in a particular manner. But, yes, decent point: they seem to need the actual physical object. Let me keep thinking."

While his grandfather was absorbed, Alex crouched to inspect the spring-heels. He picked one up. It was even heavier than it looked. After a moment, he sat and fastened the mechanisms around both feet, pulling buckles tight, then stood, testing the feel. His gaze fell on the moss-covered rock they had stopped beside. He tried a step, then hobbled heavily to stand before it. A broad boulder, about five feet high. Alex bobbed at the knees, trying to get a feel for the kind of force he might use to get up there.

He glanced at the old man's back, took a breath, crouched, and jumped – then felt stupid when nothing happened. With the weighty apparatus around them, his feet barely left the ground. He frowned, then brightened, remembering the last little movement his grandfather had made, swivelling the heels toward each other.

"Must set the mechanism," he muttered, licking his lips.

"Hmm?" his grandfather said over his shoulder.

At the same moment the old man turned and shouted – "Alex! No!" – Alex moved his feet quickly inward. Then something punched him so hard in the stomach that he couldn't breathe.

XII.

OUT ON A LIMB

HE STILL COULDN'T breathe. He was beginning to panic about that. He couldn't see, either. His eyes were streaming. The world was a grey-green smear, waving strangely up and down. Blood was rushing to his head. And possibly out his nose. He wheezed uselessly.

"Alex?" His grandfather sounded far away.

White spots sparked across his blurring vision. The weight pressing into his belly grew heavier. There was a jagged, tickling feeling there, too, as though something was struggling weakly, trapped against him.

"Alex?"

Trying to move away from it, he felt himself lurch forward and steadied himself by flinging out a hand, grabbing something rough. The agitation at his stomach was gone.

"Alex?"

Gulping fishlike, he finally found a shallow, shuddering breath. Then another, deeper. His vision cleared, but he couldn't understand what he was seeing. To his right, an enormous grey pipe stretched off into a great greenish-brown wall, about sixty feet ahead. Something was waving oddly in the air nearby. Two things. Turning his head slightly downward, they seemed familiar. It took him a second to identify his own feet.

With sickening clarity, he realised. The grey pipe wasn't stretching ahead into a wall. It was a tree trunk, and it was going straight down to the ground. The very hard ground. Sixty feet below. He was hanging bent double, flung over a high branch.

"Hang on, old chap, I see you now. I'll get a rope from my bag."

Alex opened his eyes and squeezed tighter to the branch as he felt himself slip. The weight of the machines around his ankles was dragging him back. His arms were beginning to ache. He didn't know how much longer he could keep hold.

His mind was suddenly taken off that problem by a small scratching sound to his right. He stopped breathing again as he looked in that direction.

Just along the branch, a small grey robot was trying to stand, but every time it pulled itself to its feet, it went toppling woozily onto its back again. It was almost comical, but Alex didn't feel like laughing. The scratching sound was the noise of its hook-hand, digging viciously into the bark to stop it falling.

Flier. The word buzzed into Alex's mind with a sting. The robot was badly mangled. One of its razor-edged wings had been bent, almost torn off. On its head, a tiny propeller jerked uselessly, then died. Its lamp-eyes gave only the faintest amber glow. But the hook and scalpel blade that served as hands still seemed sharp enough.

The thing had given up trying to stand. It sat staring dully at him. Alex noticed a new detail: around its hook-arm hung a small patch of black cloth. Before he could think further about it, his attention was snagged by a more pressing point. The flier had started crawling toward him.

It clawed at the branch, sinking its hook into the wood with a hollow little *thunk* and pulled itself forward. Then repeated the manoeuvre, drawing closer in tiny increments.

Thunk.

Alex tried a kick at it, swinging one leg up. His foot hit the underside of the branch, and he swayed terribly backward as it dropped away again like an anchor. He held tighter. With the dead weight around his feet, it was all he could do to hang there and watch the robot closing in.

Thunk.

Thunk. Nearer.

Thunk. Seven inches away.

It raised its scalpel-arm as though testing it, making a slash at the air.

Thunk. Five inches.

Slash-slash.

THUNK.

This was a sound of a different, more violent order. With it came an explosion of splinters that Alex had to duck to avoid.

When he turned back, the little machine was lifeless, lying impaled by one of the three sharp prongs of the grappling hook that had embedded itself into the branch about three inches from Alex's face.

"Sorry, old chap," his grandfather's voice sailed up from below. "That was a little closer to you than intended."

The rope tied to the hook tightened as Alex's grandfather started hauling himself upward. The branch trembled and groaned.

"And that's why," the old man grunted as he swung himself over the limb, "it always pays to ask permission." He sat straddling the branch with his back against the trunk, catching his breath. "If you had *asked* me, I could have told you that the spring-heels are rather carefully calibrated for a specific user's weight and height. In this case: mine. Plus, I think Albert might have been a wee bit overenthusiastic about tightening them up."

He rubbed distractedly at his left arm, stretching his bicep then flexing his hand. "Have to confess, that climb took it out of me. Feeling my years, ha. Hold up, what's this?" Spotting the dead flier, Alex's grandfather leaned forward, scrutinising the thing. "Where did he come from?" He scanned the sky in alarm.

"Don't know," Alex said. He could barely feel his arms. "Uh. Could you help? I can't hold on much longer."

"Oh. Of course. Give me your hand, old bean."

With help, Alex manoeuvred until he was sitting facing

his grandfather. The old man sat studying the robot pinned between them. Moving with great care, Alex bent to join him.

"I think I crashed into it, in the air, when the heel things threw me up," Alex said. "Or maybe it was already on the branch and I landed on it."

"In bad shape," his grandfather mused. "What do you make of that?" As he flicked the scrap of black cloth, Alex suddenly remembered Carl, in his bedroom, holding up his hooded top, the rough little square hole cut out of the back. *Gremlins come when they're out on the washing line.*

"I think that's . . . *mine.* Cut from my hoodie." Moving with great care, Alex pulled at his hooded top to display the spot.

"Hmm. Wear it a lot?"

"All the time."

His grandfather nodded. "Beginning to make sense. When I met you, you said you'd had a feeling you were being followed. You were. By this. How long did you say you'd felt it?"

"A week, maybe?"

"Uh-huh. They must have sent it to keep track of you. My father or Zia, but most likely him. He knows where your house is now. He knows *you exist* now, more to the point. He didn't before the golem business; I'd always tried to keep you— Well, anyway, this explains how they knew we were going to Harry's office. Why they were waiting."

"They can see us through these things?" Alex asked, shifting on the branch. "I've never really understood it."

"Well, depends on the type of device, and how close to us

it got. And, most of all, who's operating it," his grandfather said, still distracted. "Ah, what kind of skill, what power they have. It's a combination of natural talent, study, and practice, like most things. A low-level practitioner could just give the machine a basic instruction and would then have to watch and direct it: like operating a remote-control plane, say. But, yes, at higher levels, when you learn to section off your mind, and have the strength, you can send out part of your awareness. A psychic extension—"

The old man considered Alex seriously, as though debating what more to say, then shrugged. "These machines started as a by-product of my father's experiments into extending life, Alex. He was exploring the possibility of *migrating consciousness*. Throwing your mind into another body. So if you were near the end, you could just slip your personality into someone else, take them over.

"Trouble with *that* is, it would take a lot of effort to suppress the mind of whoever's body it was. Personally, I don't find the idea appealing on any level. I mean, I find it hard enough getting comfortable staying as a guest in anybody's *house*. I like my own space.

"But the robotics line was something Hans Beckman developed, using elements of that technique, and . . . other methods, under my father's guidance."

Alex nodded, trying to ignore the disheartening creaks the branch gave out with every movement they made. This was more than his grandfather had ever told him about the tall man's eerie machines. Despite their precarious position, he was keen to keep him talking.

"So Beckman made them," Alex prodded, picturing the unsettlingly ingratiating little toy shop owner who had once held them at gunpoint, a man whose eyes were perpetually hidden behind the shining lenses of his glasses.

"Well, the basic mechanics. Beckman was an engineer originally," his grandfather went on. "Rather clever at it. He investigated creating an artificial body, you see, and transferring the mind into that. That's how the life-sizers started. I think my father quickly dismissed that idea. But Beckman's work proved useful.

"They first bought the toy shop in Prague to keep tabs on any discoveries concerning *our* old toy robot. While he was cooling his heels there, Beckman had the idea to miniaturise his process and started creating the machines you've seen.

"As far as this one goes –" the old man gestured at the flier – "I'd guess my father used it to do more than just watch you. He, well, tried to put a hex on you. It took that scrap of material for a focus: something of yours, something close to you. Just be thankful it didn't get something even closer – hair or nail clippings or blood, y'know. I'd venture he's been trying to probe your mind, size you up, or wear you down. The attack in the street when I met you was probably an angry surge, trying to get at you before I could.

"Thing is," the old man continued, "far as I know, they were busy on the continent while this was following you in Britain.

So even if he only devoted a little attention to it, using the machine across such a long distance, over that length of time, would have cost enormous mental energy. The machine would have been growing weak by now, in any case. They need, ah, topping up every now and then. Could you give me the spring-heels, Alex?"

Fascinated by the old man's account, Alex had almost forgotten where they were perched. Moving with care, he unfastened the apparatus and handed it over to his grandfather, who began strapping it to his own feet. When the old man straightened again, he looked bleak.

"They know where we are. And they know we know. We have to assume they'll be coming after us—" He stopped as the branch emitted an unmistakable crack. "Ah. Probably not a good idea to hang around up here, Alex." He held out the rope. "Think you can shimmy down?"

Alex considered the drop doubtfully. The branch splintered again and shuddered alarmingly. His grandfather raised his eyebrows. Alex swung down, starting to lower himself.

"Good man. Probably best to take as much weight off this branch as possible. So I'll see you down there."

Alex felt the trembling relief of the branch through the rope as the old man jumped off and went plummeting past him. He shinned down as fast as he could, the rope slick with rain.

"That's the style, Alex," his grandfather called from below. "Keep it up."

His hands were raw, his biceps trembled, his mind reeled,

and the branch above kept shivering. Pausing for an upward glance, Alex was disappointed to see how close it still was. As he watched, the branch snapped from the tree. Suddenly, he was falling, fast.

Something springing up just as fast slammed into him. He had a jumbled awareness of being wrapped in his grandfather's arms. Then they were hitting damp green ground, hard. They tumbled forward in a heap together, then spilled apart.

Alex ended on his back, panting. He lay looking up. The slow grey sky framed by trees.

"You know, as first lessons in jumping with spring-heels go," his grandfather said from somewhere nearby, "could've been worse."

Alex felt rain on his face, tasted grass in his mouth. He heard sudden laughter. It took him a moment to recognise it as his own.

XIII.

UP THE HILL

AFTER THEY CHECKED there was no damage, they headed back to the car. Alex was about to get in when his grandfather stopped him.

"Just been thinking. If the flier got close enough to take a cutting from your clothes, it could have got close enough to plant something else."

Alex hurriedly emptied his rucksack and pockets, going through everything he had brought. Clothes, phone, keys, wallet, toothbrush, notebook with a pen attached, old toy robot carrying the name of God inside. There was nothing.

"Might be an idea to give your mother a call," his grandfather said, nodding at the phone. "Maybe not mention being up the tree, though," he added as Alex held it ringing to his ear.

"Hello, you," his mum said. "What're you up to? Is your grandfather behaving?"

"I heard that!" the old man shouted.

"We're out walking in . . . Paris. Going to get some . . . balloons."

"That sounds nice." She yawned. "Does Harry still have no idea you're planning his birthday?"

"Uh, no. Mum? Listen. I'm sorry I've been a bit, eh . . ."

"Moody."

"Yeah."

"S'all right. You should've seen me at your age. You're barely an amateur."

"Can you tell Carl I said sorry, though? I was a bit of an idiot to him."

"Yes, you were. He can handle it. Have you eaten?"

"Uhm, we're just going to do that."

"Okay. Dunk a croissant for me. Keep in touch. Love you."

"Love you."

He ended the call, stood staring at the phone, then pulled up the abrupt message Kenzie had sent him.

Don't.

It had just come back to him. The night before, when he was trying to make contact with the power, pushing through the doors of his deep dreamlike state – the dim figure he had seen, trying to talk to him.

It was Kenzie.

He typed back:

What?

126

He stood waiting, trying to will a reply to appear, then put the phone away. His grandfather stood scowling at the sky.

"Foul weather. That reminds me, there's something I was going to give you." He dug through his bag, finally producing a rolled-up olive-green bundle. Shaking it loose, he held it out for Alex's inspection: an old army-style parka coat.

"Used to be your father's. I remember he got it when he was a couple of years older than you. Wore it constantly for a while. Yours, if you'd like."

After a moment, Alex nodded, lost for words. Something burned behind his eyes as he brushed a palm over the fabric.

"Might be wise to get rid of that," his grandfather said, tapping his cane gently against Alex's hooded top. "They used it to target you, who knows, there might be some residual hexing hanging around. A hoodoo in your hoodie."

Alex barely heard him. He shrugged out of his top and absently handed it over, then slipped one arm into the old coat, fully fascinated. The parka was too big and musty from storage, but he didn't care. As he pulled it on, he felt himself wrapped in a strange sensation, something simultaneously close and far away.

"Thanks," he said. "It's great. It's really cool. I mean, I love it."

"Well," his grandfather said, turning away abruptly. He cleared his throat. "Not quite my style."

Alex packed his belongings away, gathering up the toy robot last and slipping it into the coat's deep pocket. Meanwhile, the old man worked at his discarded top with his cigarette lighter and a small can of fluid. He soon had it burning, a small strange fire, bright in the dull morning. Alex stuck his hands in his new pockets and watched it burn.

Fire burn and cauldron bubble.

The words just popped into his head. The witches' spell from *Macbeth*. He tried to recall the rest. All he could get was, *By the pricking of my thumbs.*

He frowned, seeing the blood shining on his thumb by lamplight in his bedroom on that very first night, when he'd accidentally cut himself on the old toy robot's ragged tin edge, his blood leaking inside, toward the ancient tablet.

His grandfather used his stick to poke away the last embers in the smouldering heap. With the tip of the cane he drew an obscure pattern through the ashes, then scrubbed it away.

"Onward."

❁

"HOTEL UP AHEAD," Alex's grandfather said.

They had shot through a series of small towns that were barely more than bright little buildings scattered along the roadside. Now they were in empty country under swollen clouds. The terrain was changing, hills growing on the horizon, dark with trees. The hotel nestled alone in a dip by the road, a cheerful white building bearing wooden balconies brightly planted with meadow flowers.

"That's the way to the Kandel," Alex's grandfather said, as if wrestling with a decision. He gestured to the road snaking into the solemn hills ahead. "I had hoped we could grab some rest at the hotel before we try for Harry. Can't risk it now. We need to keep going. Are you up to it?"

Alex nodded.

"Good man. Don't know if *I* am, mind you. Suppose we'll find out. Still—" At the last moment, rather than bypassing the building, Alex's grandfather spun them in a sudden screaming turn into the hotel's sandy carpark. "We can always book rooms for *afterward*. Give us something to look forward to, eh? Excellent food in this place, I seem to recall. Ah, keep watching the road for unwanted company, Alex, shan't be a moment."

As the old man headed into the building, Alex stepped out of the car to stretch. Fine rain hung in the air. The hotel looked old-fashioned and friendly, yet, standing bright and small as the last outpost against the forest towering darkly beyond, it made him think of the flickering taverns in the creaky old black-and-white horror movies his mum and Carl loved to watch late at night on TV: the little inns where locals warned strangers to stay away from the woods after nightfall. The memory didn't seem so funny now.

A blue banner ran the length of the balcony, emblazoned with one word in big, pumpkin-orange letters, WALPURGISNACHT, accompanied by a date and time: APRIL 30, 19 UHR.

Tomorrow night, Alex thought foggily, not entirely certain he

still had track of the days. In the car park, smaller posters advertised the same thing, illustrated by photographs of people clustering happily in fancy dress: red devils stroking pointy beards,
witches making wizened pouts and shaking broomsticks.

The road remained empty. Alex looked to the infinity of
trees looming above and shivered, recalling Harry's last desperate phone call from somewhere up there. He checked his own
phone. A reply from Kenzie.

```
Sorry. Had the dream again bad.

I was shouting don't stand up. You were going
to stand up and something was going to get
you if you did. Sent it before I was proper
awake. Keep seeing things don't know what
they are. Not feeling well. Sorry.
```

Alex read it three times before he remembered, with a cold
feeling, hiding outside Harry's office and watching the tall man
just feet away – thinking about standing up and calling out. He
typed:

```
Let me know if there's any more.
```

He hesitated before sending. Exchanging messages like this
with Kenzie was a new experience. The other boy's meek tone

was entirely out of character – but it was entirely in keeping with the way Kenzie had been behaving in recent weeks, and Alex was increasingly troubled over just what was causing it. He added:

```
Please. I mean it.

Hope you feel better.
```

He read it over, feeling awkward, then blew out an exasperated sigh and shrugged and sent it on its way. His thumbnail tapped the screen as he tried to straighten his scrambled thoughts. He put the phone away, leaned into the car, and fished out his notebook and pen from the rucksack before he lost the thread of his thinking. He scribbled down:

> USING POWER
> UNCONSCIOUS REFLEX: bedroom homework (my blood got inside toy robot)/guys on train in France/ turning invisible/sending thought to golem(?).
> POWERFUL PLACES: Prague on bridge/Prague sending thought to golem(?).
> UNKNOWN???: David's house, when his great-gran screamed at me.

He thought for a few seconds, then added:

KENZIE???: bullies beating Kenzie up in park/the
time Kenzie tried to beat me up after school.

He chewed the pen. There was another moment, he realised,
back at the very beginning of his strange journey with the old
toy robot. He added it to the last list:

Kenzie on bus to school (morning after my blood got
into robot), when he took the robot off me, but then
just gave it back.

He looked at what he'd written, couldn't think what to make
of it, sighed, and closed the notebook. Then he hurriedly opened
it again, scrubbed out the section headed UNKNOWN, and
added to the KENZIE list:

David's house, when his great-gran screamed at me
— Kenzie was there again!! Just outside the window.

He read it over, wondering what it meant. His grandfather
came loping out from the hotel, a newspaper under one arm
and a distracted look on his face. He stopped by the car and
studied the sky. "Rain's going to get heavier. But with a bit of
luck it'll keep too many people from going up the mountain."

"Are we going to climb a mountain?" Alex asked.

"What? Oh, no, no," the old man said. "We can drive up.

There's a parking place up top. Then we'll walk back down the other side for a bit. There's a remote spot on the slope we have to get to. That's where Harry is."

"You think he's still up there?" Alex said as they climbed back into the car. "You don't think they'll have taken him somewhere else?"

"No, shouldn't have thought so. Now: they were sorting out the morning newspapers in there, Alex. I had a glance through." He held up the paper, folded to an inside page. "There was another painting taken last night. In Paris. The Louvre itself. *Interior of a Kitchen*, painted by an artist named Martin Drölling in 1815."

The photograph accompanying the story showed a painting that matched the title, figures sitting in a cluttered country kitchen before a high window that framed trees against a bright morning sky.

"You think . . . ?" Alex said.

"We have to assume so," his grandfather said, starting the engine. "And if Harry was right, that means there's only one more painting left to go. Unless they have it already and we just haven't heard about it, of course." He shot Alex a sudden grin. "Still. The *good* news is, if they were busy in Paris last night, we might have a lead on them."

They swung out of the parking lot. The road soon narrowed, twisting upward between trees that pressed in heavily all around. They passed only a couple of lonely cars coming down, the drivers offering waves as they slowed to edge by each other.

As they climbed, the rocky slopes falling from the roadside grew steeper, until finally they were turning onto a high, bare parking area at the top of the hill. A trio of cyclists passed them, ringing their bells, starting on the road back down.

Alex's grandfather killed the Citroën's engine. The grey sky hung vast and low. Beyond the car's bonnet, a grassy slope dropped away to frame a far-off vista of tree-covered peaks poking blackly through mist. A little way down the hill ahead, four small helmeted figures were working to fold up what looked like massive sheets of red-and-yellow fabric, the colours so intense against the surroundings they seemed to pulse.

"What d'you call 'em? Paragliders," Alex's grandfather murmured, watching them. "The Kandel is a popular launching spot. Giving up because of the rain, probably." By the time the pilots had packed and gone, there were only a handful of other empty cars left around.

"You have the, ah, tablet?" Alex's grandfather asked quietly.

Alex nodded.

"How are you feeling about it?"

"Not sure." Alex took a deep breath. "I think I might have an idea. I can try, anyway."

"Good man. Where we're going is just a little way down the hill." The old man pointed. "There's a path over there."

Towering trees closed in as they picked their way along a thin track that wound muddily down a steep, stony slope. Birds chattered and called. After a while they came upon a small grey hut, sitting oddly alone in the forest, perched out on a high rocky shelf above a valley. There was a bench outside, sheltered by the overhanging roof. Alex's grandfather sat wearily and beckoned Alex to join him.

"Always worth taking a moment for something like this," the old man said, gesturing ahead. "Remind yourself you're alive."

The view was devastating. The world spread out beneath them in jagged ranks of blue-black hills and mountains that rolled away through a thin ocean of fog toward a horizon where earth and fog and cloud all melted together. On distant slopes, mist rose from the darkness of the trees in massive, mysterious columns that glowed strangely where they met scattered shafts of sunlight.

"'Course, you need a clear day to really appreciate it." Alex's grandfather waved a hand at the vista, then removed his hat, produced a handkerchief, and mopped his face. "In good weather, you can see as far as the Swiss Alps. But even on a day like today it's quite something. Maybe more so on a day like today. Over there is Freiburg, that's an interesting town, and down there Feldberg, where they do a lot of skiing, for some reason. Can't say I've ever seen the attraction. Just another way to break an ankle, if you ask me. Oh, and you see that big hill, they call that . . ."

He broke off and looked at his feet.

"Hah. Name escapes me. You're in the centre of it all here, Alex. The Black Forest. This is where all the stories come from. All the tales of big bad wolves and magic mountains that open and swallow people and witches and demons. And wicked old people who eat children. There's a reason for that. You can feel it when you sit among these trees and look out on a view like this. Remember I told you, there are places on Earth where things get thin? Well, this is about the thinnest of all. The Black Forest . . ."

The old man suddenly tensed. "Hold on." It was barely a whisper. "I hear something."

The forest suddenly seemed abnormally silent, as if even the birds were holding their breath. A moment later, Alex heard it, too, the soft, steady tramp of footsteps coming nearer.

The old man stood and held his cane ready.

XIV.

THE DEVIL'S PULPIT

ALEX SAW DIM figures through the trees, disappearing in and out of the dappling light. He searched the ground, spotted a rock the size of his fist, and quickly stuck it in his pocket, just in case.

The approaching party gradually became more distinct. They were strangers, three men and two women. Alex saw his grandfather's stance relax, but the old man remained wary.

"Hallo!" one of the women called out, spotting them.

The group joined them by the hut. They carried backpacks and ropes, and wore bright hiking gear appropriate to the terrain and the weather, taking in Alex's grandfather's elegant grey suit and coat with a mixture of surprise and respectful amusement as he greeted them.

"Excuse," one of the men said, speaking English with a German accent. "We left our reward hidden here." He bent and reached into a hole in the planking beneath the hut, pulling out a six-pack of beer: "The treasure of the mountain!"

He shared the cans among his friends, offering the last to the old man, who raised it in salute as they drank.

"We have been climbing," the man said, gesturing behind with his thumb. "At the Kandelfels. You know the story of the pulpit?" He said this last part to Alex, who shook his head.

"So. You are on the witches' mountain, you know, my lad," the man went on, winking at Alex's grandfather. "A place of legends. Now, there are rock crags just up there, the Kandelfels, very wonderful for climbing. And at the very top, there *used* to be a . . . what is the word . . . a natural outcropping? A great, massive black rock that hung out. They called it *die Teufelskanzel* – the Devil's Pulpit! Because the legend says it was where all the witches from this area would gather on their special nights, and the demons and devils would come to them there from the other side, and they would all dance beneath the moon and perform . . . well, whatever wild rituals dancing witches and devils might perform."

"Please accept our apologies," another of the men interrupted. He wiped foam from his moustache and grinned. "This is Richard's favourite story. We have banned him from discussing it with us, and so he bores any strangers he encounters at any opportunity."

"Silence." The first man made a mock scowl and raised a finger. "This is the good part: now, in 1981, you see, the Devil's Pulpit suddenly disintegrated overnight. Tons and tons of rock – *whoosh* – it all just came falling down, for no reason. And there were two more *very* strange things about it. First, this collapse occurred on *Walpurgisnacht* itself. And second, when they investigated, buried among all the rocks and rubble below, they found a . . . what is the . . . a broomstick! Good, eh?"

"This is a very true story," the woman who had first called out said to Alex, widening her eyes. "The experts, of course, came up with rational reasons to explain it away. But still: you will never find me up here after dark!"

"And definitely not tomorrow night," the man added, finishing his beer as the rest of their group laughed. All but one. Alex noticed that the other woman just looked away. She wore a bobble hat in bumblebee stripes of black and yellow that caught his eye as it moved.

"Tomorrow?" Alex asked.

"Walpurgis Night," his grandfather said quietly. "I'll explain later."

"It's no game," the woman in the striped hat blurted out. They all looked at her.

"An older cousin of mine." She shrugged and made a pensive frown, as if she'd regretted speaking. "She was up here that night. She and her friends only barely escaped the rock fall. I saw her the next day."

"You've never mentioned that, Hannah," the first man said.

"No. I was just a child. It scared me. She just kept saying the same thing. That they saw something appear that night. An . . . imp. She never spoke of it again. But I believe this –" she gestured weakly – "this is a troubled place. I would never come here alone. I would rather we never came at all."

"Well, so." The first woman nodded brightly after a second. She turned, hoisting her backpack, and raised her eyebrows secretly to Alex and his grandfather, rolling her eyes. "We must be going. We will leave you to enjoy the view in peace. Oh, you see that hill?"

She pointed out the distant peak Alex's grandfather had mentioned a moment earlier, looming in the misted landscape like a marker.

"They call that the *Toter Mann*. The Dead Man! Strange minds we have here, eh?"

Alex watched them go, vanishing with a final wave through shadows and pale tree trunks. The old man bent to his Gladstone and started uncoiling his rope.

"Was that story true?" Alex asked.

"About the tip of the mountain collapsing in '81? Yes. Thin place, Alex. The surface breaks easily. Things can fall through the cracks. Or slip out of them. Back when it happened, I always meant to investigate more, but, y'know. Time flies away from you."

"What's Walpurgis Night?" Alex asked. "I saw posters about that down at the hotel. Looked like a party."

"Ha. Yes, well, in a way it is. *Walpurgisnacht* is the night between the last day of April and the first of May. Tomorrow night," his grandfather said, searching for a solid spot to anchor his grappling hook.

"It was named after an English saint. St. Walpurga. She came to do holy work in Germany during the eighth century.

Interesting stuff. Some legends say that if you speak her name to an angry dog correctly, it will calm the animal. Anyway. Walpurgis Night coincides with a point in the calendar that's been considered important for thousands of years in many countries – people giving thanks they've survived another winter and banishing the last of it to welcome in spring and summer, you know.

"But around these parts, it's all rather more . . . potent. Some also call it *Hexennacht*: Witches' Night. The stories go that *Walpurgisnacht* was when witches would gather on the mountains for, well, strange celebrations, like the fellow said. A second Halloween, if you like, when ghosts and ghouls run free.

"Just as there are places where things get thin, Alex, there are *times* when things get thinner, too, when half-remembered old beliefs come bubbling up to the surface. Tomorrow night, in this area, you'll have both things happening at once: a *thin place* at a *thin time*.

"And all of this worries me." The old man paused to secure his rope around a tree trunk. "The timing of it, the way it all seems centred on the Black Forest. This place, at this time. There are coincidences in the air I don't like. The story about the mountain disintegrating, the old Shadow Gate legend about a castle falling. Two great unexplained collapses."

"Could it have been here? The Shadow Gate? Is it connected to the collapse of the Devil's Pulpit?"

"Hmm? Oh, no. I mean, the Shadow Gate legend dates from, what, five, six hundred years earlier, Alex. And it was supposed to have happened in a castle somewhere."

"Could that be it, then?" Alex said, trying to fit pieces together. "If there's a code in the paintings, maybe it tells you *where* it happened. Where the gate was. Like, I dunno, you . . . follow a path through the locations in the pictures, or *where* they were painted?"

"Decent thinking, Alex. I had thought something similar." The old man grunted, still fussing with the rope. "But it's led me nowhere yet." He straightened with a puff and slapped his hands.

"Now," he said. "There's just a *little* bit of climbing to do. Need to get down there." He pointed opposite their bench, where the ground simply dropped away. Alex stepped gingerly over and peered down: an almost vertical cliff of jagged granite.

"Just be careful, it'll be slippery," his grandfather said, "but it's not far down." The old man crouched at the edge. He had tied the end of the rope around his Gladstone and lowered it before following after, disappearing swiftly from sight.

Alex started to follow, then stopped. He checked his phone again. His scalp tingled when he saw a new message from Kenzie.

Can't remember.

You need to go to the right I think.

He rubbed his forehead and looked out on the view, trying

to shake off thoughts of witches and devils and dead men. It didn't work. He grabbed the cord and started climbing. A few minutes later he stood catching his breath beside his grandfather, thirty feet below the hut on a wild slope where no path could be seen. The old man led away, threading between trees.

Soon they came to a silent place where the trees stood back to form a ring around a large area entirely covered by broken rock and massive boulders. It was a picture of devastation, a gallery of shattered stone. More smashed rocks formed great cracked steps on the slope stretching upward through the trees toward a towering grey cliff face.

"What's all this?" Alex said. Granite shards shifted under his feet.

"Where the rocks fell," his grandfather said. He gazed up toward the serrated peaks above. "The night the mountain collapsed. We're standing among the pulverised remains of the Devil's Pulpit, Alex. Ah, let's not hang around."

They continued down the wooded slope. It grew so steep that Alex marvelled that the trees managed to stay standing. He concentrated on keeping his footing. In places the ground had dissolved to mud.

"Okay, Alex," his grandfather said, suddenly halting. "It's time to try to get Harry now."

Alex swallowed. He felt a heavy weight pressing down on him, did his best to ignore it. They had come to a small clearing. He noticed a rough mounded spot by his feet, covered in leaves and broken branches.

"Okay," Alex said. He peered past his grandfather into the trees ahead. Some kind of secret lair hidden down there? He dropped his voice. "I'm ready. So what's the plan? Where's Harry from here?"

"Hah. Well. That's the thing." His grandfather stood pulling at one ear, then offered a curious, apologetic smile. "Ah, you're . . . Well, you're standing on him. More or less."

Alex stared blankly. He searched around his feet, the disturbed ground, the pile of dead branches and leaves.

"Huh?" An underground lair?

His grandfather rubbed at his brow, covering his face for a moment. When he dropped his hand, he looked more tired than Alex had ever seen him. The old man gave a hopeless shrug.

"I, ah . . ." His voice was hoarse. "I had to bury him. Here. The other night."

Alex stared, uncomprehending.

"They killed him, Alex."

The words took a long time to travel across the clearing. Alex felt as though the slope tilted steeper, dropping away under his feet. He stumbled, then sat on the damp ground. Still, the world kept lurching downward. He looked up, trying to steady himself. Sunlight glinted among black leaves. Birds cawed to one another not far away, ravens maybe, and his grandfather spoke again.

"They killed him, Alex. Harry's dead."

XV.

THE TROUBLE WITH HARRY THIS TIME

"DEAD . . . ?" ALEX FINALLY whispered.

"Yes." The old man lowered himself by Alex's side. Water dripped from his hat brim as he bowed his head and turned up his coat collar. "Afraid so."

They sat in silence. The sensation that the world was spinning slowed. Alex felt tears spill out, briefly hot among the cold rain on his face. More gathered like acid in his throat. He swallowed and moved his hands in a useless arc.

"Why didn't you tell me?"

"Didn't want you worrying."

There was no answer to that.

"Okay," Alex said. He noticed he had picked up leaves without realising and was twisting them between his fingers. He let them drop. "But I don't understand. Why are we up here, Grandad? What do you want to do? Do you want to try to . . . move him?"

"In a way." His grandfather looked off down the slope. "That is, I want you to try to move him."

"I, uh . . . what?"

"I can't remember how much we spoke about the golem legends," the old man said. "Invisibility and all that. Well, one of the *other* powers it had, according to many stories, was the, ah –" the old man cleared his throat, half burying the rush of words – "abilitytoraisethedead."

Alex tried to blink away the sting in his eyes.

"We talked about this before," his grandfather went on, warming slightly to the task of delivering a lesson in strange history. "What powered the golem is a force of *life itself*. There were tales about trials in the old Prague courts, you see, where the golem would, ah, summon up dead witnesses to appear and give evidence—"

"Wait." Every inch of Alex's skin was suddenly crawling in different directions, as though trying to get away. "Hang on. You want me to . . ." He searched for words. Nothing sounded right. "Bring him back? To life? Harry. From being dead. You want me to try to bring him back."

"Well . . . yes."

"That's . . . I can't do *that*," Alex stammered. He had started to protest that the idea was impossible, ridiculous, but these words no longer meant much. Indeed, what horrified him most was that he knew his grandfather was entirely serious. "I thought we were going to rescue him. Break him out of somewhere. I thought you'd want me to . . . I dunno. Smash down walls or blast robots or . . . but *this* . . . I can't."

"Alex, you don't know *what* you can do until you try—"

"I've *been* trying! I can't do anything with it! I've lost it. I've lost the way to it. Or maybe it just doesn't want me any more. I can't remember how I did any of it. I can't do it."

"Maybe not." His grandfather shrugged and smiled. "I'll admit, it's a long shot. But it's got to be worth a try, hasn't it? You got *something* from the tablet not long ago."

Alex shivered. "That's another thing," he said, frowning. "You've told me how dangerous it all is. Magic. Forces not to be dabbled with. Old voodoo for another time, you said. Had to be destroyed. The whole point of everything you've done, everything *we've* done, was to stop your father getting his hands on the golem's tablet, stop him doing . . . this kind of thing. And now you want me to try to do exactly the same—"

"This is very different."

"How? How's it different?"

"It's just different, that's all. Anyway, a person has a right to contradict himself. And, Alex, this is *Harry.*"

"But other people died . . . my *dad.*" Alex's throat tightened. "You never tried to bring him back . . . did you?"

"No." The old man stared into the trees, focused on something else. "I had no chance to try. I had nothing like the tablet then. Maybe it's for the best I didn't. And maybe I shouldn't be asking you now, but—"

"But if I could," Alex broke in. His mind was racing into new territory. "If I *was* able to do what you're asking – I could try to get my dad back, too, couldn't I?"

"Ah, no, Alex, I don't think so." Taking up his cane, the old man began quickly tracing patterns on the ground. "I don't know much about the whole resurrection game, but from the little I've gleaned, it seems three or four days is the optimal time. Four was the magic number for old Lazarus, for example. You know, chap in the Bible. That's why I didn't want us to leave it any longer: it'll be three days for Harry tonight. I mean, he's hardly been away, ha. Your father has been gone too long. He's gone, Alex.

"Perhaps I'm just being foolish now. I have no idea what might happen if you manage to succeed with Harry. All the stories about this kind of thing – well, few end well. But Harry knows . . . Harry *knew* things about what's going on that we don't. I have a very bad feeling about it. If there's even the *slightest* chance, we have to try. And, anyway: Alex, this is *Harry*. And it's my fault he . . .

"Alex." The old man turned to him with new intensity. "If I could do this instead of you, if I could take it away from you, I would. In a heartbeat. But all this is beyond me, son. I've never studied the golem stories the way my father did. The procedures. The rules. The name of God. I never *wanted* to know. And besides: the golem's tablet, the power, seems to have formed some particular and peculiar connection with *you*. You told me your blood had touched the tablet. I think maybe it was that: you . . . woke it, and it latched on. It sought out a master. But this is where we are. I need you to try. Just *try*."

Alex hunched forward, hugging his knees. Even in the weird circumstances he'd grown used to, it seemed unthinkable. Suddenly, he felt trapped, as if the world and everything in it had conspired to force him into this spot. He was ready to rebel against all of it.

And he realised: there was his solution. Simply refuse. He felt certain that if he just said no right now, his grandfather would accept it. He sensed that the old man hated asking him to try this as much as Alex was loath to think about it.

So that was the answer. Say no, ditch the toy robot, give it to his grandad to get rid of, let the old man get on with his senseless escapades. Alex could leave all the insanity behind. Get back home. Back to life. He looked at his grandad, looking back at him, and made his decision. He would refuse.

"All right. I'll try."

Even as he said it, Alex wondered why he was agreeing. Perhaps because of the look in his grandfather's eyes. Perhaps because he felt certain nothing would happen. Or perhaps because he suddenly thought of Harry as the cheeky little boy in the old photograph, surviving alone through a world at war, smiling. He would try.

"Good man," his grandfather said quietly. He gave Alex's arm a squeeze. "Who knows, we might be lucky because of where we are, and when. Powerful place. Things are thin, and getting thinner as Walpurgis approaches. If it doesn't work, well. We'll just go back to improvising."

"Should we . . ." Alex nodded toward the mound of earth. "Uncover him?"

"I don't think so. I should think that if you can get him all the way back from . . . If you can get him *back*, the details will take care of themselves. There's not much over him, anyway. Now, take this. It was Harry's. Something close to him. Might help you focus."

He held out an old wristwatch on a worn leather strap. Taking it, Alex found himself staring at the second hand, still moving after its owner had stopped. He pulled the watch on.

"You just do whatever it is you have to do. I'll give you space," his grandfather said, rising. "In fact, I think I'll go prowl around, just in case. I won't be far." The old man smiled, nodded, then headed into the trees, leaving Alex alone among the shadows swaying gently with the breeze.

XVI.

SOMEWHERE IN THE LIGHT

ALEX TOOK OUT the toy robot. He knew the clumsy face so intimately he could draw it blindfolded. He closed his eyes, holding the image in his mind, lining it up as the first door he had to pass through in the experimental process he'd worked out. First the toy. Then the tablet. Then the light.

He sat like that for what felt like a long time, trying to move his mind. Eventually, he opened his eyes. To judge by Harry's old watch, nearly an hour had passed. It was useless.

He shifted where he sat, trying to get comfortable, and tried to think what he would be doing at this moment if he were at home and not sitting deep in the woods in Germany, trying to raise the dead for his two-hundred-year-old grandfather. Double maths. He still couldn't decide which was worse.

He lay back and pulled out his phone. Nothing new. He tapped a message to David – Hey, I'm away just now with my grandad. Short notice trip. Back in a couple of days. I hope – just to send some contact back to normality. It would be nice to keep in touch. The message wouldn't go. "No signal," Alex said, and laughed bleakly.

Raindrops spattered the screen as he scrolled through the pictures of the stolen paintings. He stopped at the one called *The Great Last Judgment*, struck by the blues and reds of the garments some of the figures wore, very vivid in his gloomy surroundings.

"The dead have risen . . ."

He stared at the last message from Kenzie.

You need to go to the right I think.

He shook himself. He was putting off what he had to do, just like he always did with his maths homework. The Prince of Procrastination, his mum called him. He pulled out his notebook and puzzled over the lines he'd scribbled to himself, searching for a clue. He hesitated, uncertain. The idea that was forming didn't make sense. He decided not to think about that – what did make sense any more? – and just follow the feeling that it somehow seemed to fit.

He resolved to make one last try at contacting the power, give it everything. But this time, he would line up a new set of mental doors to guide him: the old toy, then the tablet, and then . . . Okay – something to do with Kenzie Mitchell. *Then* the light.

He cleared his mind, put those thoughts in order, and focused.

The forest was hushed around him, and before long he was sunk inside his mental journey. He passed the old tin toy and opened the door that led on to the old clay tablet. Now he held the tablet in his mind. For a moment, he glimpsed himself from above, a boy sitting in the woods in flickering light. The mountain quietly urged him on. He opened the door and pushed his thoughts through.

And now there was Kenzie.

Alex concentrated hard on the other boy. It was easy to bring him into focus. The face had given him nightmares during the long years Kenzie had bullied him. Kenzie was trying to talk, but he didn't seem to know how.

Alex directed his entire concentration at Kenzie. He told him to be quiet. He could see the door that led to the light behind Kenzie now. Kenzie was blocking the way. He couldn't get around him. There was only one thing to do. Alex gathered his mind and used it to shove Kenzie. Kenzie made a protesting gesture, but he fell easily backward, fell against the door, opening it, fell through the door, fell into the light.

And now the light came surging at Alex. Or he was moving toward it, moving away from the lonely mountain. All he could hear was the relentless ticking of Harry's old watch on his wrist. Minutes ticked by without him. Alex had the impression of riding on the watch's second hand, sweeping around a massive golden dial made of light, pushing time away. And somewhere in the light was Harry Morecambe.

Harry, he thought, and attempted to recall him in as much detail as he could – light in his eyes, lines on his face. *Harry Morecambe. Old Harry. Child Harry, hiding in your bomb craters. Where are you hiding now?*

As that question formed, Alex felt it move out from him, into the light.

He kept focusing on his vision. Two new doors had appeared. *You need to go to the right.*

Right-hand door. It was locked. But Alex knew that the key to open it was shaped like the sound of the words in the name Harry Morecambe, and as he formed the words, the key was in his hand and the lock was turning and the door was opening and—

A sharp sound shocked him back into the forest clearing with a rush that left him dazed. The light through the branches had grown dim, tinged with red. The light flickered. There was a faint hissing on the air, dying away. But it hadn't been that which had alarmed him. Alex looked in panic to the pile where Harry lay. Nothing had changed. The noise had come from across the clearing.

His grandfather stood alert in the shadows there, cane in hand, head cocked, listening to the woods.

"Grandad." Alex rubbed his aching neck. "How long have I been sitting here?"

"Going on seven hours," the old man said, then gave a blunt

silencing motion. After a second, Alex heard a crack from the forest interior. A heavy foot stepping on old wood.

"How did you do?" Alex's grandfather whispered. "Feel anything?"

"Yes. I'm *sure* I did. But nothing happened." He gave a defeated shrug. "I tried. I don't know how."

"Stay. Try again. Keep trying. There's still time." The old man sounded as though he was trying to convince himself. He spoke quickly, leaping from one thought to the next. "If it's them, if they've tracked us down . . . I'll lead them away. I'll buy as much time as I can, then circle back and come get you."

"But—"

"Alex. Please. Keep trying. Just a few minutes more." With that, he was gone.

Alex stared after him, then bent over the old toy and strained to find focus again, but another noise off in the trees wrenched away his concentration. A sound like a cane striking metal. A violent crash came from another direction, further away. Alex stood, brushing dirt from his clothes. He looked at the mound on the ground.

"Sorry, Harry."

There was nothing he could do for Harry. But he could help his grandfather. The rain came on harder. Alex put the toy away, turned his back on the grave, and started running up the hill in the direction the old man had taken.

XVII.

ESCAPE FROM WITCHES' MOUNTAIN

ALEX CREPT THROUGH a labyrinth of trees in the failing light. The branches above made black scratches against a deepening midnight-blue sky. It was difficult to see very far. He listened hard, but all he could hear was his own too-loud footsteps and rain on leaves.

As he came within sight of the rock face they had climbed down, his grandfather suddenly appeared, off to his left, running out from the trees. Alex started toward him, but something about the old man's hunted look told him to take cover. He crouched among scraggy growth at the foot of a tree.

His grandfather reached the cliff, stopped, and whipped around, peering back into the shadows. Alex followed his glance. Nothing.

The white rope hung beside the old man. He dropped his bag, hooked his cane's handle over his coat collar, and began climbing as the bushes behind him burst apart. A life-sizer came stalking from the darkness.

Alex felt himself freeze. It was like watching something walking out from his nightmares. The huge metal man closed in on his grandfather and took a savage swipe, gouging a lump from the rock face just as the old man hoisted his heels beyond its reach. The machine grabbed the rope and gave a wrenching tug. Alex's grandfather was shaken but clung on, hauling himself up, more than halfway to the top now.

"Go on, you're going to make it," Alex whispered.

The cord tightened as the robot pulled harder. To Alex's dismay, the old man paused in his ascent, bracing his feet against the cliff. Hanging there one-handed, he extended his other arm and began swiping furiously at the rope above with his cane.

By the time Alex spotted the hovering flier chopping at the cord, the little machine had sliced almost all the way through. The life-sizer gave another savage yank. The rope snapped.

As he started to fall, Alex's grandfather pushed hard with his feet against the cliff and twisted in the air, turning his helpless plummet into a precision dive, aimed directly at the life-sizer. He cannoned into its chest. If his plan had been to topple it over, it almost worked. But the machine was too massive. It rocked back, dealing out a vicious punch that caught the old man on the side of his head. With piercing clarity, Alex saw things scattering from his grandfather's coat pockets as he bounced on the ground. The old man landed hard, face down on top of his Gladstone.

"Get up, Grandad," Alex whispered. He looked rapidly around, trying to form a plan. There was nothing. He thought about trying to connect with the tablet, but if it hadn't worked during all those hours with Harry, it wasn't going to happen in the next few seconds. Maybe he could run out, distract the robot, lead it away. But his legs refused to move.

"Get-up-get-up-get-up."

The life-sizer strode over to the motionless figure, paused, then bent low, raising a huge fist. As the blow came smashing down, Alex's grandfather rolled, spinning fast onto his back, flinging up an arm as he turned. Something flashed from his hand and smashed open on the machine's face. A salt shaker: the image of the old man casually pocketing it in the café back home popped into Alex's head.

The robot lurched back in a frenzy as a pained scream sounded from above. A portly shadow stood at the top of the rock face. After a second, Alex made out a face he had last seen in Prague: Baron Willy von Sudenfeld, the sly, maniacal antique toy collector who had become one of the tall man's followers.

Von Sudenfeld stood gasping, bent, clutching his head, stung by the touch of the salt on the machine he controlled in a way Alex had seen before. No longer under his direction, the life-sizer staggered backward, then stood planted, arms blurring as it chopped blindly, savagely, at the air around it. Alex's grandfather stood shakily, looking stunned. He leaned against the cliff face for support.

Forcing his legs to cooperate, Alex stood to run to him, then froze again.

Movement to his right. Close. He pressed against the tree as another life-sizer came smashing through the undergrowth, heading for the old man. Von Sudenfeld had straightened and stood staring down, concentrating furiously.

Alex's grandfather spotted the new machine. The old man stood muzzily shaking his head, trying to focus. The robot moved cautiously, circling to head him off whenever he tried to move. It was gradually closing in, cutting down any options for escape – and steadily forcing him backward, toward the thrashing arms of the salt-crazed machine behind.

Above, von Sudenfeld stepped closer to the edge, directing the action. He yelped in delight. "See what I can do now?" He sounded both amazed and triumphant. "See?"

The tubby man was fully caught up in it, Alex realised, too focused on his machine to notice anything else. Alex studied the rock face. "Move," he ordered himself.

He circled right, fast, keeping under cover of the trees until he was pressed against the cliff base, out of sight of the man above. His grandfather's bag lay on its side a little ahead. One of the heavy spring-heels had fallen out. Scattered on the ground, Alex saw the things that had spilled from the old man's pockets. His wallet, a few cards that had come loose. Half-consciously, he scooped the wallet up, tucking cards back inside. One caught his eye: a small, plain white rectangle bearing a single word.

DEATH

Frowning, he turned another.

DEATH

Half a dozen, all the same.

The clatter of the old man's cane snapped him back to attention. His grandfather ducked woozily away from the life-sizer's blows, dazed, yet somehow fighting on instinct. Still, he was being gradually forced back toward the other machine lashing lethally behind him.

Alex stowed the wallet away and searched the sheer rock face for a step, a handhold. He looked up, considering the task. It was impossible. He started climbing anyway.

Rain showered down. The granite was slippery. His arms and legs tightened and burned. Twice in quick succession, he missed his grip and knew he was going to fall. Each time, he saved himself with an instinctive grab and kick, forced himself on.

The cliff was pockmarked with places to grip. As he neared the top, Alex told himself it was easy after all. He had almost managed to stop picturing the fall beneath, the ragged rocks. Looking up, he could see von Sudenfeld now, a few feet to his left, rocking with excitement at the cliff edge as he steered his machine in on Alex's grandfather, some twenty-five feet below.

Alex worked along until he was directly beneath him. There, he paused, arms trembling, forehead pressed to the rock. He watched a single raindrop run down there as he thought over what he planned to do, testing actions in his head, feeling the motion. Then he stopped thinking, hauled up fast, grabbed von Sudenfeld's ankle, and pulled down hard, putting all his weight into it.

Von Sudenfeld had time to say "Huh?" before he fell.

The life-sizer spun from Alex's grandfather and stumbled to try to catch the falling man. It didn't succeed, but it managed to break his fall. As von Sudenfeld crashed onto it, his wig flew from his head. Man and machine collapsed in a heap together, then lay still.

Alex hung by one arm, gazing down at what he had done, then turned to the rock and pulled himself over the top. He crawled forward and slumped face down, gulping damp air, wondering if the pain in his arms would stop.

"Alex?"

At his grandfather's voice, he stood shakily and stepped to the edge. He could see the old man peering up, bag in one hand, stick in the other. Just behind him, the other life-sizer still lashed around on the spot, furiously fighting nothing.

"Are you okay?" Alex called.

"Ha, just what I was going to ask you! Stand back, I'm going to try this." The old man raised one foot and indicated with his cane. He wore the spring-heels. Alex stepped back, there came the familiar creak, then his grandfather was there, tripping a step on landing, stumbling forward. Alex caught his arms, supporting him until he steadied.

"That really was a sterling effort, Alex." A dark brown bruise was growing on the old man's face. He looked as drained as Alex felt.

"Is he . . . ?" Alex gestured below. "Von Sudenfeld. Is he . . . ?"

"Eh? Oh, no. Unconscious. He should be okay, I think. Well, as close to okay as that man ever comes."

"I . . ." Alex pulled out his grandfather's wallet and the cards. "I found these. You dropped them."

"Marvellous, thank—" The old man broke off and tapped one of the cards against his nose, then flipped it around so it faced Alex.

DEATH

"You read that, then? Recognise it?"

Alex nodded and pulled out his wallet, taking from inside the fortune cards he'd been given by the Marvastro machine at Harry's office. He held one up.

POWER

Unmistakably from the same set.

"Well, don't read *too* much into it, Alex." His grandfather tucked the cards into a pocket. "It's the oldest trick in the book. Fortune tellers, prophets, politicians, poets, charlatans of all stripes do it: offer some vague statement that seems to mean something, then let you fill in the blanks yourself, until you think they've said something profound.

"Anyway, if you're idiotic enough to have your fortune told and you pull the death card, the great mystic *charging* you for the experience will always tell you *death* doesn't actually mean death, it means . . . change. One thing ending, another beginning. Or something equally open to infinite interpretation."

"But the card Marvastro gave me said *power*," Alex pressed. "That came true." Along with his growing concern for his grandfather, frustration was beginning to build inside him at the old man's eternal evasiveness.

"Well." His grandfather scratched an ear. "Like I say, depends how you interpret it, Alex. What if it meant . . . will-power? The power to know your own mind. You've shown a bit of that, too, and maybe that's more important, eh?"

"I just don't get you!" Alex exploded, frustration quickening into anger. He gestured around them. "We're in the middle of all this, this . . . *magic*. You've been up to your neck in it for over *a hundred years*. You've dragged me into it. And it's like you still pretend you don't *believe* in it."

The old man winced. "Well. I told you before, Alex," he said quietly. "I'd much prefer that all these old stories were just that: interesting old stories. I'd prefer to live in a world where all of this was gone, consigned to the past. There's enough magic and mystery to be found in life without wasting time on this nonsense. And enough horror."

"But you just asked me to . . . you must believe in it. You've seen the *proof*. You *are* the proof."

"Alex." The old man sighed in exasperation. "Look. There are countless people on this planet today perfectly content to believe all manner of things without any proof for any of it. Faith, they call it, right? Well, I'm just like that, except in reverse. I've *seen* the proof, and I'm happier *not* believing. Get the idea? It's like . . ." He stood searching for words, then brightened. "It's like rugby."

"*What?*"

"Yes. One of the sports I hate most. Now: I know that rugby *exists*, okay? But I can perfectly well choose to live my entire life without ever having to think about it or get involved. See?" He beamed.

"No." Alex kneaded his forehead. "No."

"Well, maybe rugby's not such a good example." His grandfather frowned. "I'll think about it some more, and we can have a good old philosophical discussion about it once all this is over—"

The old man suddenly dropped his bag and spun, swinging his stick hard at the air. There was a rattling, clashing noise and something fell whining to the ground before him, jabbing out with sharp little arms. A flier. Missing one wing, which now lay severed off a few feet away. He placed a boot on the thing, holding it down as it buzzed furiously.

"So: Harry?" Alex's grandfather sent him a searching look. Alex shook his head.

"No." The old man sighed. He stood head bowed for a moment. "Well. Can't be helped. Could you take my bag?" He lifted the Gladstone and handed it to Alex. "And I'll grab this." Gingerly, taking care to avoid the slashing hook and blade, he picked up the flier, pinning the arms down. He wrapped a handkerchief around its amber eyes like a blindfold, then gave Alex a nod.

"Let's get going, then."

XVIII.

DOWNHILL

UNSEEN THINGS BUZZED among the trees as they ran up the track. Alex noticed his grandfather was leaning harder on his cane, growing short of breath. But carrying the incredible weight of the Gladstone, he still gradually trailed behind the old man.

As he struggled to keep up, something caught and tangled around Alex's ankles, and he stumbled and fell. Bending to free his feet, he was puzzled to find it was some kind of fabric. In the dim light it took a moment to identify it as a jacket. Squinting around, Alex picked out five strange piles on the forest floor: backpacks and ropes and hiking clothes. Nearby lay a woollen bobble hat in bumblebee stripes of black and yellow.

He stared in bewilderment, remembering the climbers they'd spoken with. Somewhere beneath his confusion, another memory was struggling, but he couldn't quite reach it.

"Alex!" His grandfather's voice came as a concerned hiss from the darkness ahead. "Are you there? Are you okay?"

"Yeah. I'm fine, I just—"

"Well, if you wouldn't *mind*, we *are* in a bit of a hurry."

Alex scrambled up to join him.

Coming into the parking area, Alex saw two vehicles parked together some distance beyond their Citröen. A black transit van and another vehicle, long and low, indistinct in the murk. A hulking bald man hunkered by the van, staring fixedly at them while massageing his temples. Another of the giant robots came striding from the darkness, but too far away to trouble them.

As they ran for their car a vicious whine filled the breeze. Fliers came streaking from beyond the parking area, rippling fast through the rain in the frail light. Alex stopped as he saw Zia appearing blackly over the rise behind them, gesturing madly.

"If you pop the bag open," Alex's grandfather said, "there's a pocket at the top. Should be a couple of salt sachets in there. Last of the emergency supply."

Alex fumbled at the Gladstone's silk lining. The pocket seemed empty.

"Soon as you like, Alex," the old man said.

Alex felt the little packets, so thin his fingers almost missed them. He pulled them out.

"One should do," his grandfather said.

"Eh?" Alex held it up. "What do you think we're going to do with this?"

The fliers were three-quarters of the way to them.

"Well, if you could do the honours," the old man said, proffering the wingless flier struggling like a hostage in his grip. Alex understood. He ripped open the salt and sprinkled it directly over the machine.

In the distance, Zia faltered, then started twisting sharply, as if being stung repeatedly.

"Thaaaaank you," Alex's grandfather said. He tossed the dazed little robot high and swung his cane as it fell, batting it away with a mighty crack. Zia stumbled to her knees, clutching her head. Her fliers dropped from the air with a great rattle. But within seconds she was groggily standing again. Her metal swarm started weakly rising.

Alex and his grandfather were already in the Citroën.

"What now?" Alex said as he slammed his door.

"Play it by ear on the roads." The engine roared as they accelerated out of the parking area. "Try to lose them. Then I'll get you safely on a train or a plane back home."

"*What?*"

"I need to get you out of it now. It was worth taking the shot, Alex, but we've tried, we've failed, and there we are. I can't risk you getting hurt. Or worse. You're right, I should never have dragged you into this. We'll get you home. Leave the robot with me. If I can get through this, I'll see it's destroyed."

"I'm not leav—"

"Then again." Alex's grandfather's brow creased uncertainly. "Maybe I shouldn't send you back home alone. They had their eye on you. Maybe I should keep you close so I can protect you.

That's partly why I dragged you into all this in the first place, Alex, to try to keep you safe from . . . Sorry, Alex. I'm finding it a little hard to focus. Bit of a fog on the brain."

"You can forget it, anyway," Alex cut in. "It's not happening, Grandad. I'm not leaving you."

"Alex. No. I—"

"*I'm not leaving you.* That's *that.* I'm sure I can reach the power again, if I can only work out . . . and even if I can't, I can still help you."

"Okay," the old man said after a minute of silent driving. "Good man, Alex. Well. Here's the immediate plan, then: we need to lose them, but *not* lose them. We need to get them off our tail, but we need to get on theirs, follow them. Failing that, we need to work out the significance of the paintings."

Alex thought again about the reds and blues glowing from the picture on his phone by Harry's graveside. "I had another idea about that," he said as the car bounced wildly down the crooked road. "I don't know if it's stupid. We said that maybe they needed the actual physical paintings, right? So, could it be something in the paint itself?"

"How do you mean?"

"I was trying to remember." Alex pulled the phone out to spark his memory. "A lesson our art teacher gave us, about, like, Renaissance artists. How they used to make colours for paint back then. Reds and blues. The pigments were really valuable. They did it by crushing up minerals and even, like, insects and things. Some of the stuff was dangerous, toxic."

As he pulled up the picture of the rising dead, Alex noticed he was getting a signal on his phone. "It made me think about what you said, about snake venom," he continued. "The different *ingredients* your father used in his potion, besides whatever this . . . *flower* gives him. So, maybe there's something else he needs, but he can't get any more? Like, it's extinct? But he can get it out from the old paint?"

Alex's grandfather was silent, navigating a sudden bend. "Not bad," he said at length. "I should have thought of that. My mind is a little slow at the moment, Alex. But that's not a bad notion." He winced as though something unpleasant had been put under his nose.

"You know . . . there *was* a pigment they used back then, *Caput mortuum*. Used to be very popular, right up into the twentieth century. Gave artists nice rich browns and lovely, ah . . . flesh tones. And they made *that* by, well . . . grinding up old mummified bodies."

"What? *Human* bodies?"

"Yes. Pieces of people. They'd dig up mummies from Egypt, then pulverise them and mix it all up with—"

"And *paint* with it? That's completely gross. That's *horrible*."

"Well, yes. But galleries are full of it, Alex. Bear that in mind next time you visit a nice posh museum. Point *is*, though, it was the ancient Egyptians who first got really serious about the whole immortality game. My father had an entire section of his library devoted to early Egyptian texts, techniques for eternal life. Now, I have a friend in Berlin, a scientist. If we can get the painting Harry saved to her lab, we could run some proper tests, try out your theory, and some others. I wonder . . ."

His grandfather fell silent. There was one new message on Alex's phone. From Kenzie. Sent a few hours before:

Look out your window.

Alex glanced to the side, then behind. Nothing.

"Harry," he said after a bit. "I'm sorry I couldn't."

"You've nothing to be sorry about, Alex. I know you tried. I'm sorry for asking."

"You told me before," Alex went on, still puzzling over the message. "About your father, I mean. You told me once: *People were getting hurt, killed* . . . I guess I didn't really take it in properly at the time. I was still caught up thinking he was *my* dad. Maybe that's why I didn't get it. I still wondered why you first went against him. What made you leave him. You know: why *not* try to live forever, if you can? But I know now. If people get in their way, your father and sister, they just kill them. Like the museum guard in the video you showed me. Like Harry."

"Well, yes." The old man stared grimly ahead. "That kind of thing has happened more than once. But, Alex, that's not why I *first* went away from them. That's not the only reason people . . . were dying."

They reached the foot of the mountain and turned onto a country road that was all blue shadow.

"You see," Alex's grandfather continued, "the reason I left was, I discovered—"

A heavy thump on the roof sent a shudder through the car. They turned to each other. The ceiling over Alex bulged, buckled, then split open as a huge gloved fist smashed through. He ducked just in time to avoid it. A second fist ripped through, closer to the old man.

"Hold on!" Alex's grandfather started spinning the wheel frantically, slamming the car from side to side, trying to shake off their unwanted passenger, then stamped on the brakes, stopping them with a force that sent Alex's seat belt biting into his chest.

It was no use. The enormous hands had taken a tight grip through the ragged holes in the roof. Now, with a sickening wrench, they started ripping the roof away.

The old man threw the car forward. Alex stared up. He saw a life-sizer, peeling the car open like a sardine can. But his attention was grabbed more forcefully by what was in the air behind it.

Zia.

"Peekaboo," she called.

She flew along just above them in a cruciform pose, fifteen or so fliers lined up along her outstretched arms, holding her aloft with hooks through her black coat. Her pale face glowed like a second little moon racing through the sky, black hair streaming across it like thin clouds in a storm.

She blinked, her thrumming machines shifted, and she

darted close, tossing a powder over Alex's grandfather. The car swerved sickeningly as he tried to clear his eyes.

"Get," she said, nodding at the huge robot.

The big machine reached down, and, as Alex tried to squirm away, snapped his seat belt, then started hauling him up, ignoring the punches he rained on its iron arm.

With desperate inspiration, Alex reached quickly into his pocket and threw the old toy robot to the floor of the car, saw it bounce out of sight under his seat. Then he watched his kicking feet rise above the mangled roof. It took a stunned moment to realise he had been lifted into the air. Flying. He was aware of a whining noise all around, saw dozens more fliers labouring to support the life-sizer that carried him.

Below, the car skidded, careering off the road. It smashed through bushes and went crashing into the ditch around a dim, rutted field.

"Grandad!"

He was lifted higher. Cool rain bathed him. A rushing noise came close. He looked around to see the moon face looming in.

"*We're waaaalking in the aiiiiiir*," Zia trilled. "Come on, join in."

Alex found his notebook in his pocket and flung it at her end over end like a ninja star, then kicked out wildly as she dodged easily away.

"What? Don't feel like singing? Okay." She moved in, shoved a small fist under his nose. When she uncurled the fingers, more grey powder lay in her palm.

"Night-night, then," she said, blowing it in his face. Alex jerked back, but the stuff was already in his eyes, up his nose. A heavy, spicy smell.

Blinking to clear his vision, Alex saw, far below, the beams of the car's headlights stretching forlornly across the field, lighting up a group of horses that stood startled in the darkness, watching the strange flying formation. He started to feel warm and full, cold and empty, moving slower as the world rocketed faster away from him.

Eyes closing. Opening. Closing. Opening.

The horses were galloping below, running after him, looking up, as though they were trying to catch him, tell him something he'd forgotten.

Closed. Open.

The world rushed away. He thought about his mum waving him off to school, his grandfather falling from a roof, Kenzie Mitchell falling into the light, witches dancing on collapsing mountains with their thumbs all bleeding, cars crashing everywhere, bye-bye.

He saw horses . . . horses . . .

And then his eyes closed and would not open again.

XIX.

DOWN IN THE HOLE

THE MOON WAS enormous, blindingly bright in the black sky. A halo of light echoed around it.

Alex lay on his back, staring up, until the glare made him turn away. Shielding his eyes, he looked again. There never was a moon so big. As he blinked, a shadow moved across its lower edge.

"Morning, bunny," the shadow called.

Alex flinched and his head struck something hard and cold. There was a smell of time and dampness. It took several seconds to work out what was going on. The glowing white disc above wasn't the moon in the night sky at all. It was the morning sky: grey-white clouds, framed within the circular opening of a deep, dark well.

And he was lying at the bottom of it.

He lurched up, stumbled, stood staring around. A dingy bed of twigs and leaves rustled beneath his feet. The well was about five feet across. The dank brick walls were furry with moss, but otherwise depressingly smooth, devoid of handholds. The opening was thirty feet above. Maybe more.

"Led us quite the merry dance," Zia shouted down, her voice bouncing happily around him. "How d'you like your new nursery?"

"Let me out of here!"

"Oh, dee-*press*ingly predictable, my dreary dearie. I had a bet with myself what your first words would be."

"Let me out!" Alex felt panic closing in, did his best to fight it away.

"Don't repeat yourself. And don't whine. Besides, do you honestly imagine I would have gone to all the effort of getting you down there just to help you back up?"

"I don't have it!" Alex shouted.

"What's that? Not with you, bunny. You don't have what? Wit? Style? 'What it takes'?"

"The robot – the tablet. The name of God."

"Oh, I know *that*, Alexander. I searched your disgusting pockets before I popped you down your rabbit hole. You didn't have anything useful at all. But we can fix that; I can give you something all kinds of useful now – catch!"

Alex ducked back as she dropped something. It landed with a soft thump inches from his toes, disappearing under the leaves. He tensed, staring at the spot, waiting for something unimaginable to come crawling out.

"Well, *take* it then!" Zia finally shouted. "And a thank-you wouldn't go amiss."

"Wh-wh-what do you want?" Alex stammered.

"I want you to *p-p-pick it up*. I know it's difficult for your tiny mind to understand, but I positively *can't* make myself any clearer."

Alex thought furiously, glancing around his circular prison. His eyes were drawn helplessly back to where the thing had fallen. It seemed he had no option but to do what she wanted. It was that or nothing. But there was a thought – do nothing. He leaned back against the chill brickwork and folded his arms.

"No. I won't."

"Oh, tell you what: let's have a bet. I says you will." The silhouetted figure disappeared.

Alex stood staring up, mind racing. He had the awful, certain feeling she was going to cover the well. He stiffened as he heard another voice suddenly call out from a little further away.

"Don't listen to her, Alex!"

"Grandad!" Alex shouted.

All he could see was the bright disc of sky.

"Don't—" The old man's voice was silenced by a sharp slap. There were sounds of struggle, a pained sigh, then nothing. Zia's head popped back into view.

"Want to guess what I've done to him?"

"Leave him alone! I'll—"

"What'll you do, duckie?"

"Okay, okay! I'll do what you want! Just leave him alone."

"Well, go on then."

Alex swallowed with difficulty, then forced himself to reach down into the dead leaves. His hand closed around something jagged. When he brought it out, he was clutching a flier.

The little machine seemed lifeless. A purple-and-black ribbon was knotted tightly around it. Taking care to avoid its razor-edged wings, he warily turned the robot over. The ribbon held small sharp scissors strapped to it.

"Yes, bravo, well done," Zia called. "Now, see this?"

Alex squinted up and froze. Something was coming over the edge of the well, slithering oddly down the wall. After a moment, he realised she was lowering a rope ladder. When the bottom rung was around ten feet above, it halted.

"Now. The Soaring Spirit is all prepared, receptive and ready just for you."

"What?"

"Sorry. Let me translate into rabbit. Ahem: in your tiny right paw, you clutch a Soaring Spirit. You have seen them before. This device has been especially prepared for your use, and your use alone. Tuned to the bunny wavelength. It's all ready for you, it's *wait*ing. Treat it carefully, because we're getting to the stage that we don't have many left. Not had time to get more ready.

"If you examine it closely, you will find a hinged panel on one side. You can see in the dim, can't you, bright eyes? All the carrots you eat? You will further notice I have loaned you my nail scissors, which I expect returned in the same immaculate condition, although I will of course have to have them sterilised. Now, to prime the Soaring Spirit and thus commence commune, you must give something of yourself. As we are only trying teensy-tiny wee baby steps, a little snip of your fur will suffice."

"I–I don't understand . . ."

"Give us strength," Zia muttered. "Cut some hair off and stick it in the machine."

"But . . ."

"I see." She sighed theatrically. "We need everything spelled out. Righto. You see the ladder, above, yes? And you *have* worked out that it's too *far* above for your wittle wabbity arms to weach, even with a vewy, vewy *big* hop? Well. Should it turn out that you are able to access the Soaring Spirit, you can send it up to *hook* the ladder and drag it *down* to you."

Alex looked dumbly from the shadow above to the macabre machine in his hand.

"But I can't," he managed. "I don't know—"

"Oh, I sympathise, Flopsy, believe me." Zia yawned. "Far as I'm concerned, odds against you being able to do it are a zillion to none. If it were up to me, I wouldn't be up at the crack of dawn wasting my precious time. But *don't worry* if you can't. We won't bother you any more, and you can just curl up and have a nice big sleep in your cosy burrow."

Alex's blood had curdled to sludge. Her orders made no sense.

In his mind, a clear picture was growing, of what it would be like to be left alone down in this hole. How time would crawl past in days and nights and deepening hunger, until . . . He cut that line off.

"Find yourself in a situation, deal with it," he whispered. He pulled the scissors free. His fingers shook. He tugged out a strand of hair at his temple, cut it off, then stuffed the scissors into his back pocket.

Examining the flier, he saw the panel. Opening it with his clammy hands revealed a shallow compartment, a humdrum metal clip inside. Tiny tubes led strangely off from it, like fine blue threads, disappearing inside the robot. He tucked the hair beneath, hesitated. He looked at his hair lying there. Then he clicked the panel shut.

What now?

Screwing his eyes tight, he focused, straining to cast aside disbelief. He concentrated so completely on the flier that he stopped breathing. Finally, with a choking gasp, he had to give up.

"Oh dear," Zia called, without interest. "That was none too promising. There are things I could give you to help. Secrets and things. I've helped other little cotton brains. Did you see von Sudenfeld with his new toys? But, in your case, y'see, if you can't do *anything* on your own, there's no *point*. Tell you what, though, you can have another go, best of three. Fair's fair. I'll even give you extra motivation."

As she disappeared, Alex slumped against the wall and slid to the ground, letting the flier drop. He stared numbly at the bricks beyond his feet and thought about his mum, wondering what had happened to him, about his grandfather, captured up there.

He wondered where this well was, what the landscape around it was like. Lonely, he assumed. Forgotten. His heart thudded high in his chest. He had thought he knew what fear was, but now he understood. This now, this was fear.

And beneath it all, another feeling it took him a moment to recognise: the absence of the old toy robot. He had carried it with him constantly for months. Now that he was without it, he felt its lack like a thinning of the blood.

"No, oh, don't!"

Alex shot to his feet as his grandfather's anguished cry came echoing down.

"Stay *down* there, Alex! I'll save you, just— No! You *fiend*!" A painful groan.

Alex realised he was pacing, touching uselessly at the walls. Forcing himself to stop, he stared at the flier lying among the dead foliage. He hadn't managed to raise Harry, but he had definitely felt *something* moving when he'd tried to send his mind out to the old tablet. He had done it before. Maybe he could do this. He tried to recall the sensation of pushing a thought out. He could do this. So do it. He shut his eyes, clenched his jaw, and tried reaching out with his mind again.

He had a sense that this would require a similar yet subtly different kind of movement to the one that led his mind toward the tablet. What had his grandfather told him about how the tall man's gang powered the machines? *They use themselves.* So, then, he wasn't trying to reach out to some other force this time. He was reaching out to . . . *himself.* The lock of his hair. Part of him.

He thought of the clip of hair, attempting to picture it clearly. The sounds of his grandfather struggling continued. He tried blotting them out – then, instead, focused on them. He stopped fighting it away and allowed himself to feel it all rushing around him, through him: fear, anger, panic. *Use it as fuel. Take it in. Send it out.*

He kept trying, went far beyond the place he thought he had to stop – and then he gave up, seized by a wracking coughing fit. Alex leaned against the shabby wall, panting. When he opened his eyes, it was several seconds before he realised the flier was no longer lying where he had dropped it. Searching around in bewilderment, he found it.

The robot hovered in the air just behind him.

Its wings beat so fast he couldn't see them. Its propeller whirred hungrily. For an instant, he had a vague, unsettling impression of looking back at himself through its wavering eyes. Practically as soon as he noticed it, the machine fell lifeless to the ground.

Before he had time to think, Alex closed his eyes again. Thinking was no use. He had to feel it, deeper than thinking. Tune out thoughts but feel everything in him, everything around him. Fear and anger and panic. Put it into the effort.

Not passing through doors this time, but . . . building a bridge.

He was one end of the bridge. And he was also the other end of it, the part of him waiting over there, the clip of hair. Build the bridge, then send a thought across it.

A rustling made him open one eye. The flier's wings were moving on the ground, twitching, faster. As soon as he saw it, the movement stopped.

There was surprise now, a sliver of hope. Feed that into the mix, too. Use it all to shape the bridge, then send the thought across. *Up*, he thought, and felt the thought move.

The machine was in the air, metal wings thrumming. As soon as he thought about it, it all stopped and the flier fell. Five seconds later, he had it flying once more. Alex sensed himself trying to divide his mind, block part of it off from the rest. Shutting doors. The trick was connecting without thinking about it, almost without knowing he was doing it. Like sprinting fast down a flight of stairs – try to think about what your feet are doing, and you lose control.

In fits and starts, dipping, then climbing, he sent the machine wobbling upward.

Vague amber flashes were going off across Alex's vision. He was seeing the wall of the well through the flier's eyes. With that realisation, the connection broke again. He caught the machine, threw it back up, then sent his mind after it, building the bridge. *Up*. The ladder appeared in his flickering picture. Alex distantly felt himself reaching out a hand, felt the flier's little hook bite into rope. Now, leaning back, he dragged it down.

Looking up to see, he lost the connection, caught the flier as it fell. He stuffed it in his pocket. The bottom rung hung little more than arm's reach above.

"Close enough for a big hop now," he muttered. He pressed back against the wall, took two steps, and leapt. Catching hold, feet scrabbling against slippery bricks, he hauled up until he could grab the next rung, then the next. His grandfather's yells grew clearer as he neared the top.

"Ow, oh, ow, oh, you devil, ow . . ."

Just below the opening, Alex paused, trying to form some plan to take him into the next few seconds. There was no plan. He steeled himself to move anyway. Not thinking had carried him this far.

Alex heaved himself out of the well.

XX.

OVERGROUND

ALEX HIT THE ground and rolled into an alert crouch, surveying the scene. The sight flummoxed him.

They were out by scraggly trees at the end of a long, drab brown field. The derelict remains of an abandoned farmhouse stood close by, forest clustering behind, wooded hills beyond.

Zia lay alone on her back on a felled tree trunk, watching the clouds. Scattered on the ground around her lay objects Alex recognised as the contents of his coat pockets: his house keys, wallet, and phone. The latter lay broken beside the fist-sized rock he had picked up on the mountain, which Zia had presumably used to smash the phone to bits.

With one hand, Zia swiped a stick absently against the log, making thumps and cracks. With the other, she occasionally gave herself a lazy slap on the cheek, or pounded her chest. All the while, she sang out anguished sounds in perfect imitation of Alex's grandfather's voice.

"Ow, you villain, oh, oh— Oh." Seeing Alex, she sat up

and frowned. "Well, that's disappointing," she said, still speaking with the old man's voice.

Something about it turned Alex's stomach. Acting on instinct, he whipped the flier from his pocket and threw it hard. As it sailed away from him, he caught it with his mind, put life in the wings, and aimed at Zia. He moved a finger. The machine raised its scalpel arm, going into attack

"Now, don't be silly," Zia said flatly, using her own voice.

Two silvery blurs burst from her coat and slammed into Alex's flier from either side. It felt as if his brain had been squeezed in a vice. The pain made him almost black out. He fell, faintly aware of his flier dropping stunned before him. He didn't think he would be able to move again.

"He was right," Zia mused.

Alex could vaguely see her through his watering eyes. He heard a whirring. Something was pulling at his coat. Lots of things. A team of fliers, lifting him. The pain in his head was too intense to fight back. He hung limp between them.

"We'll just pop you safely back in your pot to stew a bit."

Alex felt himself carried up and back. His head hammered, but he forced himself to start struggling. As his wavering vision cleared, he saw that the machines held him directly over the well's yawning mouth. He stopped writhing in case they dropped him, then started worrying that dropping him was exactly what they intended, anyway. Instead, they lowered him softly to the bottom, then flew off, one pausing to lift the rope ladder out as it went.

"Where's my grandad?" Alex yelled up at the empty sky. "What have you done with him?"

"Hmmm?" Zia's shuddering silhouette reappeared. "Oh, he's away over there somewhere." She waved a hand idly. "Not done anything to him, bunnykins. What to do with *you* is the question now." She paused, as if considering options, then clicked her tongue.

"Plan *was* to just keep a wee eye on you, then come visit you later in your dreary suburban burrow back in Blighty, bunny, once we'd concluded our current business. But my doddering old brother *would* keep bringing you closer and closer, and, well, if he *insists* on serving you up on a platter, seems rude to refuse. What did you think you were doing poking around the pulpit pieces? I'd've thought the old man would know better by now. How many friends is he willing to lose? The gate will open regardless, child. It's all coming together.

"Anyway. Father's awful keen to meet you, little leaping lepus. He reckoned you have *an interestingly shaped mind*. Reckoned it might be worth the cultivation. Family blood and all that. *I* reckoned your mind would be about as interesting as a wet lettuce on a Wednesday, but there we go. I will grudgingly concede there might be some very limited potential for teensy talent of an extremely minor kind.

"Shame the *old man* didn't see you with the Soaring Spirit, though," she went on. "Oh, brother drear wouldn't like you playing with toys like that *at all*, bunny. But maybe you do, eh? You're allowed secrets, Alexander. You've already kept secrets, haven't you? We all have secrets. Even your wonderful old grandpapa. . ."

Alex's vision shook as the pounding between his ears pulsed faster. The shadowy figure above seemed to stretch and lurch strangely in the air.

"Bet he never told you . . ." The voice came and went on waltzing waves of pain. ". . . your daddy, eh? Bet he nev . . . daddy . . . even brighter bunny than *you*. And bet ol' Grandad never told . . . Daddy *died*, hmm?"

"What?" Alex whispered. He couldn't make out what she was saying. He sank back on his heels.

"*My* father would never let *me* die," Zia continued haughtily. "But s'pose it takes all sorts. Anyway, you just take another little nap now, until we're ready to begin your schooling."

She turned away, and then something was hovering in the well's opening, slowly descending. Alex tensed and got unsteadily to his feet. His head felt like the inside of a drum being battered by an angry toddler, but he rubbed his eyes as clear as he could.

Another flier, but there was something about the shadowed shape that was different. Eventually, he saw. The flying thing carried a second machine: thinner, with a head like an elongated egg, and arms that tapered to pin-sharp points.

He'd seen one before, when it had tried to stab him in his bed, just before his world turned inside out – a stinger, his grandfather had called it, warning its needles would put him to sleep. Or worse. The little arms were already cycling hungrily, making enthusiastic jabbing motions as it drew nearer.

Alex backed away and slipped off his parka. When the machines got within range, he jumped, whipping out with the coat. The flier dodged, but he swatted again and caught it a glancing blow. The robot bobbled in the air, then recovered and shot upward, disappearing out the well. Alex felt a tiny, grim thrill of victory. It dissolved as he realised that the departing flier no longer carried the stinger.

The leaves at his feet rustled, and a silvery little arm broke through, making a stabbing lunge at his toes. With a yelp, he leapt across the well. The thing disappeared. Alex stood frozen, searching the ground, listening. Risking a glance up, he saw Zia leaning over, watching. A noise brought his attention back down in time to catch a stirring of the leaves. He dived for the spot, spreading out his coat and pressing down hard.

Alex knelt staring at the blank green fabric stretched between his fists. A needle jabbed through, wiggled meanly, then vanished. A second later it came knifing out again, nearer his left hand.

Half his mind screamed, *Let go, get away.* The other half showed him images of the stinger instantly getting free and springing for his face. He felt the thing moving under his hand. With an involuntary shudder, Alex threw himself back, stared down at his coat, and waited for the machine to emerge.

Nothing happened. He caught a faint noise from above, then another. A rushing whirr, rapid clangs. A pained gasp that could have been the cry of a small girl. He looked up. Zia had vanished.

Alex stood perplexed. Maybe his grandfather had tracked him down. Or maybe this was another trick. After a second's more hesitation, he snatched up his coat, jumped back, held it ready.

The horrendous thing just sat there, scratching its needles gently on the leaves. It no longer seemed interested in him. Alex took his chance, grabbed for the robot and smashed it hard against the brickwork. The egg-head cracked. Something yolky oozed out. He heard Zia's shriek from above, sounding further away.

He tossed the machine aside and stood waiting, looking up. Solid silence radiated down on him. Clouds moved slowly high above. Then the silhouette of a man's head appeared in the well's opening. Not his grandfather, he knew instantly.

"Eh . . . hello?"

No response.

"Hello?" Alex tried again. "Can you help?"

Still no answer. The figure disappeared.

"Wait! Don't—" Alex stopped as he saw the rope ladder flung over the well. It lowered until it hung just before him. He glanced around. The broken stinger robot lay lifeless amid the dingy leaves. Staying down here was not an option, whatever waited above. He pulled on his coat, tested the bottom rung, and began climbing. As he reached the top, his arms shook, and not just from the exertion. He drew a breath, then gingerly raised his head above the wall.

A thickset man who looked to be in his late seventies or early eighties stood by the well, making sure the ladder was secure. The man chewed his lip uncertainly, watching Alex.

"'Allo," he finally said, then paused, wincing in doubt. "It's, uh . . . *Alex*, innit?"

Alex stared at him. He couldn't remember how to speak. Finally, he found one word.

"Harry?"

XXI.

FLIGHT

THEY STARED AT each other. Then Alex hurled himself from the well and flung his arms around Harry. One big arm wrapped around him, squeezing back. Alex wiped his eyes as he stepped away.

"Harry! You're—" He broke off as new apprehension washed through him. He had been going to say something like, *You're safe, you're all right.* But now it hit him. He didn't know *what* Harry was.

"Uh," Alex tried again. Waves of fear pounded at him. "Harry. Are you . . . all right?"

"Eh." Harry looked to the sky, then furrowed his brow. "Eh, yeah. Think so. I mean, I'm kind of . . . foggy-feelin'. But it's beginnin' to clear a bit. I just can't remember 'ow . . . I found myself in gloomy woods, but I can't remember 'ow I got there. I was just walkin', tryin' to think, listenin' to the birds. Somethin' made me come in this direction. Then I heard voices and saw . . . wassername, the girl."

He broke off, frowning after a memory. His eyes widened. "Zia! Gawd. Yeah. I 'id in the trees watchin'. There were, eh, whatsits, little flyin' blighters . . . *fliers* sittin' around, but she was too busy lookin' down the well at you, I guess. They were dozin'. I managed to grab a couple and smash 'em before she knew I was there. Stunned 'er for a moment. I thought I'd be in for it then, but when she saw me – well, it was *weird*. She just kind of froze, starin' at me. Like she was . . . *scared* of me, just for a second. So I took the opportunity to smash another couple of her machines. She went stumblin' away, then she got 'it by another bigger shock and ran."

Harry gestured at a few badly damaged fliers lying around the ground, then pointed out the direction Zia had taken, into the trees behind Alex. "I reckon we shouldn't 'ang around too long, though."

"Harry . . ." Alex paused, picking his way carefully. He held himself tense, ready to run. "You don't remember *anything* before you found yourself in the forest?"

"Well, yeah," Harry mused. "I mean, I can remember most things. I just can't remember what 'appened . . . just before. Do *you* know?"

"You, uh. There was an accident. With your car," Alex said tentatively. He stole a glance at Harry's clothes, looking for signs of his recent burial. They seemed immaculately clean.

"Oh yeah." Harry stood scratching his cheek. "That rings a bell, right enough. Must've banged me 'ead . . . Lessee, I was . . . up on the Kandel. And—" He stiffened, snapping into slightly sharper focus. "'Ere, where's your grandfather, Alex? There's things I need to tell 'im. If I can remember what they are."

"We have to find him," Alex said, glad to change the subject. "He crashed. Over . . ." He trailed off as he looked around, lost. He cast another anxious look at the big man and decided he was glad he was there. Harry seemed like Harry, after all. Leaving aside that he had returned from the grave, there was nothing different about him as far as Alex could tell. So far, anyway. He made a quick bargain with the part of his mind that was screaming: they could get together and freak out about it later. There were more important things to do now.

"But what *do* we do now?" Alex said, speaking more to himself than Harry.

Harry shrugged, then started patting his pockets. "I've lost me phone," he muttered. "Mind you, wouldn't be much use for tryin' to get 'old of your grandad, anyway. Just can*not* persuade 'im to carry one. I mean, 'e's *fanatical* about it. *Those things mark the end of civilisation* was 'is exact quote last time I tried."

Alex wandered to the felled tree where Zia had dumped his possessions and lifted his own pulverised phone. Smashed beyond repair. Prying it open, he managed to pull the SIM card free from inside. It looked okay. He pocketed it along with the other items, then stood massageing the tension knotting his neck.

His eyes drifted until they stuck on a small grey shape nearby. Another dead flier. But this one had a purple-and-black ribbon tied around it. The machine he had briefly controlled. The sense-memory of operating it – of *being* it – hit him. He had done that. Just like them. With his *interestingly shaped mind*.

He crossed over and picked it up. It seemed undamaged. He pushed the panel open. His hair was still in there.

"Alex, what're you doing?" Harry's concerned voice came from behind him. "Careful with that."

"It's all right, Harry," Alex said, trying to convince himself. Some deep instinct compelled him to remove Zia's ribbon from the machine. Searching the ground, he found a pebble and stuck the strip of cloth under it, before stamping the stone down into the soft earth.

He studied the flier. It couldn't hurt to try again. Could it? He had to try to find out where they were, and then how to find his grandfather. It probably wouldn't work, anyway. He hefted the machine and closed his eyes and sought to remember how to build the bridge.

"Alex?"

He sensed Harry's anxiousness. He put that into the mix, along with his own simmering fears. Before long, he heard the little thrum and whirr.

"Alex!"

He ignored Harry's alarmed cry. Ignored everything. It was

getting easier. He felt the robot rise, him rising with it. Green-grey-brown flared in his mind: glimpses of trees, a momentary sight of himself standing there, eyes closed, Harry behind him, staring in dismay.

Up, he thought. He tried to send *up* across the bridge. The flier responded, climbed higher. Alex tilted his head, and the flier banked, as he knew it would. The landscape spread below like a map. He saw himself down there with Harry beside the black spot of the well. He circled. No sign of Zia. He moved off, fast now, flying over the ruined farmhouse, a huge brown field, the woods.

His flickering vision was vague one moment, sharp the next. Beyond the trees stretched another rutted field. He flew higher, scanning the landscape. There, the hills rising, the Kandel itself. Not far. He turned in the air, trying to orient himself.

The field below was bordered by a thin footpath and then a long green meadow. Beyond that, a pale road. Alex raced toward it and swept lower, searching. There. A break in a hedge. And there. Tracks. A wrecked car. No sign of life, he thought, then stopped thinking it as the cold weight of that thought caused him to stall and waver dangerously in the air. He righted himself and mapped it out. If they walked in a straight diagonal, they should get to the car before too long.

He climbed again, partly trying to fix the location in his mind, but partly just luxuriating in his sense of flight, soaring and looping above the treetops. Something else caught his attention. Something moving further along the road, away from the wreck: a grey figure.

With a surge of delight, Alex tore through the air to catch his grandfather. He appeared fine but tired. The old man must have heard him, because he turned. Alex swooped in and raised an arm to wave. The old man lifted his cane in reply, then, just as they were about embrace, dropped his Gladstone, leapt up and thwacked Alex square across the face.

Alex's mind flashed deep, stinging black. He was sent spinning backward, blind, out of control. He crashed, reeling from shock and pain. Opening his watering eyes, he was bewildered to find himself kneeling at Harry's feet. His brain was vibrating in his skull. He'd lost all contact with the flier. Harry grabbed his shoulders.

"Alex! You all right?"

"Uh, yeah. I saw my grandad, Harry. He's okay. But I, uh. I forgot I wasn't me. Hang on."

He didn't know if he could find the flier again. It was too far. The bridge he'd need to build was too long. He put that fear and worry into the effort, and, after a while, there it was, still the same bridge, still there. But he could see nothing but black.

Look, he thought, and sent *look* across.

Images came, faint, then clearer. Black spikes towered above him, jagged against the sky. Not black, green. He was lying on his back in long grass. Movement. His grandfather's head appeared above the grass, not far away, moving stealthily, a giant hunting him, cane held ready to pulverise him. Alex sent an urgent *up* across. The old man swiped as he took flight, but he was already too high.

Alex called the flier back, reeling it in until the thing sat in his palm, wings shivering, amber eyes warm. Head dented.

"Alex, what did you do?" Harry said anxiously. "I don't think you should—"

"We need to get a message to Grandad," Alex said, suddenly aware he was breathing heavily. This had taken more out of him than he'd realised. "He's going the wrong way. Have you got a pen?"

Harry shook his head, frowning gravely. Alex thought hard. He slipped Harry's watch from his wrist.

"Is it okay if I use this?"

"'Ow'd you get that?" Harry pulled back his sleeve and stared in surprise at his empty wrist. "Your grandad been teachin' you pick-pocketin'? But, yeah, go on. Whatever you're doin'."

Alex double-checked the strap was fastened, then hung it over the flier's upraised scalpel-arm and sent the thing flying again. He slowed when he spotted his grandfather, heading determinedly along the road. The old man halted and lifted his stick as Alex descended, then paused, hovering at eye-level ten feet in front of him. His grandfather glanced around, turned back, regarding him cagily.

As slowly as he could, Alex lowered himself almost to the ground and let Harry's watch slide gently to the tarmac. He bobbed back up and retreated another ten feet.

The effort of controlling the flier was really beginning to tire him. He could feel every beat of a wing, every inch of the distance between himself and his machine. Hovering motionless like this took it out of him more than anything else.

The old man scowled, then lowered his stick and stood leaning on it, regarding the scene. Eventually, he came cautiously forward. A few steps from the watch, he dropped to a crouch and reached out, poking it warily with the cane. Finally, with care, he fished it up and pulled it to him. He straightened, examining the watch, pulled at his bottom lip, then cast another searching glance Alex's way.

Alex turned slowly in the air, seeking inspiration. Nearby, the scraggy hedge ran along the field. He buzzed quickly over to it, scanning the ground, until he found a slender broken twig, almost a foot long. After a few efforts, he managed to work his clumsy hook into it and carried it back.

His grandfather stood watching. Alex approached gingerly until he was within five feet, then shook the twig free so it fell to the road. The old man pushed back his hat, baffled. Alex hunted for another twig much the same and dropped it on top of the first, then repeated the operation with a third, smaller, twig.

After making sure his grandfather wasn't going to smash him to pieces, he hovered low, pushing and pulling the twigs on the road with his scalpel until they formed an *A*. He retreated several feet. His grandfather stared at him. Alex bobbed forward slowly, trying to nod at the *A*. The old man rubbed his chin.

After a few seconds, Alex moved in again. He hooked up the smaller twig and pulled it away, then rearranged the remaining two: X.

His grandfather stared at it dubiously, then gave Alex a long, pensive look. The old man moved to the side of the road by the spot Alex had marked, dropped his Gladstone, and, with a curt nod, sat on the bag, waiting.

The strain of using the machine was getting unbearable. Alex called the flier back as fast as he could, limbs raw from flight. He had to let it drop when he was still a little distance away from himself and Harry. The abrupt feeling of hitting the ground jolted harshly through his body. He pulled his aching mind away from the robot, and hugged himself, kneading his stiff shoulders.

"Alex, what did you do?" Harry repeated sadly.

Alex stood panting. Thinking about what he had done unsettled him. Yet using the flier had been easy. And it had got him what they needed. After a moment more of indecision, he walked over and picked it up, tucking it away in his coat.

"C'mon Harry. It's this way."

The boy and the dead man set off across the fields.

XXII.

REUNION

THEY MARCHED THROUGH the morning rain. Alex cast nervous looks behind and equally nervous looks at his companion. Harry seemed lost in trying to piece memories together.

"S'funny," he said. "Like, I remember clear as a bell what I 'ad for dinner last Tuesday: pie 'n' mash night. But the past few days, it's all muddled, bits missing. Still, I'm sure your grandad'll fill in the blanks."

"Uh, yeah." Alex nodded. The ache had faded from his head and limbs, but he remained shaken. As his mind cleared, he tried replaying what Zia had said, about his grandfather and secrets. *Bet ol' Grandad never told . . . Daddy died, hmm?* She was trying to mess with him. He resolved to ignore it and concentrate on getting to his grandfather. At least it was a problem he could understand.

Eventually, he saw horses ahead in the field they were walking through. The big animals came wandering softly over.

One nodded to them as they passed. Alex began to feel a faint prickling running through him.

"'Orse goes into a bar," Harry said. "Barman says, 'Why the long face?' One of me favourites, that. That and the one about the 'ippopotomus."

Not far beyond sat the battered Citroën, ripped roof hanging out like a ragged black sail. The tingling in Alex's blood tightened.

"Blimey." Harry gave a low whistle. "What a mess. Wait." He squinted at the wreck. "I'm remembering bits. Yeah. I crashed, like you said. Life-sizer in the road. Then I ran. Into the trees. Then . . ." He grimaced. "Nah. Nothin'."

Alex only half listened. The feeling singing through him sharpened again as he hurried toward the car. He leaned in, searching the footwell. His hand found the old toy robot, stuck beneath the seat. Relief flooded him, along with something else: a sense like being whole again. Now all he needed to do was find his grandfather.

Heading along the road, Alex grew increasingly puzzled. He was certain they had come the right way, but there was no sign of the old man. He stopped when he reached a spot where two twigs formed an X. Two stubbed-out cigarettes lay nearby.

"Hands up." His grandfather's voice came out of nowhere.

"Grandad?"

"Hands. I don't like guns, so don't make me have to use this one."

Alex and Harry raised their hands. Alex's grandfather's head lifted warily above the hedge further along the road. His eyes glittered coldly as he studied them. He flicked a quick, unreadable glance at Harry, then turned his steely gaze on Alex.

"Over here. Slowly."

Alex did as he was told.

"Grandad—"

"What was the name of the film I sent you for your birthday?"

"What? Uh . . ." Alex struggled to remember. Something old, black and white. *"Night of the Hunter."*

"And what did you make of it?"

"Not much. It was a bit silly."

"Hmm." His grandfather squinted at him. "Sounds like you, anyway. Come closer, hold out your hand."

Alex did it. His grandfather lifted the last of his salt sachets in one hand, ripped it open with his teeth, then reached quickly over the hedge to sprinkle grains onto Alex's palm. The old man watched Alex's face carefully while nothing happened.

"Lisssen," Harry said. "Can I put me bloomin' 'ands down?"

Moving as though he suddenly couldn't contain himself any longer, Alex's grandfather grinned wildly, ducked out of sight, and burst through a hole low in the hedge. He carried no gun, only his cane, bag, and Alex's rucksack, all of which he dropped to clutch Alex by the head. He stared into his eyes with a serious, searching look, then wrapped him in a hug.

"Grandad, are you okay?" Alex asked, rubbing salt from his hand.

"Fighting fit," Alex's grandfather replied. He let Alex go then spun to embrace Harry. "Question is: how's *this* chap? Unbelievable! Harry! Let me look at you." The old man stepped away, gazing in wonder. "My *word*, man! Harry . . . how are you?"

"Yeah, fine," Harry said, embarrassed by the attention. "Just a bang on the 'ead. Little woozy."

"Harry can't remember much after his *crash*," Alex said pointedly. "He came to in the *woods*."

"Just amazing," Alex's grandfather said. "Ah, now, Harry. I need a quick private chat with Alex. Something his mother wanted me to check. Teenager stuff, you know."

"Sure thing," Harry said.

"I thought you said you couldn't do it," the old man murmured as he drew Alex aside.

"I didn't think I *had*," Alex whispered. "He just . . . turned up."

"What'd you tell him?"

"Nothing. I was waiting until we found you."

"We have to tread carefully here, Alex," his grandfather murmured. "Break it to him gently. Extreme delicacy required. There's no telling what the shock might do. But first thing's first, young man: am I correct in thinking you just sent a *flier* for me? That was you? *Controlling* that thing?"

"Yeah, but—"

"What on *earth* were you thinking? How stupid can you be? Do you know the risk . . . What happened after she took you?"

Alex told him as best he could. He could see his grandfather growing more worried by the word. And angrier.

"Agreeing to use the flier when she asked was bad enough," the old man snapped. "But I can understand that: you had no option. But doing it *again*? Of your own free *will*? Do you have any *idea* what you might have opened yourself up to? How do you even know Zia couldn't also connect to the machine, get to you through it? When I saw you, I thought maybe they had you under some control."

Alex hung his head, stung by the scolding, partly because he agreed with most of it. Using the flier had been foolish. Yet he felt certain only he had access to this particular robot now. And, after all: it had worked.

"It's only me who can use it," he muttered. "She said so. She said it had been prepared—"

"*She?*" his grandfather exploded. "*She* said? After *she* grabbed you and threw you down a *well*? *Zia*? You believe a word that drops from her mouth? If she told me water was wet, I'd think twice. I can't believe you could be so *stupid*."

"Okay," Alex snapped back. "I get it. I'm stupid. What was I supposed to do? I was lost, I needed to find you, and the flier was there, and I knew how to do it, and so I *acted accordingly*, like you keep saying.

"Oh, and *talking* of your advice," Alex went on, yelling now, "what am I supposed to think, anyway? You're all *over* the place. One minute you're telling me all this stuff is dangerous and needs stopping, the next you're getting me to magic Harry back up from the dead. I mean, make your mind up. Anyway, what's so bad? It was easy to use the flier. I'm good at it. It's really useful, we can use it."

"Oh, *easy,* was it? Just you listen to— Wait a minute. What do you mean we can use it? You don't still *have* it?"

"Yeah, I—"

"'Ere, 'ang on."

Alex and his grandfather turned irritably as Harry stepped toward them.

"Just a minute, Harry," the old man said. "Alex and I have some—"

"No, wait. What did the lad mean? *Magic me up from the dead.* What's 'e on about?"

In the heavy silence that followed, Alex and his grandfather exchanged a look from the corner of their eyes.

"Ha," the old man said eventually. "Now, Harry. I was planning to talk to you about all this. Yes. You see, well, you, ah – I mean, it sounds silly even *saying* it – but you . . . Are you sure you're feeling okay, old chap? Quite yourself?"

"I'm feelin' fine," Harry said. "And I'd feel even better if you'd get to the point."

"Of course. Well, thing *is*—" The old man threw another look at Alex. Alex shrugged helplessly. His grandfather turned back to Harry and tried a reassuring grin. "Thing is . . . Harry. You died."

Harry looked at Alex, then back to Alex's grandfather. "Eh?"

"Died. Dead. They killed you. Snapped your neck, far as I could tell."

"This is us breaking it to him gently, is it?" Alex said.

"I think you'll find," his grandfather said, "it was you who let this particular cat out of the bag. Are you okay, Harry?"

Harry was staring at the ground. He looked up. "You *sure*?"

"Well, yes. I, ah, buried you. A little."

"But, when . . . I mean . . . 'ow long?"

"Three days. More or less."

Harry looked away, at the sky, grey patched blue where the clouds were thinning, at the damp green fields, trees hugging the horizon. His lip trembled. He rubbed quickly at one eye with the heel of his hand, then sniffed and straightened.

"I'm not sure 'ow I feel about that."

"Well, no." Alex's grandfather nodded sympathetically. "I mean, of course."

They stood in an awkward silence broken only by the sound of the old man tapping his boots with his cane to dislodge some dirt. He glanced up at Harry from under his hat brim.

"Mind if I try your pulse?"

Harry shrugged, held out his hand.

"Strong as a horse," Alex's grandfather said after testing Harry's wrist. "Oh, by the way, here's your watch back. Harry, do you feel *any* different?"

"Hmm." Harry stretched, then rolled his shoulders and flexed his knees. "Pain in me 'ip."

"Pain in your hip?"

"Yeah. It's totally gone. It's all cleared up."

"And after you . . . woke up, you just found Alex, by chance?" the old man asked.

"Eh, well, yeah. I mean, I was walkin' and just 'ad a feelin' about the direction to go."

"Uh-huh. Harry, try something for me, would you?" Alex's grandfather said. "Close your eyes and don't open them until I say. Now let me just turn you around on the spot here."

Gripping Harry gently by the shoulders, he spun him slowly around three times. "Good man. Keep your eyes closed. Now, Alex, quietly as you can, could you walk over there?"

Alex shrugged and went a few steps in the direction the old man pointed.

"Okay. Now, Harry: keeping your eyes shut, could you point to where you think Alex is?"

Harry blindly aimed a big thumb over his left shoulder, straight at Alex.

"Hmm," Alex's grandfather said. "Let's try it again."

They repeated the procedure four times in random directions. In each case, Harry knew exactly where Alex was.

"Fascinating. Ah well." The old man slapped his hands together, dismissing the issue. "Back to business."

"What? No, *wait*!" Alex said. "What does it mean?"

"Beats me," his grandfather said. "Interesting, though. Harry, are you hungry at all?"

Harry pursed his lips. "Now you mention it, I am a little peckish."

"Marvellous food at the hotel not far from here," Alex's grandfather said eagerly. "Shouldn't take too long to walk."

"We don't have time for *that*," Alex spluttered. "We—"

"We need to regroup, Alex, refuel. Besides, we're not much use on foot, and unless you suggest hijacking a passing vehicle, which is something I've tried to give up, our best bet is to arrange another car at the hotel. But before that: Alex, I need you to do something. You still have the flier?"

"Yeah."

"Then you need to give it up. Here and now."

"But—"

"No buts. Yes, I heard what you said: you can do it, and it's useful, and you think you can control it, and control yourself. I wonder though. If you get a taste for this little machine, then what about the *next* thing you're offered? Something a little more potent, perhaps, something that takes a little more out of you? Or something that requires you to give it something else, *not* of your own? How far down that road do you think you can go before there's no turning back? You have no *idea* what you're dealing with, and I'd prefer to keep it that way. I have a basic rule, Alex: if we have to resort to using the other side's methods to win, then maybe winning's not worth it."

"You stick by it when it suits you," Alex muttered.

Harry said nothing. He stood watching them pensively.

"I have neither the time nor the inclination to argue, Alex," his grandfather said. "Give it up here, or we go no further together. So. You have a decision to make."

Alex looked from the old man, very tired but doing a good job of hiding it, to Harry, who shuffled from one foot to another. It seemed as if the whole world was watching, waiting. The weight of it all came down on him, and then, as if in response, came a sudden light, exhilarating memory of his soaring flight with the machine.

He sighed, sagged in defeat, and pulled the flier from his coat, offering it to his grandfather. "You're right. What do we do with it, then?"

"Well." The old man straightened, as if a burden had been lifted. He gestured to the roadside. "Burying it should do the job."

Alex hesitated. The little robot seemed to look at him from his hand. He shook himself, then bent and started scooping out a hole in the ground under the hedge. As he placed the flier inside, a sharp memory of being trapped down the well shivered through him. He covered the flier, being very careful about just how he did it, gently patting the dirt down.

"Okay," Alex said, when he was satisfied.

"Thank you," the old man said quietly. "And thank you for Harry. What you did was extraordinary, Alex. And I know it wasn't easy for you, in more ways than one. I'm sorry for snapping. But I'm very glad you've decided to give this up. When we get through this, I want you to be done with all of this business. Out of it. It's . . . not for you. Come on, let's go."

As they started walking, Alex's grandfather put an arm around Harry's shoulders, speaking in a confidential tone. "Harry, just out of interest: can you remember *anything* about when you were, y'know. Out. Away . . . Dead."

Harry chewed his lip, head bowed in silent concentration, then looked up. "Coconut."

"How's that?"

"There was a coconutty smell," Harry said decisively.

"Absolutely *fascinating*."

Alex sighed and dropped behind a few steps, leaving them to it. He closed his eyes and concentrated. Back along the road, the patch of dirt he'd left as loose as possible trembled, and his flier came bursting out. Damp earth fell away from it as it climbed for the sky. Alex held it high in the air behind them as they walked, far enough back that no one would see.

XXIII.

DEAD MAN TALKING

THE DRIZZLE BECAME a mist over the country. Alex's grandfather kept up a largely meaningless conversation with Harry, mostly, Alex suspected, just to get the dead man's mind working. Harry was still having trouble with his memory.

Alex let them talk, more focused on scanning the roads around them using the wavering overhead images coming to him from his flier. They seemed safe, so far.

He hated lying, but he was sure his grandfather was wrong. The old man had said as much, more than once – his thinking wasn't clear. There was something wrong with him, Alex was increasingly sure. With his grandfather's concentration waning, and with Harry . . . being in whatever state Harry was in, Alex had taken the decision, to protect them all.

With his flier, he could watch for anyone following, anything waiting around the bend. It was eating up his energy, but the more he used the machine, the more he understood how to control it. It could prove useful in whatever lay ahead. Then, once it was all over, once he was out of this deranged dream life, he would give it up and get rid of it.

He would.

Before long, in his high mental view, he spotted the hotel, the busier roads beyond. Arriving at a crossroads, his grandfather hesitated over the way to go.

"It's left, I think," Alex said.

"Think you're right, Alex."

In the small lobby, the old man and Harry called a car rental company, then gave the hotel's bemused owner details about where to find the wrecked Citröen, and instructions for having a local garage transport it to Albert in Paris, along with extra cash not to ask questions.

Alex's grandfather slapped his hands in satisfaction. "So: car's on its way, they'll fix us an early lunch, and lunch'll do us good."

The small dining room felt more like someone's home than a hotel. They took a table by large windows that framed a panoramic view across the valley, the world vibrating in shades of green beneath bulging clouds so dark they were almost blue.

Look out your window. Alex sat thinking about Kenzie's last message, still not understanding it at all.

It was barely nine in the morning. The place was almost empty, just one other couple finishing breakfast in the corner. "I propose," Alex's grandfather said happily, examining the menu, "we make the most of this. Nice big lunch. I'm hungry, and we need the energy. Now, this trout sounds rather delicious, eh?"

Alex tried to relax. The coast seemed clear, anyway. He had the flier perched on the hotel roof and flicked his mind across the bridge into it every few minutes, turning it on and off. After a while, he realised that, with a slight increase of effort, he could keep a small part of his consciousness active in the machine without having to focus entirely upon it: a kind of standby mode, like keeping a finger tapping. He recalled something his grandfather had said, about *sectioning off the mind*. This must have been what he'd meant.

When it arrived, the meal the old man had ordered – crispy fried fish, with creamy sauce and generous mounds of salad and potatoes – did something to restore Alex. As Harry started eating, Alex and his grandfather both stopped and stared, mesmerised.

"Somethin' between me teeth?" Harry frowned.

"No, no," Alex's grandfather said. "Sorry. It's just – how is it?"

"Yeah." Harry waggled his fork. "Tasty."

"No, I mean *eating*. How's it feel? Is eating still something you can do? Want to do?"

"Eh? Oh, yeah. Forgot for a second." Harry took another bite and chewed thoughtfully. "Yeah, reckon so."

"How's about a drink?" Alex's grandfather hurried away and returned bearing two brandies. "Shall we do the toast?" The old man raised his glass "Remember, man, that thou art dust—"

"An' that's why you always feel so thirsty," Harry replied. They touched cups and drank. "Oh, that's a lovely drop," Harry said, smacking his lips.

"Taste buds seem in order, anyway," Alex's grandfather said. "Now, Harry. We were in the middle of something, remember? The stolen paintings?" He quickly filled Harry in on what had been happening in his absence, including his vague recollections of the Shadow Gate story and the news of the most recent painting stolen in Paris.

"We're still in the dark," he continued, speaking lightly. Alex sensed him working hard to hide his desperation, trying not to put too much pressure on Harry to remember. "So, can you recall what you've been up to since the last time I saw you? I mean, before your, ah, accident. We split up, remember? We were trying to track down any trace of my father's movements."

"Oh," Harry said quietly. He nodded at Alex. "You've told 'im then. About . . . your father."

"More or less. But back to the point: I headed for Italy. You stayed in Paris. And then you found something, you got onto their trail."

"That's right," Harry said dimly. "Yeah. We'd put word out on the concierge network – that's the people who run the front desks in all the 'otels," he explained, catching Alex's uncomprehending look. "Receptionists, concierges. Pays to keep in their good books. Add in all their connections with taxi drivers and restaurants and everything, it's still the best way of knowing what's going on in a city. Grapevine. We'd circulated descriptions 'alfway across Europe. Bit of a long shot, but I got an 'it: a message next afternoon that someone matching Willy von Sudenfeld's description 'ad been spotted arriving in Paris from London. Willy's not very good at the cloak-'n'-dagger stuff."

"Arriving from Britain. The Schalcken picture," Alex's grandfather muttered. "The painting that was stolen in Cambridge, Alex, waffle lady. Must've been Willy. Might have been him that carried over the flier that was sent to watch you."

"Yeah." At mention of a flier, Alex shifted slightly, feeling guilty.

"It's coming back," Harry went on. "I got on their trail at the 'otel they'd checked into. Willy and the bald bruiser. I tailed 'em when they left that night. They left Paris, drove east. I followed them to an 'ouse, a château. I 'id nearby. When they 'eaded for the 'ouse, I stuck a GPS tracker under their car."

"A what now?" Alex's grandfather frowned.

"Cheap little gizmo, tells me where the car is. Sends messages to me *mobile phone*. I showed you one before, but you said you weren't *interested*." Harry turned to Alex, gesturing to the old man. "See, unlike your grandad, I try to keep up with technology."

"Well, what was wrong with the little electronic bugs we always used to use?" Alex's grandfather said petulantly. "The beepers. I liked those."

"These're better," Harry said. "Anyways. This château. They

went over the wall and were prowling the gardens. Casing the place – 'ere, that's it!"

"What's what?" Alex and his grandfather spoke in unison.

"That's where the painting is! The last one! They said so. It's in this château. I followed, close as I could. They got right up to a ground-floor window – but then there were people coming out from the 'ouse with guns and . . . *dogs*.

"Willy and his pal ran. Next thing I know, dogs are coming at *me*. I got over the wall in time to see Willy's car racing off. By the time I got to my car, the people from the château 'ad come out in a motor and were after me. They didn't look like they were in a mood for explanations, so I floored it. It took me *ages* to lose them. Then I picked up Willy's location again using the GPS and went after 'im."

"Admirable." Alex's grandfather tapped his nose, thinking. "So you headed for Germany, racing after von Sudenfeld?"

"Yeah. Eventually, I saw they'd stopped beneath the Kandel. I parked further down the road. When I crept up, they were still in the car, waitin', then the others arrived, in a van, and I think another car, a kind of . . . Not sure. I was a good distance away, but it looked like Zia, and your old man, standin' with a couple of life-sizers. Uh." Harry rubbed big fingers gently over his brow.

"It's 'azy. It's like, the closer I get to . . . to what 'appened to me, the blurrier it is. It was dark, raining. They were carryin' things. They 'ad some of the stolen paintings, two at least. But the robots, they was carryin' something *else*. Something bulky, long and low. They 'eld it flat between 'em, one at the front, one at the back. They all 'eaded up the 'ill, into the trees. I went after them."

"You couldn't see what the life-sizers were carrying?"

"Can't remember."

"Okay. Remember this, Harry?" Alex's grandfather unfurled the painting from his bag, held it close to his friend, as though trying to physically prod his memories with it.

Harry nodded slowly. "Yeah, that's one of the paintings they 'ad up there. 'Ow did you get that?"

"You got it, Harry," Alex said. "You got it back from them."

"Did I?" Harry scratched his chin. "That was good, eh? They took the paintings and the other thing to a place in the woods, I remember that. Place under a cliff. Big rocks all over the ground everywhere. Masses and masses."

"Under the Devil's Pulpit?" Alex asked his grandfather. "Where the rock fell and smashed?"

"Sounds depressingly like it." The old man nodded. "Go on, Harry."

"They took everything to these rocks," Harry said slowly, going step by step. "I 'eard them talking, just snatches. Von Sudenfeld told them about the château and 'ow the people 'ad chased them off. Zia said something about leaving it till they were ready to go together, somethin' like that. And then they were doin' something. Moving among the rocks, chanting, you know, the usual malarkey. Yeah, that's right: that's when I grabbed the painting, they were too busy to see me, and it was just lyin' there. But then there was a glow . . . something glowing . . . and then . . . I was running through the trees . . . and that's all I can remember." He shrugged apologetically.

"But the Shadow Gate, Harry," Alex said. "You said they were talking about the Shadow Gate."

"Yeah . . ." Harry turned to Alex's grandfather. "That was as much as I 'eard though, just those words."

"That's *it*?" Alex said. "This is hopeless."

"It's not," Alex's grandfather said.

"It is," Alex said. "Completely hopeless."

"No, no. I mean, 'It's not.' Remember, Harry?"

"Eh?"

"The message you left on my answer machine. You were trying to tell me something. You said, 'Two things: it's not . . .' Ring any bells?"

"It's not," Harry repeated. He shook his head. "Sorry." He tapped at his skull. "But there's more . . . lurking; it'll come back."

"Not to worry," Alex's grandfather said, weary but determined. "You've shown us our next move. We need to get to this château for the last painting, and hope they haven't already beaten us to it. Think you could find it again, Harry?"

"Ah." Harry raised his eyebrows. "Got that. Memorised the address. Château de Saint-Clement, in Marsilly. Moselle, near the French-German border."

The hotel's owner came with news that their car would be arriving within twenty minutes.

"Just time for coffee and cake." Alex's grandfather beamed, grabbing for the menu again.

As dessert arrived, the old man rubbed his hands eagerly. "There are a million good reasons to visit this part of the world. But the *Schwarzwälder Kirschtorte* ranks among the greatest." He took an ambitious mouthful, then waved his spoon in bliss. "I don't care if it's touristy: you won't find finer Black Forest gateau anywhere other than in the Black Forest. Stands to reason. It's a pudding that seems to have fallen out of fashion in Britain these days, Alex, but who knows what anyone is thinking any more."

"These cherries are top-notch," Harry mumbled.

While the old men fell into reminiscing about great desserts of yesteryear, Alex pushed away his plate, too full for more. It chinked against the bowls of sugar and salt on the table. The sugar packets bore a print of a pen-and-ink drawing. He pulled one out to study it: an ancient castle, turrets against a clouded sky. He reached to examine a salt packet, then dropped it, pulling his hand back sharply.

A dim flash of pain had tingled across his fingertips, like a chill electric shock, so faint and brief he wasn't sure he had felt it at all. He glanced quickly at his grandad and Harry. Neither seemed to have noticed.

Alex sat looking uncertainly at his hand on the table, feeling shadows crawling on his spine.

❂

THE CAR ARRIVED. While Alex's grandfather and Harry were busy with the delivery drivers, Alex slipped outside and around the side of the hotel. When he was sure he was unobserved, he allowed his weary body to sag and called his flier down.

He was exhausted, both from the effort of controlling the thing, and from the strain of not letting it show. As soon as the little robot landed on his palm, he let life fall away from the machine. He removed his hair from inside and tucked it into the watch pocket of his jeans, then blew into the panel, taking care not a single hair remained.

He was by now uncertain whether he had really felt a sting when he'd touched the salt, or just imagined it, a phantom pain brought on by his overworked nerves and mind. But he was deeply unsure that using the flier had been wise. He tied a sock around its head like a blindfold as he'd seen his grandfather do, then hid it away in his rucksack.

He found Harry inspecting the rental car. A 4x4 in a gleaming metallic flame colour, it looked expensive and brand-new, the latest model. Harry kicked a wheel disapprovingly as Alex's grandfather emerged from the hotel.

"Look at the state of this."

"Well, yes." The old man gave a sympathetic smile. "But needs must, Harry."

"It's embarrassin'. I wouldn't be seen dead in the likes of this. It's like a blummin' clown car."

Rain rattled the roof as they climbed inside. Harry turned the key and grumbled as he listened to the engine.

"Are you sure you're okay to drive?" Alex's grandfather asked. "I mean, what with . . ."

Harry turned and raised an eyebrow.

"Forget I said anything," the old man said.

They sped northwest through a damp green world. The roads grew busier. Despite the fizzing in his mind, the combination of the big meal and his enormous fatigue soon had Alex nodding toward sleep. Just before he dropped off, the thought really struck home: he had brought Harry back. And that meant he had finally succeeded in contacting the power in the tablet again, directing it.

His process, the curious detail of focusing on Kenzie Mitchell, worked – even if he didn't understand why or how. He was learning to control his power. It had taken seven hours, but he was sure that now he knew the way, he could find it faster. He could do it again.

XXIV.

OVER THE WALL

ALEX WOKE AS the car bumped to a halt by a country road-side. His grandfather was already getting out.

"Are we there?" Alex said. The dashboard clock showed it was not long after noon.

"House is about five minutes back that way." The old man pointed with his cane. "But it wouldn't do to just drive up and ring the bell. Bit of sneaking seems in order. So, I'm going in, you and Harry can wait—"

"No way. You're not going in alone. I'm coming. Harry said they had *guns*. We might need . . . this." Alex took out the toy robot.

"You've really worked out how to use it?"

"Kind of. Well. Not sure. It takes time. But looks like I can." Alex nodded toward Harry. "It's got to be better than nothing."

The old man stood pulling his lip, then nodded. "I'm not keen on you trying to use that thing any further, either, Alex . . .

but, this is the situation. And it's a different kind of power from my father's creations. Yes, okay, agreed. Grudgingly."

Alex thought about the flier hidden in his rucksack, the faint sting of salt on his fingers. *A different kind of power* – he wondered just what his grandfather meant. He recalled the definition he'd read on his phone in the café, when he'd looked up the name David's great-grandmother had yelled at him: *sorcerers who may practise both light and/or dark magic*. Light and dark. It was beyond him. But the idea of using the flier again filled him with apprehension.

And yet, it could prove valuable, and he knew he could do it far more easily than reaching the power inside the ancient tablet. He moved to pull the rucksack over his shoulder.

"No, leave that," his grandfather said. He hoisted his Gladstone. "Got everything we need here. I'd rather you were able to move as fast as possible. Just in case. Okay, Harry. Keep watch for them to arrive. If we don't come out in, say, twenty minutes, then . . . well. Improvise. Feeling up to it?"

"Practically bionic," Harry said.

There was no way to retrieve the flier without giving away that he still had it. Alex reluctantly put the rucksack down, and climbed out after his grandfather.

Five minutes' walking brought them to a stand of thin trees, through which eventually loomed a stone wall around nine feet high. His grandfather boosted him, and Alex sat straddling the top while the old man stretched to hand up his Gladstone.

Alex's grandfather considered the climb, then stepped back.

"You know, I'm getting too old to be climbing walls. I think I'll make life easy on myself. Could you toss down the spring-heels, Alex? They're in the bag."

Alex dropped them down one after the other. His grandfather fumbled the second, and it fell heavily by his feet. The old man stood staring at his left hand, flexing the fingers. The hand trembled. Alex watched with growing concern. After a moment his grandfather gave it a quick, dismissive shake, then leaned against the wall, deftly strapped the spring-heels over his boots, and leapt to join him.

He landed unsteadily, swayed, then straightened and winked reassuringly. Alex wasn't buying it. Something was very wrong. He felt it like a jab in his stomach.

They sat among the branches that pressed around the wall, each surveying the landscape that lay on the other side: more trees, a glimpse of grass beyond. Scanning the scene, Alex found himself looking at the back of his grandfather's head. The old man turned, their eyes locked, and it was as if they came to an unspoken agreement to acknowledge what they both knew: something was wrong.

"Are you okay, Grandad?" Alex asked. "You're not, are you?"

"Hmmm? Oh, yes, I—" His grandfather started brightly, then stopped and gazed down. "Well," he said, without lifting his eyes. "Truth is, I have been a little under the weather." He paused again, considering. Finally, he looked up and smiled.

"Might as well tell you straight," he said. "Although none of this has been how I imagined it would be when I told you any of it – I had pictured us sitting in a nice room by a roaring fire, with something good to eat. But here we are. So. I told you that I took my father's potion for a little while, his *elixir of eternal life*. And then I stopped.

"I was about twenty-one when he first brought it to me. He explained what it was. Some of it, anyway. He told me he wanted me to take it, too, join him, and I was raised never to disobey my father. It sounded exciting, I suppose, this great secret. At first.

"His plan was to wait until Alexia was around twenty-one, too, and then tell her. But she was always one for sneaking around, snooping and spying. She must have overheard, because it turned out she found the stuff when she was about ten, and started taking it secretly on her own. Probably took far too much. She later said she'd decided she didn't want to grow any older, because she 'didn't like the look of it.' Funny thing is, Alexia *hates* children.

"It was a few years later that I left them. I was still a young man, and I stopped taking the brew long before I would have noticed any difference, anyway. For several years, well, things just seemed normal – I mean as far as my body went. There were no effects from the potion I could see. I had assumed that when I stopped taking it, that would be an end to it.

"Turns out I was wrong. Years later, I gradually started to notice I wasn't growing any older, even though it had been a long time since I took it. Or, at least, if I *was* ageing, it was happening very slowly. Some kind of lingering effect of the potion, you see. It was in my system, replicating in my blood, and, ah, keeping me . . . *frozen*.

"And, well, that rather complicated life for me. You learn that you, eh, have to disappear from your friends before they start to notice, y'see? Avoid having your photograph taken, that kind of thing. Keep moving. You end up rather alone.

"Harry was the first person I ever told, actually. I had him help me out in a bit of an escapade when he was a boy – there was a chimney and he agreed to climb down the inside, and it all got slightly more . . . *supernatural* than I'd anticipated. Harry seemed to take it in his stride, though, so I thought I might as well tell him about me.

"But then something marvellous happened. In the years after the Second World War, I noticed I *had* gradually started ageing again, after all. I monitored the situation for a decade or so, to be certain, and it seemed like everything was back to normal. I thought the effects had finally worn off. Or, at least, I allowed myself to pretend that I believed that. And that's when – well. That's when I met your grandmother and . . ."

He broke off and cleared his throat. Alex felt his own tightening. The branches of the trees shushed around them.

"Well, that's a whole other story," the old man continued. "But, to get back to the point: seems I was wrong *again*, ha. The potion's effects returned. I eventually noticed my ageing processes had stopped *again*. But this time something was different.

"There's been an odd cycle at work in my body, Alex. For years, nothing changes. Nothing ages. But then, well, it's as if I go through a sudden *rush*. It all catches up with me and, eh, I can put on years, almost overnight. I can tell when it's due to happen, because I go through a period beforehand where I begin to feel run-down – like flu, y'know. For some reason, it seems to affect one side of my body more than the other. A little numbness and stiffness in the limbs, lack of dexterity, general butter fingers.

"And, well, yes: I've been feeling that way recently. These exertions have been taking it out of me more than usual. You might find I'm not thinking at my clearest. Missing things. My decisions might not make much sense."

"But then what happens?" Alex was lost listening to his grandfather's tale. "I mean, how *many* years older do you get?"

"Well, hard to say. Varies. Four or five, a few more, a little less. Anyway, point is: when it really comes on, I'm not much use for a few days. It's like a fever. That's why the timing of all this is so bad – well, that and the fact that it's the last day of April, which wouldn't be good for this kind of thing under any circumstances."

"But, Grandad, I mean, how many more . . . how much older can you *get*?"

"Oh, don't worry yourself over that. Besides, I'm not feeling too bad yet, Alex, just a little peaky. Plenty of time. After it happens, after I age a bit, I usually feel particularly spry, actually.

In the meantime – how's about a lemon drop? I found a little place still makes them the right way. They're really incredible. Give us a bit of a boost."

Alex half-consciously took a powdery yellow sweet from the paper bag his grandfather proffered. It was indeed delicious, although it did nothing to ease his anxiety. But the old man had already dropped down the other side of the wall, impatient to move on. Alex did his best to push his worries away and followed. There was nothing else to do.

They crept with caution until they stood at the edge of the trees.

"This must be the place," Alex's grandfather whispered. "Ugly old pile."

Ahead, across a stretching lawn and past an ornamental garden gone to weed, stood a stern grey three-storey house. A single door and four large shuttered windows were the only decoration on the ground floor facing them, a few more windows behind louvred slats above. Discoloured concrete patches marked where repairs had been attempted. At the top left, stray creepers curled round from the side of the house, where Alex could see that the bare facade was relieved by a thick, green-red flourish of ivy.

"Hmmm." The old man nodded, sizing it up. He pulled binoculars from his coat. "There's a second-floor window around the side looks promising. Ledge looks large enough for me to jump up and get a grip. Think you could climb

that marvellously convenient ivy? I reckon it should take your
weight."

"You want us to break *in*?"

"Seems the thing to do."

"But are you—" Alex looked from his grandfather to the
sombre house and back. "Are you up to it?"

"Now, listen. Don't start trying to wrap me in cotton
wool, Alex," his grandfather muttered, surveying the building. "Lots of life in this old dog yet. Okay. I'll jump up and
pop the window open while you climb up after me, and in
we go. The question is whether there will be anybody in that
room. But we can deal with that when the time comes. If
we're lucky, though, the place is big enough that we should
be able to prowl around in there undetected for a while if
we're careful."

"Are you sure?"

"Oh, yes. Depends how many people are inside, of course.
But back in my house-breaking days, this is exactly the kind
of place Harry and I liked doing best. I'll teach you a trick for
walking quietly."

Alex was doubtful in the extreme. The plan didn't seem particularly solid, but he couldn't tell whether it was because of his
grandfather's "fog on the brain," or his usual recklessness. He
glanced again at the drab château. The bleak afternoon light
gave it a menacing aura, like a place waiting for bad things to
happen. Birds were singing in the trees above. He wished they
would shut up.

"But then what? We don't even know what this painting looks like."

"Ha, well. Decent point. But we're not going to learn that sitting here. I'm rather hoping it might all make itself clear once we're inside," the old man whispered, raising the binoculars again.

"So, essentially," Alex said after a moment's more processing, "the plan is: break in and see what happens."

"That's the idea. Improvise. Now, let's get moving."

Alex made no reply. He was more concerned with the enormous dog staring at him from the shadows beyond his grandfather's elbow.

It was a German shepherd, so large that the top of its blocky head came almost to Alex's chest. It regarded him silently with sad dark eyes set in a black mask of fur. As Alex took a reflexive step back, the dog bared its teeth. Alex's movement caused his grandfather to lower his binoculars and look down at him. His eyes widened.

"Ah, don't make any sudden movements, Alex, there's a good chap."

"What?" Alex spun around, to be met with a discouraging bark from another, even bigger dog at his back. These eyes were reddish brown, highly intelligent, and not friendly.

Noiselessly, five more dogs of the same breed and powerful build emerged from the bushes, surrounding them in a hostile, growling circle. Alex saw his grandfather's fist tightening around his cane.

"Any plans forming," Alex whispered, "about how to improvise our way out of this?"

"Well . . ." his grandfather began grimly, but the tension in his voice suddenly shifted into bright cheerfulness as he glanced off into the trees. "Well, I suppose we just do what the lady says—"

"What la—"

"Hello!" The old man raised a hand in a wave, then dropped it as the dogs reacted by closing in as one.

"Good afternoon!" a deep, cheery, English-sounding female voice called back. A second later, its owner came striding into view. Slim, just a little shorter than Alex's grandfather, she wore a long, loose, charcoal-coloured coat with a hood hanging down. Straight hair fell in a shoulder-length swoop of dark auburn flecked with silver. Alex guessed she must be in her late-fifties. She smiled pleasantly and held a shotgun pointed in their direction.

XXV.

KINGDOM

"LOVELY DAY." ALEX'S grandfather beamed. "Apart from the rain. Out walking the dogs, were you?"

"Not really." The woman grinned back. "We came out especially to meet you two."

"Well, isn't that wonderful," the old man burbled brightly on. The largest dog was now sniffing his hand. The rest stared fixedly at Alex.

"Beautiful animals," his grandfather continued. "Well, it was lovely to meet you all. I suppose we'll just be on our way, then."

"Oh, please." She lifted the shotgun, just slightly. Her smile remained, but the gleam in the brown eyes was sharp and edgy. "I was going to invite you up to the house for a chat."

"Oh, we'd be delighted! After you?"

"Before me, I think. Guests first. I insist. And keep your hands where I can see them, if you wouldn't mind."

"Come on then, Alex." The old man raised his hands and

strolled off across the lawn. Alex hesitated, reluctant to uncurl his fist from the toy robot in his coat pocket. He clenched it tightly, frantically trying to get his thoughts together in order to access the power. The woman stooped to lift the Gladstone, grunted as she felt the weight, then motioned him sternly with the gun. He let go of the toy and lifted his hands.

As they marched toward the house, Alex was intensely aware of everything around him: a smell of rain and wet earth; the noises of grass then gravel under his feet; the complicated patterns of the curious melody his grandfather was whistling quietly through his teeth as he walked ahead; the panting of the dogs prowling beside the old man, ears pricking up at his tune; a sudden dampness of fur and the solid muscle beneath it as the animal on Alex's right brushed against his fingers; the swish of the woman's coat; the sense of her shotgun at his back.

The house's wooden doors stood open. Waiting inside, scowling up from an old and rickety-looking wheelchair, was a man with silver hair and a stern, square face. Clad in a heavy wool cardigan, he sat with a tartan blanket covering his legs. One glowering eye was ringed by a fresh, purple-black bruise. An old scar that ran through it stood out vivid white. The hand resting on his lap clutched a revolver.

Without a word, he used the gun to nervily wave them across a hallway with a chequerboard floor into a large, wood-panelled room. The windows had been boarded up. A massive chandelier hung from a high ceiling, dousing the place in dusty light. The seven dogs swept in to take positions along the walls, sitting like sentries to watch whatever the humans did next.

The room looked as though it had once served as a hall for banquets and dancing, black ties and bright ball gowns. Now it stood bare, with just a few melancholy pieces of furniture: a wall lined with bookcases that were three-quarters empty, save for more dust; two drab sofas angled shabbily around an ancient TV; several hard, ornately carved wooden dining chairs pushed against the far wall, looking bereft without the table they must once have accompanied.

A plain table bearing two more shotguns, seemingly abandoned while being cleaned in preparation for imminent use, did little to brighten the atmosphere. A long, thin, padded case with a shoulder strap lay beside the guns. Alex felt he recognised it, but couldn't place it.

In a corner stood a well-stocked drinks trolley, toward which Alex's grandfather was now striding with genuine interest. After scrutinising it, he turned. The old man's face betrayed nothing, but Alex caught a momentary signal from his eyes, flashing briefly upward above his right shoulder.

Glancing that way, Alex noticed that the wall above the bar cart was patterned with faint rectangular patches where framed pictures had once hung. Amid all the empty spaces, one last painting remained: a depiction in oils of the same house they stood in, wreathed in mist on a moonlit night, trees bending in the wind. Staring at it, Alex had a woozy sensation of being simultaneously trapped inside the ghostly house in the image and outside of it looking in. He pulled his eyes away and tried to look blank.

He was still desperately trying to think his way toward the tablet in the old robot in his coat, but panic was getting in the way, and he realised he had grown used to holding the toy as part of his ritual. He had a hunch the people with the guns wouldn't react well to him reaching into his pocket.

"How about," his grandfather said, gesturing toward the drinks cart, "we all have a little glass of something, toast our new acquaintance?"

The man in the wheelchair ignored him and rolled to the centre of the room. The woman closed the door, dropped the Gladstone, then moved to stand close behind him, cradling her shotgun. They regarded one another in the piercing silence.

"Just the two, after all?" the man finally asked. He spoke with a tense French accent.

The woman nodded, then turned to Alex: "Here." She indicated a place at her side. Moving stiffly, Alex did as instructed, then stiffened more as she lifted her gun and rested the barrel gently against his forehead.

"Now," she said, addressing Alex's grandfather, "*very* slowly, remove your coat, jacket, and waistcoat and throw them to the floor there. Then empty your trouser pockets and pull the lining out."

For a moment, Alex's grandfather hesitated. His eyes glinted coldly as he regarded the shotgun threatening Alex. Then, with a shrug, he obeyed. Both coat and jacket hit the floorboards with heavy thuds. Turning out his trouser pockets produced coins, a folded handkerchief, a compass, and a set of keys on a small, luminous green keyring shaped like the head of Frankenstein's monster.

He held this last up with great seriousness for their inspection and squeezed it, producing a pattern of absurd rubber-toy squeaks that caught the dogs' interest. Then he tossed the keys on top of the pile.

The woman lowered her gun and swiftly patted Alex down. He stopped breathing as she took the toy robot from his pocket, but she only frowned at it, then him, before throwing it on top of his grandfather's coat.

The man wheeled to face Alex's grandfather. "Where are the others?" he snarled.

"Ah . . ." The old man shared a puzzled glance with Alex. "Not quite with you, old bean. Where's wh—"

"The others who tried to get into this house last night. The others who came prowling through my gardens a few nights before that. The man who was with you when you attacked us in the offices of Harry Morecambe – the *tall* man, who gave me this." Whipping back his blanket, he revealed his left thigh, wrapped in a padded bandage through which a fresh bloodstain seeped.

"Oh, I *see*," Alex's grandfather said. "That was *you* at Harry's the other night. Didn't recognise you without your devilishly stylish masks. But I think we might have our wires crossed. You've made a mistake: yes, Harry is with us. But the *others*, we're not with them—"

"So what were you doing at Morecambe's place together, then?" the woman interrupted.

"Well, I could ask you the same thing."

"I think you'll find this gives me first go." She smiled, waggling her gun. "And what was Morecambe doing here with them the other night? Beyond prowling around the grounds looking to break in. Like you were again today."

"We caught you on the monitors," the man in the wheelchair said. From his cardigan he produced a thick black remote control and clicked in the direction of the bookcases.

With a grinding of gears, one section spun to reveal a bank of nine bulbous, 1970s-era televisions, stacked in a grid of three per shelf. The eight outer sets displayed a single dotted white line against a black background – it ran along near the top of the uppermost three screens, down the left and right sides of the TVs on the left and right of the second shelf, and along the bottom of the trio at ground level. In the centre screen on the middle shelf, a large, pale, rectangular block flickered. Alex stared incredulously at the archaic assemblage, vaguely reminded of clips he'd seen of the earliest computer games. *Pong.* The name pinged oddly into his head.

"My father's work," the man said with a hint of pride. "This alarm system monitors the estate's entire perimeter."

"That's fiendishly clever." Alex's grandfather sounded genuinely impressed. "And that's the house in the centre, there, is it? Isn't that marvellous, Alex?"

"Yes. It's. Amazing." Alex ground his teeth. The dog nearest him growled reproachfully.

"It's how we spotted Morecambe, the first night he tried to get in," the woman said, watching the old man closely. "We went out with the dogs. And the guns. They ran. Left in two separate cars. We followed Morecambe. He lost us, but not before I got his number plate. It took me a couple of days and several favours to track him down, and then we thought we'd repay him the visit, to find out what he was up to. Which is when we first met you. We searched Morecambe's place to try to discover how much he knew. But, as you know, we were interrupted."

"And you say you were attacked here again just last night?" Alex's grandfather asked.

"Enough. Who are you?" the man snapped. He aimed his pistol at Alex's grandfather. The gun shook. The man wetted his lips and swallowed. "Who is this Morecambe? How did you learn the secret?"

"Secret?" Alex's grandfather wrinkled his nose as though trying to think. "Do we know any secrets, Alex?"

"Please don't waste any more of our time," the woman said. Despite the lightness of her tone and the steadiness of her hands, she shared her companion's anxiety. She directed the shotgun at Alex's grandfather. "And please don't think I won't use this. I saw you looking at the painting as you came in."

"Oh." Alex's grandfather's shoulders sagged. He ran a hand across his brow, looking suddenly utterly drained, defeated. "Game's up, then. Ah, would you mind terribly if I sat down, my dear?" He gestured weakly at the dining chairs pushed against the wall behind him. "When you get to my age, the legs tire easily."

She narrowed her eyes, considering. "Fine. But talk. And don't call me dear, or I might shoot you anyway."

"Thank you. Apologies." He walked slowly across the room and sat heavily. "Okay. The *painting*. No point trying to deny it now. I confess, we are very interested in your painting."

He sighed and leaned far forward, rubbing wearily at his forehead. As he did, Alex saw him lift both feet slightly, bracing the soles of his boots hard and flat against the front legs of the chair he sat in. Alex realised the old man was still wearing his spring-heels.

"You see, thing is—" Alex's grandfather said. Then he rocketed across the room in a flashing grey blur.

The force of his launch smashed the chair into a shower of splinters behind him as he cannoned head first into the man in the wheelchair, sending him rolling backward at a speed that knocked the woman to the floor. A deafening stray shot went off as the guns fell skidding from their hands and the wheelchair tipped over on top of her, leaving the pair struggling in a tangled heap.

By the time the woman had jumped up, Alex's grandfather had collected their weapons and the others from the table, and was in the process of casually pouring himself a drink from an ornate round bottle on the cart. Leaning the shotguns against the trolley, he lifted the bowl-like glass, sniffed it, sipped, and sighed contentedly.

"Oh, unbelievable cognac, well done. Now—" he began.

"Sic, Maia," the woman said. The next thing Alex knew, he had been pushed roughly back against the wall behind her. The largest of the dogs stood on its hind legs with its huge front paws on his chest, pinning him there. It weighed more than he would have thought possible. Its mouth was drooling against his neck.

"Guns back, please." She smiled at the old man, extending her hand. "Or I'm afraid Maia will rip the boy's throat out."

"Oh, I can't imagine she'd do a thing like that. Splendid dog like her?" The old man twirled the pistol carelessly on one finger and took another unconcerned swig of brandy. "And anyway—" He muttered something Alex didn't catch. One word, repeated seven times.

"Grandad?" Alex said. The dog lifted its head until they were nose to nose. He caught the meaty flavour of its breath as it growled, long, low, and wet.

"I'm absolutely serious," the woman said. "One word from me and—"

"C'mere, girl," Alex's grandfather said.

The dog abruptly lurched at Alex's face, licked his nose, then jumped down and padded to stand at the old man's side. Alex's grandfather whistled a brief snatch of a strange tune that Alex forgot as soon as he heard it. Silently, the other six dogs came from the walls, lining up in a loose arc behind the old man.

"Sit," he said, and, as one, they did.

"How—" The woman said after an uncomprehending second. She stopped, staring at the dogs, then tried again. "How did . . . ?"

"Oh, me and dogs go way back," the old man said. Bending to retrieve his jacket and coat, he squeaked his keyring again. In response, the seven animals simultaneously lay down, flattening happily out on their bellies.

"Just need to know the right name and the right tunes and the right tone of voice. I'll teach it to you some time, Alex. Now, listen," he went on, smiling at the woman. "It strikes me we've all got off on the wrong foot here. Let's try again, and stop wasting time."

Setting down his glass, Alex's grandfather hoisted the shotgun, spun it, broke it open, and emptied out the cartridges, dropping them into his pocket before tossing the weapon to her. She caught it one-handed, open mouthed.

Unloading the revolver, the old man let it fall, deftly trapped it with his foot, then sent it sliding across the floorboards, where it came to a rest just in front of the man, who had righted his wheelchair and pulled himself back into it, clutching his thigh.

"I think now's the time for introductions," Alex's grandfather said. "This is Alex, and I'm his grandfather, and I'm deeply sorry about breaking your chair." He raised his glass to the woman, smiling expectantly.

"Kingdom," she said, after a moment. She gave an involuntary laugh. "Evelyn Kingdom."

"Charmed. And you, sir?"

"Philippe de Metz."

"An honour." The old man nodded and took another sip. "Now, are you sure you won't join me in a drink while we sort this out? Alex, there's ginger beer over here."

A few minutes later, they sat like opposing camps on the two sofas. Kingdom and Metz regarded them warily across an uneasy silence, trying to work them out. All four held glasses, Alex's grandfather having poured everyone a measure and given himself a healthy top-up, but only the old man was drinking.

"Your dog," Alex said to Kingdom in an attempt to break the impasse. "Would it really have . . . ?" He traced a finger across his throat.

"Maia? No," she said, after a moment. She gave a shrugging smile, like she'd been found out. "She's a big softy. Growling's usually enough to stop anyone in their tracks."

Alex's grandfather turned to Metz. "How bad's your leg?"

Several seconds passed. "It feels worse now than when he stabbed me," the man finally muttered gloomily. He tugged the tartan blanket around his wounded thigh. "A huge man, and hugely powerful. I suppose adrenaline gave me strength to fight on at first. His blade went deep. Evelyn has stitched it as best she could. I don't think there is too much damage, but it will be several days before I can do much walking. This wheelchair belonged to my grand-mère." He nodded sadly to where it stood by the sofa. "The junk one keeps lying around an old house that has seen better times."

"Indeed." Alex's grandfather smiled sadly, then grew serious, watching the pair carefully. "To old junk, then. Tell me: by any chance, does your painting have some connection with nine others that have been stolen over the past few months?"

As the old man began listing the stolen paintings by name, Kingdom and Metz exchanged a panicking look. The woman started to speak, but Metz grabbed at her wrist. "You mustn't," he hissed.

Alex's grandfather considered them, then pulled from his pockets the ammunition he'd removed from their guns, placing it softly on the sofa arm beside Kingdom. "Token of good faith," he said. "We'd like to help. And we would like *your* help."

"You *mustn't*," Metz repeated, staring at Kingdom.

"Oh, Phil," she said. "*Calme-toi*. What other choice do we have? Almost all the pictures have been gathered. I'm beginning to have the feeling these two are the only help we have coming." She turned back to Alex and his grandfather, still cautious. "How much do you know?"

"Ha." The old man scratched a finger around his shirt collar. "Well, let's pretend, just for conversation's sake, we don't know much at all. But we do know the paintings have been stolen – and we know who's doing it. Harry and Alex and I have been on their trail. The night you saw Harry outside, he'd followed them here. We're trying to stop them. We, ah, we've tangled with them before, in other matters. They are a strange little group but extremely dangerous."

He paused and sipped his drink, as though weighing how much to say. "And we also know they aren't stealing these paintings for, shall we say . . . the *usual* reasons?"

Metz turned to Kingdom with new alarm. She did a good job of pretending not to notice.

"Not money, for instance," Alex's grandfather pressed. "I mean, no offence, but, pleasant as it is, that –" he gestured to the painting hanging above them in its heavy wooden frame – "can't be worth very much. We know they're stealing them for something . . . else."

"Something bad," Alex added.

Kingdom threaded her fingers and leaned forward, staring at the floor. Her eyes moved slightly from side to side, as though scanning through a list of possible ways to proceed. After a moment, she smiled at Metz with the air of someone who had made up her mind.

"This decision is mine to make," she said. "The responsibility lies on me. But if you really disagree, I'll say no more. So: shall we?"

After a moment, Metz spread his hands in resignation.

"Why not?" he muttered bleakly. "It seems this is the end of it now, in any case."

He spoke with such a final heaviness they all fell quiet.

"The end of what?" Alex finally asked, just to fill the silence.

Kingdom paused while refilling her glass and gave him a flat flicker of a smile.

"Of everything," she said.

XXVI.

THE FISHING CLUB
OF LONDON

"WHAT I'M ABOUT to tell you is a very *old* story and a very *strange* story," Kingdom continued. "And I fully expect you will not believe a word of it."

"Might be surprised," Alex's grandfather said.

"Yeah." Alex rubbed a hand wearily over his face. "We kind of specialise in those."

Kingdom blew out a small laugh. "Well, in that case, gentlemen." She raised her glass high. "As president, I welcome you to what looks like being the last meeting of the London Fishing Club Limited. Established 1893, and dissolved, well – any time now."

Alex and his grandfather looked dumbly at each other, then back at her.

"You've never heard of us? Well, no reason why you should." Kingdom took a sip of cognac. "There was a time when the club was the toast of European society. But the club is not what it once was. It formally ceased to function in 1913, you

247

see, during the buildup to the First World War. The leadership back then decided to take advantage of all the chaos and slip back under the radar. Before that, though, they had advertised widely: 'Trout Fishing in the Black Forest!'" She waved her glass, giving the line a theatrical flourish. "That was the big selling point, that and the baths: 'renowned natural healing waters, proven since times ancient for the treatment of rheumatism, gout, and skin disease!'

"To all appearances, it was a health resort, you see," she continued. "Hidden in a remote valley, not far over the border in Germany. A spot called Bad Boll, outside the small town of Bonndorf."

"The Black Forest." The old man nodded grimly.

"Is it near the Kandel?" Alex asked.

"Well, near is a relative concept, Alex," his grandfather said. "Relatively speaking, the moon is near the Earth. But I wouldn't want to walk it. The place Evelyn is talking about must be a good twenty miles from the mountain, at least. Please go on," he added to Kingdom, who was watching them with a look of puzzlement.

"The original Fishing Club was a group of eleven international investors operating out of London," she continued. "They bought Bad Boll in 1893, taking over from the previous owners – who were actually themselves, under different names. The club has had many names over the years, sometimes no name, and many members, although only ever eleven in the core circle, stretching right back to the 1600s. Membership has been passed down since then, usually from parent to child.

"In the late 1800s, they built an elegant hotel out there in the Black Forest, advertised as a health spa, a retreat for those seeking to soothe their nerves in nature. They opened paths through the woods for the first time: hiking trails under great chestnut trees among ancient rocks and rare orchids. Sounds rather idyllic, doesn't it?" She directed the question to Alex.

"I guess. But you said: 'To all appearances.'"

"Very good. Now. Isn't it curious that a group from London would make such fuss around some anonymous little spot buried in the woods in Germany? They even had a telegraph station built out there, so they could stay connected with the outside world. They brought in electricity, using a waterfall to power a generator so they could light the place by night. They built a chapel. I mean: how good could the trout be? And isn't it *curious* they managed to attract some of the world's most influential people to this obscure place? Guests included royalty from around the globe, politicians, thinkers, artists, writers. Winston Churchill stayed there. You know that name?"

"Sure." Alex nodded. "British prime minister, he was in charge during the Second World War."

"Right. So isn't it *most curious of all*," Kingdom went on, "that after being such a fashionable, internationally renowned resort, the place simply *vanished*? The First World War brought an end to the Fishing Club's official ownership of Bad Boll, but the club kept secret watch over the place afterward, and they made sure it disappeared. The spa was gradually allowed to fall into wrack and ruin – or, perhaps, *steered* into it.

"Mysterious fires destroyed buildings and so on, until by the 1990s it was decided what was left should just be demolished, let wild nature reclaim the area. Today, apart from the chapel, which still stands in the forest – abandoned, overgrown, and rotting away – there's no sign Bad Boll ever existed. As if it had been completely wiped out of history."

"Okay." Alex's grandfather sat forward. "Very interesting for students of the history of European tourism, I'm sure. But I feel you haven't told us the part we're not going to believe. So. What's the *real* story?"

"The real story –" Kingdom leaned toward him until their faces were twelve inches apart – "is that the resort was just a cover, of course. Simply an excuse for the club to go about its true activities out in the woods. What I haven't mentioned, you see, is that, perched on a hill *above* their hotel, deep in the forest, were the remains of an ancient, long-ruined castle."

"Oh, this sounds more like it," the old man said, rubbing his hands and grinning at Alex, who failed to share his enthusiasm.

"The ruins are there still," Kingdom continued. "Just a single wall with a few empty windows, part of a crumbling tower. Some people call the old castle Burg Boll, others Burg Neu-Tannegg. It was built around the year 1160 and stood until around 1460 – and then it was destroyed by . . . well. Some tremendous calamity. Yet for long periods of that time, it's a place almost entirely without a history – again, as though it had been *deliberately wiped from the records*. For many years now, entry to the castle ruins has been forbidden: the risk of further collapse is high, there are loose rocks, steep plunges into old vaults. A wrong step could be fatal."

"But that's not the only reason entry is forbidden, I take it?" Alex's grandfather said.

"And what was the tremendous calamity that destroyed the castle?" Alex asked. He had leaned forward too now in anticipation.

"That," Metz said with a sigh, still slumped back on his sofa, "is the secret the Fishing Club has sworn to protect." He held his glass to the light, watching the chandelier's glow shimmer and shift through the brandy.

"Our society was formed to guard that ruin, keep watch. You see, something terrible was done inside that castle in the fifteenth century. Something unearthly."

He suddenly turned to them, speaking faster, a wild glint in his eyes. "Something that caused the earth to *revolt* and a pit to open under the place and *swallow* it. And if it was ever done again, it would cause a destruction that this time could *not* be stopped. The end of this *world*."

Metz paused, catching himself, embarrassed. He regarded them and seemed surprised to find they were taking him seriously.

"Sounds ridiculous," he went on quietly. "But this is the legend. My father, who was not a man given to flights of fancy, believed this story sincerely, and that made me believe it, with all my heart."

"Same deal here," Kingdom said. "My father was convinced of the danger. He was genuinely scared some great horror was waiting to be unleashed, and then—" She drained her glass, tossing back her head. "Ka-blooey."

"The earth revolted," Alex's grandfather repeated to Metz. "A pit opened. Are those the words your father used?"

"*Une abîme,*" the man replied, nodding. "A phrase from childhood that is hard to forget."

Alex's grandfather sat tapping a thumbnail against his teeth. "Please go on. I don't see the connection with the paintings."

Metz exchanged another look with Kingdom. She nodded.

"In the years following its destruction," Metz continued, "many legends sprang up about the ruin of the destroyed castle in the forest at Boll: that some great prize lay buried in there. And so the place became a target for treasure hunters across the sixteenth and seventeenth centuries. For many years, the first incarnation of our society worked to keep curious eyes away – while simultaneously working among the ruins to conceal all traces of what *had* happened.

"In the early 1600s, they finally removed something from the site and hid it safely elsewhere. And to prevent this knowledge from falling into the wrong hands – what it was, where it was taken – the society scattered the information. They hid the key to it all in the paintings, which were then spread across Europe: those you already know about; this painting here above us; and—"

"And one other," Kingdom quickly cut in.

"Another?" Alex and his grandfather spoke in unison.

"Yes." She regarded them carefully, not quite masking her relief at their surprise. "One more. Put all the paintings together, and, *the ancient secret can be known again.*" She said the last words in a singsong, like a poem she had learned by heart.

"*Something* was removed." Alex's grandfather said, catching Alex's eye. "So, ah, what was that? You've trusted us with this much, you may as well tell us the rest."

"That's the problem." Kingdom sighed. She hung her head, then smiled ruefully up through a curtain of hair. "It's not a matter of trusting you. We can't tell you much more because we don't *know* much more. You see, around the time the society became known as the Fishing Club, its leadership came to a great decision: that the best way to *protect* our secret was to let it be *forgotten*.

"The society always guarded its knowledge religiously – very few outsiders were ever told this story. But in the 1880s it was suspected that one member of the club had betrayed us. Nothing was proved, but it was thought he had been persuaded to reveal the secret to someone: some outsider. And so the

Fishing Club built their hotel out there at Bad Boll at that point, as a way of increasing protection of the ruins: they could run regular patrols, even light the forest by night, without anyone wondering why.

"As the years passed, however, nothing happened. No one came, no one tried to break into the old castle. The club's leadership decided then to simply let the secret wither and die, and the club with it. Each new generation of members would be told only part of the story and instructed to tell the next generation even less. In the meantime, the dwindling club would keep silent watch over the ruins and the paintings, just in case the rumour about an outsider knowing the secret was true. But, by now, of course, any such outsider would be long dead."

As Kingdom said this, Alex and his grandfather shifted uncomfortably in their seats.

"It was decreed that if we kept ourselves hidden, if we let the story fade, and if nothing happened for a hundred years," Kingdom continued, "then we could safely assume all was well, and simply disappear. Let the club die out. And so, Philippe and I are the very last members. Until recently, there were three of us left. Our comrade Ralf was from the family assigned to watch over the Rubens, *The Great Last Judgment* – the largest of the paintings. Ralf was president before me. He actually worked as a guard at the Alte Pinakothek museum in Munich. He was killed there the night it was taken, attempting to stop the theft."

She paused before going on. "So. While we have sworn our lives to our cause, we only have fragments of the story left: *first*, that something once happened at the castle in the Black Forest, which must never happen again; *second*, that to prevent it happening, the paintings must never be brought together – and now, when we have no strength or influence left, it seems that they are being. This group you mentioned have already taken nine. And now they are coming for this one. We drove them off last night, but I have no doubt they will return."

They all followed her gaze to the picture on the wall.

"Where's the eleventh?" Alex asked. "The last painting?"

Metz started to reply, but Kingdom cut him off.

"No." She shook her head. "The eleventh painting is our last secret. Trust can only stretch so far. To earn more, you have to give us something in return."

"Why don't you just take this painting and hide it?" Alex said. "Or destroy it. That'll put an end to it, won't it?"

"Perhaps," Kingdom replied. "Perhaps not. There are two problems there. For one, as the last of the club, Philippe and I are sworn to stopping anyone who tries to gather the paintings together – not to *run* from them, not to *hide* from them, but to *stop* them. Stop the secret from being known. And so here we are, waiting for them to come." She nodded sadly at the shotgun leaning against the table. "Who are they? Who's doing this?"

"Oh, we just call their leader the tall man, don't we, Alex?"

Alex's grandfather said distractedly. "Two problems you said. The other?"

"Yes. Well." Kingdom winced. "It gets more complicated yet, I'm afraid. It seems our forerunners in the club were an extremely devious bunch. There have always been eleven paintings, yes, eleven paintings that hold the secret. But they've not always been the *same* eleven."

"What?" The old man stared at her.

"The original list was drawn up in the 1600s. But a few pictures were replaced over the years. This, for example." She nodded to the painting on the wall. "It dates from 1760, so it can't have been one of the original eleven. But the titles of the originals that were removed from the list were not passed on to us. We don't know why now. We can only assume the . . . code changed, too. But perhaps not – so we must also assume that there's a danger those unknown original paintings could still somehow be used to make up the eleven. If this . . . tall man of yours knows enough about the secret to have already gathered nine, he may know about the originals. He may know more than we do."

"Wouldn't be hard," Alex's grandfather mused. He stood to scrutinise the painting, then suddenly spun and pointed to Kingdom.

"Shadow Gate."

She stiffened. Metz looked from her to the old man and back. "What?" he said. "What is this now?"

"Where did you hear that?" Kingdom asked, visibly shaken.

"You said we had to earn your trust," Alex's grandfather said. "So I'm giving you what we know. The great secret you're sworn to keep hidden. It's the Shadow Gate, isn't it? This castle ruin at Bad Boll, it's where the legend took place."

"I have no idea what you're talking about," Kingdom said. She sat grinding her jaw over some internal argument. "But . . . yes. I know the phrase. At least, the German equivalent: *Schattentor*."

"What *is* this?" Metz demanded.

"Each time the Fishing Club took a new president, the successor was also selected," Kingdom said. "As a precaution. When Ralf became president, he selected me – and he passed on that phrase. *Schattentor*. A password, secretly handed down from one president to the next, over decades. You see, we don't *know* what the eleventh painting is. It was decided a century ago to keep its identity hidden even from the club. Another insurance measure: if members don't *know* what the painting is, they can't *reveal* it. A letter containing that information, the title of the painting and its location, has been locked away in the vault of an old law firm in Stuttgart for decades. But if needs be, the president can be told it, by contacting the lawyers and speaking that phrase. But how did you know it? I'd thought it was just a made-up word."

"Well, seeing as we're swapping unbelievable stories," the old man said. "You've already said that your fear is of something . . .

unearthly happening. I'm afraid that's exactly what we're dealing with."

As Alex's grandfather relayed what he knew of the Shadow Gate legend, Metz started to squirm. Kingdom pursed her lips in a thoughtful frown.

"So, yes," the old man summed up. "Seems to me that your Castle Boll was the lair of this great and greatly evil medieval magician. He supposedly created this thing as his way of thwarting death. But when he used it, your great calamity occurred. The castle fell, the pit opened, and all of that."

"Well," Kingdom said at length. She shrugged. "Why not. I try to keep an open mind. Phil?"

"This madness makes as much sense as any other part of it ever has," Metz muttered.

"What about the Kandel mountain?" Alex asked. "The Devil's Pulpit? Do you know if there's a connection with the castle?"

Metz and Kingdom looked blankly at him. "You mentioned the mountain before," Kingdom said, shaking her head. "Why should there be a connection?"

"The people who are stealing the paintings have been, uh . . . doing . . . something up there, too." Alex shrugged apologetically. "We think."

"Means nothing to me," Kingdom said. "As your grandfather said, the Kandel must be . . . what, twenty-five miles away from the castle ruin."

"Twenty-five miles and several hundred years away, to be

precise," the old man mused. "Well, here we are. So, what was your plan? You figured you'd just hole up in here and wait for them to come, using the painting as bait, and then – all or nothing? The Fishing Club's last stand?"

"More or less," Metz muttered, looking at the guns.

"Well, I admire the courage, but I would propose that, for the time being, discretion is the better part of valour. I say we take the painting down, get out of here, and try to come up with a better plan. Preferably one that ends with us all going out for a nice supper afterward, rather than going out in a blaze of glory."

"But how many are in this gang?" Kingdom asked seriously. "If Harry Morecambe is your friend, then we've only ever seen two, maybe three figures. Surely between us we could handle—"

"There will most likely be five," Alex's grandfather said. "But there could be more. And, ah, they'll have things with them."

"Things?" Kingdom frowned.

"Yeah," Alex said. "You know how you said you had a story that *we* wouldn't believe? Well—"

"We can come back to that if needs be," his grandfather cut in. "But my point is, given that they already have nine of the paintings, let's not offer them the chance to get another. Although, they actually only have eight, of course."

"What do you mean?" asked Metz.

"Hmm? Oh, didn't I say? Yes, they only have eight. Harry got one back. *Way to Béziers*. It's over there in my bag."

Kingdom and Metz looked shocked all over again.

"You have it *here*?" Metz said.

"That's right." The old man slapped his hands. "What say, before we take your painting down, we get this other one out and try holding it up alongside it? Maybe if we see two together in the flesh, something might become clear."

The pair sat speechless.

"Okay?" Alex's grandfather said, striding across to his Gladstone. "Alex and I have come up with so many theories I've lost count. Maybe it's something in the paint, maybe it's a map, maybe it's something to do with the trees . . . More trees in this new one, Alex. To be honest, I can't see the woods for the trees any more, ha-ha."

As the old man stood happily unrolling the painting, Kingdom was first to recover her voice. "Did you miss the part where we mentioned we were members of a secret society who have taken a sacred oath passed down the centuries to devote our lives to keeping these paintings from ever being brought together?"

"Oh, pshaw," Alex's grandfather said. "What's the worst could happen?"

Metz and Kingdom's anxiety was genuine, and contagious. Alex had joined them in staring at the old man in silent apprehension. Seeing their faces, Alex' grandfather hesitated, glancing from the picture in his hands across to the painting on the wall. The lonely mountain road. The old house shrouded in mist.

"Ah . . . just what *is* the worst could happen, do you think?"

The air filled with a deep, low pulsing sound that set Alex's teeth on edge. The dogs sat up. Flat and ominous, the vibrating tone seemed to be coming from all directions at once.

"What's that?" Alex said. "What's happening?"

Metz drew himself unsteadily to his feet, face ashen.

"The alarm," he said, sounding already defeated. "It seems they are here."

XXVII.

LAST STAND AT CHÂTEAU DE SAINT-CLEMENT

ALEX'S GRANDFATHER AND Kingdom ran from the room toward the front doors of the house, dogs following. The pulsing noise continued.

Alex shrugged his coat on, shoved the toy robot deep in a pocket, and joined Metz where he stood, gazing at the bank of TVs. On the screens, numerous small white blips were gathering together to form large, vibrating white dots at the centre of each stretch of the wall around the house, north, east, south, and west. After a moment, the large dots began breaking up again, spreading into swarms of spots that started closing in on the central grey block representing the building.

"The end of it," Metz whispered.

The front door slammed and there came the sounds of keys and of bolts being rammed home. Kingdom, the old man, and the dogs reappeared, all looking serious.

"What's happening?" Metz gestured at the rash spreading over his screens.

"Trouble," Alex's grandfather said. "We're already surrounded."

"But by *who*—" Kingdom started. She paused when she saw Alex's face. "Or . . . *what*? I couldn't see anyone, maybe some movement at the trees."

"Yes, well, you'll see soon enough," Alex's grandfather muttered.

The alarm kept pulsing, maddening in its monotony. On the monitors, the first wave of blips was almost at the grey block, more coming behind. As the spots lined up around the building, the picture across the screens suddenly changed, zooming in from a map of the grounds to now show a rough plan of the house itself, its outline flashing in distress as the first dots touched it.

From the hallway, there came a strange scratching at the front doors.

It grew louder, as though more and more sharp little blades were joining in to hack at the wood. The alarm's flat, steady tone was augmented now by a new note of a higher, more urgent pitch.

"Is there any chance," Alex's grandfather said, "we could turn that noise off? I think we've got the general idea now."

Metz, standing gazing vacantly, took a moment to respond. He clicked a button on his remote and the alarm ceased, allowing a stark new appreciation of the sharp chatter thudding into the door. The noise echoed oddly around them, behind them. Then Alex realised it wasn't an echo.

"They're at the back, too," he said.

"The kitchen door!" Kingdom turned and ran.

Following her, Alex and his grandfather found themselves in a modest kitchen that lay just off the ballroom along a narrow corridor. Low ceilinged and dim, its single small window was thick with dirt and covered by iron bars inside and out. Beside it, the old wooden back door looked solid and heavy. Amplified by the acoustics of the tiled walls, the scratching noises from the other side of it grated harshly.

"Door should hold for a little while," the old man said. "But if there are life-sizers coming, it won't last long."

"Life . . . sizers?" Kingdom repeated.

"Mmm," Alex's grandfather muttered, raising his eyebrows as he went back past her. "Big as life. Bigger."

Kingdom turned questioningly to Alex. He tried thinking about the best way to explain it. After a second, he shrugged. "Robots."

Even in the circumstances, it felt slightly stupid saying it aloud. Kingdom opened her mouth and narrowed her eyes. Then she simply nodded.

"Okay, then." She thought about it a second longer. "Although I don't know how Philippe will feel about that."

"No," Alex said. "He's close to losing it already, isn't he?"

"Maybe. I don't know him that well, to be honest. We've only met a few times over the years." She gestured around. "You have to understand, for us, all this was always just a strange horror story our parents told us. A kind of secret game. But now it's all coming true. Phil always struck me as a man fighting a battle with his nerves. I don't know how he will react. Or how I will, come to that."

The chopping commotion at the door suddenly grew louder. "I suppose we'll see," she said.

They ran back into the main room. Alex's grandfather stood at the door to the hallway. He leaned out and craned to look up the stairway that curved to the next floor.

"As we were coming in," he said over his shoulder, "I noticed a concrete outbuilding around the side of the house. Garage?"

"Yes," said Metz. He had sat back in his wheelchair, looking like he had given up.

"Car in there?" the old man went on.

Kingdom produced keys, twirling them around her finger and catching them with a slap in her palm. "All filled up and ready to go. But can we make it out there?"

"I think upstairs might be our best bet. Out a window, maybe over the roof . . ." He trailed off, turning gravely to consider Metz in his wheelchair. "Ah. Do you think you could—"

The sound of breaking glass from upstairs cut him off. Alex's grandfather crept into the hall, heading toward the staircase. Alex and Kingdom moved to the doorway, in time to see him turn wildly from the bottom step and come sprinting back.

"Shut the door!" he shouted as he hurtled past them. But Kingdom had already stepped out, and stood peering curiously up the stairs. There was a whishing whirr from above, and a silvery cloud came sweeping down around the curve of the staircase, rushing at her.

Alex lunged, grabbed her arm, and hauled her back in as his grandfather slammed the door, turning a key in the lock. They heard several objects hitting the other side of the door, followed by the now familiar scraping of small blades against wood, closer than ever.

"What in the name of—" Kingdom said. Her eyes were round.

"Fliers," Alex said. "They, uh. Fly."

"Help me barricade it, Alex," his grandfather said, running to drag a sofa over. "If you'd be so kind as to lend a hand," he added to Kingdom, with a grunt.

The hellish scratching at the door continued as they worked to pile everything they could against it. The dogs stood in a semicircle, watching. Metz sat behind them, eyes wide, staring at nothing.

"Philippe," Kingdom called matter-of-factly, as she moved a chair across the room. "Maybe you could finish preparing the weapons?"

Metz blinked. "Of course." He rolled his chair to the bare table where the extra shotguns lay and started loading them from a box of ammunition. Alex noticed the man's hands trembled.

Alex's grandfather joined Metz, picked up a red shotgun shell, and stood studying it. "Do you have much in the way of salt in your kitchen?"

Metz frowned, bewildered. "There is a container from the supermarket, I think perhaps half-full."

"Could you pop in and fetch that, Alex?" The old man had found a Swiss Army-style knife in his bag and was picking carefully through its attachments.

"In the cupboard nearest the outside door," Metz said to Alex, utterly perplexed.

The metallic scraping at the back door continued as Alex entered the kitchen. A little chip of the black paint fell away, leaving a pale scar near the lock. A second later, there was a dull glint as the tip of a scalpel-like blade pushed through. The scrabbling noise intensified around the spot.

Alex did his best to ignore it and opened the cupboard, running his eye hurriedly over its contents: scales, a blender, a small blowtorch of the kind he'd seen countless TV chefs using, a dusty rolling pin. He finally found a plastic tub of salt lurking behind a box of sugar. He paused, then grabbed it, relieved when he felt no sting. He ran back through, the scratching from the door singing after him.

"But it is senseless," Metz was complaining. "It will cause almost no damage."

Alex's grandfather stood over him, working at one of the shotgun shells with his knife. "Bingo," he said, prying open the casing. Tipping the cartridge up, he poured out the lead shot from inside. "Salt please, Alex."

Alex sat the tub on the table, then watched as the old man briskly packed the shell with salt. Using tiny pliers on his knife, he crimped the casing closed again, then held up the finished article for Metz's inspection.

"Trust me, a shell like this will do us a world more good against anything coming through that door today."

"But—" Metz looked to Kingdom for help. She shrugged.

"We always knew this was a strange business, Phil," she said. "I think it's safe to say we're through the looking glass now. These two seem to know what they're talking about."

"Very well." Metz took the proffered knife and started opening another cartridge. The task seemed to calm him.

"You empty them, I'll fill them," Alex said, moving to stand at Metz's side.

"Meanwhile," Alex's grandfather said to Kingdom, "we can have a think about what's the best way to get out of a locked room with no windows when there are things at the only two doors trying to get in and kill you. I used to love trying to solve puzzles like this."

The old man and Kingdom stood surveying the room while Alex and Metz worked on the cartridges. As Alex bent to fill the first, he froze. The salt definitely burned his fingers faintly. The plastic tub must have protected him. The sting wasn't too bad. He gritted his teeth and filled the shell faster, resolving to worry about it later.

The scrabbling at the door had been joined by a faint, low buzzing. After a while, the dogs padded to the centre of the room and sat there together. Watching them, waiting for the next shell to be filled, Alex realised Metz had stopped working.

Glancing around, he saw the man was staring at the monitors, fresh horror spreading over his face.

"Eh, you okay?" Alex asked, knowing he wasn't.

"There." Metz pointed a shaking finger. "You see?"

Alex squinted at the old TVs. As far as he could tell, the display looked depressingly the same: the flashing plan of the house, like a terrible video game adaptation of Cluedo, the swarming dots moving around it.

Kingdom had noticed them. "What is it, Phil?"

"They're here," the man said, still pointing at the screen. His voice and his arm both shook. "They're here."

Alex, his grandfather, and Kingdom exchanged a worried look.

"Yes, Philippe," Kingdom said gently. "We know. That's why we're all trying to figure a way out of here."

"No," Metz snapped. "They are *here*! Look! According to the monitor, they're already *here*!"

The three of them looked at him dumbly.

"In the *room*!" Metz screamed, looking around wildly. "*This* room. They're in this room *with us*!"

XXVIII.

SPIDERS, FLAME, WOOD

FOR A PANICKY few seconds they danced a silent twist in the old ballroom, ducking and turning rapidly to scan in all directions, finding nothing. Alex's grandfather called them to a stop.

"Shhhhh." He held up a finger. They froze. The scraping at the door kept up. The buzzing was louder. Nearer. The dogs suddenly stood, forming a circle around the spot where they had been sitting, all staring intently at the floorboards, ears up.

"Ah, call the dogs away from there, please, Evelyn," the old man said. "Everyone, take what you need and back up to this side of the room." Grabbing his Gladstone, he gestured toward the far wall, where the painting hung.

"What is it?" Alex said as they gathered under the picture, backs to the wall.

The old man scratched his forehead and winced apologetically: "Diggers. I'd forgotten about them."

"You mean . . . ?" Alex stared back to the place in the floor the dogs had found so interesting.

"'Fraid so."

There was a muffled but mighty crash from the hallway – the sound, Alex was certain, of the main doors smashing open under a life-sizer's fists. The buzzing grew louder, a depressing, toneless song from under the floorboards. His grandfather took the box of salt and strode over, surrounding the spot with a thin circle, then pouring a larger mound at its centre.

"Should buy us some time," he said, returning and spreading another line on the floor in a semicircle before them. "Well, a few seconds. Still, better than nothing. We can save these last handfuls of salt for throwing. How many shotgun shells did you manage to prepare?"

"Six," said Metz, setting them out on the blanket over his knees. He was breathing fast, Alex saw, but holding himself together.

"Three each then," Kingdom said, pulling her sword sheath across her back and breaking open a shotgun. As they worked preparing their weapons, Alex stepped closer to his grandfather.

"How's the improvising going?"

"Have to confess, I'm having a bit of an off day on that front, Alex."

Alex noticed the old man's hand was trembling badly. Sweat stood out on his brow. "Grandad, couldn't you just . . . take the potion again? To stop you ageing?"

"Hmm? Oh. No." The old man wiped his brow, then looked down at his shaking hand, tightening it into a fist. "No, I'll never do that." His voice dropped to a murmur. "Alex, you asked me why I left my father. Why I turned against them. Well then. It was because I found out the truth. I found out about the deaths."

"Deaths?" It came out as a dry whisper. The scraping sounds from the kitchen were now joined by a mighty banging. The barricade at the door across the room shuddered as something slammed against it from the other side.

His grandfather nodded. "I told you, my father uses an extract from the flower, the flower we took from the Black Forest that awful night. Ghastly stories surrounded the thing, Alex. It grew out at an abandoned crossroads, under a tree that had once been used as the local gallows. Legend was, it had grown there by absorbing the lives of all the killers and thieves that perished over it. It was said its roots ran . . . very deep. But there were other legends about it."

The buzzing beneath their feet had become a high, horrific whine, shuddering angrily as it bored into wood.

"After we brought it home, I became aware my father was going out some nights, going out late. Going out with his spring-heels. My suspicions grew. I started following him, or trying to. Long story short, one night I finally saw it happen. It was all part of the hideous bargain of keeping that demonic flower alive, and the flower keeping him – us – alive."

They watched the floorboards. There was a puff of sawdust. Wood began coiling away in strips

"Every once in a while, Alex, the flower produces a ghastly new leaf. And when this leaf grows, my father must cut it off, then press it to the neck of . . . a victim. The leaf takes the . . . life force away from a person. It absorbs it – totally, and at once. Every mote of energy in the body. Instant decomposition. Nothing left, not even bones. Then the leaf is pulped into their mixture and . . ."

For a moment the old man seemed unable to go on. "That night, the night I finally put it all together, is the night I left them, Alex. I was almost out of my mind. I stole his spring-heels, hoping it might hinder him in his hunting, and I ran—"

With a sudden final scream from the wood, a metal awl came tearing through the floor. Alex caught a glimpse of the robot attached, like a happy toy mole, with this nightmarish drill-bit as its nose.

As it touched the mound of salt, the machine fell back through the hole it had created, roughly four inches in diameter. More salt fell in after it. Scuttling sounds came from under the floor, then silence.

Alex's grandfather raised his cane. Across the room, the barricade collapsed a little as the door was forced open a crack. The dogs gave a low growl.

"*Mon dieu*," Metz whispered, on the verge of blind panic. Alex followed the man's wild, wide-eyed stare.

What looked like two pieces of long, thin wire had appeared out of the hole. They reached up from below, wavered in the air a moment, then bent to start tapping delicately around the opening, testing the ground. After a second, they were joined by another six wires – then the strands stopped moving, braced against the floor, and something came hauling itself up through the hole, followed rapidly by another, and then another and another.

More kept coming. Spiderlike things. Fat, fuzzy black bodies supported on glistening, hairlike wire legs. Each sported a pair of cartoonish felt eyes. More than twenty had come out and were scurrying toward them.

Metz suddenly rolled his chair forward and laughed, half-hysterical. "*These?* These are what we are hiding from? No need to waste ammunition on these," he said, turning his shotgun and holding it by the barrel, like a club.

"Ah, please be careful," Alex's grandfather called. "Probably safer if you just come back here, old chap."

"What do they do?" Alex asked.

"No idea," the old man replied. "These are new to me. What'll we call them? I've already used *crawlers* for something else. Spiders?"

The spider-things had come to a stop at the salt semicircle. They lined up along it, fat bodies bobbing grotesquely on spindly legs. Then, with a sudden flex, one jumped, fast and high.

Metz swung his gun. When it connected, the little machine

exploded with a ferocious blast that ripped off the shotgun's stock and sent Metz crashing to the floor, lying across the salt line.

A flier shot out from the hole in the floor straight for him, fastening itself to his neck.

Eardrums ringing, Alex ran with Kingdom to help Metz. The little machine buzzed hungrily at the man's throat like an awkward metal vampire bat as they tried to drag him back. Alex flung more salt. The robot darted off, disappearing beneath the floorboards.

Alex's grandfather leapt forward, scattering salt at the rest of the spiders. Most jumped out of reach, but two were caught and started sprinting crazily, before running into one another with another horrendous explosion. Alex felt the heat on his face. Kingdom bent to inspect what was left of Metz's mangled weapon, then kicked it away.

The barricade across the room fell in as the door was shoved open wider. Two life-sizers could now be seen, struggling in the doorway. One managed to reach in and began shifting the blockage, tossing chairs away.

"C'est la fin." Metz lay cowering on the floor, staring at the giant robots. He kept repeating the phrase, hoarsely, woozily, fainter all the time. "C'est la fin."

"Philippe," Kingdom said. "We need you. If you can. Philippe?"

She spoke without looking at him, holding her shotgun

trained on the door, studying the life-sizers as they dismantled the barricade. Alex's grandfather stood with his box of salt, not much left now, watching the spiders warily.

Alex glanced at Metz. He lay motionless, a red, raw spot on his neck. Alex knelt to listen at the man's chest.

"Alex?" his grandfather said.

"He's alive. Unconscious."

Alex stood and pulled the toy robot from his pocket. His fist tightened as he screwed his eyes shut, picturing the toy, picturing the tablet, lining up the doors he needed to move through. He strained to connect.

There was a sudden wispy scuttling on the floorboards. Alex looked to see spiders darting forward, then stopping as his grandfather scattered a meagre handful of salt. He closed his eyes, pushing harder. No use. No time.

He opened his eyes at another sound. The last of the barricade had been pushed away. A life-sizer was striding across the room.

When it was ten feet away, Kingdom fired. The giant robot went into a frenzy, then fell, landing on four of the spiders. The resulting explosion ripped off its arm and sent the metal limb flying across the room, where the ragged shoulder embedded itself into the wall. The disembodied arm hung there, hand groping hideously for a few seconds, before falling lifeless.

"That's one," Kingdom said. She suddenly lifted her gun higher.

A flier was racing at her. She shot again. The thing rocked

back, dropped dead. A shower of salt from the cartridge rained down with it, sending three of the spiders running into the wall with another ferocious blast.

"That's two." Kingdom levelled the shotgun again, aiming toward the other life-sizer that hulked unmoving in the doorway, seeming to watch her. Other things gathered at its feet and in the air behind it. An awful pause settled.

Alex felt his back touch the wall. Looking up, he realised he was directly beneath the painting. The target of all of this. He looked down at the toy robot, absurd in his hand, then gave up, stuffing it back in his coat.

His dad's old coat, he thought. With the thought came a stray memory: his grandfather burning his hooded top. Across the room, there was another small fire burning, blackening the wall where the spiders had exploded. Fire flashed across his mind. He started for the kitchen.

The nearest spider came scurrying at him.

"Alex!" his grandfather shouted, chucking salt. The thing jumped safely back.

"Just hold them another second!" Alex shouted over his shoulder.

In the kitchen, the furious scratching at the door continued. A huge gloved fist came smashing through the wood, started searching blindly for the handle. Alex ignored it, tore open the cupboard, and grabbed the little blowtorch, checking that it worked.

Another gunshot sounded starkly from behind, followed by Kingdom's apologetic voice: "And that was three."

Sprinting back to the ballroom, he was aware of his grandfather's confused, questioning look, and, beyond the old man, of a brightly coloured torrent of things pouring in through the door, swarming around the prone body of another life-sizer: small things, flying things, things rolling and crawling. But he focused on the painting. He clicked frantically at the blowtorch. The little flame caught the second time, strong, sharp, blue.

"Stop!" he shouted, holding it up to the old wooden frame. The varnish started to blister. The parade of robots froze instantly. The banging from the kitchen halted. The silence was absolute.

"Anything moves, the painting's getting torched."

Alex's grandfather frowned. "Why didn't I think of something like that? I really am losing my touch. Evelyn, would you mind helping me take the picture down from the wall?"

As Alex moved slightly for them to get at the painting, he accidentally let the flame go out. Instantly, the machines started closing in. It took three attempts to click the blowtorch to life. The robots halted.

The old man held the framed picture awkwardly under one arm. Kingdom hauled the prone Metz into his wheelchair.

"So, we all ready?" Alex's grandfather said. "Oh, actually, hang on." He reached to the drinks trolley and slipped the cognac into his coat pocket. "Shame to let that go to waste. Okay. Let's go."

They made their way toward the wrecked door. Kingdom led, pushing the unconscious Metz with one hand, rapier drawn in the other. Alex walked behind his grandfather, keeping the blue flame held close to the picture frame. The seven dogs pressed around them as Kingdom shoved aside the last of the barricade.

Alex had his other hand in his pocket, clutching the toy robot. He ordered his panic to calm. He thought about the way he had controlled the flier – that sense of sectioning off his mind, so different parts did different things. He tried it again now while he walked.

First the robot, then the tablet, then . . . Kenzie. Then the light.

In the hallway, they threaded through a frozen army of machines.

"Looks like they've brought everything," his grandfather marvelled quietly. "All or nothing. Why so desperate?" The only other sounds were the squeak of Metz's wheelchair, the whine of fliers hovering motionless in the air.

Outside in the pale afternoon, yet more things lined up silently along the path. Fliers sat on hedges and on the shoulders of four more life-sizers. The lifeless eyes watched them pass.

Figures had gathered far across the lawn, at the tree line: the bald man; a tubby blur that must have been von Sudenfeld; the dark smudge and pale, round face of the ancient little girl. Behind her stood the tall man in black, massive, motionless, merging with the shadows. Kingdom was studying them closely, Alex noticed. He could almost feel Zia's vehemence on the breeze.

But one missing, Alex thought distantly, trying not to disturb the process of his other thoughts. All this time, he had seen no sign of little Hans Beckman, he realised, the toy shop owner who had helped design all these robots in the first place. He recalled the little man's unctuous, treacly voice and shivered. He supposed Beckman must be around the back of the house, directing operations at the kitchen door. He stopped wondering about it when he realised his flame had gone out.

The dogs growled as the frozen tableau around them came to life. Machines started moving, crawling, rolling, jumping. Alex clicked uselessly at the blowtorch. It spat sparks, but nothing more.

"Really would be awfully good if you could get that going again, Alex," his grandfather said. The old man whipped his Swiss Army knife from his pocket and held it to the canvas. The machines kept coming. After a second Alex got the vicious little blue flame going. It guttered alarmingly, then steadied. The robots froze again, as though they were all playing a hellish game of Statues.

"I think it's almost out of gas," Alex said. He tried to swallow.

An engine roared, coming closer. Through the trees that lined the driveway, Alex saw their rental car, moving fast.

"Harry," he said in reply to Kingdom's questioning glance.

The dark, distant shape of a life-sizer stepped from the trees to meet it, raising its hands. The car rammed into the giant robot and was halted. There came a grinding, complaining sound as Harry gunned the engine uselessly, car and machine locked in a growling stalemate.

One part of Alex's mind had gone past the tablet and opened the second door. He was getting faster. And there was Kenzie ahead, standing quietly, not even trying to speak now. Alex could sense the door to the light beyond the other boy. But it seemed much further away than before. He thought briefly about his grandfather's theory of powerful places, boosting the signal, bringing it closer. He'd just have to shove Kenzie back harder, for longer. He tensed his thoughts and pushed.

As they crept on through the garden, Alex watched the blue flame he held by the painting's frame. He thought about the varnish bubbling. He thought about the way the machines hadn't stopped when his grandfather had threatened to rip the canvas with his knife. Why? *Can't see the woods for the trees.* Seen this close, the wooden frame looked very old. Can't see the woods. Can't see the wood. The wood.

"The Shadow Gate," Alex suddenly gasped, striving to keep everything going in his mind at once. "I mean – what was it?"

"Eh?" His grandfather grunted grimly. "Well, I told you, some magical doodad. A portal the magician conjured up, an opening."

"But was it an actual *gate*? I mean, did he build a . . . structure? What would it have been made of?"

"Well, I don't know. But back then, I suppose they probably used iron, or wood, or . . . Is this really the time, do you think?"

Alex fell silent. In his thought journey, Kenzie was staggering backward as he shoved him again and again. But Kenzie was struggling, and the distance to the last door was much too far. He was never going to get there in time.

They were at the garage. It looked like it had once been a stable. More fliers perched on the roof. As Kingdom struggled to get Metz inside, Alex's blowtorch died again, for good.

Things started coming at them, fast, from all directions.

"Get inside, Alex," the old man said, then suddenly spun, hoisting the painting. Alex realised he was going to throw it, Frisbee-like.

"No, don't!"

Too late. The old man sent it spinning over the heads of the nearest robots. The fliers lifted from the garage roof and darted after it, caught it in the air, and carried it away. Then the rest of the machines rushed at Alex and his grandfather.

Alex was almost at the last door, the door to the light. He shoved Kenzie with a wild mental force that drew strength from his fear. The door slammed open as Kenzie fell back into the curtain of light beyond. Alex felt the light roaring at him. He took it in, sent it roaring back out, shaped it with words as loud as the sun.

The light flickered, Alex heard a hissing on the wind, and, for a second, the old tin robot moved in his grip. Then he and his grandfather were lifted from their feet and thrown back against the rough garage wall by a concussive wave. For a moment, the day was blindingly bright. Kingdom leapt from the garage, shielding her eyes, and started helping them inside. The light faded. She slammed the door.

"Alex," the old man said. "What did you . . . Are you okay? Can you hear me?"

Alex nodded. He couldn't do much more.

"What just . . . What did he just do?" Kingdom said. She stood with her back to the door, staring at Alex as though she had never seen him before.

Alex's grandfather shook his head. "He saved us. Let's leave it at that. I'm more worried about what it might have done to him."

"Good lord," Kingdom whispered. She stood peering through the small garage window. The old man helped Alex to his feet and they joined her.

Machines lay lifeless everywhere, spread over a vast arc of scorched white grass and smoking black gravel. The figures across the smouldering lawn had been knocked to their hands and knees. Slowly, groggily, Zia got to her knees. Some of the paralysed fliers began twitching weakly.

"Best to get moving," Alex's grandfather muttered. He considered Alex with grave concern. "You okay?"

"Just need a minute," Alex said. "Or two."

Kingdom bent by his side and whispered confidentially. "When we tangled with you, back in the office in Paris . . . I was never sure, the light was so bad, but . . . did you turn invisible?"

"Uh . . . yeah. Kind of."

Kingdom nodded. "Strange day. Still, glad to know my eyes are okay."

Alex's grandfather turned to the big car behind them. "Oh, Rolls-Royce Phantom! Little ostentatious for my tastes, but a decent old tank to have in the circumstances. Harry'll love this."

The old man practically carried Alex and put him on the back seat beside the prone Metz, then ducked into the front as Kingdom started the engine. The car was spacious, but most of the space was filled with a tangle of dogs. The one named Maia put its chin on Alex's lap and gazed at him, grumbling contentedly.

"All ready?" Kingdom said. Without waiting for an answer she threw them rocketing forward, smashing through the garage doors. Small machines crunched under their wheels and bounced off the windshield. Then they were on the main driveway. As they approached Harry's ruined car, Kingdom accelerated. The woozy life-sizer turned weakly and was knocked sideways, leaving a dent in the bonnet. Harry extricated himself from the other car and clambered in.

"Pleased to meet you," he puffed at Kingdom as he squeezed in beside Alex. "Nice motor."

"Shame we had to give them that painting." Alex's grandfather sighed grimly, as they headed for the open gates.

"Ah, but we didn't," Kingdom said cheerily as the car shot out onto rough country road.

"Eh?"

"The painting we gave up was a decoy," she said. "Bait. When we heard about the first paintings being stolen, I had a copy made. I took the *real* painting out of the frame and replaced it. So that's what they have: a fine old frame, holding a useless new forgery. The real painting's rolled up in here." She patted the sword sheath propped beside her leg and changed gear.

"What an entirely devious woman," Alex's grandfather said. "We're absolutely delighted to make your acquaintance, aren't we, Alex? Alex?"

For a moment, Alex said nothing. He was utterly drained by the narrowness of the escape, shaking from the power he had finally unleashed, and still unsure about quite how he had done it. The Kenzie connection was certain, but it perplexed him. But, for the moment, he was far more concerned with the other idea he had just finished putting together.

"It's not," he panted.

"Eh?" His grandfather turned.

"I've worked it out," Alex said bleakly. "What Harry tried to tell us. *It's not.* I think he meant it's not the *paintings*. It's not the paintings they're after, Grandad. Right, Harry?"

"Aw, crumbs." Harry's face fell. "Lad's right. I've just remembered."

"What?" the old man said. "Not with you."

Alex looked at Harry. They spoke in unison:

"It's the *frames*."

XXIX.

GET THE PICTURE

"AN THAT'S 'OW I managed to grab back the painting I rescued."

Harry had been going over his story while the car tore eastward. They had joined a flat, busy highway.

"They were taking the frames *apart*," Harry went on. "They'd chucked the painting aside. Then, lessee . . . Yeah, they were *touching* pieces of the frames against rocks, like dowsing sticks. All the broken rocks. The whatchamacallit, pulpit. Chanting, low. Yeah, an' that's when the glowing started."

The Rolls growled contentedly. Dogs snored. The unconscious Metz made a small, unhappy sound deep in his throat.

"The paintings don't add together to reveal where the Shadow Gate *is*," Alex said. "They *are* the Shadow Gate. The frames are, anyway. I think the gate was an actual wooden structure the sorcerer made. Just like with the golem's tablet: you need the tablet to hold the power or . . . reach the power; the object is part of the magic. I think the sorcerer made the gate as part of his . . . spell. Then it was dismantled and the pieces were disguised as all these frames and scattered all over the place. That's why they needed to steal the physical objects. That's why it's not always been the same eleven paintings on the list, like Evelyn said – they've sometimes switched the frames to different paintings. And that's why the robots kept coming when you were going to slash the canvas, Grandad, but stopped when I was going to burn the frame. Well? What do you reckon? Are you all right, Grandad?"

Alex's grandfather sat repeatedly clenching his left hand, then stretching it wide, wiggling the fingers. He looked up and smiled.

"Never better. Although, I feel a little embarrassed at not putting that together myself. I think you're right, Alex. Seems rather obvious now you say it. And I just gave them one of the frames they need. Old fool. Well, regardless, our immediate job remains the same: we have to get to the final painting – the final *frame* – before they do. Evelyn?"

"I have to make a phone call," Kingdom said. She pulled into a large and depressing-looking service station. While she stepped out and got on her phone, Alex's grandfather and Harry disappeared toward the shopping area.

The dogs grew alert as Metz groaned again. His eyes opened. He sat staring, trying to get his bearings, and traced a finger gently over the fresh wound on his neck.

"You okay?" Alex asked.

"Like coming back to life," Metz croaked, then smiled. "And what is happening out in the world, young man?" The dogs stared at him curiously.

"Evelyn's finding out about the last painting," Alex said. He gestured out the window. "Or trying to, anyway."

Kingdom was making animated, frustrated gestures in the rain, clearly in a heated argument with whoever she was speaking to over the phone. She clutched her head, then bent double. A few moments later, she killed the call, sat back behind the wheel, and let out a small but heartfelt scream through clenched teeth.

"Infuriating old duffer," she said. "Sounded about two hundred years old."

"Uh, did you . . . find out?" Alex asked. "What the painting is?"

"Not yet. Honestly, it was like pulling teeth. Like he was doing me a favour. With a lot about 'the protocols, young lady, the protocols.' But he told me *where* it is. Staatsgalerie museum, in Stuttgart." She checked the time. "He's asked to meet us there. We should just make it before they close. Oh, hello, Phil. Good to have you back with us. How are you feeling?"

"Weak but well," he said. "Getting stronger."

Alex was happy to note Metz seemed calmer, more assured. His grandfather and Harry reappeared. The old man clutched a bulging paper bag that turned out to contain chocolate-coated marshmallows. Harry brandished two cheap new phones, handing one to Alex.

"Harry tells me you can put the something-or-other from

your old phone into this new one," Alex's grandfather said through a full mouth.

"Just need to find a place to charge 'em," Harry muttered.

"Oh," Kingdom said. "I had a couple of outlets added to the dashboard."

"You modified a Silver Phantom?" Harry gasped. "That's sacrilege. But 'andy."

Alex's grandfather fished a new road map from his pocket and folded it to show a particular area. "Could you mark where your ruined old Castle Boll is?" he said, offering Kingdom the map and a pen. She hunted around, made a spot, and handed it back.

"And here's the Kandel, where our pulpit collapsed," Alex's grandfather said, adding another dot. "They're around, ah, twenty-two miles apart, as the crow flies." Using the blunt edge of a blade from his Swiss Army knife as a ruler, the old man drew a diagonal between the two points. They all crowded forward, staring down at it, as if something might become clear. The enigmatic line glistened blackly across the landscape.

"Clear as mud," Alex's grandfather eventually said. "So, Evelyn. Do we know where we're going?"

"Stuttgart," she said, starting the engine. "Staatsgalerie."

"Oh, lucky us." The old man hummed happily, folding the map away.

As the car moved into traffic, they fell silent, everyone following their own thoughts. Alex left his new phone charging and leaned against the window.

He considered what he had done at the château – not only calling up the blast of power but directing it just as he had wanted. Protecting them. It had exhausted him to the point where he could barely stand, but he had *done* it, and he had succeeded in making the connection faster than ever, even though it had taken more effort. His technique was working. He could learn more, he was sure. For the first time, he felt they had something on their side.

He jumped when his grandfather suddenly spoke.

"And . . . we're back in Germany . . . *now*."

Alex hadn't realised he'd been dozing. He opened his eyes to find they were crossing a huge concrete bridge spanning a wide bend of river. The landscape on the other side seemed much the same.

Soon they were rolling through a town in a shallow valley, the streets looking sleepy as another afternoon wore itself out. The pastel-coloured walls and red-tiled roofs gave the place a toytown look that reminded Alex of a little wooden village that had accompanied a train set his grandfather had bought him as a kid.

He remembered how he had enjoyed laying out the houses and shops in different arrangements as much as he had setting the engine snaking through them, using blankets and cushions and books to create a bumpy landscape of hills and tunnels around the tracks. Building worlds on his bedroom floor. He settled sleepily into the memory, oddly comforted by it.

He hadn't thought about it since he was a little kid.

He'd played with it a lot back then, during the years when he'd had his endless appointments with doctors and hospitals, running tests, taking blood, because his mother was constantly worried about how small he was. By the time he'd started school, he still only looked about three years old, but he'd finally taken a sudden spurt and . . .

Alex sat bolt upright. A thought had dropped onto the surface of his mind, hard as a diamond. It took a few panicking seconds before he could whisper the words.

"It's in *me*."

"Hmmm?" his grandfather murmured.

"Stop," Alex said. "I need to get out."

"What?" Kingdom spoke over her shoulder. "We don't really have time—" She broke off as she caught his eye in the rear-view mirror. "Hang on."

Alex was out of the car before it stopped. He ran along the grass verge, staggered, then dropped to his knees. A moment later, his grandfather's shadow fell across him.

"It's in *me*," Alex said, staring at the ground. "In my *blood*. Isn't it? The whole thing you were talking about: not ageing properly, being frozen for years without changing, then suddenly growing years older all at once. It's what was going on when I was a kid, not growing, all that time with the doctors. You were *always* there, I remember. You were always watching. You *knew* what was happening. It's in me! It's been . . . passed down."

"Ah." His grandfather hesitated, made a painful wince, then sat sadly by his side. "Well . . . maybe, Alex. But, then, maybe not. Your father, you see, when he was born, exactly the same thing happened. He was tiny as an infant, for years. But then, once he reached around nine, it all seemed to work out. Same as you, Alex. Everything started running normally. So there's every reason to believe that will be the case with you. You know: you're one more step removed from the *source*, so whatever inherited effects there are will be much weaker, diluted. If there are any inherited effects at all."

"But my dad . . ." Not for the first time, Alex found a racing new landscape of thoughts opening and struggled to keep track. "Dad was still quite young when he died. Maybe if he'd lived longer, it might have started in him again, like it did with you."

"Well," his grandfather said after a long pause. "We'll never know. But, Alex, the potion, it's not just a question of biology and chemistry. It also required a magical element to ignite it. And you've not had that. But, yes: it may be lying dormant in you. That's perhaps what the golem's tablet responded to in you, actually. It's maybe *why* it responded when your blood touched it. It's two different types of magic being brought together that shouldn't have been. Alex, I–I'm sorry. I should have never started any of this, son. I should never have thought I could have a fam— Well, I'm sorry, that's all. But here we are."

A heavy silence fell between them.

"Those deaths you talked about," Alex said after a while. "That's part of what's in me, too. In my blood. Those deaths. Murders."

"Alex. Listen very carefully. This is our history, but it wasn't our choice, and it's certainly not *your fault*. It's good to know the history, but you're not chained to it, son."

"No. I know." Alex paused. Amid his jittering jumble of thoughts, two more memories suddenly linked up. "There's nothing left of the victims' bodies, you said. The flower, the leaf, it absorbs everything . . . That newspaper story I asked you about in Harry's office, about the railway worker that went missing from the train. They just found his uniform in a heap. Was that . . . ?"

"Ah, I reckon so, Alex. I clipped that story. I've tried to keep track over the years."

"I think it's happened again," Alex whispered. "The climbers we met on the Kandel. I think I found their clothes just lying . . ."

The old man opened his mouth, but no words came. His head fell forward. "All five?" he finally managed.

Alex nodded.

"So soon," his grandfather said after a moment. "So many. That's much faster than ever before. There used to be years between . . ." He let the thought drift into silence.

"How many?" Alex said.

"How many?"

"Lives. Deaths. In the . . . potion. I mean, before you knew and went away from him. While you were still taking it."

"I don't know, son." The old man still sat with his head bowed.

"Grandad. It's not *your* fault. It's all just . . . it's horrible."

"That it is, Alex." His grandfather patted his arm. "That it is." He looked up. "And that's all the more reason for us to keep going and try to stop it. If you can."

Alex looked around, blinking. He saw Metz watching them from the back of the Rolls. Beyond the car, a castle ruin rose starkly on a hill above the village roofs, a single tower poking up like a crumbling finger thrust accusingly at the heavens. It wasn't the ruined castle Kingdom and Metz had talked about, he knew, but it seemed a menacing premonition and intensified the chill in his blood. His grandfather noticed him staring at it.

"Oh, I do love a derelict castle," the old man said, forcing cheer into his voice. Then he frowned. "Well, most of the time. Now. We really should get moving. Alex?"

Alex took a breath. He felt history pressing at his back. But the only way to go was forward.

"Yeah."

"Good man."

ALEX'S GRANDFATHER CHECKED his wristwatch as they hit the outskirts of Stuttgart. "Almost four thirty. Sunset's around half past eight. Then it's officially *Walpurgisnacht*. Although midnight will be the centre of it all, of course. That will be when they're hoping to open the gate and conduct whatever madness they're up to." He brooded darkly then shot Alex a bright smile. "Gives us almost eight hours. That's loads of time."

Alex watched the stately city passing behind the raindrops on his window. Cars nudging one another, a police car, a hearse, tourist coaches. People on the streets. Eventually, Kingdom slowed, searching for a place to park.

"Here we are," Alex's grandfather said. "The Staatsgalerie. It used to be just the old museum, Alex." The old man pointed out a stern, classical-looking building across the road. "They added this extension a few years ago."

The newer structure looked as if its designer had started to build an imposing fortress, but at the last minute a child had snuck in and scribbled happily over the plans with crayons.

For the most part it was a solid, sombre construction of heavy-looking sandstone in tones matching the old museum. But here and there were sudden wild angles, changes in level, curves and incongruous splashes of colour. Big, friendly plastic tubes of bright pink and blue marked stairs and ramps that led up from the street to the entrance, where the main facade was punctured by a huge, undulating curtain of glass in a Day-Glo-green frame, as if the wall had melted.

Harry helped Metz out. Metz tested his leg, tentatively putting weight on it.

"'Ere you go, lean on me," Harry said, offering an arm.

Metz considered him carefully, then accepted. "Thank you. My leg is better but still just a little weak."

"We won't be long," Kingdom cooed gently to her dogs. She wound down her window and closed the car door. "I have a feeling that's our man," she added sourly, nodding to the entrance.

A small, thin, elderly figure in a shabby charcoal suit and black raincoat stood by the glass wall, stooped beneath a huge black golf umbrella. His bald grey head was encircled by a white fuzz that suggested his barber was either wildly imaginative or long past caring. But, when they got up to join him, Alex saw his black eyes were sharp and watchful. The man studied them impatiently.

"Herr Morgenstern?" Kingdom said, holding out her hand. "Evelyn Kingdom, president of the Fishing Club. We spoke on the phone."

The birdlike little lawyer made a show of turning away, lifting his runny red nose, and staring haughtily at the sky, as if he hadn't heard her.

"Really?" Kingdom muttered. She traced a finger delicately over one eyebrow as if a migraine was taking root there. "Okay: *Schattentor.*"

"The museum closes in twenty minutes." The man spoke in a high, brittle bark. He produced a large fob watch on a tarnished chain and shook it under Kingdom's chin. "You have no conception of the value of my time. Who are all these people?" He flourished a pale hand without looking at them.

"They're with *me*. I'm the *president*."

"You are a very rude young woman, is what you are. But I have no time for this. Come."

"Would you mind if we borrowed your umbrella?" Alex's grandfather said.

Morgenstern looked horrified. He stepped toward the old man and drew himself to his full height, his dribbling nose now level with Alex's grandfather's chest.

"If you have the *impoliteness* even to *ask*, I don't see how I can refuse."

"Thaaank you. We'll take good care of it." The old man rolled the umbrella up tightly, then proffered it to Metz. "Not as good as a proper walking stick. But close enough." Metz took it and gave the air a small, testing swipe before leaning on it like a cane.

"Come!" Morgenstern led them inside and across the foyer, over a dimpled rubber floor the same vibrant green as the frame of the high, rippling window. Daylight poured in like liquid, the collision of light and colour setting the air singing with emerald hints.

They went through large white exhibition spaces. People struck curious poses to consider sculptures from various angles. Voices murmured. Phones clicked. A small semicircle of kids around five years old sat beneath a large abstract canvas, busily drawing with felt-tip pens, copying bright splotches of colour onto big sheets of paper. Alex watched them with a pang. It looked like fun.

Leaning on their sticks, Alex's grandfather and Metz walked together like mismatched mirror images. Metz limped slightly but moved easily enough with the aid of the umbrella.

"You feeling better?" Alex asked.

"Much," Metz said, taking in a deep, satisfied breath. "There is some pain in the leg, but it just takes a little mind over matter to ignore it. It feels good to be up and moving around again."

Eventually, they arrived in a dimmer, more traditional gallery room and gathered before a painting hanging on a burgundy wall.

"*Bohemian Landscape*, by Caspar David Friedrich," Morgenstar said fussily. "And with that, my job is done." He turned to Kingdom. "You will be receiving a bill for the umbrella. Good day."

They watched him stalk off, then turned back to the painting, except Harry, who seemed more absorbed in studying the ceiling and walls.

A landscape indeed, roughly three feet wide by two feet high. Empty green fields rolled toward a range of mountain peaks that rose in a glorious light on the horizon beneath an enormous, hazy sky. Near the centre of the image, two tall trees stood side by side alone in a meadow. Darker woods lurked beyond, on the way to the distant mountains. Just a simple, silent country scene.

"'The deeper meaning of this work lies in its composition,'" Alex's grandfather said, reading from a card on the wall. "'The two old oaks in the middle distance seem to form a gateway—' Yes. Very droll."

They stared closely at the frame. It looked old but, beyond a faint impression of scratches beneath the thick varnish, there was nothing notable.

"What do you think?" Kingdom said, scanning the gallery.

"Harry's the man for that. So, Harry?"

"Oh." Harry brightened. "Yeah. Easy peasy. Smash 'n' grab'll do it. Can we risk waiting until the place is closed?"

"It's beginning to look that way," the old man said, frowning. "Maybe they didn't know about this picture after all." He looked around, then knocked a knuckle at his forehead in frustration. "I'm constantly plagued by the feeling I'm missing something obvious."

"Smash and grab?" Alex asked.

XXX.

SMASH AND GRAB

"ARE YOU ABSOLUTELY sure about this?" Alex asked for the third time.

Rain bounced off the Rolls-Royce. Alex sat inside with his grandfather and Harry. They were parked across the street from the Staatsgalerie, in a space behind a grand building Alex's grandfather had pointed out as an opera house. A four-lane road cut between them and the now-dark museum. Little traffic moved. It was now past nine o'clock. Night was deepening. *Walpurgisnacht*, Alex thought.

"Absolutely," the old man said. He bent forward, fastening the spring-heels around his boots.

"Some jobs, Alex," Harry said, "quick and simple's best. Thing about art galleries is, they like to splash natural light around. That means skylights. Now, the power in them 'eels –" he pointed as Alex's grandfather finished attaching the second device – "means your grandad can break through the glazing and roof structure no problem. Soon as 'e does that, alarms'll go off. But 'e's only after the one painting, so that's no worry."

"Once the alarms are triggered," the old man said, shrugging into a harness with dangling, strap-like attachments, "it'll take the police at least three minutes to respond. Bags of time."

"But there must be guards in there," Alex said.

"Oh, somewhere." His grandfather nodded. "But it's a big place. And, in our experience, night guards at museums tend to be underpaid, undertrained, and undermotivated. They're basically only there to call the police if anything happens."

"So, yeah," Harry went on, counting off points on his fingers: "'E bounces up onto the roof. Smashes a nice big 'ole. Drops down inside. Nips along and pries the painting off the wall. Straps the frame over 'is back with the 'arness. Then 'e runs back along, jumps back up through the same 'ole, and bounces away. Soon as we see 'im coming out, we get movin', and then we all meet up in the park 'alf an hour later."

"It *can't* be as easy as that," Alex complained.

He supposed that the idea of his grandfather breaking into the museum would have set his nerves buzzing under any circumstances. The pressing sense that the tall man's gang lurked somewhere multiplied his anxiety infinitely. He held the old toy robot in his pocket, readying himself to begin reaching out. Better to be prepared.

"Maybe I could do it," he suddenly said.

"Eh?" The old man and Harry looked at him.

"Like, I could turn myself invisible or something. I'm sure I can do it now. If you just give me a minute to work it out."

"What? And spoil my fun?" His grandfather tutted, raised a foot, and turned his ankle so the street light caught the apparatus around the heel. "No, no. This is my job, Alex. You know, Harry, I'd almost forgotten how much I used to enjoy this."

"Like old times." Harry beamed.

The old man lifted his cane, pushed open the door, and stepped outside. Rain danced around him. "Okay, Harry. What does Evelyn say?"

Harry lifted his phone. "'Ow's it looking?"

"All clear," Kingdom's voice came over the speaker from where she was positioned as lookout behind some abandoned roadworks further along the road.

"And, Metz, Alex?"

"Uh, hello?" Alex said into his own phone to Metz, who was stationed off in the street behind the big museum. "Seen anything?"

"All quiet."

Alex's grandfather turned away, considered the buildings across the road, then suddenly turned back. He had slipped his black eye mask on. "Listen, do you hear?" he said, cocking an ear toward the opera house. Beneath the sigh of rain on the streets, Alex caught a distant swell of music.

"They're doing Puccini. Shame we're busy. Ah well. Here goes nothing. Although, eh, you shouldn't really go around robbing museums, of course, Alex."

He crouched, then leapt, touched down briefly in the middle of the road, then sprang again, to land near the museum's raised entrance.

"That really is quite impressive," came Kingdom's disembodied voice.

"Harry," Alex said. "Do you think he's up to this? I mean, he's been getting weaker and . . ."

"I know. But 'ave you ever tried talking your grandad out of something, Alex?"

They both sighed. Alex held the toy robot and prepared to begin his process of contacting the power. A thought struck him. "Did you ever remember the other thing you found out, Harry?"

"Eh?"

"When you left the message for Grandad before . . . before your accident. You said 'two things, it's not.' One was about the frames. What was the other?"

"Oh." Harry thought for a second. "Nah. Sorry."

A third jump and the old man stood on the roof above the museum doors. Alex placed his phone on the seat alongside Harry's. As he did, he noticed a new message. When he'd checked earlier, hoping for more cryptic clues from Kenzie, there had been nothing. This was from David.

> Sort of bad news here. Kenzie Mitchell's in
> a coma or something. They just found him in
> his room. Can't wake him up. Guy's an idiot,

but not good stuff. Doctors don't know what
it is yet. Tricia Babcock says it's touch and
go. Weird biz.

You okay? What's happening there?

Alex stared at the screen. It felt as though everything was
draining out from him. He sat staring at the dark floor of the
car. In the shadows there, he saw Kenzie staggering away as
he pushed him through the door in his mind, Kenzie falling
backward, disappearing into the roaring light. He let go of the
robot as if scalded.

"There 'e goes," Harry muttered, jolting Alex from his
thoughts.

Alex grabbed the binoculars Harry proffered. It took a
moment to find his grandfather, a faint grey phantom in the
dark, moving toward a wall where the level changed again.
Another great leap and he was poised on a much higher roof.
A glazed skylight ran the length of the building. The old man
padded along in a catlike crouch, hunting for a particular spot.

"Everything okay?" Harry spoke to both phones at once.

"All clear."

"Clear."

Alex's grandfather had stopped. Rain blurred in the binoculars' lens. With a curious combination of movements, he lifted
one leg and slammed a foot down, then repeated the action.
Alex heard no alarms, yet he felt them going off. Then his

grandfather was simply gone, having dropped down through the hole he'd made.

"Three minutes," Harry muttered, checking his watch.

Alex glanced around. Harry was clearly going through every moment of the job along with Alex's grandfather, acting out the movements. His head nodded silently as he counted off the footsteps from the place where the old man had landed to the wall where the painting hung.

From the corner of his eye, Alex caught a change across the road. Lights had come on behind the crazy window of the museum's foyer. Shadows flitted inside.

"Uh-oh."

"Eh?" Harry looked up, then dismissed it. "No worries. Two minutes twenty."

Continuing his mime of the robbery, Harry lifted his hands, turning them as though working with some tool.

"Hurry up," Alex whispered.

Harry ignored him. He slipped off an invisible harness, worked to secure it to the invisible painting, then pulled it back on. He paused, motionless for several beats, then started nodding again, marking each step of Alex's grandfather's return to the point where he had broken in.

"Here we go," Harry murmured happily. "Back out any second. And still a minute left."

Alex trained his binoculars on the museum again, trying to locate the right place. A distant siren sounded. Rain stirred restlessly.

"Do you see something?" Kingdom's concerned voice suddenly sounded over the phone.

"Where?" Harry said gently and seriously, lifting his binoculars.

"On the roof. Wait. Maybe it was just the rain."

The siren was getting closer.

"Metz?" Harry said.

"No sign of anything here."

Alex shifted his glasses frantically. The only movement was the steely shiver of rain – then he tracked back. There was something else, behind the rain.

"Oh no," Kingdom breathed.

A dim, massive figure rose from a crouch and stepped stiffly toward the ragged opening where Alex's grandfather had broken in.

"Bloody Nora," Harry whispered.

"What'll we do?" Alex said.

"Too late."

Alex lifted his binoculars again in time to see his grandfather come springing up through the hole in the roof, wearing the painting like a flat turtle-shell on his back. The old man landed lightly and bowed theatrically in their direction. The tall man came forward, fast, lashing out.

Alex's grandfather must have heard something. He ducked, not quite far enough. The swiping stab caught him on the shoulder, sent him spinning, tripping toward the roof's edge.

Alex threw open the door. "Grandad!"

Up there, his grandfather recovered, balanced, then jumped, springing from the high roof to a flat section beneath, where he instantly leapt again to escape the dark figure bounding down behind him.

Alex grabbed for his rucksack and frantically searched until he found the flier. Then he was running, already in the road, ignoring Harry's calls.

He hurdled the barrier in the centre, dodged a lone car that swerved around him, horn blaring. All the while he squinted up, trying to keep his eyes fixed on the two vague figures bouncing around the museum complex's roofs.

His grandfather suddenly changed direction, springing back the way he had come, flying past his pursuer. Mid-leap, at the peak of their arcing jumps, the two dark figures struck out at each other. The old man's thrusting cane caught the tall man under the chin, snapping back his head. At the same time, Alex's grandfather shuddered and spun from an unseen blow.

Both fell, disappearing from Alex's sight. He was too close to the building to see them now unless they were at the very edge of the roof. Far along the road to his right, he caught the blue glimmer of a distant police car's flashing light.

Almost by instinct, he pulled out the old toy robot. It grinned up at him.

Kenzie. He couldn't do it.

He stuffed it away, pulled out the flier, unwrapped the sock from its eyes, and rammed home the lock of his hair from his jeans pocket. He hesitated as his skin remembered the sting of salt on his fingertips in the hotel the last time he had used it. "Always a price to pay," he whispered. Very well. He'd pay it. He steadied his mind, then threw the little machine up, building his mental bridge faster than ever, chasing the flier with a thought that took it higher.

A vague aerial view of the roofscape came to him in staccato flashes. Two figures fighting and jumping wildly. His grandfather was trying to head toward the old section of the museum. The tall figure crouched and sprang, hurtling ahead, cutting him off.

Alex sent the flier plummeting toward the tall man, barely thinking about what he was doing. Seconds before he struck, the figure turned his face up, sunglasses staring. The distraction was enough for Alex's grandfather to hop away, but he was caught by a vicious swipe from somewhere as he jumped – it seemed to have come from behind, but Alex couldn't work out how. The tall man was too far away. Did he have a flier of his own in the fray?

Alex abandoned the question as he went into attack with his own machine, striking out with his hook and blade. The dark figure flinched, dropping his knife to clutch at his face with both hands. Then Alex was struck by another wicked blow he hadn't seen coming, and sent spinning sickeningly through the air.

Below, the real Alex sprinting along the street stumbled and fell as his mind flooded with pain. His vision bled to black. He lay groggy on the damp pavement, then pulled himself up and stumbled in the direction his grandfather had gone.

The old museum extended to a corner where another road cut across. Alex looked up, hunting the roofline, then down, scanning the ground. A border of tangled bushes and trees ran along the other side of the street. In the shadows beside it lay an odd, motionless heap, half on the road.

Alex ran over and knelt. His grandfather was out cold, face down on the wet pavement. The painting remained strapped to his back. The fingers of one outstretched hand still curled loosely around his cane

"Grandad. Grandad!"

He shook the old man's shoulder. Nothing. Trying to contain his panic, Alex bent to the old man's mouth and listened. A thin breath. He tried rousing him again, to no avail. He looked back to the roof looming across the road. Nothing. Yet.

Beyond the corner, the whooping police siren abruptly fell silent.

Alex searched around, hunting for inspiration. Traffic was coming along the road at them, fast. He grabbed his grandfather's shoulders and hauled him safely onto the verge as a truck rumbled heavily past, inches away.

With difficulty, Alex slipped the harness from the old man and propped the painting against the bush. He took the old toy robot from his pocket, thinking hard about his options.

He could try to connect, rush to find the light, work some

mighty blasting wonder, end all this now. But that might end Kenzie with it. He was almost certain of that.

Even before, when Alex had used the tablet barely conscious of what he was doing or how, Kenzie had started growing quieter, weaker. Now that he had started using it consciously, calling up greater and greater forces – creating the blast at the château, raising Harry – Kenzie had fallen into a coma. Somehow what Alex was doing with the tablet was taking a toll on Kenzie.

There's always a price to be paid. The memory of his grandfather's words hit him again like a dead weight. Maybe Kenzie was paying the price that Alex should have been for using the tablet.

He crouched, frozen, looking at the old man lying helpless before him. Sacrifice Kenzie to save everything else. That seemed to be the choice.

"No," Alex said to himself. Then again. "No."

He wouldn't do it. He refused. And he couldn't risk having the tablet near him. He might use it by accident. Or in desperation.

He slipped the old toy into the inside pocket of his grandfather's coat. Then he rolled the unconscious figure into the undergrowth as far as he could.

Alex looked back. A chill ran through him as a silhouette came striding to the edge of the museum's roof and paused. The tall man stood against the bulging charcoal sky, head turning slowly, hunting.

He only had a few seconds before he was discovered. Save his grandad. Save the frame. Save everything. How?

He looked to the corner, hoping for Harry or Kingdom. The road was empty. The painting stood to his right. Pattering rain drummed pleasantly on the canvas. To his left, his grandfather's feet stuck out from under the bush. The spring-heels glinted dully.

Alex forced himself to start moving before he had time to talk himself out of it. He worked at the spring-heels with fast, trembling fingers until he had them fastened around his own feet. He examined the harness, then pulled the painting across his back.

On the roof across from him, the tall man suddenly stiffened, peered, crouched.

Alex cinched the buckle tight at his waist. Too late. The shadow had launched in a high, arcing jump. The leaping figure passed over him and landed close behind.

Alex turned to face him, only to be knocked aside as Kingdom came sprinting past, her dogs right behind her. Without breaking stride, she pulled her rapier from its sheath on her back.

"Go, Alex, get it away!"

The tall man swung his knife at her in a ferocious swipe. In one fluid motion, Kingdom ducked, moved forward, and thrust at his throat. He backed up. She attacked again, dodged another lethal blow – then her foot slipped on the wet ground and she was on her back.

The tall man closed in. One of the dogs bolted from the pack.

"Maia!" Kingdom shouted. "No! Stay!"

The big animal ignored her. It crouched to leap. The man flung a savage fist to meet it – but it was as if the dog had predicted his reaction, because she feinted left, only jumping when the tall man had already started his swing and was off-balance. Maia pounced and crashed into him with all four paws, sending him sprawling. The dog skipped safely away, trotting happily back to her owner.

"Bad girl," Kingdom said affectionately. "Alex, just get it out of here! I'll hold him off."

Alex started running back across the road toward the old museum as fast as he could, although with the heavy equipment at his ankles, it was more an ungainly stumble. He glanced up, urgently calculating distance and height. He crouched, turned his heels in the motion he hoped would engage the mechanism, and pushed hard.

Alex leapt.

XXXI.

OVER STUTTGART

AN EXPLOSION WENT off beneath him, but this time he was ready. For an instant, as he rocketed upward, Alex experienced a thrill similar to that which he had felt when soaring with his flier. His elation was whipped away on the wind as he realised he had been flung far too high. He saw the old museum dropping away beneath him. Then he was plummeting toward its roof, arms and legs windmilling wildly, trying to grab the air.

His flailing right foot hit first. Part of Alex's mind briefly noted how the machine strapped around it acted to absorb the shock of the impact with a violent hiss. Then he was sent tumbling forward.

He hauled himself up, panting, surprised to find he could stand, and surveyed the strange terrain. The sky felt close and cool. City lights gleamed low around him. A section of peaked roofs stretched dimly away toward the new part of the museum. He searched for the best spot to land, gauging the distance, and tried to recall everything his grandfather had told him about the devices, which wasn't much. *Basically, the spring-heels multiply the force of your leap. Although it gets a little exponential after a certain point. . .*

A sharp hiss from behind announced the tall man's arrival. Alex didn't look back. He jumped.

This time he put less force into the leap. He told his body it was just like jumping over a large puddle in the road. As he sailed through dark air, a gust of wind caught the canvas at his shoulders, slowing his flight, dragging him back. He landed lightly, the heels sighed, and for a millisecond he was pleased with himself. But he had undershot. Now he was sliding backward down a slick slope of tiles, the edge coming up fast.

In frantic reflex, he stamped down hard with one foot, forgetting what would happen. The single spring engaged. The lopsided eruption sent him somersaulting high and helpless, heels over head.

His feet slammed down on another part of the roof, then flung him up again. He shot toward a sheer wall, curled instinctively, forcing his legs to lead, kicked and cannoned away. As he bounced like a rubber ball, the next few seconds were a jumble of rushing impressions. Walls and roofs, Stuttgart spinning, night sky and street lights.

Some calm section of his mind was determined to solve the problem. In his desperation, he was trying to cushion the expected shock instead of just letting the heels do their work. That was his mistake. With a huge effort of will, he forced himself to surrender control. Suddenly, he was falling, straight down, but he hit the ground almost gently, the spring-heels exhaled, and he flopped forward onto his hands and knees, gasping.

Lifting his head, dizzy, Alex shrank from a group of tall people gathered around him. Then he realised they were statues.

He had dropped down into a circular courtyard in the middle of the museum complex, its high walls open to the cloudy sky. The pale statues stood on plinths, robed stone women with staring blank eyes. Arched windows loomed behind them. A curving ramp ran up around the walls.

And at the top stood the tall man.

The dark figure launched at him. Alex got to his feet and jumped – or tried. Something grabbed his leg, just for a second, but it was enough to pull him slamming back down onto the paving slabs.

Alex dragged himself behind a statue and risked a look from behind its legs. The tall man stood in the shadows on the other side of the circular arena.

"Please, now. Come out where I can see you. Let us stop this foolishness. We can talk, you and I, and avoid further unpleasantness. Please."

Alex flinched back in confusion. This wasn't the voice he had been expecting. But the soft, treacly tones were all too familiar.

He snuck another glance. The figure took one stiff, heavy

step into the courtyard, peering in Alex's direction. The man removed his large sunglasses to reveal round, wire-framed spectacles beneath. He wore a yellow-and-black spotted scarf around his throat. His long black coat hung open. Faint shapes moved strangely inside.

"I wish you no harm. Please."

It took several seconds for Alex to process what he was seeing. This wasn't the tall man at all. This was little Hans Beckman. Yet somehow he stood massively tall and broad. There was a look of intense satisfaction on his face.

Alex could just make out vague, horrible details. As far as he could tell, Beckman had hollowed out the body of a lifesizer robot, and attached himself hideously inside, wearing the machine's colossal carcass like a mechanised suit of armour – an awful, powerful extension of his body.

Medical-looking tubes ran from grubby, bandaged spots around Beckman's head and neck, disappearing inside the machine. The things Alex could see writhing softly within his coat were thin, coiled wire attachments, like Slinkys. They hung from Beckman's robotic torso as ghastly extra arms, six in all. At the end of each bobbed a twitching, glove-like hand.

One of the hands suddenly came shooting out, the coiled wire stretching across the courtyard with a fast, stinging *shish*. As Alex stared at the padded white fist flying at him, he found himself thinking dumbly about the cheerful hands of Mickey Mouse, until he remembered to duck.

The wire wrapped around the statue above him. He heard a grating, slicing sound. Something fell crunching down beside him.

The marble head lay at his feet, shorn clean off.

"Apologies." Beckman sniggered. "This is only a rough prototype. I have yet to refine control. See?"

Another fist lashed out. This one a cartoonish boxing glove. Another stone head dropped heavily to the ground.

"I always had trouble controlling the *big* machines, you see," Beckman murmured, gesturing humbly at his great mechanical physique. "My mind doesn't have the muscles. I needed always to stay close to keep control. So I thought: why not get as close as I can? Wire myself in? Hard-wired. Like this, my thoughts go directly through the mechanism. I really don't know my own strength. This is how I killed your friend Morecambe. It was an accident. I only meant to knock him out. I gave him just a tap, like this."

Beckman lashed a huge arm at the wall behind him, gouging a hole in the concrete.

"But I mean you no harm. Quite the opposite. Please, now."

Alex said nothing. He was furiously concentrating.

"Very well." Beckman came striding toward him.

Reaching out his mind, Alex finally found his flier. It lay not far away on the roof above. One wing was damaged, so it kept veering left as it haltingly flew. He fought to compensate, urging the flier to move faster, up. Looking down from its eyes, he saw the circular courtyard below, the shadowy figure stalking across it. He dived at Beckman in a jackknife.

Beckman somehow sensed the attack. He turned, sending a glove-hand shishing up to meet the flier midair. In the same moment, the dark windows behind the broken statues blazed with light. Inside the museum, shadowy police and guards came running. Beckman whirled around to them.

The distraction was enough. Alex took his chance and leapt. Beckman swatted the flier spinning away over the roof with a blow that left Alex feeling like his mind had been stabbed with a glass shard. He slammed against the top of the wall and hung clinging to the edge, scratching at slippery stonework for a grip. The weighty heels were dragging him down. A padded white fist smashed into the wall, inches away from him. Alex heaved himself over, pain ringing in his head.

He could just make out the road where Harry had parked ahead. Alex saw his stunned flier lying between him and the roof's edge. Another fist pounded down behind him, sending up a dust cloud of pulverised concrete, glittering in the moonlight. This glove resembled the clawed, furry paw from a Wolfman costume. It began scuttling like a crab straight for him.

Alex lurched up and ran stiffly, staggering as he picked up the unresponsive flier. Wind tugged at the painting on his back as he hurled himself off the roof.

He jumped wildly, arcing over the street in a leap that sent him crashing down into the roadworks opposite, sprawling face-first in a mound of damp sand. Abandoned tools scattered about him as he tumbled forward.

He sat up, wiping grit from his eyes. There was a strange heaviness pressing down on his neck. A traffic cone had wedged itself firmly around the top of his head. No sign of Harry or Kingdom or the Rolls-Royce. But a group of well-dressed people now stood outside the opera house along the road, staring at him open-mouthed. Many clutched wine glasses and cigarettes. It must have been the interval. Some started coming toward him.

More footsteps were sounding from his side, closer. Police were running, almost on him. No one seemed to notice Beck-man watching, crouched like a shadowy gargoyle atop the museum.

Alex grabbed at a broom lying amid the debris and, with a desperate yell, swung it wildly to ward off the nearest police-man, then crouched and jumped hard, passing over the opera-goers. Dumbfounded faces swung up to watch him go.

When he touched down, he instantly sprang back up, leap-frogging along the dark street until a blast of wind threw him off course. His ankle twisted as he hit the ground. The traffic cone dropped from his head. Rain lashed down.

Alex gingerly tried a step and gasped at the pain. Not far ahead, he spotted a narrow alleyway between buildings. He still held the broom. Ramming it under his arm for support, he made a hopping run for cover.

Stumbling into the alley, he cursed as the edge of the paint-ing cracked against the wall. Beckman couldn't be too far behind. The picture frame scraped the brickwork again. It was hampering his movements, both on the ground and when he tried to leap.

Shrugging out of the harness, he dug from his pocket the nail scissors Zia had thrown him in the well. The little blades were honed to wicked sharpness. He looked at the painting. If he could remove it, it wouldn't catch the wind. He paused for just a moment, then stabbed the blade into the canvas, cutting it from the frame.

He thought he heard a hiss in the street, not far away. Several inches of painting remained attached. Alex ripped it out. He left the painting rolled against the wall, tucked the frame under his arm, then ran for the far end of the alley.

He came out onto a tree-lined street. A few people hurried along, hunched in hoods or hidden behind umbrellas. Cars swished past. Alex limped fast, head down, forcing his thoughts into order.

He'd left his phone in the car, where they had been keeping the line open to Metz on lookout. Why hadn't they spotted Beckman on the roof? They had planned to meet in a nearby park after the robbery. He tried to recall the map he'd been shown and work out where he was. Maybe he could use the flier, if it wasn't too badly damaged. But when he tried, he couldn't feel anything from it.

As soon as he got his bearings, he would double back to where his grandfather had fallen. Harry might have found the old man already, or maybe his grandfather had come to. But he had to check. If there was no one there, he would head for the rendezvous. It was as much of a plan as he could manage.

Through the traffic ahead, he spotted the headlights of a car flashing quickly on and off as it came toward him. Then again. With a surge of relief, he recognised the car. It was unmistakable. Kingdom's Silver Phantom.

Metz was behind the wheel.

"I got it," Alex gasped as he clambered in and slammed the door. "The frame. Is my grandad okay? Where's everyone else?"

"Hmm?" Metz glanced over as they started moving. "Oh, looking for you. Yes, the old man is fine. We split up. They're on foot. We decided I should take the car. My leg, you see."

"I think I know what Harry was trying to say," Alex panted, talking more to himself, trying to calm down. "When he said, 'It's not . . .' he meant, it's not the tall man."

"Oh yes?" Metz turned a corner and slowed, searching the street ahead. "The tall man?"

"It was Hans Beckman," Alex went on. He dropped the broom into the seat behind without looking, and bent to free his injured foot from the cumbersome mechanical springs. Metz stopped the car. They sat, engine idling.

"Beckman," Alex repeated, still working it out for himself. His racing thoughts kept colliding. "I can't remember if we told you about him. . . But then, that means we've not seen the tall man at all. Even when I thought I saw him, outside Harry's office in Paris. It was Beckman. It was Beckman who stabbed your leg. I heard him laughing. Giggling. So where's the tall man?"

"He's right *here*, silly bunny," said a voice from behind. Alex felt something sharp scratch gently at his Adam's apple. In the rearview mirror, he saw Zia sit up, grinning. She held one arm curled around his neck, her little hand clutching a huge, old razor at his throat.

"That's Father in there, see?"

Alex looked dumbly in the direction the triumphant purple fingernail pointed. Metz smiled back at him.

"A very weak mind, this one. He was almost grateful to give up," Metz said. Except, Alex suddenly realised, it was no longer Metz at all.

With piercing clarity, he recalled his grandfather speaking as they sat together in a high tree, telling him horrible, impossible things about the tall man: *He was exploring the possibility of* migrating consciousness. *Throwing your mind into another body . . . just slip your personality into someone else, take them over . . .*

"All it took was the teensiest wee sample of his blood," Zia bubbled. "Father's Soaring Spirit got it during that nonsense at the big house in France. And weren't *you* showing off back there with your exploding head, magic bunny. You should be careful with that, Alexander. You might almost have hurt me. And then I would have been very mad *indeed*. We'll have to teach you to use it properly. And I still want my scissors back."

A towering figure was coming along the street, walking stiffly in the rain. As Metz signalled him, the car's flashing lights reflected from round glasses lenses.

Alex watched Beckman approaching. He felt as though he were drowning in slow motion.

"Now," said the man who wasn't Metz. He patted the frame Alex had brought him. "The gate."

XXXII.

TOWERS AND MOONS
AND EVERYONE FORGOT

THE CAR TORE south, Stuttgart fell behind, and neighbouring towns passed as smears of light. Then they were out on a highway between fields under the enormous sky. A racing moon kept pace above, playing peekaboo through ragged clouds.

Alex had been forced onto the back seat beside Beckman. His hulking robotic body perfumed the car with scents of oil and metal tinged with sweet, medicinal overtones. Beckman had removed the hand from one of his spring-arms, and the razor-like wire now looped thinly around Alex. Any time he moved, Beckman's grip tightened threateningly.

The possessed Metz drove like a demon, but from what Alex could see in the mirror, the man was exhausted. Sweat beaded his grey brow over red eyes. Zia sat alongside him. Once, she placed a hand on his arm.

"Father?" She spoke in a tender tone Alex had never heard from her.

"I find even a will as weak as this tiring now." The man

gestured contemptuously at himself with pale fingers. "I must rest. Rebuild energy."

"I could drive," Zia said.

"We're almost there." The engine grumbled as he accelerated.

Zia had searched Alex and taken away his damaged flier. Now she wound down her window and stuck her hand out. Between thumb and forefinger, she held the lock of Alex's hair. He watched it blowing in her grip. Then, with a flick of her wrist, she let it go into the wind. "Stop you getting any ideas." She smiled over her shoulder as she stowed the little machine inside her coat.

Eventually, the tall man turned onto a side road, driving over a gravel track, then a narrow dirt trail, the car shuddering as the surface changed. They came to a sudden stop, and he instantly slumped forward as far as his seat belt allowed, hanging limp over the steering wheel, out cold.

Alex could make out two vehicles waiting in the lonely blue gloom ahead. The transit van he had seen on the Kandel, and a large, long car it took a moment to identify.

A hearse.

Zia jumped out and ran to it. She pulled open the door at the back then clambered inside, out of sight. As Alex leaned forward, trying to see, Beckman's coil constricted around him in warning, cutting into his arms

"Don't move, please," Beckman said pleasantly. "We will be on our way soon. You are very privileged, you know. You will be there to witness the opening of the gate. Something no one has seen in centuries. The Shadow Gate of Boll," Beckman said the phrase in a soft, happy singsong, as if reciting a favourite lesson. Alex felt a nauseating shiver of excitement pulsing through the wire loop that bound him.

"They took it apart," Beckman went on, gazing into the night. "All those hundreds of years ago, they took the gate apart. Too scared to destroy it, you see. Or maybe too curious. But, of course, you can understand that. You had the chance to destroy the name of God, after all, and you chose not to. Perhaps, in their hearts, they secretly always longed for the gate to be opened again. And now we have put it back together. And I helped."

Alex peered at Beckman, morbidly fascinated by the wounds around the little man's neck, bruised areas from which thin tubes ran down into his mechanical torso. Thick liquid quivered inside the transparent plastic lines as Beckman turned eagerly to Alex, his little head swivelling around on top of the unmoving body.

"You will see soon," Beckman said. "The unseen. It's only right you should be there. It's because of you the gate will be opened again, you know."

"What? What do you mean?"

"Your meddling brought the fire down on him. In Prague." Beckman spoke as though patiently explaining something very obvious. "*That* led us to *this*. He has studied the gate stories for such a long time but always hesitated to make the attempt. Until now. Too dangerous. Only to be tried as a last resort. But now, here we are. At the last resort. Or second last, maybe."

Alex jumped in his skin as the car door was pulled open.

"What are you saying to the rabbit?" Zia demanded, nodding at Alex. Beneath her arm, she clutched a thick padded cushion brightly patterned with picnicking teddy bears.

"Nothing," Beckman protested placatingly, bowing his head.

"Loose lips sink little tin men," Zia scolded. "We will begin Alexander's education when the time is appropriate. If such time ever comes. In the meantime: *shtum*. Now, move that one." She pointed at Metz's limp form. "We'll take him, in case Father needs to use him again."

Obeying, Beckman stepped out, dragging Alex on the end of the wire. Flexing his massive mechanical arms, he lifted Metz from behind the steering wheel, carried him around the car, and dumped him on the passenger seat, then worked hurriedly to bind Metz's hands to the door handle.

Von Sudenfeld stood by the van, watching them. The bald man sat at the wheel. They had opened the van's side door, and by the stark light inside Alex saw it was kitted out as a mobile workshop, a mix of electrician's tools, engineering gear, and medical equipment. Robot parts were stacked on shelves. Fliers hung upside down from the ceiling. Von Sudenfeld straightened as Zia brought him the old empty wooden frame. He inspected it briefly, slanting it in the light, then slipped it inside the van, slamming the door.

Zia returned to the Silver Phantom, balanced her cushion on the driver's seat, then perched on it, impatiently watching Beckman and Alex until they were all inside again.

"If we're quite ready."

She stretched to reach the pedals, the engine roared, and soon they were on the main road, hurtling southward, the other vehicles following. At a certain point, the van bearing von Sudenfeld, the bald man, and the old picture frame peeled off onto a road that split away in another direction. Zia tooted the horn jubilantly as they went.

"There it goes," she sang, bouncing on her cushion. She revved the engine. "Vroom-vroom! What a lovely big motorcar! I think I'll keep it. If there are still any roads left after."

Metz's limp form bobbed beside her as she enthusiastically spun the wheel, changing lanes. He gave one faint, confused groan, then fell silent again.

At spots along the dark horizon, distant fireworks flowered, reds, golds, and greens flashing and fading. As they slowed to enter a village, a giant flare exploded just above, sending down a sparkling shower of intense purples and blues.

"Look, bunny," Zia said as they crawled along the main street. "Celebrating Walpurgis Night. See how funny they are? Happy little fruit flies."

The town's Walpurgis Night celebrations were in full, noisy swing. Cavorting forms crammed pavements in the wavering light and shadows of swaying lanterns. Music pulsed. It seemed as if half of the town's inhabitants had dressed up for the occasion. Everywhere Alex turned, people loomed at the car in outlandish masks of painted wood and papier-mâché: merry gangs of devils, witches, and wolves, alongside other, weirder, more obscurely grotesque and twisted faces.

"'When people put masks *on*, they're really taking their masks *off*,'" Zia announced in a haughty, professorial tone. "Has your grandaddy bored you with that philosophical pearl yet, Alexander? That used to be one of his very favourite bits of puffed-up windbaggery. Although, to be fair, on nights like this, I can see what he means."

A small bonfire had been set up at an intersection. As Zia nudged the Rolls past, happy witches and devils took turns leaping through the flames, using pitchforks and broomsticks like little vaulting poles. A circle of people cheered them on, waving bottles. In the flickering firelight, the masks seemed alive.

Reaching the town's outskirts, Zia accelerated through a stretch of unlit country, then stopped as the road ran out. The Black Forest loomed ahead, solidly filling the horizon, blacker than the night. The hearse rolled up behind them.

"C'mon, walkies." Zia jumped out.

"I can't walk like this," Alex complained angrily as Beckman dragged him from the car. He gestured at the wire looped around him, pinning his arms to his sides. "I twisted my ankle. I'll need to use the broom or something as support."

"Little knocks and sprains." Zia wrinkled her nose in disdain. "Coughs and colds and lumps and bumps. What a ridiculous way to exist. We do without them." Her face suddenly fell. "It's only the really big hurts hurt us."

She nodded to Beckman. "Let him take his stupid brush. Hold his other arm. If he tries anything, knock him out. Oh, but do be careful not to *kill* this one quite so much, hmmm?"

She grinned horridly, then almost skipped to the hearse. A life-sizer climbed from the driver's seat and strode to the back. Beckman moved to join it, pulling Alex along behind. The robot opened the hearse's back.

There was indeed a coffin inside, a huge one of heavy black wood, intricately carved with spiralling galaxies of countless numbers, letters, and symbols that Alex could just make out.

Atop the casket, tied in place by black-and-purple ribbons, sat a similarly inscribed plant pot. As Beckman pulled the door wider, Alex saw the flower. It was an unimaginably hideous thing: a single, ugly bloom, glowing pale in the moonlight, and, growing from the stem, a solitary new leaf that horribly suggested a kind of living green flesh.

Zia measured the leaf between her fingers, then turned smiling to Alex. "Soon be time for its dinner again. It's always hungry just now." She clambered inside to retrieve the flower, then jumped back down, clutching it to her chest.

"Come on."

They walked in line, Zia leading with a bright torch. The life-sizer and Beckman went next, carrying the enormous coffin between them. Alex came stumbling after, tugged along on Beckman's wire. As he crossed into the forest, the trees glimmered red, reflecting another mighty firework hanging like a distress flare above the little town behind them.

The woods closed in. Aside from the torch's beam dancing on the trees ahead, the darkness was absolute. A heavy, spicy smell clung to the air. The track grew thin, the ground treacherous and rocky. Once or twice, as they trudged deeper, came the growling, splashing sounds of waterfalls nearby. All the while Zia cooed a gentle song to the plant.

Eventually, they left what path there was and started labouring up a steep slope. Alex dug into the wet earth with his makeshift crutch and dragged himself forward, reluctantly using his weak foot. Each step still sent pain flashing through him, though it wasn't as sharp as before.

As they neared the brow of the hill, the trees thinned and suddenly he had his first sight of the ruined castle that lay hidden in the forest, stark and alone on the ridge above.

Perhaps it was the darkness he had emerged from, but the moonlight seemed stronger. The pale, crumbling stone almost glowed. A sign cautioning against going any nearer stood planted beside a fence blocking the way.

Really, though, Alex felt there was little need to ward people away from this place. For one thing, its hazardous condition was plain to see. The ancient ruin had been corroded by the centuries. The decomposing relic of a once-strong tower poked up like a blunted old fang, riddled with rot. Alongside, the high remaining walls were like unsupported curtains of stone that might collapse any moment.

But that wasn't it. Something about the ruin itself, the very way it sat there, seemed to generate its own forbidding atmosphere. The place lay shrouded in a thick, silent sense of time and decay best left undisturbed. Mottled by moss, the cracked grey facade had a strange, organic look. The empty black windows made Alex think of skulls that had been petrified in wide-eyed, open-mouthed grimaces, crying out frozen warnings. Everything sent the same ominous message: *stay away*.

Zia moved aside to let the life-sizer kick down the fence, then hurried on, passing beneath a high archway, torch beam bouncing.

"Mind your paws on the way down, bunny," the disappearing shadow called. "We don't want you snapping your neck."

It was not an unlikely prospect. Beyond the arch, the ground fell away steeply. As they went lumbering down, Alex found himself sliding helplessly, caught in a mini-landslide as loose rubble gave way. Beckman's loop of wire bit into his arm, saving him.

Finally, they stood down in a desolate space strewn with strangely shaped rocks that Alex realised weren't rocks at all but fragments of long-destroyed walls. The area must once have been the castle vaults but now lay open to the elements. The broken tower loomed above at the top of the slope they had come down. The full moon hung almost directly over it.

"Towers and moons," Zia said, catching his glance. "And everyone forgot but us." She turned to Beckman. "Quickly now."

As Beckman and the life-sizer lowered the coffin, Alex noticed a new detail. There was a small glass panel in the lid, about where the face would be on a body.

The glass was misted from inside.

Beckman's wire arm lengthened, unspooling with a shivering

sound as he and the lumbering robot disappeared off into darkness beyond the moonlight, leaving Alex leaning on his makeshift support. He glanced down and saw that he was standing on something. It took a moment to recognise the discarded old painting covered in footprints. A woman holding out a plate, forever offering a waffle nobody wanted.

Zia placed her plant pot down and started fussing with two large black pebbles that lay near the centre of the space, some distance apart. Smooth and shiny, they seemed out of place amid the dirty old rubble, as if they were recent additions.

She produced a compass and measuring tape. Studying the needle, she shifted the stones, making tiny, just-so adjustments. Finally, she took a small rock from her pocket and firmly tapped each stone three times before nodding and stepping back, dusting her hands. She turned to Alex, closed her eyes, then raised a finger, pointing to the sky behind her.

"Here it comes."

Alex looked up, mystified. Then he saw it. Two fliers were approaching, carrying the empty old picture frame between them. As the little machines landed, the life-sizer and Beckman reappeared, dragging a massive form shrouded in tarpaulin. Zia stepped forward and pulled the covering away, then helped manoeuvre the object into position between the two stone markers.

It was a strange assemblage, but Alex knew instantly what he was looking at: all of the stolen frames, broken into pieces and joined together to form one huge structure.

The frame that had held the enormous painting stolen from

the museum in Munich – *The Great Last Judgment* – was intact, surrounding the rest. Within it, the other pieces had been lashed together in a rough, crisscross arrangement. At the bottom left corner, Alex saw the space for the last frame, which the fliers had just dropped by Zia's boots.

"The Shadow Gate of Boll," she said, kneeling to begin knocking the final frame apart. "You honestly *don't* know how lucky you are to see this, rabbit. It's been over five hundred years since it stood intact."

With a weary blink, she sent the two fliers up and off, vanishing toward the trees. She finished tying the wooden strands into place and stood. "Look, see how happy it is?" As she spoke, she took the rock from her pocket and gently touched it to the structure. For a second, the entire gate pulsed with glimmering, white-blue light.

"Now, now, not yet," Zia said soothingly, removing the rock. The light died. She squinted up at the moon over the tower, wielding her thumb like an artist gauging a measurement. "Soon, though. Hans, toss me the astrolabe."

Beckman threw something she caught easily. When she turned back, Alex saw it was a flat, brassy metal disc. She held it up at arm's length and sighted along it toward some point in the sky, then drew it back toward her and fiddled minutely with it, muttering. Within the outer disc, several flat concentric plates were housed, all elaborately inscribed. She dialled one around a few notches, held the thing to the sky again, and nodded, satisfied.

As she tucked it away in her coat, she caught Alex's eye. "Not seen one of those before? That's a *computer*, rabbit. A proper computer, one that tells you important things, not like the distractions you play with." She turned away. "Continue, Hans."

Beckman and the life-sizer had removed the casket's lid. Now they slid away the side panels to reveal the body stretched out within.

The tall man.

He lay on a red velvet base, arms folded across his chest, hands loosely joined over his cane's silvery handle. His black coat was folded like a pillow under his head, and his shirt-sleeves were rolled up over his forearms, exposing pale skin covered in interconnecting swirls of illegible black writing. The edge of a thick, dark patch of scars just barely showed on the underside of one arm.

But it was the man's face that made Alex shiver most. Or, rather, the lack of a face. A rigid white mask covered his visage entirely, from hairline to chin. It appeared moulded to replicate the features hidden beneath, but was utterly, eerily, expression-less. There were two eyeholes cut in the mask.

The body seemed lifeless. But Alex thought about the thin layer of mist on the window of the coffin's lid and stared harder, then started in fright when the eyes behind the blank mask snapped open, as dark and wild as the heavens above.

XXXIII.

GATE, LOCK, KEY

"LOOK AT YOU, all lost in the woods," Zia called to Alex. She shifted the flower so it stood by the gate structure with its single leaf touching the old wood, then scooped up some of the surrounding dirt and poured it into the pot, patting it around the stem. As she worked, she sang reassuringly to the plant: "We're poor wittle wabbits who've wost our way . . ."

"Scared, yes?" she continued happily, smiling over her shoulder. She stood, wiping her palms on a silk handkerchief bearing a chequerboard pattern of purple and black.

"What's . . . wrong with him?" Alex still stared at the figure on the ground. The eyes behind the mask burned with an awful frenzy. The flesh Alex glimpsed around them looked ravaged.

"What's *wrong*?" Zia suddenly exploded. "Look at him, dumb-dumb! See what you did! The fire came down on him. It would have killed anyone else. Straight to dust. But we have protection, Thumper." She gestured to the plant.

"Still," she continued, forcing herself into a calmer voice. "Even so. His body is badly damaged. He's kept it going through sheer will. But he can't keep it going much longer. He's going to use what he has left to open the gate."

Alex tried to swallow. He looked at the wooden structure.

"Confused?" Zia said. "But, oh, *curious*, too, eh? And that's stronger, really, isn't it? You want to know. Father saw it in you. You kept the name of God and didn't tell anyone and tried to learn all by your lonesome. Aw. Father thinks maybe you'd like to learn properly, one day. Which is very forgiving of him, if you ask me. It's the reason I haven't popped your head off your shoulders yet. Would you like to learn about this?" She pointed a jaunty thumb over her shoulder at the wooden construction.

Alex looked up from under his brow. He hated that she was right. Even after everything, a large part of him wanted to know about the gate very badly.

"My old brother hasn't taught you anything, we know that," Zia said, with another quick glance toward the moon. "But we can't blame him for not telling you about this one. This one's ultra-top-super-secret, bunny.

"Storytime, then," she went on, slapping her hands in a gesture Alex had seen his grandfather make countless times. The longer he spent with Zia, the more he could see an awful resemblance between them. "Has brother dear told you about the weak spots yet?"

"Powerful places." Alex nodded. "Places where things . . . get thin."

She rolled her eyes. "Is that it?"

"Yes." Alex fixed her with a direct stare. "That's it." Despite the hopelessness of his situation, he felt a sullen, rebellious anger growing. She scared him, she sickened him – but, above everything else, she simply *annoyed* him. He yanked roughly at the wire around his arm but stopped when Beckman tightened it to the point where Alex thought it might draw blood. He looked at the fine line trembling between him and Beckman.

"Ooh." Zia grinned. "Getting mad. Maybe there is something of the family buried deep down inside you after all, *Alexandah*. Though I remain to be convinced it's worth the effort of digging up. Wasted time on that before with your papa."

"What?" Alex said.

"Oh yes. Your daddy, rabbit. He was sharper than you, but a wishy-washy weakling in the end. Although, your grandaddy has to take his share of the blame there. Gave the game away too soon, before the boy was ready to understand. Always a spoilsport.

"But what has the old man been *doing* with you all this time if he's taught you nothing at all? Weak spots on the *Earth* and in the *sky*, bunny. The places where things get *lost*, and things get *out*. Places where things can slip *through*. Holes, from this side into the other, and vicey-versy. Into the Elsewhere!" She barked out a deep, booming man's cry, like a circus ringleader introducing his greatest act: *"The Great Beeeyond!"*

Throwing her arms wide, she made a pirouette, before

continuing in her own voice. "Get the gist? The Black Forest's riddled with holes. German woods are like Swiss cheese. And you're standing at the thinnest spot of all. Or you will be in a few minutes," she added, checking the sky again, "when everything all lines up.

"This old castle was built *around* the weak spot by some little scared people. To keep it secret and keep all the happy peasants safe and stupid. Why else build anything in such a dreary dull nothingy place? But once upon a time, a very wise and very powerful man realised *this* spot was *particularly* special, and so he and his men took over the castle and settled in so he could examine it properly.

"So. He settled in with his old books and stuff and got all comfy and studied the weak spot for years and years and *years*. And here's what he found. Most weak places are one way. Either things can go *in*, or things can get *out*. Like Hamelin. You must know that one, bunny?"

"Hamelin," Alex said, reluctantly. He knew the name from the fairy tale that had always creeped him out most as a kid. "The town from the Pied Piper?"

"The town from the Pied Piper?" Zia repeated in a maddeningly exact imitation of his voice. "Yes. Go through that door in Hamelin, and it's bye-bye, little kiddiewinks. See? But *this one*, this one's so very, very close to the *next* one that when it all lines up –" she pointed to the sky – "they become two sides of one. One door. One gateway. Right here is one side, and it's a way *in*. Now, big test, see if you've been paying attention. Can you guess where the other weak spot is? Where the other side comes *out*? Here's a clue: this comes from there." She tossed the rock in her hand.

"The mountain," Alex said after a moment. "The Kandel."

"By George, I think he's got it!"

"No," Alex said. "I don't. I don't get any of it."

"Suffering catfish on a bike," Zia said with an exasperated sigh.

"I . . . I'd like to know," Alex said, quietly, as if he didn't want anyone to hear him admit it. He kept his eyes down, studying the ground, their feet. "I'd like to understand."

"Hum." Zia narrowed her eyes, suspicious, but faintly surprised. "Well. We don't have all night. But okay. In simpleton speak." She raised one hand in a fist and impatiently tapped the thumb clenched at the side with her other forefinger. "We're out here, on this side, okay? *Alive,* sonny. Right?"

Alex nodded. He took a step toward Zia, peering intently at her hand.

"If you're foolish enough to *stop* being alive, you, all the fizzly energy of you, drains through and gets trapped inside, in here." She shook her fist roughly, then turned her hand over, opened it, and held it under Alex's nose, with the fingers wiggling violently.

"You're sucked into eternity. Join the hot cosmic soup. Go where the wild things are. Dissolve into *death*, child."

"Okay." Alex managed a hoarse whisper.

"Death's supposed to be a one-way street, rrrright? Go through the door and it's locked behind you. Cheerio! You know about that. But at *this spot*, where we're standing, when everything all lines up, just for a teensy-tiny moment, there's a little gap, a hole."

She curled her fingers and held the hand to her eye, blinking through it at Alex like a child playing with an imaginary telescope, then snapped the fist closed tight again. "You can step *in* this side here, at the castle." Zia tapped the knuckle of the thumb. "And step *out* again over there, on the Kandel." She tapped the curl of her little finger. "And in between, you've stepped right *through* death, without getting caught *in* death." She gestured to Beckman. "Get Father ready."

"The gate is at the weak spot," Alex said, trying to piece the madness together. "You step through here. And you'll come out on the Kandel mountain. But, in between, you'll have . . . passed through . . . death."

"Through death without dying." Zia nodded, watching as Beckman and the big robot moved the tall man so his head lay centred at the foot of the gate. "Through fire without burning."

"Can I look closer?" Alex said. "The gate, I mean. Now that I know what it is."

Zia knotted her brow. "Maybe you *are* curious. Your daddy was. Okay. Slowly. But quickly. And keep away from Father. No monkey business, rabbit, or Hans'll snap your paw right off."

Beckman gave the loop around Alex's arm a friendly

squeeze, then let the wire fall loose so he could move. Alex hobbled past Zia, leaning on his broom and wincing with each step, a little more than he needed to. The wire trailed slack along the ground behind him. He inspected the varnished old wood, letting them see how interested he was. But he was also studying the layout around him from the corner of his eye, the positions of Beckman and Zia.

"How does it . . . work?" Alex asked, not really sure what he was asking.

"Well, my little *blödes Kaninchen*," Zia said. "The gate is made from old trees that had grown here, right by the weak spot, and sucked up the atmosphere. It was crafted by an extremely mighty sage. Back when people knew what's what. Before they started splitting knowledge up. When the hole opens, the gate will hold it and keep it open," Zia said, distracted, speaking faster.

She pointed up at the moon and circled her finger in a spiralling motion. "You know everything's all spinning around all the time? Yes? Planets and moons and such? Always in motion, always in different arrangements? Well, when everything lines up *just so*, just for a moment, that forms the *lock*. The gate is the *door*. All you need then is the *key*, and to know how to turn it."

"The key?"

"That's the artful bit. The key's your fizzly energy. Your life force. That's what death demands before you can pass through. So you have to give it up, to trick it."

"Give it your . . . life?" Alex said.

"You know what I mean, rabbit." She rubbed irritably at her forehead. "*You send it out.* You've done it yourself with the Soaring Spirit. But what's needed here's much more subtle, much more powerful. Much more dangerous. The gate takes your fizzly energy and uses it to keep the hole open. But you need to know how to give it *all* away, to the very last drop, then be able snatch it back as you pass through. Like breathing out and breathing in at the same time. Timing. Takes the very greatest skill and learning. Get it wrong and you—"

She fell suddenly silent, staring down at the tall man with a desolate look. Moonlight glinted from her dark eyes as they briefly brimmed with tears.

"But Father can do it. He's studied more than anyone ever." She sounded as if she was trying to convince herself. "Anyway. Time's here. Come back away from the gate. Begin, Hans."

Alex stumbled to stand on the other side of Zia from where he'd started. At the gate, Beckman began a soft, whispering chant.

"But why's he doing it?" Alex said, trying to keep Zia talking. His mind was racing. He was playing actions out in his head, gathering courage to move. "If he's so weak and it's so dangerous?"

"How stupid are you, stupid?" Zia muttered. "To fix him, idiot. Go through death without dying, it takes the bad stuff away. Like a filter. You come out all fixed and clean. Better than before. And once you've gone through and come out, death can't catch your fizzly energy again. Ever. That's what the gate-maker discovered. To gain eternal life you must give your life away. Father calls it a conundrum of faith. It's highly poetical."

Beckman's breathy singing became higher, faster. All at once, he stopped, raised a mighty mechanical finger, and tapped the gate.

Tap-tap.

A second later, like a delayed echo in the woods, the sound repeated, but it was slightly different.

Tap-tap—tap.

"It's working!" Zia beamed, actually jumping and clapping. "That's little William von Sudenfeld. He's on the other side of the gate. Up on the Kandel. Its shadow is falling there now. See?" In the brightening moonlight, Alex could clearly see the shadows of himself, Zia, Beckman, and the life-sizer. Yet the gate cast no shadow at all.

"We took all the pieces of the gate to the Devil's Pulpit first, to charge it on the rocks, remind it where it had to open," Zia said. "It was so happy. Go on, Hans."

Beckman started singing new words. Zia looked to the sky and straightened, preparing herself.

"Immortality?" Alex asked, playing for time. "So why hasn't he done it before? If he's known about it all this time."

Zia ran at him fast and rapped him hard on the forehead with a sharp knuckle.

"Knock-knock. Hello? Are you listening? 'You-have-to-give-your-life-away.' Understand? *That's ve-ry dan-ger-ous.* Father has

studied the gate for years and always held back. But now there's
no time left. No choice."

"So, where is he?" Alex put weight onto his weak foot, testing it.

"*What?*" Zia snapped.

"Your gate-maker," Alex said. "If he was supposed to have
found the secret to eternal life here, then where is he now?"

"Oh. He made a mistake. Surrounded himself with idiots.
Scaredy-cats. Unable to believe. Father will be the first to go
through. We'll be next."

"We?"

"Yes, big ears, we. Father will give the gate his life, then the
gate will hold the hole open, and we can *all* pass through with
him. It's a great gift. The greatest. Immortality's on offer: of
course we go through! Besides, you wouldn't want to be left out
here when the gate opens and everything starts falling."

"The castle." Caught by a new rush of panic, Alex barely
heard her. He looked up at the shattered tower. "It collapsed."

"Yes, yes. Keeping the hole open long enough to go through
is like ripping it open over and over again. There's energy
released. Everything's energy and vibrations, Alexander, that's
the first secret. The energy has to go somewhere. It goes rumbling into the earth."

"But the story said, if it was opened again, it would . . .
destroy the Earth. The end of the world."

"Poppycock. Don't be such a drama bunny. Why would we
want that? Father's calculated it. The fault line will only open

from here to the Kandel. Just twenty-five miles long or some-thing. And only a few hundred miles or so wide either side. *Some* things'll fall in, yes. But we'll be sheltered by the gate."

"A few hundred miles either side – but all the towns!" Alex cried. "The cities, all the people! There are thousands—"

"But all the peeeeople!" Zia mimicked. "They're all going to die, anyway, Alexander. They don't seem to mind. None of them think about it much at all. No, what you should *really* worry about isn't them all falling in. It's the things that might come climbing out."

"*What?*"

"Things, Alexander. Things. Things from the wild side. Things with wings and things you don't have words for. You'll see. But it'll be fun. It'll give Father and me something to hunt and study. Now. Shut your mouth."

She turned to walk to the gate. The moon hung directly above the broken tower.

Alex had barely half a plan. Less. But he was out of time. He dived in front of her feet, scrabbled around fast behind her again, then threw himself back hard in the dirt. With the sleeves of his coat over his hand like gloves, he pulled desperately at the wire that was already tightening around his arm.

Zia shrieked, tried to move, fell on her face.

Beyond her, Beckman, still chanting, reeled his wire in faster. Alex yanked it in the opposite direction with everything he had. Between them, Zia lay in the dirt, with the loop Alex had man-aged to throw around her leg cutting tightly into her ankle.

347

"Stop pulling, moron, loosen it!" she screamed at Beckman. He continued murmuring his ancient song, sounding nervier now. More wire started spooling out from under his coat.

Alex got to his feet, shoved the broom under his armpit for support, and hobbled backward, straining to keep Zia caught tight between them. He cast a nervous glance at the motion-less life-sizer, then jerked away as another spring-arm came flying at him. But Beckman was too absorbed in his ritual to shoot accurately. The flailing white fist missed and fell writh-ing to the ground. Alex pinned it down with the brush handle and leaned on it hard.

"How long do you think you can keep this up, idiot?" Zia yelled. "What actually is your point?"

"Doesn't have to be long," Alex muttered. "I don't understand what you're doing, but I know enough to understand it has to be done at the right time. You said you only had a *teensy-tiny* moment to open the hole. So, a teensy-tiny moment will do."

"What?" Zia gave a despairing chuckle. "It's already happen-ing, bunny-brain. Look."

The gate was glowing steadily brighter. Alex saw that the light seemed to come from countless burning letters and sym-bols hidden beneath the layers of varnish, spelling out some long, indecipherable message. Within the structure, the dark air was shuddering. The shuddering began to centre above the tall man's head.

"You won't stop it. Father can't stop now. And he doesn't need *me* to do it. He just needs Hans singing on this side, Willy calling from the other. So, all that's going to happen now is, if we aren't over there – me *and you,* bunny – in the gate, we'll be caught out here when everything starts falling."

Alex pulled tighter on the cord. "I don't care. We'll go together—"

He heard the whirr of her flier a millisecond before it slammed into his temple. A blade slashed his cheek and his grip on the wire loosened momentarily. Zia instantly slipped free, leapt up, and ran to touch the gate.

"Bring him, Hans. Try not to damage him. Too much." She bent to lift the flower.

The ground vibrated, very faintly.

The white hand jerked out from under Alex and grabbed his ankle. The wire round his arm bit hard. Then he was being reeled rapidly, helplessly, in toward the blazing gate.

The ground rumbled, stronger this time.

Within the gate structure, the vibrating air was spinning, spiralling, forming a wormy whirlpool. Slivers of the white-blue light emanating from the frames seemed to get sucked into it, whirling around. A low, rhythmic whine started from somewhere, growing louder, faster, like the gears of some vast, far-off machine beginning to turn. Above it, Alex thought he heard the barking of dogs.

The life-sizer stooped to the foot of the board the tall man lay upon and began pushing him. The eyes behind the mask were wide in furious ecstasy. The gate swung open inside its huge frame, setting off shivering cascades of light. As the tall man's head passed within the frame, the air around him burned solid white. Slowly, the robot pushed him deeper through.

Beckman was whispering feverishly as Alex arrived at the gate. The ground bucked and complained. It seemed as if the moon was shaking in the sky. There were figures moving on the slope beneath the tower. Dogs ran before them, barking ceaseless warnings. His grandfather was there, looking old and tired, but lifting his cane high.

The big robot kept pushing steadily, until the soles of the tall man's shining boots were swallowed up and disappeared. As soon as he vanished, the machine fell lifeless.

"Now!" Zia shouted. Alex felt her take his elbow. Beckman's mechanical hand crushed around his other. Then they were moving, forward, into the light.

The grinding noise was racing, deafening. Alex strained to look back over his shoulder. It was perhaps a trick of the light crackling blindingly around him, but, for a second, he thought he saw the quaking old castle change – phantom hints of long-vanished walls re-forming, rebuilding. He tried to call out.

But he was already touching the light, stepping over into eternity.

XXXIV.

MEETING THE MAKER

THE FIRST THING he thought was that the pain in his ankle was gone.

The second thing he thought was that there wasn't any air.

Being underwater was as close as Alex's mind could get to understanding the sensation. A feeling of the silent environment pressing in, simultaneously surrounding him and supporting him. But it wasn't like being underwater at all. After a few panicking seconds, his body relaxed.

The stormy night had vanished. It was a bright but dismal day, and they stood on a small ledge jutting out from a high cliff. Behind them, where Alex would have expected to see the gate they had just stepped though, stood only a sheer, solid wall of rock, stretching up out of sight.

Far below, a pale landscape spread out like a desert of snow, vast and featureless, save for a black forest clustered darkly along the distant horizon. Their narrow shelf led off around a curve in the rock face, just a few feet away. And there, just where the path turned, the tall man stood, pulling on his coat.

Father. It worked! . . . Did it work?

Zia's voice sounded inside Alex's head, horribly intimate.

Yes. Alexia. I am well. All is well. The tall man removed his hard white mask, letting it drop without a sound. The smooth skin of his face practically glowed. Silver-black hair shone thickly as he swept it back from his high forehead. Alex knew that his father would have looked very much like this man. He tried to stop thinking about that.

Zia ran and hugged the tall figure. He patted her head.

Well done, Hans. The man looked at Beckman. *A perfect incantation under less than perfect circumstances. You learned well. We must see about getting you out from your exoskeleton soon. Too much longer, and you may never be able to remove it.*

Beckman smiled and pulled back his coat collar and bright polka-dot scarf. The wounds in his neck were gone. The tubes connecting him to his robotic body had fused seamlessly with the skin. *Already too late, I think. Passing through the gate has . . . healed things together, ha-ha. But I like this body. I like being strong.*

The tall man pursed his lips quizzically, then nodded, before turning to Alex.

And, Alexander. You are with us. As it should be. Taking your father's place.

Alex opened his mouth to speak and found he couldn't. He tried thinking a reply and sending it out, wondering if they would hear. *No. I'm not with you. I'll never be with you. My dad would never have been with you.*

The tall man's smile broadened sympathetically. *Well. We knew your father better than you ever did, child. As for you: we shall see. There is lots of time to come. For the moment, we shall treat you as a guest, if you behave like one. But first, we must complete. Come.*

He turned and strode beyond the corner. Zia and Beckman hurried after him.

A few seconds later, Alex followed. There was nowhere else to go.

He found them standing only a step around the curve, staring in wary confusion at what lay just ahead. The path simply ended at another sheer cliff wall. And there, with his back to them, crouched a grey-headed figure, pressing his hands to the rock, as if searching for a hidden doorway. He wore a heavy purple cloak, intricately embroidered with tiny black writing much like that Alex had seen glowing around the gate.

Who— Alex thought, before Zia could signal him to stop.

The man whipped around, wild-eyed.

What manner of devils are these now? He started moving his hands frantically, tracing strange signs. *Back, I say, or—* The warning dissolved into a long, convoluted singsong, rhyming lines of words Alex could not catch.

The tall man stepped forward, hands aloft, palms up. *Hold, please, brother. Peace.* Alex could see him thinking, fast and calm. Then: *Could you really be the master who crafted the Shadow Gate of Boll?*

The stranger paused and regarded Alex's great-grandfather with a combination of fear, suspicion, and pride. *Aye, creature. I am he.*

The tall man dropped his hands in a placating gesture. *Then you have been held here many years, friend. So. Let us help you now get free.*

The cloaked man scowled, angry again. *Seek not to confound me, demon. I passed through my gate but seconds ago. I wait now only for my men to call me through.* He lifted his hands, forming clawlike shapes, pointed toward them.

The tall man dropped to one knee. *Hold. Please. I know you are mighty. I have studied your book and know it is great. I am a fellow student of those same arts. I have other lessons I can share. Some of the high secrets and some of the low. My own discoveries and inventions. We should join together. Your men betrayed you, friend, abandoned you. They sealed you in and pulled your gate apart behind you in fear. We have built it once more, by your design. But hear me: many hundreds of years have passed since you walked through that portal.*

They fell into a tense stand-off. The old gate-maker glared at them, keeping his hands held in their strange and oddly threatening gesture, but there was an uncertainty in his gaze, as though he was trying to remember something and couldn't.

Alex glanced nervously out from the path. The empty white plain below, the dark woods far beyond. He had a distinct feeling something had changed down there. He stepped closer to the edge, peering harder.

Betrayed . . . The cloaked figure lowered his hands slightly. *Hundreds of years?*

Gazing over the landscape, Alex's eyes widened. *Wait*, he thought, urgently. *Look* . . .

Zia spun. *Shut up.*

Alex shook his head and pointed. *Look.*

The blackness along the horizon. He had taken it for some vast forest. But now he saw: it was creeping closer – still a great distance away but coming fast. As he stared, he began to see the tangled darkness consisted of countless figures, running furiously in their direction. Now some of the creatures seemed to stretch out wings and take flight.

Things! Zia thought at him, with a grin. Then, glancing again at the approaching wave, she pursed her lips in a pensive frown. *Father—*

TAP-TAP—TAP.

The sudden knocking sounded huge and hollow, booming from within the cliff behind the gate-maker. As they all stared, the shadow of the gate began to materialise, appearing in the rock face like a developing photograph.

Curse your trickery, creature. The gate-maker had an exultant, furious look. *My men call me now!*

The tall man stood. *No. It is my man, and he calls for us.*

Die, vile entity. The cloaked figure twisted his hands violently in opposite directions. The tall man gasped and

staggered, clutching painfully at his chest. Zia sprang for
the gate-maker as Beckman shot two fat white fists at him,
wrapping his hands in wire. Blue light crackled back along the
coils, causing Beckman to arch his back in a long spasm. The
tall man straightened painfully, lifting his cane.

The four of them started fighting in a flailing, struggling
scrum.

They crashed into Alex, almost sending him over the edge.
He backed up, looking from them to the ocean of figures seep-
ing across the plain, the shapes hurtling through the air, getting closer.

He looked to the gate made of shadow. It was fully there
now: sharp, solid black. Already, a whirling tunnel of light was
growing within it.

Nowhere else to go.

Alex watched the fighting figures blocking the thin path
between him and the gate. Every few seconds, as they lurched
back and forth, there was just enough space at the edge for him
to squeeze by. He poised himself, then darted forward.

As he shoved past, Beckman knocked into him, causing his
right foot to slip over the precipice. Alex stumbled. He refused
to fall. He drove down hard with his left foot and used his
broom handle like a cane to drag himself forward, and then
he was past them, and he was jumping into the swirling light,
and there was a faint voice calling him, growing louder, guid-
ing him, and he grabbed at that voice like a lifeline and pulled
himself on.

XXXV.

THE IMP

AND THEN HE was falling forward, shocked by the rush of air in his lungs and a suddenness of darkness and cold. The voice was gone. There was a curious, blaring sound, high and tinny, and a flicker of flame.

But Alex clung to his racing thoughts. He knew von Sudenfeld was waiting beyond the gate, probably the bald man, too. He'd have only one chance to get past them. But he had surprise on his side.

Still blinded by the dark, Alex started screaming and lashing out wildly with his broom. He felt it connecting with a satisfyingly solid blow and heard a gasp of shock and pain. He kept swinging as his eyes adjusted to the faint light.

It was not the scene he had expected.

Before him on the rocky ground, groaning and holding a hand to his head, lay a young man of around nineteen, with long dark hair, a ratty moustache, and a startled expression. Sitting behind him were five other teens, three boys, two girls, similarly attired in T-shirts, jeans, greasy hair, and astonished looks. They held hands around a small fire and gawped at Alex in fearful silence, with the air of children caught doing something they shouldn't. Empty beer cans and coiled climbing ropes lay around them. A cigarette dropped as one girl's mouth fell open, scattering tiny embers.

As he stared back, utterly perplexed, Alex dimly realised he recognised some of the band names on their T-shirts. The noise in the air was a frenetic heavy metal guitar solo, screaming from a battered old boom box.

"Was habe ich getan? Verzeih mir," the boy on the ground whispered. *"Verzeih mir!"*

They were on top of a flat, very high rock that jutted out like a balcony over a sea of black trees. The woods below spilled thickly away down a steep slope. Off to the right, beneath the full moon, the tiny lights of a little town twinkled against surrounding miles of darkness. In other circumstances, the view might have been enchanting. Alex stole a glance behind. He could just glimpse the gate's quivering outline.

"Get away from here!" he yelled at the group, who still regarded him with dumbstruck awe. "Run!" He glanced around wildly. No sign of von Sudenfeld.

"You speak . . . English?" the boy on the ground said weakly. "Forgive me. Please. We were only . . . fooling. I did not mean to summon you . . . Do you *all* speak English?"

"What?" Alex thought he detected a faint tremor beneath his feet.

"Well . . . demons . . . imps. Whatever you are. Forgive me. We always heard the stories about this place. That the witches summoned you here. But we never believed, we were just joking about it. Please, you must forgive us."

"Yes. Okay. Right. You're all forgiven. But only if you get away from here *right now*. I'm very, eh, very *upset* at being . . . disturbed." Alex wagged his fist at them and stomped a foot. As he did, the rock quaked under him again. This time, the others felt it, too. They exchanged fearful looks.

"Be GONE!" Alex thundered, shaking his broom in the air. There came a glaring blast of blue-white light from behind him and he spun to see one of Beckman's fake fists bursting from the darkness. The white hand swung at nothing, then disappeared through the gate again. When Alex turned back, the last two teens were disappearing on their ropes over the edge of the rock.

"Forgive us!"

The music ended as the tape in their machine ran out. A second later, there came a low, distant breaking sound. Not from below this time.

Directly above, a thin line of white-blue light now shone through the clouds, as if a crack of daylight were breaking into the night. As Alex watched, transfixed, the crack lengthened, ripping across the sky in a jagged, sinister diagonal. From miles away, he could just see another glinting path of light tearing toward it, on a course to meet as one. He remembered his grandfather drawing a diagonal line on the map. The Kandel mountain at one end. The ruined castle at the other.

"Fault line," Alex whispered.

The rock beneath him groaned, shifted, settled. He stared at his feet, at the landscape around him. With a slow, horrifying sense of realisation, he recalled the story told by the climbers on the Kandel:

"At the very top, there used *to be a . . . great, massive black rock that hung out. They called it* die Teufelskanzel – *the Devil's Pulpit . . . Now, in 1981, you see, the Devil's Pulpit suddenly disintegrated overnight. Tons and tons of rock . . . it all just came falling down . . ."*

Before he could recall any more, he was flattened by Zia, who came flying through the gate and crashed into him as if she had been thrown. They collapsed in a tangle together.

"Where's Willy?" she said, sitting up and glancing rapidly around. "What did you do?"

"I don't think he'll get here for a while yet," Alex managed to croak.

"Eh?"

The rock was shaking steadily now. Alex could hear a hard rain of pieces falling from the edges. The rip in the sky was breaking open, and there were things moving up there, beyond the sky, flying things. Shafts of blue-white light slanted down across the landscape. He lurched as the mountain quivered horribly again.

"There's all sorts of monstrous things in there now." Zia nodded urgently toward the gate. "We need to help Father, get him out."

"But we can't stay out here!" Alex gestured frantically. "This whole part of the mountain is about to collapse. I think we've . . ." He fought to catch a breath and get his head around what he was going to say. "We've come out into 1981."

Zia frowned, then dismissed it. "Close enough. Just out by four decades or so. Considering we were aiming across all eternity, rabbit, that's like hitting a bull's-eye."

"No, but *look*!" Alex pointed at the fracture growing above them and tried to straighten his scrambled thoughts. "That . . . crack. It's running from here to the castle. But you opened the gate in . . . the future. I mean, I think the crack is running from here in 1981, to the castle in *our time*. Maybe even back to the magician's time, too, hundreds of years ago, when he first opened it. All at once. It's all breaking open at once across . . . time *and* space . . . I mean, it'll swallow everything. Everything'll be wiped out. We have to *close* it."

"Oooh." Zia clapped her hands. "A fracture in existence! You could be right, brainy bunny. That's exciting, eh? The crack of doom!" She paused and fell silent. Her brow furrowed as the rock swayed sickeningly to the side then slid back again. Zia looked seriously around them, taking in the increasingly apocalyptic scene. Turning to Alex, she considered him curiously.

"Here." From her pocket, Zia pulled the flier Alex had previously used. She frowned at its mangled wings, then fished in her coat and produced a tiny silver hammer. Holding the little robot to the rock, she quickly battered the wings straight, then thrust it at Alex. "Looks like we'll need to give you this."

"What?"

"Well. There's things to fight in there. Help or don't help. You won't be much use, anyway." She moved toward the gate, staring at it impatiently, hands on hips.

Alex looked helplessly at the flier in his hand. "I don't have any hair to give it," he said.

"You've got a headful, idiot."

"Oh." Alex pinched a lock between his fingers, braced himself, and ripped it out. He fitted it inside the machine as carefully as he could with the world collapsing. "How do we go back through the gate?"

"I call, and I think we have to wait for someone to open it from the other side."

"You *think*?"

"Stop *whining*. Something'll turn up. I'll call them."

Alex looked around as she started chanting. The rock bucked beneath them. The crumbling sound was constant as the great crack in the sky yawned wider, brighter.

A sudden thought struck him. If he really was somehow standing in 1981, as he felt certain he was, then his father was still out there in the world somewhere, still just a boy, several years younger than Alex himself.

He staggered as another tremor pounded the mountain and Zia was thrown against him. They stood in a fearful embrace as half of their rock platform simply sheared off and fell away, leaving them perched atop a slender column that teetered alarmingly. Zia shook him off and began singing louder.

Alex turned back to his thoughts. He had minutes left, perhaps seconds, and so he would use them to think about this: his dad, a kid out there, safe somewhere, far away. At least until the chasm in the heavens widened further.

Maybe, Alex thought, if he had worked it out a little sooner, he could have got himself down from this place alive. Maybe the crack would have been closed somehow, and he could have found his father, eventually. Maybe. And then maybe . . . then maybe what?

"Alex!"

The desperate voice pulled him back into the moment. Alex looked to the vague gate. Kingdom was leaning through, reaching out, light fizzing around her. Zia was already scrambling past her, vanishing to the other side again. Kingdom scowled after her, then waved her hand frantically.

"Come *on!*"

The ground fell away as Alex grabbed her hand. He swung there for a second as the last of the crag beneath him collapsed, tons of rock falling like a booming black waterfall. He saw his abandoned broom swallowed in the deluge. Dust rose up in a choking cloud.

And then he was being pulled up, through the light, into silence.

✸

THE FIGHTING ON the narrow path was furious.

Alex's eyes adjusted to the light to see the gate-maker being lifted into the air by . . . by something. It wasn't a bird. More like a giant, single, fleshy wing thrashing fast. Yet it had claws and a beak. Perhaps two beaks. The cloaked, ancient figure seemed to be screaming. But there was no sound here. Then the creature and the man were gone, shooting up out of sight.

Alex's grandfather stood shoulder to shoulder with the tall man, the two of them working together, slashing silently with their sticks to battle off an attack from a flock of similar flying beasts. Beckman balanced precariously at the edge of the precipice, his great metal arms struggling furiously with a number of writhing tentacles that reached up from below. Alex couldn't tell if they were the limbs of some enormous entity down there, or vicious, wormy creatures themselves.

Zia stood clutching the plant pot, frowning furiously. *Father?*

Yes, child, he answered without looking.

We must go back.

The tall man paused in his fighting a fraction of a second. *Certain?*

Zia nodded.

Very well.

But that means we will not complete. Zia's voice wavered. *It will all reverse, and you . . .*

I will have to find another way. He slashed at the air. A flier shot from Zia's coat and jabbed at the wing menacing her father, driving it away. Kingdom leapt past Alex, rapier held high.

Ah, Alex, there you are! Alex's grandfather's voice rang

brightly in Alex's mind. *I was just saying to Evelyn, perhaps we should get out of here. After you, son.* He nodded back toward spot where the gate had first opened.

Get off, get off, get off, get off!

Alex turned in time to see Beckman pulled screaming silently over the edge by a group of flailing grey hands that had appeared among the tentacles. Alex, his grandfather, Kingdom, the tall man, and Zia formed a huddle. Still fighting, they headed as one back along the path.

As he rounded the corner, Alex saw that Harry stood inside the gateway, light smashing against him as the portal tried to close. He was holding it open, but despite his efforts, even as Alex drew closer, the opening narrowed. The sparking light intensified. Kingdom sprinted forward, ducked through, and vanished.

Let's go, Alex, his grandfather's voice urged him on. They ran for it together.

No!

Alex halted as Zia's simple, terrible cry pierced his mind.

Looking back, he saw the tall man fall. Zia's flier flew slashing at the wing flapping above him. The flying creature plucked the robot from the air with a beak and disappeared upward with it. Zia stumbled in pain. Her father lay motionless.

Alex!

Harry's voice. The gate was closing. Alex's grandfather grabbed him roughly by the shoulders to push him through, then paused. The old man and the boy looked back. Zia knelt at the prone figure, uselessly trying to drag her father by his feet. She looked very small.

Alex and his grandfather exchanged a serious look. The old man nodded. Alex threw his flier into the air and built his bridge to it as another wing swooped toward Zia. He slashed the creature hard with his blade and hook, holding it off.

His grandfather jumped over the tall man, then bent to lift him by the shoulders. *You two. Grab a foot each.*

Zia balanced her plant in the crook of her arm and they took the man's legs. The flower jiggled as they started moving. The tall man was heavier than Alex could have imagined. But together they shuffled closer and closer to the gate. A horde of figures came climbing onto the path behind them. Alex slashed at the wing again and called his flier back. Then light was crackling all around him, angry and intense, like a static electric field barring his way.

Before, passing through these openings had taken only an instant, but this was different, the going much harder, as if he was forcing himself against a raging ocean tide. Swimming lattices of light formed before him and linked up, bleeding into one vast, incandescent corridor that warped and stretched out infinitely ahead. Beyond its edges, he had the vaguest impression of rushing, twisting landscapes, wild swarms of star fields colliding in blinding explosions of colour, then gone like matches struck in the night. He was gripped by a sudden, seductive sense of insignificance that bloomed into an overwhelming sense of wonder, and then the urgent sense that he had to go on, push forward against the weight of time and distance. He heard the great gears grinding slower, felt himself moving faster. The pressure grew unbearable, as if the air was trying to slam itself together around him, crush him out of existence, smash his atoms and make them pop.

And then he was through.

The pain in his ankle returned. He was wheezing for breath in the dark and the rain, and the ruined castle lurched above him. The ground shook and the ripped sky shone and roared painfully as unearthly lightning flashed across it.

The whole world howled. Alex looked up to see his grandfather standing in the blazing gateway with Harry. The old man took his cane, considered it for a second, then swung two-handed at the old wooden structure, beginning to smash it apart.

A thin, flailing tentacle reached through from the other side and curled tightly around Alex's grandfather's ankles. He staggered as it started dragging him back in. While he struggled, another, greater limb emerged, knocked Harry flat, then wrapped around the lifeless life-sizer that had been abandoned by the gate and lifted it through. The dying light of the broken gate flared brighter and rushed over Alex's grandfather in blue-white flames. He bent in pain.

Alex threw his flier and sent it diving at the tentacle that held his grandfather. He struck out with his hook. As the metal plunged into the pale, sticky flesh, Alex felt a sickening, burning sting on his mind and had to let go. His flier dropped. But it was enough. The tentacle uncurled, releasing the old man, and shot back into the place beyond. The last of the light winked out as the gate collapsed.

The earth stopped shaking. Alex stood panting. The sky had healed. The moon shone down, tinting the black clouds silver, and the rain rattling the leaves of the Black Forest sounded like endless applause from a vast, unseen audience.

XXXVI.

OUTSIDE/INSIDE

ALEX'S GRANDFATHER LAY face down, surrounded by pieces of broken old picture frames. Harry and Kingdom were already by his side. As Alex limped to join them, Harry glanced up anxiously. He shook his head.

Alex knelt. "Grandad?"

Silence. Rain fell steadily. Alex touched the old man's shoulder. He shook him gently, to no response, tried again more urgently, then let his hand fall to his side.

He knelt staring at the body before him, watching raindrops land on his grandfather's coat and disappear, absorbed. His mind was blank and heavy.

"Aw, Gawd." Harry stood and turned away.

"I think I'll take a bit of a holiday after this one." The voice was faint, but the old man managed a grin as he turned his head. "Somewhere with a bit of sun, I think. Nice café by the water."

"Grandad," Alex said. Relief beat through him. "Grandad, I—"

"There should be a first aid kit in the Rolls," Kingdom said. "And blankets and things. I saw it up there, not far from where we left the car we, uhm, borrowed. Philippe was out cold inside, tied up. I couldn't wake him. I should check on him. I'll bring back what I can."

"Now, Alex," the old man said weakly as Kingdom and the dogs ran off. "I really wish you hadn't dabbled with using the flier. We'll need to have a serious talk about that later. But in the meantime: thank you. Give me a hand to sit up, eh?"

Alex helped Harry manoeuvre him upright. He was sure his grandfather's hair had grown even whiter. Alex sat back. His ankle ached. He noticed the old man's hand trembled badly on his cane. Alex looked over at the space where the gate had stood.

"Beckman," he said bleakly.

"Yes. Well, don't shed too many tears, Alex. Hans Beckman made his bed a long time ago," his grandfather said. His breathing was ragged. "Now he's gone to lie in it. I mean, leaving aside everything else – he *killed* Harry."

"Yeah," Harry said grimly. "I'm not one to 'old a grudge. But I'm 'aving an 'ard time forgiving that one. Mind you, came in 'andy."

"Huh?" Alex said.

"The opening that the gate made started closing behind you when you went through," Alex's grandfather said. He was mopping at his face with a handkerchief. "Nothing I did could stop it. But it opened again when Harry reached into it. It's just a theory, but I think it's because he has a different kind of energy about him now. A different kind of life force – when it tried to close around him, it was like, you know . . . like two magnets forcing each other apart."

"I'm officially repulsive." Harry beamed.

"I think Harry might have been responsible for the damage that was done, actually," Alex's grandfather continued. "His holding the gate open for longer than it should have been, that's what caused the convulsions, the rip in the sky, the earthquake, all that."

"The collapse of the Devil's Pulpit back in 1981." Alex nodded.

"Eh?"

"I'll explain it later. If I can work it out." Alex sat still gazing fixedly at the empty spot. The memories of what had happened in the strange, pale place were still vibrating in his head. But even as he thought about it, he realised, the images were fading, slipping away from him. He tried to hold it all in his mind before it vanished.

"Is that it?" he said.

"Hmm?"

"Is that what's coming? At the end? When we die. The things we saw through there, through the gate. Is that where we go?"

"Oh." The old man pulled a wrinkled paper bag from a pocket. He fished out a sweet, popped it in his mouth, then held the bag toward Alex.

"Lemon drops. Exactly what's needed. Ah, to answer your

question, Alex: I don't think so. It's just another theory, but I think that . . . that –" he wiggled his fingers at the wreckage around them, searching for words – "that *place*, where we were, that should never have been opened, and we should never have been in there. Think of it like a wound being opened in a body, and us as bacteria getting in. An infection. The . . . *things* were like . . . what's the word . . . antibodies produced by the body's immune system, coming to get rid of us. Get it?"

"No." Alex rubbed his head. "Sort of. Not really. Grandad . . . what do you think does happen, then?"

"Oh, no idea," the old man said, dusting sadly at the dirt coating his clothes. "That's the whole fun of it, don't you think? Not knowing? I suspect it'll be calmer, though. But let's ask an expert. Any thoughts, Harry?"

"Oh," Harry said. "Well, yeah, I mean, it didn't seem to do me any 'arm. I don't remember much about it, Alex. Eh . . . but I do know it smells like coconut."

"There you go." Alex's grandfather smiled. "I've never yet encountered anything bad that smells of coconut. Could you help me stand?"

Alex and Harry got his grandfather to his feet. The old man took a second to steady himself, then brushed off their support and walked slowly toward his father and sister, leaning on his stick.

Zia sat with the tall man's head in her lap. The ugly flower drooped in its pot beside them. From what Alex could see, the man's face was entirely burned and ruined once more. Zia had placed a red silk handkerchief over him, like the mask a bank robber would wear in an old western movie. Above it, the staring eyes fell in and out of focus.

Moving stiffly and with difficulty, Alex's grandfather lowered himself to one knee.

"How bad is it?"

"Body's done now," Zia answered without looking at him.

The tall man lifted a hand in a faint, beckoning gesture. Alex's grandfather bowed lower.

"You saved us. From in there." The ghastly voice was less than a whisper.

"I had to."

"How could . . ." The words faded. The tall man coughed, tried again. "How could . . . I . . . ever . . ."

Alex's grandfather bent toward him, face ashen. "Yes?"

"Have raised such a *fool*?"

"Plan B," Zia said. Her head snapped up. "B for *bunny*. Let's see how predictable you are. Catch, old man."

There was a flier coming out of her coat, going for Alex's grandfather. The old man fell backward. Alex instantly reached out with his mind toward his own little machine, lying nearby amid the gate's debris. He built the bridge across to it, faster than ever. It was becoming second nature now.

"He's doing it!" Zia whooped.

Something was different, Alex realised. There was something

else at the other end of this bridge. Something dark, charging over the bridge, racing toward him. A cloud. The same cloud of heads he had encountered at home. Surging around him, through him. Then the bridge was folding up toward him with a slamming sound, closing in, getting smaller until suddenly it wasn't a bridge before him at all but . . .

A door. He was in a small grey room, looking at a door.

And there was something behind him.

IN THE FOREST, Zia called her flier back to her. She smiled sadly as the last frail breath left her father's body.

"Alex!" Alex's grandfather yelled, staring up at him in alarm. "Harry, help me to him."

Harry and the old man cautiously approached the boy, who stood rigid, rooted to the spot, staring wide-eyed at the ground between his feet.

"Alex?" Alex's grandfather said again. "Are you okay?"

The boy stumbled a step, then reached out to touch the old man's cane. Alex's grandfather let him take it.

"Alex?"

With abrupt ferocity, the boy swung the stick up so the heavy handle caught Harry square in the side of the head, knocking him out cold. The boy grinned at Alex's grandfather.

"My *name* is Alexander. But you shall call me Father."

Zia clapped her hands.

INSIDE THE GREY room, Alex turned and found the tall man standing there. His face was healed and clean once more. Alex looked around the small space in bewildered fright.

"What's . . . where are we?"

"Don't you recognise it?" The man spread his arms. "Your mind. You opened the door to me when you opened yourself to the Soaring Spirit, child. I've only glimpsed it from afar before, but I was right: you have an *interestingly* shaped mind. Great potential. A combination of your physical inheritance and some innate talent that warrants further study. We can do very good work together."

"What?"

"Fair is fair. Twice now, through blind ignorance and sheer luck, you have managed to damage my body. This time, you have destroyed it. This angers me, but I see no profit in that. So I will allow you to make amends.

"Alexander, the situation is this: I believe that the mind and the body are one; can you understand the concept? I have done all I can – and I have done truly *astonishing* things, boy – to keep my mind and my body together *as* one. But if I cannot go on in my own body, I will have to go on in the next best thing. Yours. The blood in your veins is my blood, after all.

"That is why it is so easy for me to reach out – you have used the Soaring Spirit, so you understand, yes? A lock of hair was enough for you there. Now: imagine how much more potent it is for me, with my blood beating through every part of you. Diluted a little, yes, but still stronger than any other.

"The power in that blood is a power I cultivated and can call. Even your features are my own. You are as close to an exact replica of me as could be. Certainly better than any of the toys Beckman ever produced. So I propose we share."

"What are you talking about?" Alex shouted. "Let me out of here!"

"Listen," the man said patiently. "Try to understand. It is much better that you do not attempt to fight, Alexander. You can never win. The proposal is this: join with me. There is plenty of room for two of us here. Infinite space. Although, only one can be dominant, of course. But I will develop your body and your mind, and we will both profit. We shall let the body age naturally a little while, and then, at the optimal moment, we shall stop ageing forever. And then we will go on, until we have solved all the secrets and created new ones.

"I realise you will need a little time to think this over. To understand. I will give you that time. Say, thirty years. I am not cruel. And in the meantime, I will give you a whole world to keep you satisfied and occupied. A world of wonder. Visions of dazzling happy endings, where all the darkness disappears, and you become a legend. Or, no: perhaps I will simply give you a small world of contentment. Give you the thing that you have always wanted most, with the pitiable lack of ambition my son has allowed to fester in you. Yes. This will be your reality for the time being. Honestly, you will never know the difference."

The man stepped past Alex and pulled open the door behind him.

"Thirty years of . . . What?" Alex flinched away. He was getting lost in panic. "Just let me go. . ."

"Are you lost, son?" the man said in a kindly tone. "There, behind you. Isn't that your parents?"

"What?" Alex looked behind, uncomprehending.

He was in a little dark street and he was five years old, and there were his mum and his dad at the corner where the sun was shining, calling him to come.

He turned back to the thing he'd been looking at.

A crammed old toy shop window. Behind the glass, there stood a grinning tin robot that he had wanted to show them. But when he looked at it now he realised it was just old and battered and very dusty. He turned away and ran to catch up with his parents.

They each took him by the hand, one on either side.

AT THE RUINED castle in the forest, the boy who called himself Alexander winced as he took a step.

"Damaged his foot, too," he muttered to Alex's grandfather, indicating the offending ankle. "Tiresome child. I fail to understand how you put up with his bleating."

"Bunnies don't bleat, Father," Zia chirped, delighted. "They make squeaking sounds."

"And look at you." The boy jabbed Alex's grandfather roughly with the cane. "You've allowed yourself to become decrepit. Ridiculous." He threw the stick down as the old man collapsed.

"Nothing to say? Wits failing you now, too?" Alexander gestured toward the flower, which seemed to move its head slightly on the breeze, as if following their conversation. "There's still time, you know. You could come back to us. Play the repentant prodigal. But, no. You and I have been through that."

The boy limped across to the tall man's lifeless body. He stood staring down at it for several seconds. Then he stooped to retrieve the man's shiny black cane. He swished the stick in the air with satisfaction, then twisted the silver handle to withdraw a long, swordlike blade from inside.

"I'm already growing stronger." He smiled at Zia. "Far sooner than I thought. It's because the body feels so familiar, you see? I can even spare a little energy to dull the pain in this wretched ankle now." He called across to Alex's grandfather – "Mind over matter!" – then leapt in an almost dancerly fashion at him, landing lightly on the injured foot.

As he came down, he swept his blade violently at the old man on the ground, who just managed to parry it with his cane.

✿

ALEX WOBBLED BUT kept going.

He was almost seven, and he was determined to do it, even though it was impossible. Most of his friends already knew how to ride a bike, but no one had been able to explain the mystery to him.

They were out on the street in front of their house. His mum stood away ahead, urging him on, beckoning him. His dad ran behind, holding the saddle with one hand, keeping him upright.

Stop thinking about it so much. That was supposed to be the secret. His elbows and knees stung. He knew he would be sore if he tipped over again. He leaned forward, pedalled faster, and saw his shadowy reflection flitting through the windows. His mum was clapping. She lifted her hands above her head. Yay.

You're doing it.

His dad had let go without telling him. But he still felt him just behind him, his presence, the sense of him there, just in case.

Alex kept pedalling forward and it felt like flying.

ALEX'S GRANDFATHER SCRABBLED backward on his elbows.

The boy who called himself Alexander frowned, then sighed. "What to do with you is a question indeed. But first: the name of God. I can take it from you, of course. But I think I would rather that you *give* it to me. Just for the symbolism of it: the last belated gift from a dutiful son to his father."

He walked toward Alex's grandfather, holding out one hand expectantly, raising his blade with the other.

As sword struck stick, Zia raised a hand to her mouth and giggled.

AND ALEX WAS twelve and it was almost Christmas.

They had gone away for the holidays. Just a cheap little cottage by the sea, but they had brought loads of food and there were endless nights of old films and no homework and a real fire. It was cosy and it felt like they were the only people left on Earth.

It was evening. Alex was in his room. His mum and dad were in the big room just beyond the half-open door, getting dinner ready. A smell of roast potatoes.

He sat at a desk by the window, wrapping the presents he'd bought them. Books and a Johnny Cash mug for his mum. For his dad, a weird-looking toy robot that Alex had found lurking in a stuffy second-hand shop.

Rain rapped against glass. If he looked out his window, he knew he would see the black curve of the shoreline, and off in the distance, the slow turning beam of a high, lonely lighthouse. But he didn't want to look out his window.

He glanced down suddenly as his finger jagged on the robot's rough old tin.

He had to be careful. In places, the ragged edges were sharp enough to draw blood.

✺

THE CUT ON Alex's grandfather's brow bled freely. Alexander stood over him, pressing his sword to the old man's breast. Dogs barked somewhere off in the forest.

"The life I could have given you," Alexander said.

"You've never lived," the old man whispered. His eyes were closing. "You've spent two hundred years trying not to die. It's not the same thing."

"Enough," Alexander said. "Give it to me, and I will end it quickly. I may even allow Morecambe to live on. Although . . . *live* isn't quite the word now, is it? Actually, he has become quite the subject for study, hasn't he?"

The old man drew in a breath, let it go with a long sigh. He closed his eyes and his head fell back. Rain ran in the lines of his face. He reached a weak hand toward his coat, trying to clutch protectively at the old robot inside. But he didn't have the strength left. His hand fell back down.

Alexander bent to take the toy.

ALEX WAS STILL sitting in his room in the cottage by the sea, still staring at the toy robot in his hand. His mum and dad called in unison for him to come join them. Dinner was ready. Don't let it get cold.

"Just a minute!" Alex shouted. He dimly remembered: he *had* cut his thumb on the old toy once. His blood had gone inside.

"By the pricking of my thumbs," he murmured, wondering where he had heard that.

Another memory was coming now. There had been another boy who had cut his finger on this old toy robot once, too. Not long after Alex had. On the bus to school, that same morning. This other boy had grabbed the robot, and then his hand was bleeding, running red. What was his name?

Kenzie. Kenzie Mitchell.

The lighthouse lamp must have been turned directly toward the cottage, because the raindrops on the glass suddenly glowed with a fierce brightness. Alex stepped to the window and looked out.

There was a figure lying on the ground out there, blurry through the rain. He looked hurt.

Alex opened the window. "Grandad?"

He'd almost forgotten he had a grandfather. Alex looked back over his shoulder as his parents called again, sharper. His dad stood right behind the half-opened door now. He could see his shadow falling on the floor. All Alex had to do was close the window, walk over there, and he would be with him.

He turned toward the frail figure lying in the rain. A little white card had been left on the window ledge outside. Alex squinted to make out what was printed on it.

POWER

His dad wasn't really there. He knew that.

Everything in him wanted to turn back, back to Christmas, back to his mum and dad. But instead, Alex looked straight into the harsh glare beaming at him from the lighthouse and stepped forward. The light surrounded him, blinding him. He walked further into it, reached both hands out into the light, picturing a face.

"Come back out." He sent the words out like a lifeline tossed into the sea. Hands touched his, he gripped them tight, then used all his strength to pull Kenzie gently back out from the light and into the room.

"Sorry, Kenzie," Alex said.

Kenzie stood trying to speak, but didn't seem to know how. Alex focused on him, helping him.

"Alex," Kenzie said, dimly. "There's something behind you."

"I know. Stay here, Kenzie."

Alex thought about the techniques he'd learned while using the flier, about moving his thoughts, about sectioning parts of his mind off from each other. With that, he put a wall around Kenzie, shielding him. Then he turned. The little cottage melted away, and he was back in the small grey room. The tall man stood before him, intently studying the toy robot. He noticed Alex with surprise.

"Get out," Alex muttered, still weak. It felt as if his mind had been injected with something like the anesthetic the dentist used to numb his jaw. "Out of my head."

"Don't be ridiculous." The man held the robot aloft and smiled. "The name of God. It *recognises* you. Which now means, of course, it recognises *me*. And I know how to access it fully. Decades of deep learning, child, not your feeble fumbling at the edges. You could barely begin to understand a millionth of what might be done with this. I know all the words and what they mean. Shall we conduct a little test first, so you can see, before I lock you back in your box? I'll set the rain on fire, make the forest burn, how about that?"

The tall man began whispering long and low. Satisfaction

spread across his face, then disappeared, replaced by confusion, anger.

"Something's wrong. Something . . . *missing*? What have you *done* to this, child?"

The man shook the toy, then closed his eyes as he devoted his full attention to the problem.

His full attention.

At once, the fug cleared from Alex's mind. Thoughts, memories, and feelings came pouring through him, along with a sharper sense of the tablet than he had ever experienced before. He knew exactly what was wrong, the missing piece the tall man would never find.

"What's that behind you?" the tall man asked suddenly. "What are you hiding back there?"

Alex took the wall away. Kenzie stepped out to stand by his side. From behind him, the raging light came pouring around them. Alex gestured toward the tall man. A door appeared behind him.

"This guy," Alex said to Kenzie, "is a real idiot. I need your help. We just need to tell him to get out."

"Right." Kenzie nodded and shrugged. "Uh. Get out."

"Don't be rid—" the tall man stopped speaking as one foot stumbled back half a step. He paused in surprise, then gathered himself, stood straight, and began chanting quickly and quietly.

"Get out," Kenzie repeated. This time, Alex threw his mind after Kenzie's words, caught them, aimed them, and set them flying, dragging bolts of the light with them. Then he sent his own, weightier command racing brightly behind them.

"Get out," Alex said. The tall figure flinched as if he'd been hit by a combination punch.

Alex gathered his thoughts. The white-blue light was there for him, behind him, before him, waiting to be used, hungry for direction. He knew how to reach the power, and the power knew him. He knew how to move his mind from all his flights with the flier. Two different kinds of magic, light and dark. He took both, pushed them together, and put it all into his words. "Get out. My mind. Get out."

The tall man staggered back against the door. He stopped chanting and looked helplessly at Alex.

"No. *No.* Wait. Alexander— Alex," he said pleadingly. "Don't you understand—"

"I understand," Alex said. "Get out." The door opened.

"Get out," Alex and Kenzie said, now speaking as one voice, with words of fire.

The tall man lifted a hand in a beseeching gesture. Then he fell backward through the doorway, out of sight. There was no light there.

Alex felt something move in his mind, like a gust of wind passing through a house, all the doors slamming shut behind it. The door vanished.

"Alex," Kenzie whispered after a long silence. He stood blinking, looking around. "What—"

"Later, Kenzie," Alex said. "You should get back home.

You've had a bad dream. We both have. But it's over now. Let's leave it alone. Go home. Wake up."

"I—" Kenzie started. But Alex closed his eyes and stepped back and he couldn't hear him any more.

His ankle was aching and he was very tired. He felt wind and rain on his face, wet clothes sticking heavily around his limbs. He opened his eyes.

No grey room. No Kenzie. No tall man. Just trees and rain, wild night and a ruined old building. A scratched tin robot in his hand, and his grandfather bleeding on the ground. Alex threw the sword-stick away and dropped to his knees.

"Grandad, I—"

The old man gestured weakly. "The toy robot, Alex, the tablet," he said as Alex bent an ear to his mouth. The voice was as faint as a breath. "You must promise to . . ."

"I will." Alex nodded fast. "I promise. Don't worry, just . . ."

"Dawn soon." His grandfather patted his hand. "Sunrise in a forest, always worth . . . Remind yourself you're alive."

Then it was as if the old man simply went to sleep.

XXXVII.

FEVER

THERE WAS SOMETHING running at Alex from behind. He wiped his blurring eyes and turned to see Kingdom's dog Maia galloping toward him. Beyond, Kingdom knelt by Harry, helping him up. The other dogs stood around them.

Alex tried again to rouse his grandfather.

"You all right, son?" Harry called warily as he and Kingdom approached.

"Yeah," Alex said. He rubbed his eyes and nose again. "I'm . . . me." He touched the side of his own head as he looked up. "That wasn't me. Who hit you. Sorry, Harry."

"Don't be daft, son, I know that."

"How is he?" Kingdom asked quietly, nodding at Alex's grandfather.

"I don't know." It come out as a fast sob. Alex looked around without really seeing anything, then noticed Kingdom carried Zia's flowerpot. His gaze stuck on the evil plant, sagging limply on its stem.

"I met her running through the trees," Kingdom explained. "Almost caught her, but she's fast. And rather more vicious than I was expecting." She displayed a long cut on her inner arm. "She dropped this, though. I thought it might be important."

Harry had knelt by Alex's grandfather. He touched his neck, then bent to listen for breath. "Still there. Fever. I've seen 'im like this before, Alex. It's when 'e, y'know . . . When 'e gets older. We really need to keep 'im warm."

"I dropped the blankets when I was fighting the girl." Kingdom set the flower down, drew her rapier, and left at a run, Maia bounding beside her.

Alex flinched slightly as one of the other dogs pushed past him. Ignoring Harry's grumbling complaints, the big animal stretched out and lay across Alex's grandfather's chest. One by one, the others followed suit, covering the old man entirely, like a heavy, living rug.

Alex and Harry stood back to watch them.

"Keep 'im warm, I suppose," Harry said, after a moment.

Alex nodded. "Harry, do you think he'll—"

"'E's come through it before," Harry said brusquely. He softened instantly and shrugged, before continuing with the distinct air of a man changing the subject. "'Ere, so, Alex. 'Ow did you, y'know, get rid of 'im? Your grandad's dad, I mean? When 'e . . . took you over?"

"He let me go for a second. He was too busy trying to use this." Alex lifted the toy robot.

"The tablet. Name of God. He knew everything about it,

Harry. I think that was what caused him trouble, though. He was expecting to find more than he could get to; the tablet wasn't working the way it should. He got caught up trying to work out why."

"So, eh – well, why couldn't 'e get at it?"

Alex frowned as he tried to explain, still trying to put it together himself.

"Grandad told me he thought the tablet had made a connection with me because of my blood getting on it, like waking it up. Because there was this magical element lying in my blood. But about the same time that happened, there was another guy at my school. Kenzie. He cut his finger on the robot, and some of his blood got inside, too. I think our blood must have got . . . mixed up in there.

"The tablet connected with me, but there was some kind of confused, faulty connection with Kenzie, too. Like, the tall man and Zia – they could focus on people if they had something of theirs, right? Hair, blood, whatever. And I had Kenzie's blood in there. It's like I was using him. I had to go *through* him to get to the power, to make the connection. Or the power went through him before it got to me – he could see things happening that I couldn't, that hadn't happened yet, but he didn't know what any of it was. All he knew was, the more it happened, the worse he felt, I guess. Grandad said there's always a . . . cost. And Kenzie was paying it. Every time I used the tablet, I was using him. Using him up. Like he was . . . insulating me from it. I got a message he'd fallen into a coma.

I think I almost killed him, Harry, without realising. But, yeah, there was this part missing, or an extra part in the way. The tall man couldn't work it out. I tried to call Kenzie so we could get to the power together, so it would go through both of us. So that I'd pay the cost. Then I tried to let Kenzie go. I wonder if he's feeling better now."

Alex took a step toward his grandfather. The dogs gave a warning growl. He sat down in the mud.

"Harry. Zia and her father, they both said stuff about my dad. What happened to my dad? Do you know? How he died?"

Harry lowered himself with a grunt. "Well . . . Well, 'e crashed in 'is car, son. You know that."

"There's more to it than that."

"Well. Yeah, a little. Not sure it's my place to, uh . . ." Harry gazed at the still figure on the ground and seemed to come to a decision. "When your dad came along, Alex . . ." Harry paused and looked off. "Blimey. Seems like yesterday. An' seems like forever ago. Anyway. When 'e was born, your grandad swore off all of this." He gestured around them with a big hand.

"Like 'e wanted to stop fightin' and just live a life, y'know. And 'e tried to keep 'is old life away. But 'is father found out about the boy eventually. 'E knew there was something of 'is potion being passed along from your grandad's blood, see, and 'e wanted to study it, use it. Although, after what 'appened with you tonight, I reckon maybe 'e 'ad other reasons for wanting a male descendant close to 'im. A convenient body to take over, if needs be.

"So, 'e watched and waited, and gradually wormed 'is way into your dad's life, without your grandad knowing. I dunno 'ow they met, but over the years, 'e showed your dad things, an' promised to show 'im more. Secrets . . . y'know. Things that would make life easier. A little more every time, drawin' 'im in.

"But listen, Alex," Harry continued urgently. "'E never told your dad about the people *dying*, or who 'e really was. Your dad didn't know *any* of that, son. What 'appened in the end was, your grandad found out about these secret meetings. 'E confronted your dad about it. They 'ad an argument and, during it, your grandad told your dad everything: about the deaths, 'ow that was what was fuelling it all.

"Well. Your dad was sent into shock. The 'orror of it, the guilt. 'Ow *close* 'e'd come to joining up with your great-grandad. 'E just ran. Drove off without looking to see what was comin'. And, yeah. That was that. Closest I've ever seen your grandad comin' to, y'know. Givin' up. But then 'e found out you were on the way."

"Why didn't he ever tell me?" Alex said.

Harry shrugged. "Your grandad didn't want to risk it 'appening again with you. All your grandad ever wanted was to keep you out of all this, Alex. But when 'e was up against it, you were the first person 'e turned to for 'elp."

"Second person, Harry," Alex said, putting a hand on the big man's shoulder.

"Yeah." Harry sniffed. "Well."

Alex watched the rain. After a while, Kingdom returned.

She considered the strange tableau and pulled up her hood. The long raincoat shrouded her like a monk's habit.

"The Rolls is gone," she said with a sigh. "I thought I heard the engine and went to look. No sign of Philippe. And the car we came in has been wrecked. Tyres slashed, windshield smashed, steering wheel ripped out—"

She was interrupted by a strange snuffling, tearing sound. They all turned to see Maia enthusiastically eating the ancient flower, straight from the pot.

The last of its roots seemed to wriggle on the wind as they disappeared. Maia snapped her mucky jaws with great satisfaction, yawned, then padded over to lie by Alex's grandfather's head.

"Good girl," said Alex.

❂

THEY KEPT WATCH over the old man until the night began to fade. Shortly before sunrise, Kingdom left in search of a fresh vehicle.

Using pieces of old picture frames as shovels, Alex and Harry dug a grave for the tall man. Harry asked Alex if he wanted to say anything, but Alex had nothing to say. They went back to sit by Alex's grandfather.

Dawn came creeping over the treetops. Alex watched it with intense concentration, trying to fix it in his memory forever. As the first sunlight touched them, the dogs got up, stretched, and padded away. Alex's grandfather seemed to be breathing steadily. The fever had broken, but they still couldn't rouse him.

"What do you think, Harry?" Alex said.

"We're not out of the woods yet." Harry smiled. "But goin' in the right direction."

Kingdom returned a couple of hours later, and they carried the old man up the slope, past the ruined tower, and down through the forest. They left Alex's grandfather in the car she'd "acquired," then returned to gather up the picture frames. Harry said he planned to have a bonfire in Albert's garage yard.

"Nearly forgot," Harry added. "You left your phone when you went runnin' from the car at the museum. I picked it up."

There were two messages from David.

```
Kenzie's woke up, doing okay. Need your help
with witches.
```

The second message read:

```
Witches from Macbeth I meant. This essay.
Can't figure out what they're supposed to be
all about: Paddock calls! What?
```

"So," Kingdom said. "Which one of you is going to explain to me exactly what just happened?"

As Alex bent to lift another armful of broken wood, he realised he was smiling. The dogs ran around them as they worked, playing among the trees.

✹

Two days later, Alex arrived back in Britain with Kingdom. They had done their best to return the paintings they'd found hidden around the ruins of Castle Boll and on the slopes of the Kandel, sending them anonymously in the post. Kingdom was on her way to dump the last, the picture they all now called *Waffle Lady*, at Cambridge University.

She dropped him in front of his home and tooted the horn of the rental car as she drove away. He balanced a large white cardboard box in the crook of his arm as he hunted for his keys. The front gate squealed when he pushed it open. He stood looking at it for a moment.

"Oh, hello, stranger," his mum said when he walked into the living room. She was at her desk by the back windows. Carl was off at work. Alex put his arms around her and stood hugging her silently for almost a minute.

"Well, that was lovely," she said, after he stepped back. "You all right, Alex?"

"Yeah . . . Uh, Mum?"

"What?"

"Would it be okay if I asked you some stuff about Dad some time?"

"Oh." Taken aback, she looked at her laptop, then tried a smile. "Of course, I . . . I used to tell you about him, Alex. When you were small. All the time. But once you got a bit older, I don't know, I thought it was upsetting you. You didn't seem to want . . . I always planned to tell you more one day, but . . . You know. Time just goes away."

Alex nodded. "Later, I mean. And about you, too."

They smiled at each other, a little embarrassed. "What're you doing?" Alex nodded at her computer and the teetering stack of papers beside it.

"Usual glamour." She rolled her eyes. "Reading through a million spreadsheets so I can tell the idiots who sent them to me what they mean."

"Fancy stopping for a cup of tea?"

"Almost always."

"I brought us this back," Alex said, and opened the box.

His mum's eyes widened in delight.

"Black Forest gateau? I've not had that in *ages*."

XXXVIII.

ALEX

FOUR WEEKS LATER, Alex was walking through London.

They had travelled down for his mum's birthday. Carl had bought them all tickets for her favourite musical. He and Alex had sworn a solemn pact that they would join in singing along. Harmonise, even.

It was mid-morning. Alex had left them in the hotel, telling Carl he was going out to pick up a present for his mum, even though his present to her was already wrapped and hidden in his rucksack. The city bustled around him, not yet at full roar. Alex was nervous. He had an appointment to keep.

Hard rain had fallen through the night, but it had stopped and now the sun blazed over the bright world. Roads shone and buildings gleamed and the river glinted blue brown as it tumbled toward the sea. One of those washed-clean mornings when everything seems new.

He found them by the river, at the café Harry had specified, two old men and one large dog, sitting at an outside table.

Alex's grandfather smiled up as Alex joined them, then turned back to watching the boats on the glittering Thames. His hair shone very white in the sunlight. A heat haze rose in rippling waves from the water, giving the day a slightly unreal look around the edges.

"You know, I quite fancy a bowl of chips," the old man said.

"You've just 'ad a bowl of chips," Harry replied.

"I have not."

"Righto." Harry raised his eyebrows at Alex. "I'll get some chips, then."

"Splendid."

Alex's grandfather hummed an odd little tune as Harry headed inside, then caught Alex's eye. "Hello."

"Hi."

"You know, you look very like my son?" The old man glanced off around them with a distracted look. "He's around here somewhere. What's your name?"

"Alex," said Alex.

"Oh! That's his name, too. He was here just a minute ago. . . Wonder where he could have got to."

"Chips are coming," Harry said as he returned.

"Oh, splendid. I quite fancy some chips." Alex's grandfather patted Maia's head, then looked at Alex, suddenly thoughtful: "I'll need some salt."

"I'll get it." Alex stood and crossed to an empty table beside them. He hesitated, then grabbed up a fistful of salt packets from a bowl. Nothing. The old man watched him.

"So, 'ow's it feel to be famous?" Harry said as Alex sat back down.

"Eh? What do you mean?"

"What? Ain't you seen?" Harry turned to the bag hanging over his chair, produced a German newspaper, and leafed through. "From a coupla weeks back. 'Ang on, not this one, but it's interesting." He tapped a story. "About towns in the southern Black Forest experiencing earth tremors on Walpurgis Night. Lots of fractures appeared in buildings. They're blaming a power company that was doin' geothermal drillin'." Harry flicked a few more pages. "Ah, this is what I wanted to show you. It was everywhere. 'Eadline says, 'The Stuttgart Witch'!"

Alex frowned at the photograph the big man pointed out. A blurry snapshot, captured at night on a mobile phone outside an opera house. The shadowy figure depicted was indistinct, but Alex recognised himself. He was caught leaping over the photographer, silhouetted against a full moon. The traffic cone wedged on his head sat like a pointy hat, and he held his long-handled broom in a way that almost looked as if he was riding on it, flying.

"Oh, witches." Alex's grandfather grinned. "I could tell you a story or two there. But you'd never believe me. Hang on, the dog wants to say hello."

The old man rose, took Maia by the lead, and walked toward the river pathway, where a young couple stood with a dachshund whose tail was wagging furiously.

"How is he, Harry?" Alex said.

"Oh, 'e's all right," Harry said. "Getting more stubborn, if you can believe that. That dog blummin' loves 'im. She's good for 'im, I reckon. Evelyn says she can stay with us as long as we all seem 'appy about it."

"Do you think he'll . . ." Alex took a breath that caught in his throat. "Do you think he'll stay like that?"

Several seconds went by. The city boomed quietly in the background.

"Who knows?" Harry finally said. "You know your grandad, son. Full of surprises."

"You sure you're okay to look after him?"

"I won't even *dignify* that," Harry said, putting on an exaggeratedly snooty voice, "with an answer."

"But *you*," Alex said. "Do you feel . . . After what happened to you. Do you think . . . How long do you think you'll be here?"

"Oh." Harry shrugged. "Dunno. Feel all right. Same old 'Arry." He rapped his head with a knuckle as though knocking on wood.

"The ageing thing," Alex murmured. "In the blood. Slowing down then speeding up . . . living such a long time. Do you think it's going to happen with me?"

"All I can tell you is, your grandad told me one time that 'e reckoned you'd be okay, Alex. 'E worried about it a lot when you was little, but then your body seemed to sort itself out. Maybe the effects were more potent when you were smaller. Your grandad told me 'e reckoned that the stuff was *dormant* in you. But if you're asking me 'ow long you've got, well, I mean:

nobody knows that, son, do they? You, me, everybody else, we're all sittin' in different seats in the same boat."

They smiled at each other in sympathy.

"And Zia too, now," Alex said after a moment. "She'll start ageing. Or will she? What will happen to her, with the flower gone, and her father – Harry, has there been any sign of her? Do you think—"

"Nothing," Harry said, shaking his head. "Disappeared. So," he went on, clearing his throat. "What do you reckon, Alex? Still want me to do it?"

"I don't know," Alex said, suddenly filled with uncertainty. "What do you think?"

"Oh." Harry leaned back, raised both palms. "Can't 'elp you there, son. Your decision now."

Alex watched his grandfather, walking slowly back toward them, bent painfully over his stick, the dog carefully taking its time not to rush him.

There must be a way to help him, Alex thought. *Make it better. Turn it back.* He knew, if he studied hard enough, if he devoted himself to it, threw himself deep into it, he could find the way, find the words, shape some power. Keep them all safe. And, like that, Alex decided what he was going to do. Then he looked at his grandfather smiling at him and he changed his mind back again.

Alex nodded. "I'm sure." He took out the old tin toy robot and handed it to Harry. "Take it. Do it. Get rid of it."

"Righto," Harry said quietly, and slipped the toy into his bag.

The chips arrived just as the old man sat down. "Oh, those smell good. Can I have one?" he said to Alex.

"Many as you like."

"Excellent." The old man took a chip, then used it to point at Alex. He narrowed his eyes. "You know, you look very like my son. What's your name?"

"Alex," Alex said.

"Oh, that's his name! Pleased to meet you. Good name, that."

They shook hands and chatted and watched the river running in the sunlight. Then it was somehow time to go. Alex had to get back for his mum's birthday lunch in a fancy restaurant. Meanwhile, his grandfather and Harry had a train to catch. They parted at a street corner, Harry promising to be in touch soon.

Alex embraced them, then turned and hurried away, walking with his head down, his hands pushed deep into his empty coat pockets, trying to keep it together. After a short while, he couldn't fight the feeling coursing through him and stopped. He turned back, searching the street desperately.

The pavements had grown busier, like a river rolling at him. It took several moments to locate them, far away now, two small specks in the crowd. He saw Harry's grey-blond head, his grandfather bent in his dove-grey suit beside him.

Alex's eyes blurred, and it seemed almost as if the old man straightened, stood elegant and tall again, and slapped Harry briskly on the back.

Somewhere in one of the towers high above, someone must have opened a window at that moment, because a sudden, dazzling glare of reflected white light blinded Alex for a second. When he looked again, he couldn't see them any more. The street seemed dimmer.

He took a step after them, then another, and then he was running, shoving through strangers. He stopped himself with difficulty and stood watching a second longer as people pushed softly past him.

Trick of the light, he thought. Then Alex turned away, promises to keep.

THAT'S THAT

A LATE SUMMER sun is sinking over Prague, the old city beginning its slow nightly display, shading through gold and red to blue and black.

On the Charles Bridge, the crowds have started to thin. Two elderly men pause in their wandering to stand by one of the statues along the side, looking down into the river. A dog sits patiently at their heels.

The taller of the two lights a cigarette, leans on the parapet, then lifts his hand to the inside pocket of his immaculate grey coat. He stands poised like that, attentive, studying the water below, the old Vltava freshly nourished by recent rains.

The other turns his back to the river to watch the people passing by. When there is no one around them, he nudges the grey man's elbow. His hand flashes out from his coat and something rather small drops, touches the skin of the water, then disappears forever as the river seals itself over it.

"And that's that," says the older of the two old men. He stands bowed a few seconds more, watching the last ripples fade. Then he straightens, turns, and considers his friend.

"How you feeling, Harry?"

"Yeah, not bad."

"It just struck me – if that thing gave you your life back, destroying it might . . . y'know. Have some effect."

"Now that you mention it."

"Yes?"

"I do feel quite 'ungry."

The old man spins happily and points with his cane toward the spiky shadows gradually lengthening from the far end of the bridge.

"About time for dinner, then, I think. Now, far as I remember, there's a place hiding along here that you just won't believe."

ACKNOWLEDGEMENTS

The quote used as an epigraph at the start of this novel – about how treasure hunters long believed there was some great mysterious prize waiting to be found buried amid the ancient ruins of Castle Boll – is a rough translation from the book *Sagen Und Schwänke Vom Schwarzwald*, a collection of strange folktales from the Black Forest region, published by the German writer Max Rieple in 1965. This tiny mention is one of the very few references to the castle I've ever come across, and Rieple doesn't say much more about it. But it's what he doesn't say that set me dreaming.

Like *Monstrous Devices* before it, this book would not exist without the help and work of many people. First and last, my greatest debt is to my supernaturally skilled agent Catherine Drayton for her encouragement, energy, belief, and apparent abilities in time travel. I owe an equal debt of thanks to Maggie Rosenthal, my editor at Viking, who shepherded *The Shadow Arts* through the perilous terrain toward creation with a meticulous eye, tireless cheerfulness, astute questions, great patience, and more than one excellent suggestion.

My gratitude again to Ken Wright and all the team at Viking, with special thanks once more to Jim Hoover, for his swellegant design and layout.

I must also thank all of Catherine's colleagues at Inkwell Management, especially Claire Friedman, for all her work and help; and Lyndsey Blessing and the foreign rights team, for giving Alex and his grandfather the opportunity to roam even further afield. Thanks also to the mighty Mary Pender of UTA, whom I'm very glad to have on my side.

For this UK edition, I'm again beholden to the entire extraordinary team at Oneworld and Rock the Boat for their enthusiasm, energy, comradeship, hard work, and scones. Heartfelt thanks to Shadi Doostdar, Kate Bland, Molly Scull, Mark Rusher, Margot Weale, Lucy Cooper, Rida Vaquas, Juliet Mabey, Katie Jennings, and – not least – Ben Summers, for his work in magicking up the shadowy new cover art. My thanks, too, to the indefatigable Philippa Milnes-Smith at the Soho Agency.

Friends and family made things easier just by being there, and by being them: thank you. Alison, again. And a final, special, and very sincere thank-you to Alex Ulyett, who set the ball rolling with *Monstrous Devices* in the first place, and gave me the chance to tell the story of Alex and his grandfather. Anything good in this book was made better thanks to these people. The faults remain all mine.

Damien Love was born in Scotland and lives in the city of Glasgow, where, even as you read these words, it is raining. He has worked as a journalist for many years, writing about movies, music, TV, and other things for a variety of publications. He has the ability to talk to cats, but there is still no evidence that they understand him. His first novel, *Monstrous Devices,* was published by Rock the Boat in 2020. Learn more at damienlove.com.